The Poet & The Maestro

By R. Patrick Taggart

Dedication

This book is dedicated to men and women who put their lives on the line every day at home and abroad to provide intelligence and security to our nation. These individuals remain unsung heroes. Their identities may never be known nor their deeds acknowledged. Yet we remain safer because of what they do.

Prologue

A young midshipman assigned to the top secret communications center enters the office of the chief of naval operations for the Russian naval fleet assigned to surveillance of N.A.T.O. naval operations.

He stands at attention before the admiral who is seated at his desk and says, "Sir, I have disturbing information from our communications liaison. It seems that they have lost contact with a Varshavyanka submarine. She failed to make her appointed rendezvous with a mother ship as planned. She was sent on a mission to the area of the Arabian Sea to survey American warships in the area. Then she was to meet with a mother ship and hand deliver a written report directly without the use of radio transmissions, so as to prevent electronic interception of her information. However, they have had no communications from her of any kind and she is more than 24 hours overdue on her rendezvous.

Sir, the communications liaison believes she may have sunk.

There has been no hostile military action in the area, but they say she seems to be gone. They fear that she may have suffered some sort of mechanical failure and sank to the bottom."

The older man sits at his desk. His face, hardened by a lifetime of military discipline shows no emotion. Silently he stands. He is an older man, but he still possesses a large and powerful body; one befitting his position of power in the Russian navy.

The chief responds simply saying, "I see. I will contact the admiralty for the details. Thank you. You are dismissed."

The midshipman replies, "Sir, do you wish to order a search and rescue mission?"

"No, I am afraid there is little we can do. At this time she could be anywhere in the Indian Ocean or in the Arabian Sea. The area is vast. We know not where she might be and a wide spread search will most certainly reveal that we have been spying on American war ships."

"But sir, surely the Americans already know that we conduct surveillance against them all the time. Even so, we have recently developed a cooperation protocol with N.A.T.O. forces for the rescue of submarine personnel in such an event. We can ask the Americans to help without recrimination. I do not understand. Why we would not make a rescue attempt?"

The chief of operations replies, "Today is another sad day for the Russian people. Under the leadership of the weaklings in the Kremlin our military has already been embarrassed in front of the whole world. A failure of an onboard fire suppression system that activated when there was no fire caused a deadly accident aboard our brand new nuclear powered Akula class submarine just last November. Many on board were killed. Among those killed were representatives of foreign nations that were considering buying submarines from us. Our military was embarrassed in front of the whole world. It jeopardized our pending arrangements to supply Akula Class submarines to India and other allies.

Now it would seem that we have lost a kilo class sub. They are considered to be our most reliable diesel powered submarines. We have a pending arrangement to supply Indonesia with Kilo class subs. Our allies in China, Vietnam and Iran also discuss plans to purchase kilo class submarines from us. We cannot tell the world that our submarines fail during routine operations. Who would have confidence that they will perform in combat?

It is not simply a matter of losing the financial profit to be gained by the sale; it is a matter of national security. How are we to maintain our military alliances with these nations if we disclose our weaknesses? Our allies must not lose faith in our strength. They must believe that they can rely upon us to deliver reliable weapons; that an alliance with us is safer than an alliance with the United States. Now we would tell the world that we need American help to rescue our submarine in the Arabian Sea? Help us find a submarine that was sent to spy on them? We simply cannot.

Our enemies no longer fear us as they the once did. Since the demise of the Soviet Union our beloved Russia has become weaker in the eyes of the world. Some of our allies have already shifted their alliances from us to America. Poland has committed troops to fight for the Americans in their efforts in the Middle East. The Americans actually have a plan to put their missiles in Poland! Poland! Poland was a

Russian ally. Today it is an ally of America. The Poles will allow America to do this right on our borders! For now we rely only on diplomacy with the current American president to deter them from doing so. Had the Americans remained committed to the project those missiles would be in Poland right now. If America should choose to resume the project, they would simply go ahead and install the missiles without any regard for us. They no longer have any fear of us.

We will tell no one. It would once again make us look weak and foolish. I am tired of seeing my country looking weak and foolish.

It is a sad thing, but a Varshavyanka has a crew of 53. Russia has millions of people who are at risk if the world were to lose confidence in Russia. Who knows what foreign powers might attack our allies or even us if they knew the true nature of our fleet, of our military. We cannot search the entire Arabian Sea and Indian Ocean without a massive amount of help. The world would know. For now we remain silent. In the near future we will develop a plausible explanation as to why the sailors do not come home. For now we do not ask for help. We will tell no one. Russia will have 53 more martyrs and millions of Russians will remain safer. No one must know."

The midshipman says, "But sir, I think I may know where to find her. She was to meet the mother ship off the coast of the Glorioso Islands. However, based on triangulating her last authorized radio communications I have concluded that she was in the area of Mozambique when her location was last known. I believe if we just search the area between Madagascar and the African coast we may find her. We can search by ourselves without advising anyone of the loss or asking for assistance. No one outside this office needs to know. We could at least do that. If you give the order I could commence a secret rescue effort at once."

The admiral says, "I see. Have you told anyone else of your suspicions?"

"No sir. I thought it best to advise you first."

After a moment of quiet contemplation the admiral begins to walk toward a large world map on his wall. As he looks up at the map he says "Come closer. Show me here on my map where you believe she might be."

The younger man points to a spot on the map and begins to speak. Then suddenly, unexpectedly, the young midshipman is unable to draw his breath! He cannot speak. He cannot utter any sound. Initially, he is confused. He cannot comprehend why he cannot breathe. He cannot comprehend what is happening. Then he comes to the realization that the large muscular hands of the admiral are around his throat, preventing his breathing, choking him, crushing his windpipe. But Why! Why!

The younger, smaller lightweight man trashes about in a panic induced seizure like struggle while the more powerful man simply holds him by the neck, pinning him to the wall, choking the life out of him. The midshipman begins flailing; punching and. kicking at the big man, to no avail. The midshipman cannot break the grip of the older, much larger and stronger man. Slowly, the look of confusion and fear leaves the face of the younger man. It is replaced by a look of resignation. He knows his life is about to end, but why?

The big man does not lose his grip on the midshipman's neck as he watches the midshipman slowly losing his grip on life. As the young man's body begins to go limp the admiral simply, softly says, "And now Russia will have yet another martyr. Fear not in death you will be honored. Your family will be told you died in heroic military action in defense of your country. Before you go you should know that soon the world will know that the spirit of the Russian bear still lives in some of us! It is too bad that you shall not live to see Russian world supremacy restored. Good-bye my good friend. Good-bye."

The Old Seaman Begins His Mission in America

This morning upon arriving in at JFK International Airport, Stanley Adamski disembarked from his plane and went to baggage claim area. He waited for his luggage to arrive at the luggage pick up area. He just stood there patiently while the luggage of the other passengers on his plane came down the conveyor. One-by-one others picked up their bags and walked away. Stan stood there, waiting, holding a book and large manila envelope. They were the only carry-on items he had. Finally, he saw his red and green plaid suitcase moving down the conveyor. He did not have to push his way close to the conveyor as he had watched others do. His bag was the last to come out and there were no other impatient passengers to block his retrieval of the suitcase; there were no people to obstruct him from retrieving his bag. He just grabbed it from the conveyor and he was on his way.

He followed the signs to the customs counter. There, a customs agent questioned him. Stanley understood English very well; he could read and write in English. He could listen and understand, however, he did not speak it so well. He would answer the questions using as few words as possible. "What is the purpose of your visit to America?" The agent asked.

"Vacation," was Stan's reply. It was a lie, but Stan knew that lies would move him along faster and more safely than the truth would.

"How long will you be staying in America?"

"One week", again a lie. The customs agent politely asked him to present his suitcase so that it could be searched. Stan was pleased that he had not placed his large manila envelope in the suitcase. He did not care who saw what was in his suitcase, but he was not yet ready to show anyone what was in the envelope. Stan hoped that the agent would not ask to see the contents of the envelope that he carried with the book he was holding. The agent carried the suitcase to a private room near to the counter area. He entered the room with Stan's suitcase and closed the door. After a few moments, he invited Stan to join him in the room.

"This is just routine Mr. Adamski. It's a random check. I hope you understand we must search for contraband." Stan stood silently as the agent went through his belongings. After what seemed like a thorough search, the agent closed the bag, zipped it up, returned the bag to Stan and said, "Please, enjoy your stay in America."

Stan grabbed the bag and rushed from the customs desk. He went directly to a nearby bathroom and stepped into a private stall. He placed his bag on the bathroom floor. He opened the zipper and slipped the envelope into the bag. Stan was glad that he had taken the envelope on as a carry on item. He would have had serious concerns if the people who search luggage ever found its contents.

Once his envelope was securely placed in the suitcase he headed for the exit. He followed the signs that said "This way to ground transportation" At the door, a man asked him if he needed a taxi and Stan nodded yes. With only a slight stammer he said, "I need go 26 Federal Plaza in Man-hat-tan."

The man said, "Don't tell me, tell the driver." The man hailed a cab for Stan. As the cab pulled up the driver activated a button on his dashboard and the trunk opened to accept the passenger's luggage. The man who had hailed the cab for Stanley reached for the bag as he planned to place it in the trunk for Stan, but Stan quickly grabbed the bag himself and threw it into the back seat. Stan followed the bag into the back seat and as he closed the door he simply said, "Twenty-six Federal Plaza, Man-hat-tan." The cab sped away. Stanley Adamski did not know that he was expected to allow the man who hailed the cab to take the bag and put it in the trunk. A tip was expected for the service, but today the cabman would get no tip from Stan. Stan was in too much of a hurry. He was not going to allow the bag to be out of his sight for one minute, not while the envelope was in it. The only tip Stan thought about was the tip he was about to give to The F.B.I.

Soon, Stan arrived at his destination. He had gone directly from JFK International Airport to the New York Office of the F.B.I.

Stan walked around the outside of the building. It was a huge structure. The building was much larger than Stan had expected and he was not sure where to enter. The building took up the whole block with many doors going out to every street on the block. Eventually, he picked one of the doors on the Worth Street side of the building and entered. He got on a line that looked as if it was the proper line for gaining access to F.B.I. headquarters. He and other people carrying briefcases were about to be shuttled through a metal detector like the one he had to go through at the airport. However, he was carrying a suitcase, not a brief case. It seemed odd to the security officer that the man carried a suitcase. A brief case was a common sight around F.B.I. Headquarters, but the suitcase seemed more appropriate for an airport. His bag was placed on a conveyor belt and sent through an x-ray machine. Stanley was not prepared for that and he prayed that the x-rays would not ruin the items in the envelope. After he and his bag were screened, he was allowed to pass on through, but he was told that he could not bring the suitcase with him. "I'm sorry sir", the security agent said, "I have a list of items that are approved for passage beyond this point. A brief case is permitted but a suitcase?…I'm not so sure…I think I'll have to ask you not to take that upstairs."

He was told that there were secure lockers on the main floor. Someone took the suitcase for him, secured it and gave him a receipt for it. Stan said, "Yes, this is, how you say?… OK…. But I must take my envelope." Stan opened the suitcase, removed the envelope, re-closed the suitcase and permitted the security man to log in the suitcase and secure it in a small room next to the screening area. . The security agent insisted on looking into the envelope. Stan's heart pounded as the security agent looked at the contents, but the agent simply looked in and returned the envelope to Stan. Stan took back his envelope, obtained a receipt for the suitcase that had been placed in the locker and entered the main lobby.

Most of the people going through seemed to know where they were going, but Stanley had no idea where to turn. The he saw a desk with a sign that simply said "INFORMATION." There, there is where I must go he thought. At the information desk Stan said, "I am here to see man in charge."

He was told that if he needed to speak to an F.B.I. agent he should wait in the lobby and the man at the desk would call for someone to come and escort him to an office where he could talk to an agent. Stan sat and waited patiently.

Michelle Thompson was not the person in charge; she was quite inexperienced, but competent enough agent. With just a little more than a year of field experience in the service of the F.B.I. she was attached to the New York Office on general assignment. She was not assigned to narcotics, or counter terrorism. She was not in the violent felony task force or organized crime control unit. She was not investigating murders or saving kidnap victims. She was a field agent who received her assignments on a catch as catch can basis. Perhaps she would handle the follow-up investigation of a bank robbery, where the local police had already captured the robber, but a perfunctory federal investigation still had to be performed. Perhaps she would be assigned to take a report on the theft of a motor vehicle owned by some agency of the federal government. There were many mundane events that required some type of F.B.I. investigation. When those mundane events occurred, she got the assignment. She was a sort of "Jill of All Trades, Master of None" who was assigned to the kind of grunt work reserved for the most inexperienced new agents.

She joined the F.B.I. with the hope of getting involved in major cases, cases with life and death consequences or international importance. So far, the stuff she was doing was routine for an F.B.I. agent. She was sure she would break out from the crowd. She would catch that big case and be recognized for some exceptional task. She would rocket to a star position in the agency. Every new agent thought that big, career-making case was coming any day now, but Michelle was more anxious than most for law enforcement stardom to come her way.

She did not know it, but today was to be her day.

Today, Thompson was assigned to interview a man who spoke broken English, who insisted that he had information that he would only reveal to the man in charge. Michelle's assignment was to find out what she could, open a preliminary case file and take the case herself. If Michelle could not handle it, she could direct the man to someone could assist him, anyone, other than the Assistant Director in Charge. The Director was a busy man.

Michelle came downstairs to the reception

area. There she was introduced to Mr. Stanley Adamski. He had been waiting in the lobby, waiting for someone to take him to head of the F.B.I.

Thompson looked at the man she was to interview. He appeared to be a man in his late fifties or early sixties; about six feet tall with a slender build, well groomed with wire-rimmed glasses. He was dressed in casual business attire. She simply said, "Please sir, please come with me." On any other day, Stan might have noticed that the woman who was escorting him through the building was an extraordinarily attractive woman. She was a little on the tall side with a somewhat athletic build. She had long chestnut brown hair and deep dark eyes, an attractive face and a soft voice. However, today Stan would make little notice of her features; he was here for serious business.

She escorted Stanley to an elevator that took them to one of the upper levels of the building and then she led him to a private interview room. She invited him to sit at a large table and she took a seat across the table from him.

"Mr. Adamski, I'm Agent Thompson, How can I help you?"

Stanley replied in harsh tones. In his halting broken English he said, "I am not here to speak to secretary; I am here to speak to agent in charge." Michelle assured him that she was not a secretary, but a fully authorized agent of the F.B.I. Although she was not the agent in charge, she could help him. She reiterated, "Now how can the F.B.I. help you?"

"No, how can I help YOU…How might I help the F.B.I.! That is question. I come many miles to help YOU…. To help America…I know something YOU need to know. America needs to know. What I to tell is much danger to me, but I will tell. I will tell when I have assurance I will be protect. I must tell top man, only top man, and that is not *you!*"

Agent Thompson had been down this road before. On any given day, people demanded to speak to the man in charge, but often it would be simple matters that could be handled by any field agent. Even a field agent with just a little more than one year of experience could secure information and initiate a preliminary investigation. However, these matters had to be handled diplomatically. The person could have some information of value. It could be a matter of minor importance, but even a small clue offered by a member of the public could be of tremendous value in an ongoing investigation.

Perhaps this person could be in real danger. Perhaps it was a matter that needed to be referred to the local police for immediate intervention. The person could not be ignored…. a witness could not be deterred from telling what he or she knew. Who knows? Maybe it might even be something for the boss's office. It was unlikely, but Thompson would find out.

"Ok Mr. Adamski, I understand what you need to tell us is important. That is why I have come down here to speak with you. We want to get your information into the system as soon as possible.

However, unfortunately the man in charge of this office is away for today. So if you could give me some idea of how we might help…." Thompson paused and then said,…"each other"….. "I think I can get the ball rolling on whatever you have for us." Thompson put on a most sincere face and said, "Once I have some idea what this is about I'm sure I can get you in to see the top man." Of course, Thompson did not intend to bring this person to see the boss.

To Michelle Thompson, the man she was interviewing seemed to be ignorant and he needed to be handled gently, but ultimately dismissed. Thompson said, "I'll try to get you in to see him as soon as possible." There was a soft condescending tone in Thompson's voice. It was the kind of voice one uses to speak to a child who might not understand the complex nature of this workplace.

Stan feigned a small smile, "Agent Thompson, you remind me of bureaucrats in St. Petersburg. They think they smarter than me. They think Russians are smarter than Poles, but they cannot build rowboat without me to show how. You act like I stupid cause I no speak English so good. I speak much Polish, very good Polish and I speak Russian very well too. I speak some English, not so good, but some. Do you speak Polish, Agent Thompson? You speak any Polish at all? How about Russian? Do you speak any language but English?"

Somewhat astounded Michelle replied, "Why no, sir I'm afraid not, not at all."

Stan smiled, "I speak very good Polish, very

good Russian and some English. You speak very good English but NO Polish, NO Russian. That makes me smarter than you. No? So, you come to my country you need to use bathroom. You go around you say 'Where is bathroom… Where is bathroom?' Because you do not know to say *Gdzie jest w łazience,* you say where is bathroom? No one understands. They no show you where is bathroom. Now who is stupid one; a simple man who cannot find his way to man in charge of F.B.I. or F.B.I. agent who cannot find a shithouse?"

"Now, I am smart man. You try to get rid of me. You say I tell you and you will bring me to see top man. That not true. I tell you and you done with me. You hope I tell you and go away. I not tell you. I tell top man. I understand top man too busy to see every kook; he send flunky first. The flunky job is to get rid of me! Does the word flunky offend you? I sorry, but you seem like young flunky to me. I think my judgment that you are young flunky is better than you judgment that I am a fool! What you think?"

Michelle was quite embarrassed. Of course, Mr. Adamski was right. She had mistaken poor English verbal skills for poor intellectual skills.

Adamski continued, "You need proof so top man will see me. Here is proof."

Stanley opened the envelope that he was carrying. From within the envelope he produced a series of old-fashioned computer floppy disks. They were of the type that was sealed in a cardboard sleeve. Years ago, when these disks were in use, one would slip the disk, cardboard and all, into a slot on the computer and the machine would read the disk through a hole in the cardboard sleeve. That type of disk had not been used in desktop computers in more than twenty years. As he handed them to Agent Thompson, he said, "Here, here is proof. You will look at this and you will know."

Michelle Thompson knew she had been rightfully taken to task. She became just a little more humble. She took the disks and said, "I'm sorry Mr. Adamski, but we no longer use this type of disk in America. In fact, none of our computers here even has a slot for these large floppy disks."

Stanley replied, "Yes, yes we no longer use them in Poland either. In my homeland I am many things. I do many jobs. I am computer expert. I can see that you no computer expert. If you know anything about computers you know you can send disks to computer expert. He will find way to convert. He will read disks and print what is on. He will send it back to you. You will show to boss. He may not understand disks. Tell boss to show to your Navy people. They will understand better than you. I will come back soon and the boss will see me then."

Thompson was somewhat relieved. This seemed like a sure way to determine if this person had anything of value. The disks would speak for themselves. She could send the disks off to the computer lab with a simple work order to convert them to an up-to-date format. She could, print whatever was on the disks, and determine for herself if this Mr. Adamski would get to see the Assistant Director. It would satisfy the complainant that at least she was doing something. She would send them to the computer lab for analysis. If the report looked interesting, she might be able to open a case. Perhaps a good case, one that would get her noticed. She said to Stan, "I can assure I will get back to you."

Agent Thompson asked, "Where can I contact you?"

Stanley replied, "I don't know yet. I not yet find hotel room."

Thompson insisted, "I'll need your phone number and address" and Stan reiterated, "I don't know. I do not have hotel yet.

Michelle insisted, "But I will need to get in touch with you."

"No," Stan said, "I get back to you. I contact you in a few days. Thompson offered to help him find a near-by hotel, but the Pole replied, "You find hotel for me, you can find me at any time. I find my own hotel you no can find me anytime. I can find you anytime right here. I like that better."

Notwithstanding Thompson's best efforts to extract more information from Mr. Adamski, he insisted that it was time for him to leave. He took Thompson's business card and left the interview room. Michelle offered to escort him to the front door. To Stan it just seemed like the polite thing to do, but actually, everyone who was admitted to the inner offices of the F.B.I. was escorted out. The F.B.I. does not allow people to walk around HQ unescorted.

Michelle followed him as he made his way downstairs. She watched him retrieve his suitcase and saw him make his way out of F.B.I. Headquarters. She was tempted to follow him out into the street but she did not. Stan walked down Broadway until he came upon a stairway that led to the underground subway station. Then Stan disappeared into the New York City Subway System.

Navigation

This was Stanley Adamski's first subway ride. He rode the subway from South Ferry in Manhattan to 242nd Street in the Bronx. Like many first time riders, Stanley was a bit nervous. Unlike other first time riders it was not the ride that unnerved him. It was not the seemingly unfriendly faces of other passengers that made him nervous. Stanley lived most of his life among people with unfriendly faces. He had no fear of the train's high speed. He was an engineer. He knew the train was not going to hit the walls or jump from the track. He was never afraid of the dark and the sound of the steel wheels grinding around turns was not about to frighten him. He had worked in the shipyards most of his life. The sounds of grinding steel were, to him, a common sound. It was neither the people on the train nor the subway ride that made Stan nervous. It was his mission; the mission he chose to undertake that made him nervous.

He knew that he had just become involved in something quite dangerous. What he was doing would make his homeland a safer place; it would make America a safer place. The world would be a safer place. Stan was nervous; another man might have been scared to death doing what Stan was doing, but Stan was just a bit nervous.

He had traveled over forty-two hundred miles from Gdansk in Poland to get to New York. He was here now. Here in America it would be safe to do what he had come to do. Here he could do what he felt he had to do. He could have gone to the authorities in Poland, but here in America it would be safer. The authorities in America could be trusted.

Today his Poland was free from the controlling oversight of the now defunct Soviet Union, but there were still many in his homeland whose sympathies lie with the communists, with the Russians. Many communists who held government posts were ousted after the Solidarity Movement; after Lech Walesa, Pope John Paul and President Reagan changed the world, but some, who still strongly believed in communism, managed to stay in powerful government positions.

They held positions of importance when the Russians were in charge. Some still did. Others had been reduced to lower government positions, but they were still scattered throughout the bureaucracy. In fact, when Lech Walesa left office a former communist leader was elected president of Poland. Poland remained more democratic, friendlier toward the U.S.A., but the communists were still around. They still had influence. Too many of them longed for a day when communism would again be a powerful force in the world. Those faces, the faces of the communists, were the unfriendly faces that Stan knew. They were more unfriendly, more deadly, than any unfriendly face on the subway. If any of them should find out what he was about to reveal, his life would not be worth one *grosz* in Poland.

Stanley believed that here in America he could do what he had to do. Here it would be safer.

Stanley was a bit nervous, but he had already started his mission; he had delivered the computer disks to the authorities. It was too late to turn back now. His mission was now in the hands of the F.B.I.

Stan had only been on American soil once before in his life and that was more than 20 years ago. He had never been in the subway system. The subway system in New York is complex, but the maps are color coded and any reasonably intelligent person can navigate their way from one station to another. He knew where he wanted to go and the maps were easy to read. Stan would have no problem.

Twenty years ago a shipboard accident caused Stan to get off a boat at a place and time when he was not scheduled to do so. He found himself temporarily stranded in America, in Yonkers, New York. He had no place to stay, no money, and no means of transportation. However, on that day he made new friends. They took him to a place called the Polish Center, wherein a number of Polish-Americans, members of the Polish Center came forward and befriended him. He would always have a warm spot in his memories for all of the members of the center, but one, young man, Adam Mickiewicz, had truly gone out of his way to help. More than simply remembering his name and hospitality Stan would never forget the man's passion for American patriotism. Since his friend hated Russian communists, Stan had disappointed his friend by doing work for the Russians at the shipyards, but things were different now. Poland was no longer a puppet for the Russians. Poland had come a long way; Now Poland was closer to America. Stanley was anxious to tell his friend that now he understood American values. Now he was going to do the right thing for America and he wanted his friend to know that. He was going to Yonkers to find his friend Adam Mickiewicz, tell him that he no longer worked for the communists; he would no longer work for the Russians. Now he was going to do a great thing for America and the free world.

The subway did not go all the way to Yonkers, but a number of the stations were quite close to the border between the Bronx and Yonkers. Stan wanted to go to the west side of Yonkers and a quick look at his subway map told him he'd need walk a few blocks to the Park Place station just off Broadway. He would take the #2 train to 96th street then switch to the #1 north bound. He would take that train to the last stop, West 242nd Street and then he would be just a few miles from Yonkers and from the home of Adam Mickiewicz.

Stanley Adamski had not seen his young friend in a very long time. Just before he left Poland, Stan tried to locate his American friend several times through the Internet, to no avail. Stan's American friend had been named after a well-known Polish poet of the 19th century. All Stan's Internet searches on the name came back to the more famous Pole of antiquity. He could find nothing about the present day American, named Adam Mickiewicz.

Nevertheless, Stan was sure that if he went to the Polish Center in Yonkers someone there would know how to put him in touch with his long lost friend.

Stanley planned to take the subway train to West 242nd Street and look for a hotel near the station. He would do that today. Today he would rest after his long journey from Poland. Tomorrow he would go to the Polish Center look for Adam Mickiewicz. He would find him. Perhaps Mickiewicz could come to his room at the hotel. Perhaps he would go to the place where he and Adam Mickiewicz shared a meal and a few drinks, The Polish Center in Yonkers. Either way he would meet Mickiewicz. They would share a drink talk about old times and catch up on what had gone on in their lives over the past twenty years.

Stanley hoped that Adam was not angry with him because of the work he had done for the Russians. Stanley remembered well how twenty years ago, Adam continually tried to convince Stanley that communism was nothing less than the most evil form of government on earth. He continually and passionately spoke about how the Polish people ought to break ties with the Soviet Union and ally themselves more closely with America. Stan was curious how Adam had reacted to the more recent events in the world. Events had, in fact, resulted in Poland breaking ties with Russia and becoming an ally of the United States in N.A.T.O. Stan was sure that Adam would be quite pleased. Now Stanley could tell Adam that he would have to admit Poland was better off as a democratic nation. He hoped that Mickiewicz did not know of the work that he had done for the Soviets, but if he did, Stan would explain. He was sure Adam would understand, in hard times a man must do what a man must do. Now there would be no more work for the Russians. Now he would work for the Americans.

Stan had a plan. Once his business with Adam Mickiewicz had been taken care of, he would come back to his hotel and rest for two or three days. Then he would get back on the subway and return to Federal Plaza. Perhaps then, the man in charge would be ready to see him.

Sailing New Waters

Stanley Adamski did not think of himself as a very political person. He rarely thought about the conflict between the world of capitalism and the socialist world of communism. There were some in his country who believed communism and a close alliance with The Soviet Union provided the stability Poland needed to remain in existence after WWII. They knew periods of time when many of their people were severely poor. When the government of Poland was unstable, they saw the poor suffer tremendously. During the war when the Nazis invaded Poland, the leaders of the country fled and set up a government-in-exile in London, England. However, after the war, a government more heavily influenced by the Soviets was imposed upon the Polish people; a communist government. Over time the dominance of the U.S.S.R. over the Polish people proved to be more distasteful than what they had known before the Great War.

Many, if not most, of his friends and neighbors wanted desperately to have the kind of independence and freedom that western nations enjoyed. They longed for a free, independent Poland, a democratic Poland, and a Poland for the Polish people.

As for Stan, it was somewhat bothersome to him that Poland seemed to be subservient to the U.S.S.R. among the Soviet bloc nations, but he rarely lost sleep over it. He, like many among his people, was quite content with the communist system. They had jobs, a roof over their heads, a good education for their children and a reasonably good life style. He himself had a very good job at the shipyards. He had worked in Gdansk and when times got hard in the Polish shipyards, he found work in St. Petersburg in the Russian shipyards. Often the Russians and Poles worked on joint design programs to build great ships. He had a good job, a good life. He was content. To him it did not seem to matter. His basic thoughts were capitalism, socialism, Russian domination or an independent Poland, who cares? As long as they left him alone, as long as he had a job, a roof over his head and food on the table he did not care about politics. Leave politics to the politicians, he would say.

Then came Lech Wałęsa and The Solidarity Movement. At first, Stan thought that Solidarity was made up of a bunch of troublemakers. Sure, they said they were simply demanding fair treatment for Polish shipyard workers, but their activities were causing the authorities to clamp down on the workers. The more trouble the union made for the communist government the more the government pushed back. The Russians were cutting back on giving contracts to Polish shipbuilders. More work was going to St. Petersburg where there was no union.

At the time, Stan feared that the Polish shipyards would be closed down. He thought that he too would have to move to St. Petersburg to get work. However, over the years Solidarity prevailed. They not only brought about more rights for union workers

31

they influenced the course of the entire nation. As Stan watched the growth of Solidarity, it stirred in him a pride unlike any he had ever known before, a pride in being Polish.

Solidarity was a labor union movement that stuck its thumb in the eye of the Soviets, in the eye of the communist leaders in Poland and it called the attention of the world to the idea that freedom could become a reality for the Polish people once again. The movement started in the shipyards and spread across the nation. In time the man who started Solidarity, Lech Wałęsa, would become the democratically elected President of Poland and Poland would take its place among the free nations of the world. Stan came to understand Polish pride like he had never known before. Now he knew the pride of a free Poland, a Poland for the Poles. He understood. He knew that Adam Mickiewicz was right. He understood why this idea of independence and freedom drives men to do extraordinary things. Now he was prepared to do extraordinary things for Poland, his homeland.

As unbelievable as it seemed, the Soviet Union fell apart. One by one, various nations that had come under Soviet domination were able to break away and attain independence. Many of those now free nations were establishing relations with the United States. It was a new world for Stan, a new world for everyone. Poland would now be joining N.A.T.O.

The North Atlantic Treaty Organization was

an organization that had been seen as the most direct obstacle to communism's world dominance. Even more surprising Poland had entered into a pact with America that would permit the U.S.A to place missiles on Poland's northern borders. Twenty years ago, this would have been unheard of. If Poland was going to be a partner with America in a military pact then the Americans needed to know what Stan knew.

Finding a Port

Stan found a hotel conveniently near the train station. It was about half way between the train station and the Bronx border with the City of Yonkers. Stan did not wish to be located if the F.B.I. was looking for him. He would meet them on his terms and in his own good time. Therefore, he decided to use a false name when he registered at the hotel. Knowing that there was a significant Hispanic population in the area, he signed the registration card as Jose Mendez of 5776 Pulaski Street, Brooklyn, NY. He had once heard that there was such a street in Brooklyn named for the famous Polish hero of the American Revolution. Stan paid for a stay of several days in cash, in advance, and the man at the desk never questioned the signature on the hotel registration card.

Stan did not unpack. He would simply take articles of clothing out of his suitcase as he needed them. In addition to his clothing Stan had a small portable bar in a leather case. It had been purchased it at the Polish Center Gift Shop. The box was covered in leather. The lid had a small brass lock and on the cover was a brass plate embossed with the Polish Eagle, a symbol of Poland for more than a thousand years.

Inside there were little compartments lined with silk, that held accessories for making cocktails. A small silver flask for whiskey, two shot glasses, four tall glasses and a small pair of ice tongs. The glasses and flask were also embossed with a likeness of the Polish Eagle. The whiskey flask was nearly full and ready to serve. The portable bar had been a gift from one of his American friends. It had been opened only once before and that was more than twenty years ago. It was the night that it was given to him as a going away present. It was the night that Adamski left Yonkers to return to his ship for the voyage back to Poland. That night so long ago, he opened the leather case, took out the two tall glasses and one shot glass, dropped ice in the tall glasses and poured some whiskey from the flask over the ice. He filled the shot glasses and he shared a toast with his new friends *"do czasu spotykamy się ponownie"* or "till we meet again." They drank up. Stan then put away the glasses and flask, closed and locked the case. Then he said, "I shall not unlock this until one day when I will come back to America, I will then unlock this box and we will again share a drink from this flask, in these glasses." Stan was sure that soon he and one of his old friends, Adam Mickiewicz, would finally share that drink. Stan had been waiting years to open this small leather box and share a drink with his friends in America.

Stan made an afternoon phone call from his room to the Polish Center. Someone, the bartender, who did not identify himself by name, answered the phone. Speaking in Polish Stan asked the bartender if he spoke Polish. The man replied that he did and the conversation continued in Polish. Stan asked the man if he knew Adam Mickiewicz. The bartender asked,

"The poet?" Stan laughed. He said no, and explained that he was looking for an American of the same name. The man at the Polish Center said he did not know any American by that name. Stan told the man that he had just arrived from Poland and was anxious to see his old friend whom he had met at the Center. He also told the bartender that he would be coming to the Polish Center the next few days in an effort to find his friend.

The bartender told Stan that he would ask around to see if anyone knew Adam Mickiewicz. He asked Stan for the phone number where he was staying and promised to call him if he found anyone who knew the fellow. Stan supplied the number, told the bartender where he was staying and told him, "If you should find Mr. Mickiewicz or anyone who might know him, please give him this information and tell him I am anxious to see him."

It seemed odd to Stan that the bartender did not know Adam since he knew that his friend had been a regular customer at the place. However, it had been twenty years since Stan had been at the center. Perhaps Adam had moved away. In any event, he was sure that he would find someone at the center who knew Adam. He would find someone who could put them in touch.

There was a desk in the room. On the desk was a small plastic pitcher, a small plastic ice bucket and two plastic glasses wrapped in cellophane. Stan took the plastic items off the desk and replaced them with the contents of his small portable bar and placed them in place of the plastic drink setting. If Adam Mickiewicz showed up, he would be ready to share that drink they talked about years ago. Then Stan placed the empty leather box back in his suitcase

Much later that evening Stan prepared to go to sleep. He stripped naked and placed his clothing on a chair next to his bed, he got in the bed and turned off the lights.

Still somewhat anxious about this business of his, he lay in bed and stared at the ceiling. There was much to think about. He wondered if he would ever see his homeland again. Perhaps the F.B.I. could handle this whole matter discretely. No one would ever have to know that he was involved, that he was the one who told. He could go home. That was what he truly wanted to do. He wanted to take care of this business, perhaps see Adam Mickiewicz and go home to Poland. He thought that perhaps his safety would never be insured if he went back to Poland. Perhaps the Americans would offer him asylum. Perhaps he would have to go into the American Witness Protection Program that he had heard about. He was not sure how to proceed. If only he could find Adam Mickiewicz. Adam would know what to do.

Stanley wondered if the fact that he would be the informer could be kept quiet. Would he be going home to Poland? Would he be staying in America forevermore? His wondering did not keep him awake too long. He had a long day behind him and he would be facing another long day tomorrow. He had questions on his mind, but when he did fall asleep, it was a deep, sound sleep.

That night he slept with questions on his mind. His primary question was would he be going home to Poland, or staying in America.

As Stanley Adamski, also known as Jose Mendez, quietly slept naked in a Bronx hotel, a fully dressed man silently entered his room. He wore a heavy dark coat, a knitted hat and leather gloves. He removed from his coat pocket a .380 caliber semi-automatic pistol. He attached a state of the art silencer to the barrel of the gun, placed the gun near the sleeping man's head. He took the extra pillow that lay on the bed next to Stan's head. In one simultaneous movement, he placed the pillow on Stan's head, put the barrel of the gun into the pillow against Stan's head and pulled the trigger.

Stan would not be going back to Poland.

Clearing the Decks

With his target eliminated, the man who cryptically called himself Sorge went about the business of assuring that he would evade detection. Keeping his gloves on the whole time, he methodically searched the room. He could hardly believe his good fortune in this endeavor. In many ways, Stan had already unwittingly taken steps that would make solving his own homicide difficult. His killer found the hotel's computer printed cash receipt for the payment of the lodging fees. The receipt was made out to a Jose Mendez of 5776 Pulaski Street Brooklyn, NY. Sorge would leave that in the room for the authorities to find. It would mislead the police. They would not even know the true name of the victim. The victim had not unpacked and he was naked. All the assailant had to do was pick up the clothing on the chair, put it back in the suitcase and take the suitcase with him when he left. There would be no clothing that might lead the police to a possible identity of the victim. No store clothing labels, no laundry marks, no nothing that might help to identify the dead man.

The police would believe that the pillow had been placed over the victim's head to silence the shot. Actually, the pillow had been placed over the head to prevent blood splatter. It had worked well. There was no blood splatter on the assailant, none around the room. Blood splatter can provide so much evidence, but this crime scene would not provide that evidence.

Since the police would think, the pillow was to silence the shot they would not be looking for a pro that might have used a silencer. They would be looking for an amateur who uses a pillow to silence a shot.

The assailant scattered a small quantity of cocaine on a table in the room. He figured that would mislead the police. Next, the assailant looked for, and found, the spent shell case that had been ejected from his .380 when he fired it. He picked it up and threw it in the toilet. One flush and that piece of evidence was gone forever.

Sorge was proud of his work. With his gloves still on Sorge grabbed one of the plastic glasses, poured himself a drink from Stan's portable bar set-up, looked in the mirror and offered a toast to himself. He drank. Satisfied that he had covered all his tracks, the man who liked to call himself Sorge turned off the lights and taking the suitcase with him he left the hotel.

When he returned to his car, he picked up his prepaid, disposable cell phone and made a call to another prepaid cell phone. It was a call to the phone belonging to Kirill Petrov.

Dangerous Seaman - Kirill Petrov

Kirill Petrov answered his phone and the voice on the other end simply said, "I found him and he has been taken care of."

"How? …."

"Judging from where I lost the signal from the transmitter I had placed in his suitcase, I surmised that he must have entered the subway system. The transmitter is a good one but, it would not send a signal from underground. I figured that he would try to get to the Polish Center. I went to the center and asked around a bit. Sure enough, he had made a call to the center. He told the bartender where he was staying. Then it was easy. I went to the hotel in the Bronx and my receiver began to pick up the transmissions from the tracking device in the suitcase. I just followed the beacon right to his room, waited for dark, and did what needed to be done."

Kirill replied, "Good, tell me, is it clean?" "It is clean." Sorge said. "There isn't a shred of evidence left at the scene."

With a slight tone of anger in his voice, Kirill went on. "It's just too bad that we ever lost contact with him. Too bad we could not have done this before he went to the headquarters of the fucking F.B.I. I cannot tell you how upset I was when you called to tell me he entered the building"

Sorge said, "Look, we weren't even sure that his trip was anything more than a vacation at first. If you were that concerned about it, you could have had your people in Europe handle it, but you did not. Now I had to handle it. Who would have thought that he would go right from JFK to F.B.I. headquarters? I most certainly was not going to be able to take care of him in there."

Kirill said, "I understand you could not kill him in F.B.I. headquarters, but it was you who lost him when he came out."

Sorge went on, "The building is huge. There are a half dozen exits on to different streets I could not cover them all. I did not see him leave the building. So he got away from us for a while, but we put a good transmitter into his bag. I found him again. It was smart to use a good transmitter."

Kirill said, "We're just lucky that no one else found it."

Sorge said, "First off it was well concealed in the bag, in the liner; Adamski wasn't going to see it in the bag. Secondly, the tracking device transmitter looks like an ordinary digital watch. If I put it right in your hand, you would think it was a wristwatch. There is no way even the best-trained x-ray screener at customs or in the TSA would recognize it as anything but an ordinary wristwatch. When you look at a bag through an ex-ray machine, there is no way to tell if the watch is actually in the bag itself or in the liner. On the x-ray, a watch hidden in the liner looks like it is in the bag proper. No one was going to find it. I am not lucky; I am good at what I do! However, a small transmitter like that takes a small battery, not very powerful, so I lost the signal for a while, so what! I found him again. Anyway, he's been taken care of."

Not completely satisfied with the answers he received Kirill said, "So what! I'll tell you so what! While he was out of our sight, he could have met with someone else. Someone could have met with him in his room. He could have told another. We know he has been trying to locate an American citizen. It is bad enough that he spoke to the F.B.I. Who knows who else he might have spoken to? By the way, speaking about the F.B.I., do you think he could have told them anything vital?"

Sorge replied, "I don't know, but I doubt it. He was only in there about an hour. If he gave up anything that seemed important to them they would never have let him leave the building, or at least they would not have let him leave without putting a tail of their own on him. I think it is more likely that he told them he had something to trade for asylum and was just arranging for future disclosure. Of course, you never know."

"Did he meet with anyone else?"

"He could have, but I don't think so."

Kirill asked, "What makes you think not?" Sorge went on, "Because he was alone. I don't believe that anyone who knew what he was doing would have left him alone. I mean he could have met with someone at his hotel during the early afternoon. He could have told someone. If he did, we will just have to deal with it. Anyway the best we can hope for is that the leak is sealed, the damage minimized."

"I suppose you're right." Kirill said.

Then Sorge asked, "Is there anything else?"

Kirill responded, "I do not think so. Not at this time. There is another person who needed to be eliminated, but I have someone better suited for this one. I believe he has already been taken care of. I'm waiting for the report."

Sorge said, "You should have let me handle it. If you want it done right, you should have let me do it. It would have been done clean. It would have been done right."

"Yes, but let us not forget that it was you who lost Adamski in the city. We needed you to take care of that aspect. There was no time to wait for you to find him then come back for another. He had to be taken care of before Adamski could meet with him. All I can hope for is that this other fellow did not meet with him at the hotel before you got to Adamski. I'm just a little concerned that this one might already know more than we would like. One way or another he will not be a problem in the future; there is no future for him."

Sorge said, "Ok, I suppose you're right... What now?"

"Just go somewhere and lie low for a while. I'll get in touch with you if we need your services again." With that said, Kirill terminated the conversation.

Kirill Petrov began to think to himself.........*Sorge..... Sorge indeed...Sorge.... this person thinks too much of himself. Too confident!*

Too confident!

The First Mate - The Maestro

Kirill then made a call himself. Again using his throwaway phone, he called another disposable phone. A man answered.

Without going through the usual salutations Kirill began to speak at once to the man he called the Maestro. Kirill spoke in demanding terms, "What about Mickiewicz? Were you able to locate him? I must insure that he is eliminated. We have been monitoring Adamski's Internet use since he left Russia to return to Poland. We know for sure that Adamski was desperately attempting to locate a Mr. Adam Mickiewicz living in America. I do not know what he has to do with this; I do not know what he knows. I do not care what he knows or does not know. I do know that he is a person Adamski met when he was last in the United States. I know he is a man who had encouraged Mr. Adamski to defect to America back then. I want him eliminated. Did you have any luck in locating him?"

"I believe I have," the Maestro said.

Kirill asked, "You believe you have?"

Maestro's reply was, "Well, actually I have, but Adam Mickiewicz is not his real name. I have very compelling evidence that the name Adam Mickiewicz is a pseudonym; it is not his real name. I have equally compelling evidence of his true identity."

Kirill interrupted, "I don't like the fact that Adamski was trying to correspond with an American person who uses an alias."

The Maestro said, "Clam down. I developed a plan for this so-called Mickiewicz fellow. I have tracked him down. I know his true identity and his whereabouts. As luck would have it, he entered a hospital earlier today for a minor procedure. You know how it is with minor procedures; sometimes they can have serious consequences. Anyway, we have someone else who has taken care of him. I believe you know who that would be."

Kirill said, "Yes, yes I can imagine who you might call for such a mission … a capable man. Still I am relying on you to make sure it is done."

The Maestro resumed, "As soon as you called and told me that Adamski went to the F.B.I. my plan for Mr. Mickiewicz was initiated at the hospital. He no longer poses a threat. Our so called, Mr. Adam Mickiewicz is dead."

Kirill said, "Very well" and then he cut off the call.

Although he said very well, Kirill was not so sure everything was in fact very well. Sorge had lost his man for some period of time. Who could know what transpired in that interval. Now he learned that his number two man had delegated the Mickiewicz matter to a third party. A reliable person, but it unnecessarily expanded the number of persons who knew what was happening. Most of all there was the F.B.I. visit. That could be disastrous, but what could be done about that now? Kirill did not like this, but as they say in America, it is what it is.

In the old days, he could have taken care of this whole matter in Poland. However, who could be trusted in Poland now? These days things are different. There were too many pro-American people in the Polish government now. Sure, he still had his communist friends in important places in Poland, but could they still be trusted? Did they have enough influence to insure that if Adamski were killed in Poland it would not be thoroughly investigated? Did they have enough influence to insure that the killing would not be traced back to Kirill himself? No, killing Adamski in America would be safer. Kirill longed for the old days, but he feared they would never come back. At least now, he was making money and life in America was not half-bad. In fact, life in America could be very good. It could be very profitable if he could stay out of jail ... if he could stay alive.

Lost at Sea

Buddy was in a state of nostalgic melancholy. He, like many men his age, was reflecting upon his youthful ambitions, his young dreams and desires. He knew very well how his simple, happy life had become complicated. The quest for vengeance will complicate a man's life. He hated the idea that his life had become so complex. He longed to once again have that carefree, youthful outlook on life. He was a realist. He knew those days were long gone, yet he still longed to regain at least some small fragment of his former life. He just wanted to be himself again. He spent so much of his time wandering around the world, but now he had come home, home to Yonkers, New York.

It was a tragic event that brought him home. He came home to attend a funeral, but he was pleased to be home nonetheless. This was the hometown of his teenage years. Buddy drove his black Hemi-Powered Dodge Charger through the streets of his former hometown. Driving that car made him feel good. The rumble in the exhaust system gave evidence of the substantial horsepower at his disposal. The sensation of power the Hemi engine provided reminded him of the cars he drove in his younger days. The days when he thought that all anyone needed for a happy life was a powerful car or a fast motorcycle. The car was just another attempt to reconnect to his past. In that car he felt he could be that young man who had simple dreams.

Being back in Yonkers was also helping him to reconnect. He sometimes referred to it as his hometown, although this was a misnomer. It was not a town at all, but a large city. It was not ranked one of the one hundred largest cities in America any more as it once was, but it did rank around one hundred and tenth or so. It was the fourth largest in New York, a state known for its large cities. Buddy had not been back there in many years, but he still had friends there. It was the home of his best friend Ray. He had not seen this friend from his younger days in about twenty years, yet he still considered him to be his best friend.

Buddy's father had been the owner of a small martial arts school located in the Fordham Road section of the Bronx. His father had been a martial arts instructor for the United States Army. He was his division-boxing champion and he held black belts in Karate and in jujutsu. He was stationed for a while in England and later transferred to Korea. The Korean War was over by the time Buddy' father was assigned there, but there was still a need for American military presence in the area. While he was in Korea, Buddy's father met a Korean civilian man named Choi Yong Sul who was teaching a new and relatively unknown style of martial art. Intrigued by what he had heard about this man teaching a new martial art form, he managed to get into his classes. Buddy's dad always said that he first began taking the lessons from Master Choi Yong Sul because he taught his art in the basement of a brewery and there was free beer available after class. The truth was that he was endlessly fascinated by martial arts and particularly Oriental martial arts. The style Master Sul was teaching had been given a number of different names, but eventually became known as Hipkido. In time, he became a champion in Hipkido and later mastered other Korean styles as well.

Buddy's mother was a Polish Jew. She was the daughter of a university professor. She had met Buddy's dad when he was still serving in the army in Europe. She had been a university student, at the Jagiellonian University in Krakow, Poland where she was studying Indo-European languages. She had hoped to become a professor of languages like her father who had once taught at the school. In fact, her father had been the chair of the languages department. She was fluent in Polish, Russian, and English and in Middle Eastern languages. She was also somewhat adept in some Far Eastern languages; Korean and Chinese were on the list of languages she was working on. Her family had escaped from Poland at the onset of World War II and immigrated to England, where her father had offered his services to the English government. He worked in the communications and cryptology sections of the military intelligence services where he worked as a translator during the war. After the war he helped to organized Rozglosnia, which was, a component of the Radio Free Europe program that was aimed at delivering a pro-democracy message to the Polish people living under Soviet oppression. He was zealously anti-communist and fought hard to restore democracy in Poland. Sadly, he never lived to see that day when democracy returned to Poland.

Although Buddy's mom had moved back to Poland after the war to attend the university there, she often returned to England to spend time with her family and some of her childhood friends who were still in England. Buddy's dad met his mom in England while he was on a temporary military assignment there. They married in England and she accompanied him when he was transferred to Korea. They often referred to their stay in Korea as their honeymoon. When his enlistment was up, Buddy's dad returned to America with his new bride. After his discharge from the service, he opened his own martial arts school and she eventually got a job at a junior college where she taught languages.

Buddy's upbringing was a mixture of his father's martial arts background and military type lifestyle and his mother's Polish roots, higher education and refined culture.

His family lived in the Woodlawn section of the Bronx on the eastern border of The City of Yonkers, New York. His father taught him all the skills necessary to become a champion martial artist. By the age of 8 years-old, Buddy was already a junior champion in several forms of marital arts. As a teen, he continued to win a number of important competitions in the Oriental martial arts. Throughout his life, Buddy continued to hone those skills so that as an adult he would be a formidable opponent in just about any martial arts competition.

He attended public schools, but his mother also home schooled him in languages, art, science, music and world politics. He was an outstanding student in all subjects.

As well educated as Buddy was, he held on to fanciful ideas as to what he wanted be when he grew up. Some little kids want to grow up to be astronauts, cowboys or pirates. Perhaps a few, wanted to be the U.S. President, but Buddy always wanted to be a racecar driver. Reading magazines about auto racing or automotive repairs occupied what ever free time Buddy had. If he was not thinking about fast cars, he was thinking about fast motorcycles. The whole atmosphere of the man, the machine and the racetrack fascinated Buddy. Although Buddy did, occasionally, give some thought to becoming a police officer, being a racecar driver was what he yearned for.

Buddy's father knew, and was friendly with, a number of police officers. Some had become students at his martial arts school. Through his acquaintance with them, he learned that the Yonkers Police Athletic League, P.A.L, had a number of sports programs for youths. At the insistence of his father, Buddy joined the P.A.L. and he became a member of their boxing team. It was there that Buddy met a young boy named Ray Cassini. Cassini was also on the boxing team. Buddy and Ray fought in different weight divisions and each were the golden glove champions for their respective division. They became inseparable best friends.

It was also through his affiliation with P.A.L. that Buddy became fascinated with the idea of becoming a police officer. Many of the officers who worked around the P.A.L. facility befriended the kids and would occasionally tell stories of exciting police actions. Many of the kids came to look up to the officers. The idea of becoming a cop was alluring to Buddy. He thought, "Wow they actually pay you to ride a motorcycle!" Of course, he was just a kid and a kid's mind did not give much consideration to the other aspects of police work. As a young boy who was fascinated by motor sports, all Buddy thought about was riding that police motorcycle or driving those incredibly fast police cars.

The P.A.L. facility was located on the banks of the Hudson River. Buddy and Ray loved to be around the riverfront. After activities at P.A.L., they would walk up and down the banks of the river take in the sights and talk about their futures. They would fish there and often take a swim. They came to know a number of persons who worked the riverfront and truly enjoyed a day by the river. Ray always talked about one day becoming a riverboat pilot and Buddy would talk about being a racecar driver.

Buddy's mother had a different future in mind for him. She hoped that he would grow up to emulate his grandfather and become a college professor. His mother insisted that he become well educated. From his earliest formative years, he was taught to speak four languages. He was masterful in Dari, Indo-European languages, Polish, and Russian as well as

English. When he spoke in those languages, even a native could not discern any unusual accent. Although, most would agree his English held a noticeable Bronx accent. Buddy often practiced the language skills he learned from his mother. It was the one aspect of his home schooling he truly enjoyed.

Buddy's fanciful teenage ambitions led him to continue to hope, one day, to be a racecar driver or a motorcycle cop. His mother knew that young boys hold such fanciful dreams, but they soon outgrow them. She did whatever she could to discourage him from any thoughts of becoming a racecar driver or following any pursuits in the automotive sports. Reading the motor sports magazines that he loved to read was forbidden. She insisted that he read the works of the grand masters of literature. She would speak of the dangers of police work and often told Buddy she would never sleep if he took such a job. She was angry that her husband had introduced her son to his police officer friends, but what could she do? It was done. Buddy did what he could to please his mother. Despite his dreams of being, a racecar driver, Buddy actually enjoyed the status of being a top student and loved learning whatever his mother had to teach. He was a sponge for education, a great student and a fan of fine arts, but he continued to read motor sports magazines behind his mother's back and continued to listen to cop war stories whenever he could.

Buddy's mom was sure that as Buddy matured, a prestigious position at a university would become more appealing. She would tell him "As boys become men they learn to appreciate different things. You will see such dreams fade and different ideas replace them."

His mother always allowed Buddy to know and understand his father's American roots, but she insisted that his Polish roots be known as well.

In Yonkers, not far from their home in Woodlawn, there was a facility known as the Polish Center. The Polish Center was opened in the 1930's as a meeting hall and banquette center operated by a group of Polish-American citizens of Yonkers. Over the years, renovations at the Polish Center redesigned the building to include a grand ballroom that could easily accommodate 700 guests. There were three additional dining rooms of various sizes for private affairs. Catering weddings and hosting political and entertainment events was the mainstay of the business, but there was also a section that was opened to the general public that housed a public restaurant and public bar.

In addition to the public bar, there were two private bars to accommodate private parties, bowling alleys in the basement and a gift shop that specialized in the sale of items imported from Poland. In addition to the Polish cultural events, there were often other events held at the center that would appeal to teens and adults of every ethnic background. One of the mainstays of the center was their athletic club program. It was a club that met at the center and it encouraged persons of all backgrounds to join in the various sports programs that they sponsored. Buddy's father was an all-round athlete and he offered his services as a coach to a number of the sports programs for children. His mother offered her services, free of charge, to teach English to newly arriving Polish immigrants. They were very involved in every aspect of the center. Buddy often would join his family at various ethnic Polish-style dances and parties that were held at the center.

As an adult, Buddy would occasionally stop in at the public restaurant for lunch. Occasionally, he would stop in at the public bar for a drink or two.

Buddy's friend Ray Cassini lived in the Park Hill section of Yonkers. His home was not far from the Polish Center and he too would often dine at the center.

Buddy had not been back to Yonkers in many years. As he cruised through the streets of Yonkers, he was quite surprised to see the recent development in the area. The last time Buddy was in Yonkers, the west side was in a serious state of depression. Now new buildings were being erected along the waterfront. Upscale restaurants had opened along Main Street and the downtown area seemed to be undergoing a rebirth. As he looked across the skyline, he could see large construction cranes lifting massive amounts of building materials to the tops of new buildings, clear evidence of a renaissance, a rebirth. It felt good to see his hometown being renewed, but Buddy sincerely hoped that some of the old would be retained. As Buddy drove past the Polish Center, he was pleased to see that they were still in business, but he wondered if his old home, the Royal Buena Vista Hotel, was still the same. Buddy only lived at the Royal for a short period of time, but still he wished to see it again. So much of his old neighborhood had met with a wrecking ball. He would be surprised if the building was still there. He would be even more surprised if it was still operating. Still he hoped.

The story of the city of Yonkers can be told like the story of many other old cities. There were the good old days of prosperity. The hard times when manufacturing centers were fleeing from the inner cities followed by a period of renaissance.

The old times were good times. Around the turn of the century in the late 1800's and early 1900's Yonkers was a major industrial city. Being just north of New York City on the Hudson River, Yonkers had its own deep-water ports, three major rail lines and an industrial work force. Elisha Otis opened his first elevator factory on the banks of the Hudson in Yonkers. It was the largest elevator manufacturing company in the world and was the single largest employer in the city. A number of foundries and cable and wire producing companies grew up around the elevator plant that was the single largest purchaser of wire and cable.   The Alexander Smith and Sons Carpet Company had a factory in Yonkers. It was composed of 45 buildings, running nearly 800 looms, and employing over 4,000 workers. It was known as one of the premier carpet producing centers in the world. Yonkers was also the headquarters of the

Waring Hat Company. At the time it was the nation's largest hat manufacturer. There was a sugar refinery that processed raw sugar cane imported, by ship, from around the world, and a wide variety of support industries that supplied materials and services to the larger corporations.

It was a boomtown known for the impressive industrial output in its southwest quadrant and it was well known as a city for living comfortably in its northwestern quadrant. It was referred to as "The City of Gracious Living," and it was a center for performing arts and leisure. The first golf course in the United States was established in Yonkers and numerous country clubs dotted its landscape. The serene lifestyle of Yonkers provided the backdrop for the famous play "Hello Dolly."

The economy there supported a large immigrant population. Workers from all over Europe came. The Irish, Italians, Poles and Portuguese moved to the city in droves, each collecting in their own ethnic neighborhoods in the city's west side. Over time, the west side became the center of the blue-collar workers and the more affluent populated the city's east side.

In the 1950's and 60's things went very bad very fast. For reasons that are not entirely clear, many of those businesses went under or moved away. Perhaps it was the ever-increasing cost of labor in the northeast, or the high cost of electrical power in the New York area. Perhaps it was foreign competition or more complex economic issues that impacted the local economy. Whatever the reasons, businesses in Yonkers began to fail and there was a serious domino effect. First, to go was the carpet factory. Overnight, 4000 people were unemployed. Next went the hat company and another 3,000 jobs. Then a Connecticut-based firm purchased Otis Elevator and moved the entire manufacturing operation to Connecticut. Then the cable and wire companies that supplied hardware for the elevator operation began layoffs. One by one, every major employer went away until only the sugar refinery was left. The entire west side of the city came to look like a ghost town. Abandoned buildings stood where great manufacturing centers once stood. The surrounding neighborhoods loomed with burned out buildings and substandard housing. The sight of empty factory buildings with broken windows and graffiti gave the west side of the city a look of desperation. There were no jobs, no hope. There was poverty and crime. It became a rust bowl city.

After many years of gloomy days for the city, there was a turnaround of a different sort. In the mid 1990's there was a renaissance of sorts occurring on the west side. People had taken an interest in the beautiful views of the Hudson. The rail lines along the Hudson that connected suburbia to the City of New York were still in operation and the interest in rail commuting was increasing as the cost of gasoline was making commuting by car less desirable.

The rail lines running through Yonkers provided quick easy transportation to New York City.

As commuting by car was becoming more and more expensive and inconvenient, the short rail hop from Yonkers to the heart of downtown New York was becoming more attractive. Investors began building condos and large apartment buildings along the Yonkers riverfront. A new and magnificent library was built in the shell of what was once one of the decrepit factory buildings. Some of the old factories were being converted to loft apartments and artist's studios. An industrial park opened on the site of the old Otis factory. Up-scale restaurants were opening. A multi-level parking garage with state of the art security was built near the train station. The transit authorities poured millions of dollars into the renovation of the downtown railroad station. Construction was going on all over the downtown west side area. Wherever Buddy looked there were construction cranes working on building a new downtown. Job opportunities were opening up and crime in the area was declining. Buddy wondered was there a place in this new revitalized area for the likes of the place he sought, the Old Royal Buena Vista Hotel?

As he turned from Main Street and drove down Buena Vista Avenue, he saw that The Royal Buena Vista still stood at its Buena Vista Avenue location, where it had stood for more than one hundred years. He soon found out that it was still being operated by the same philanthropic organization that ran it when he lived there.

It's a funny thing about names; they can be so

misleading. The Royal Buena Vista Hotel was neither royal nor was it even really a hotel anymore. It had been a hotel at one time, perhaps even a royal hotel. It was a hotel that catered to America's industrial royalty. In the old days, when this part of the city was a vital industrial area with a beautiful downtown theater district, the Royal Buna Vista served visiting VIPs who came to the City of Yonkers to do business with the various industrial moguls who operated factories and foundries in the area. It served people who attended the grand ballrooms that existed in the area in the 1930's and 40's and those who might attend a late show at the numerous theaters that once graced the neighborhood. Its ruby red carpeting, marble staircases and velvet-roped accoutrements presented a royal appearance indeed. To stay at the Royal after an evening of entertainment in downtown Yonkers was a good way to end a splendid evening of entertainment.

As the fortunes of the city took a down turn so did the fortunes of the Buena Vista Hotel. It became a home for the less fortunate, the down trodden, most certainly not the royal members of society. It had become a welfare residence of sorts in the 1960's and it still was one now. It was still the welfare home that it was when Buddy lived there. Given his younger days, Buddy would never have imagined himself living in a welfare hotel, but indeed, he had come to live in one for a period of time. Life's journey takes many twists and turns and Buddy's journey was more turbulent than most.

The city began action to have the building condemned, but it was spared from the wrecking ball in the early 1970's. A religious group obtained ownership of the building and converted it to a sort of halfway house for homeless young adults, recently paroled prisoners who were truly looking to rehabilitate themselves, and other persons seeking redemption. It became a clean and safe temporary home to the homeless, a sanctuary for reformed whores and a shelter for recovering addicts. It was not a crack house or a whorehouse, but it was a home for recovering drug addicts and reformed whores.

The two-inch thick treads of its marble staircases were actually worn thin at the center from the years of heavy footsteps. Its ruby red fine carpets were replaced by industrial carpet tiles and what was left of her velvet ropes that served as walkway liners were thread worn and falling apart. The only thing that remained impressive was the massive marble and terrazzo inlay front desk that dominated the lobby. Today, the Royal fit better into the model of the west side in its worst of times. The organization that ran the place cleaned it up. There were always clean beds with clean sheets and pillowcases. There was heat in the winter and the riverside location provided cool breezes in the summer and a spectacular view of the Hudson River.

While the name Royal no longer seemed appropriate the term Buena Vista applied well. Indeed, it had a Buena Vista. The Spanish name Buena Vista translates to good view. Situated on the east bank of the Hudson River in Yonkers the Royal Buena Vista did afford one beautiful views of the Hudson River and the Palisades. Originally, defined by Henry Hudson as a natural wonder of the world the Palisades are huge rock formations, a plateau of sorts that stood hundreds of feet high above the sea level majestic Hudson River. The plateau dropped off in a sheer drop to the river forming a straight wall all along the coast of the river, making it appear that it was held in place by a natural dam. From a room in the Buena Vista looking to the west and scanning north and south, one could see the skyline of New York City at the George Washington Bridge, to the south all the way to the Tappan Zee Bridge near storied Sleepy Hollow at the north end. The two lighted bridges at each end and the Palisades on the western shore of the view seemed to frame the Hudson. It was a beautiful sight indeed. It was a grand place to stay in the old days.

That beautiful westward view never changed. The Hudson River Valley remains a remarkable sight these days. However, if one looked out the window on the east side of the building one looked out to an inner city ghetto. Over the past several years when the industrial base of the city had eroded, it left this part of the city in deep depression. While much of the west side of the city was undergoing a renaissance, the urban renewal projects had not yet arrived at this neighborhood. Crime and criminals ruled the streets in this area. Street gangs, drug dealers and prostitutes populated the area. By the late

1960's The Royal had been converted to an SRO, a building of single room residences, a rundown welfare hotel. It was certainly no longer royal.

Yet life at the Royal was far better than life on the streets. It was better there than in much of the other substandard housing in the area. The Royal provided good meals, clean rooms, with clean sheets and a safe environment. At least it was safer than what was available in much of the surrounding neighborhood.

There was no doubt that the gentrification of the area would soon consume this neighborhood. Renewal would one day come here too. There would be no need for the services of the Royal here. They would likely be asked to move. The building would be torn down, but for now, the Royal was still providing shelter to those who needed her services.

Buddy most assuredly could afford to stay in any of the finest hotels in the world. He was no longer that lost indigent teenager who came to live at the Royal so many years ago, but Buddy wanted to stay there once again. He did not need the services of the Royal Buena Vista. He did not need its clean sheets or the reliable heat. He did not need the cool breezes from the river that kept the rooms at the Royal cool in the summer. He had no need for those things at all. Those things he could get anywhere.

He desperately needed the Royal Buena Vista atmosphere, its memories, and its ghosts. Perhaps the ghost of the Buddy he was as a teen still lived there. If he did Buddy needed to find that person, the person he used to be. He needed to reconnect to the worst few months of his life. If he could only understand himself as he was in those times perhaps, he could rebuild himself perhaps be whole again. The Royal represented the bridge. It represented the bridge from the best times of his life to the worst times of his life. Could it be his connection back to the best years of his life, his teenage years, and the years of ignorant blissful innocence? He was attempting to recapture his youth. He did not need to be physically young again, but to be innocent again. He wanted to remember what it felt like to believe in a promising future. He wanted not to have to carry the burdens of world politics on his shoulders. He just wanted to be himself again. Buddy needed to find redemption and his search would begin at the Royal Hotel.

While he firmly believed that a few days stay at the Royal would be therapeutic. He was not going to get a room there just yet. He would attend to that later. For now, he just wanted to cruise the streets. He wanted to see the sights of his youthful days. He wanted to walk the streets that he walked in his teens. He would be back. Later tonight, he would see if he could get a room at the Royal. For now, he was just going to roam the local streets.

Just a few blocks north of the Royal those streets were different now. The streets he knew there were the streets of a depressed ghetto. Those streets seemed to be gone. The abandoned factories were mostly gone. The dirty sidewalks, the graffiti were all gone. There were new restaurants where empty storefronts once were. People walked about shopping in areas where only a few years ago they would dare not go, for fear of crime. The old stores were gone. The old bars were closed. Only one of the old neighborhood bars remained in business. The old friends no longer lived in the neighborhood. Maybe you can never go back again.

But maybe you can. Some things remain the same. The Royal Buena Vista still stood where it always stood. It was still in the bad part of the city. It was still a home to the downtrodden. It was still a place for people seeking redemption. The river still flowed as it always had. The thing he wanted to do most of all he could still do. He wanted to spend a few nights in the Royal. He wanted to walk along the river, take in the sights, smell the riverfront air and reminisce. He wanted to remember his friend Ray.

A little over 20 years ago, he used to walk along the river with his best friend, Ray Cassini. They would walk along the riverbanks and talk the foolish talk that teenagers talk. They would talk about their sure fire plan to win millions of dollars in the magazine sweepstakes. They would talk about how they would cash the check; spend the money on fancy boats and fast cars. They would buy motorcycles and have delightful futures. They talked about their "very special friend," the adult man who played an important role in their little conspiracy. Their "very special friend" was the man who was helping them to make their dreams come true. It was their "very special friend" who was the man that bought them BB guns and slingshots, when their parents did not want them to have any such things. He bought them the magazines that their parents would not let them have. It was their "very special friend" who bought them beer when they were too young to have it. He got them credit and provided access to many things that only adults usually enjoy. He made all things possible. They would talk about him and all that he could do for them all the time. They would work on the furtherance of their little conspiracy to outwit their parents, their little harmless con to outwit the authorities. It was their foolish teenage prank, but it was a game they loved to play. When they became older and they no longer needed their "very special friend," they abandoned him for new friends and new conspiracies. Buddy wished the conspiracies he was involved with today were as simple, as harmless.

Back then, they would talk about their rivalry for the affection of a young girl whom they both loved, whom they both wanted. Buddy would talk of the coming days when he would become a racecar driver and Ray would talk of becoming a riverboat pilot. It was talk of an idyllic life, the kind of life and dreams that naive teenagers talk about.
He wanted to be the person he was back then.

He wanted to be innocent again. He wanted to be the person he was before his parents were killed... before his parents were murdered! ... before he had turned his life into a perpetual search for vengeance.

New bricks and mortar can restore a city of

gracious living. Can the graciousness of an innocent life be so easily renewed?

Buddy wished he could walk and talk with Ray again, talk the foolish talk that teenagers talk. He wished he could have simple dreams, simple needs, and simple plans. However, Buddy was no longer naïve. His life no was longer simple. He had seen the world and he did not like what he saw. His life was not idyllic. His dreams were nightmares. He knew that he was not going to be a racecar driver. He would not be a motorcycle cop. He would not win the millions. He would not get the girl. Ray would never become a river pilot. Buddy had become a person very different from the person that either he, or his mother, had ever imagined he would become. He was what he was … and Ray …well …. Ray was dead.

A Walking the Riverfront

Buddy spent most of his day walking around his "home town." It was a warm June afternoon, a nice day for a walk along the riverfront, although the clouds overhead suggested that rain might be coming in. Buddy walked along the riverfront to the area where the old P.A.L. building once stood only to discover that it had been torn down to make room for upscale condos. He learned it had moved to a location not far from the riverfront and that it was still a vibrant organization. It pleased him to learn that and he figured that perhaps he would go to see the new facility at another time. He walked past the location where one of his favorite restaurants, The Lighthouse, once stood. It was a classy place back then. It was perhaps the only classy place in the neighborhood. It was where he took Terri Wilkowski, on the few occasions that they went out to dinner. He liked it there, so did Terri Wilkowski. However, it too was gone.

Gone were the docks that welcomed huge ships that brought raw materials to the foundries. Gone were the riverside junkyard and the oil storage facilities where oceangoing tankers used to deliver crude. Only one of the places that held fond memories remained unchanged. It was the place where Ray often stopped to talk to his friends at the pilot station. The place were Ray would introduce Buddy to the numerous river pilots he had come to know.

The Port of New York is among the busiest ports in the world and one cannot simply steam a ship into her waters without a specially trained pilot coming aboard. When the great ships are about to enter the port, they are met by a smaller vessel, a launch that carries a harbor pilot. The launch operator will come alongside the larger vessel, he will match the speed of the bigger ship at a point along the larger ships side where there is an opening to receive a pilot. Then in a movement that requires skill on the part of the pilot and the launch operator, the pilot will transfer himself from the launch to the larger ship. Once aboard the larger ship the pilot takes over control of the ship from her captain and steers it through the harbor. The captain must have the skills to navigate the great ships across the vast deep oceans. It is the pilot who is specially trained in the small precise maneuvers needed to navigate through the more shallow waters of the harbor. It is he who must know the harbor like the back of his hand. It is he who makes sure that the ship does not run aground. It is he who maneuvers the ship to the dock.

Now, the harbor pilot can steer the ship anywhere within the harbor, but he does not take it up the rivers that feed into the harbor. A trip up the river requires a river pilot. If the ship is to travel from the harbor of New York up the great Hudson River to the Port of Albany or to any of the docks between New York City and Albany, a river pilot must take over. As the harbor pilot must know the harbor, the river pilot must know the river. He must know her shallows and the path of her deep channel. Therefore, as the great ships move north of New York Harbor and up the river, a second launch comes out to greet them where the harbor meets the river in Yonkers. Like the harbor launch, the river launch comes alongside the great ship. The captain of the launch matches the speed of the great ship. Once it is alongside, the river pilot boards the ship for the trip up river. The transfer is made while the ship and the launch remain in motion. The harbor pilot, who was at the helm since the great ship entered the port, is taken from the ship and returned to the port by the launch. From there the river pilot will guide the ship up the river. For southbound ships, the ritual in Yonkers is reversed. The river pilot brings the ship from Albany to Yonkers. There it is turned over to a harbor pilot who brings her safely through the harbor and he turns her over to her captain as she leaves the harbor for the deep seas. It is a carefully choreographed dance of great ships and smaller launches, of harbor pilots and of river pilots; a dance that is skillfully danced several times a day to keep commerce in the harbor and on the river flowing. This is what Cassini dreamed of doing. He dreamed of being part of the pilot crew; perhaps a launch captain, perhaps a river pilot. Life on the river seemed to be romantic.

When they were kids, Buddy and Ray would often walk for hours along the riverfront. They would stop at various business locations and came to know most of the small business owners and employees who worked the shops along the river. There were assorted boatyards, restaurants, diners, a bait and tackle shop and of course, the pilothouse.

Because of Ray's interests in becoming a river pilot, almost every trip to the riverfront included a stop at the pilothouse. There the boys would enjoy the company of the launch captains. All the captains knew of Ray's desire to one-day work the river and some offered to take Ray under wing. They would invite the boys in. Ray would get some short instructions on river boating. They would teach him how to read charts, how to plot a course and read a compass. They would show him how to read the tides and anticipate weather conditions. They would let the boys fish from the launch pier and, although it was strictly forbidden, they would occasionally let the boys ride with them on the launch.

Whenever the boys got to ride the launch, they felt like they were on an adventure. Even Buddy would be caught up in the excitement of taking a forbidden ride on the river. They felt like they were modern day Tom Sawyers or Huckleberry Finns. Each trip on the launch was fun for Buddy, but for Ray each trip was an education for his future lifetime.

Buddy walked up to the pilothouse. It looked the same as it had when he was a kid. As he approached, the launch was leaving the pier on its way out to meet a great ship. Buddy's hair was ruffled by the wind. It felt good. A slight misty rain started. It was an ideal setting to feed Buddy's melancholy mood. Buddy stood in the light rain and watched the transfer of command taking place on the river. He watched and he contemplated.

Somehow, the scene caused Buddy to reflect. The whole process seemed to be like a metaphor on life's choices; on the courses, we choose to follow.

The big lumbering slow ships will, like many people, move slowly but methodically making their way to a predetermined port. There is a planned course that will be strictly followed. The ship will end up where its captain planned for it to go. The small launch rapidly moves among many locations from the Yonkers piers to meet great ships at no particular fixed point. Just meet the ship wherever she happens to be as she enters the river boundary. Sometimes she brings a pilot ashore in Yonkers; at other times she returns him to the New York Harbor or perhaps to another ship. The mission and the course are always changing. There is no predetermined course. No homeport. The captains of the great ships are the supreme commanders at sea but when they come to a harbor, they must surrender to the harbor pilot and in turn, the harbor pilot surrenders to the river pilot. Any one of them can affect the final destination. Anyone of them can take her off course. Anyone of them can run the ship aground. Despite the tremendous skills of the captains and pilots, the ships can be blown off course by a strong wind or sunk completely by a raging storm. Perhaps no one is really in charge of anything; perhaps no one is really in control of his or her own destiny. Some stay the course; some go off course. Some will not come to port because of minor course changes along the way. Some are lost in cataclysmic events that change their course forever.

What happened to his dreams? What happened to Ray's? Where did they go off course?

As Buddy took in the scenery, the pilot boat returned to its dock. A man got off the boat and walked up to Buddy. "Hey pal, wadda you doin' here! This is not a public pier."

Buddy responded, "I'm sorry sir, it's just that when I was a kid I used to come here a lot with my best friend. The launch captains used to let us hang out here, you know, fishing and stuff. Anyway, I just learned that my friend has died and well ...."

The man from the launch interrupted, "Oh, ... I understand ... well look you can stay as long as you like just make sure you close the gate when you leave."

Buddy said, "Thanks." As he watched the man walk away, Buddy was glad that it was raining. He hoped the rain had disguised the fact that there were tears on his cheeks.

A Would-be River Pilot

Ray's father owned a very successful mail drop business. It was an excellent business idea for its time. Ray's father rented space in the basement of a prestigious office building at 10021 Madison Avenue in New York City. He fitted the large room with a number of post office boxes and each post office box was assigned a "suite number." Now anyone who wanted or needed a location for mail pick-ups or package deliveries, for whatever reason, would rent a box from Ray's dad. When you rented a box, you got to use Mr. Cassini's address. You could be a shyster lawyer with an office in the back room of a bodega in the Bronx, but your business card and letterhead would say

10021 Madison Avenue
Suite 463
Manhattan, New York.

Your client could easily imagine that your "suite" consisted of several plush offices. Actually, your "suite" was a box that measured about eight inches high by ten inches wide and was typically fifteen inches deep (a somewhat larger box was available at a slightly higher price) but who knew?

Your mail would be delivered to the drop location by the post office and the staff would separate the mail and put your mail in your "suite." You could come in and pick it up, or for a slight additional fee, his staff would forward it to your real address.

People used mail drop locations to disguise their actual business locations for lots of reasons. Collection agencies did not want their clients to know their exact locations. A person in debt who is being hounded by a collection agent might just try to come in when you least expect it. It is best for all concerned that the agent and the deadbeat debtor do not meet face to face. For similar reasons repo men liked to have off-site addresses. Of course, a criminal might need a remote mailbox for any host of reasons. There were other less nefarious reasons for using such a service. Some businesses were not equipped to receive large or numerous parcels at their business offices, so they have their packages sent to an-off site facility. Alternatively, persons who travel a lot need a place that will store their mail for them until they come home.

Sadly, for a number of inner city people, getting mail is a dangerous proposition. In the high rise, projects and slum area tenement houses neighborhood punks will break open your mailbox every day and steal your mail searching for anything of value. On the first and third of the month, the punks will watch as senior citizens retrieve their mail. Knowing that social security and welfare checks are delivered on those days, they will wait for a person to retrieve their mail around the first of the month and mug them. Some people find it a small price to pay to own a box at a secure mail drop where they can privately receive their mail before it is stolen from them. It is a sad commentary on urban life but sometimes the poorest of our citizens must pay a price to receive their mail.

Mr. Cassini never asked why you might need a box. You just paid your fees and received your mail at one of his shops.

Raymond Cassini Sr. also offered other small office amenities to his clients at his mail drop stores. For a reasonable fee, one could use a photocopy machine there. There was a small-scale printing press where one could have Mr. Cassini run off business cards or letterhead. His offices were authorized Western Union stations where one could send or receive telegrams, money-grams and the like. It was a thriving business that began to spread to additional locations over time. For persons who did not need such a prestigious address, other storefronts were available. One such storefront was at One Park Avenue, Yonkers New York.

When Ray was in his twenties, his father retired and gave Ray the business. In a very short time, Ray was earning serious money. His walks by the riverside became less frequent. There was no time for idle chat. Ray became a serious businessman overnight. Ray's dream of becoming a river pilot became a ship lost in a fog. It slowly drifted off course. The romance of life on the river gave way to life in the fast lane. Ray was never going to become a member of the River Pilots Association.

Buddy knew that his mom was right, "As boys

become men they learn to appreciate different things. You will see such dreams fade and different ideas replace them." Buddy could not help but wonder if Ray had made the choice that made him happiest or had choices been made for him over which he had little control. Did he choose to go into business and give up the dream or was it his destiny?

An Unknown Sailor

It was an otherwise bright and clear morning, a pleasant June day in the Bronx But there was a foul odor in the air around a Bronx hotel room. The manager at this hotel had been a hotel manager in a number of different hotels and motels over the years. One of the things a hotel manager learns is the smell of trouble. He knows the smell of death. The odor told him he needed to call the police. The first police units on the scene were from the 50th precinct, a police station usually called the 5-0 by those in the trade. The cops also knew, upon arrival, that someone in the room was dead. Whoever it was, he or she had been dead for some time. They asked the manager for the key and opened the door. They saw the body naked on the bed and the blood soaked sheets. They did not even enter the room. They knew from their years of experience that they ought not to disturb a crime scene. They secured the area and called for the detectives and the crime scene unit.

Detective Taylor was the first to arrive at the scene. He came alone. Most detectives worked in teams of two, but Taylor often worked alone. He preferred it that way. A tall large-framed man in his late forties, Taylor had gone on to the police force right out of the army. He had aspirations of being a pro football player. He had the skills and build for the job. He had been an outstanding halfback in high school. Recruited by a number of colleges he was prepared to accept a scholarship at a local college, but an injury on the field, a torn ACL, put an end to the scholarship offers. He joined the Army and upon his discharge, he joined the N.Y.P.D. Originally assigned to the 47th precinct, he made a name for himself for being attentive to small details and he was quickly made detective. Initially, he was assigned to a squad of all white males. Taylor was a proud black man, He was not what you would call an outspoken civil rights activist, but he was keenly aware of the racial divide. He would not hesitate to put a bigot in his place. However, given his large size and very apparent physical strength very few would dare to show their prejudices in his presence. He got along with others in the squad, both the white guys and the black guys, but he was not the kind of man who would adjust his personality just to fit in with others, black or white. He became a bit of a loner.

When you choose to be a loner, your coworkers do not necessarily show you the ropes. You have to learn on your own. It is not an easy task. However, learning on your own you don't pick up the bad habits of those who take short cuts. If you break in going by the book, you end up doing your job by the book. Taylor was a by-the-book detective. He was one of the best detectives in the homicide squad. He had little tolerance for those who took shortcuts. He was somewhat unyielding to the opinions of others. He was a "my way or the highway" kind of person. Therefore, he worked alone. It took him a little longer to learn the trade, but he learned it better than most. He was one of the best. He did not want a partner who might be lazy and looking for shortcuts. His superiors respected him and they often yielded to his requests to work alone.

He quickly arrived at the hotel, the site of a homicide. He decided that he would wait for the crime scene team to arrive and do their stuff. He had not yet entered the room but instead questioned the uniformed officers who had arrived on the scene before him. He was pleasantly surprised. They had not disturbed his crime scene and one of the officers, Tom Bradner, had already gathered a considerable amount of information about the victim.

With his typical Bronx accent, Taylor asked, "Ok, wadda we got here kid?" Taylor asked Tom Bradner, the younger of the two uniformed officers.

"Well, we got the call at 08:07 hours and arrived on the scene about 8:15. When we arrived, the door was still locked. The manager called us because of the smell. Neither he nor any of his staff had entered the room. We had him give us a key. We unlocked and opened the door, saw the mess and secured the scene. We did not even go into the room so I can't tell you much about the scene itself." Taylor nodded several times, "Very good."

"What else?" Tom Bradner went on, "We checked the registration card. Our victim checked in four days ago. The room was listed to a Jose Mendez, home address of 5776 Pulaski Street Brooklyn. It's a phony address."

Taylor looked a little puzzled and said, "How do you know?"

The uniformed officer replied. "I know that neighborhood. I used to work the 79th precinct. Pulaski is a short block. The numbers don't go that high. Anyway, I put a call into the precinct out there to have them double check, but I'm sure there is no such address. I also asked them to check for any recent reports of a missing person by the name of Mendez."

Taylor said "And?"

"Dozens," the officer replied. "You'll have to sort them out, but my guess is that the name, the address, the whole shooting match is phony."

Taylor nodded in agreement, "You're detective material kid." The officer smiled and said, "Don't break my balls," and they both chuckled.

"Look, I won't break your balls, but do me a favor. We are going to be here a while. We're going to need a landline phone, a bathroom, and a place to sit down and write reports. Go see the manager. See if he can give us access to one of these other rooms to use as a command center." The uniformed officer headed toward the manager's office and Taylor continued to stand at the door to the victim's room watching the crime scene people doing their stuff.

The uniformed officer returned with keys for the adjacent room. He opened the door and he and his partner took seats in the room. They began writing their preliminary report. Taylor watched the C.S.I. team wrapping up their work and he asked, "Find anything significant?" The C.S.I. team leader replied, "Not really, the room seems to have been sterilized. We gathered a few prints here and there, but it is a hotel room. There will be prints from the last dozen or so people who used the room. It will be a chore to eliminate the irrelevant prints. There are no signs of recent sexual activity. I doubt there will be any DNA worthy of analysis. We got indications of sperm and vaginal fluid all over the place, but that is not uncommon for a hotel room. I doubt if any of it goes with our victim. Nothing here looks fresh. Of course, you can't tell what's fresh by just looking at it … by looks alone but, after a few years of doing this you get an indication. I'm not getting any vibes. Hotel rooms are a nightmare for a forensic team. We'll see."

Taylor nodded in agreement. He walked into the room and began to look around for himself. He began to make mental notes: White male, about 6 foot maybe six two, about 50 or so. Tattoo ... Some kind of bird tattooed on the forearm. Tattoos can help ID victims, but with nothing else? With a quick glance around the room, he made some more mental notes. The room is too neat. There has not been much activity. The TV is off. The lights were off. The alarm clock is not set. Ok, the guy probably had no morning appointments. Nude, no suitcase, no clothes; perp must have taken everything. Shot through pillow victim must have been asleep.

A member of the C.S.I. team re-entered the room to pick up some of his equipment. "We collected some powder off the table, looks like cocaine. I guess it's a drug deal gone bad. Taylor shook his head. He walked back into the adjacent room and spoke again to the younger of the uniformed officers, "Come with me."

He took Tom Bradner, the uniformed officer into the victim's room and said, "C.S.I. says maybe a drug deal gone bad. Wadda you think?"

The officer shook his head, "I don't think so."

"Why not?" asked Taylor.

"It doesn't look right. I don't exactly know how it should look, but this doesn't look like a drug deal gone bad. I've seen drug deals that have gone bad. A person says he is selling dope, lots of it. Another person says he's buying and he's got lots of cash. They meet. Each guy brings along a little muscle, some friends to back him up. One guy is full-o-shit. Either there is no dope or there is no cash. Somebody figures he'll pull a gun and get what he came for without doing his part of the deal. Everybody has guns. The next thing you know it's all asses and elbows. Everyone is shooting there is a general panic and someone dies and someone runs off with the loot. That's how it goes. Lots of chaos lots of shots fired. The scene is a mess.

This is neat. I don't see the asses and elbows. Also, what druggie stops to clean up the scene? A druggie grabs his stuff and is in the wind. This is too neat. I say it's a professional hit."

Taylor just gave a small smile and said, "You really are detective material."

The officer said, "I thought you weren't going to break my balls."

Taylor replied, "I'm not. Here's the real test. Look around the room. Wadda ya see that's out of place?"

The officer took a careful assessment of the room and said, "Unless this is the presidential suite, I'd say our vic brought in his own glassware."

Taylor said, "Why's that?"

"All the glassware in the room next door is plastic, but here we have real glasses made from real glass."

"Excellent!" Taylor said,

"Excellent! You're right! He brought that stuff in with him. Not only is it real glass it has a bird engraved on it! It looks like the same bird that is tattooed on our vic's arm. I'd say they're his glasses and if I'm not mistaken, that's his flask. If it is his stuff, it shouldn't have any prints on it but his. If there were any trace evidence on the glasses or flask, it would not be from a previous resident of the room. Also, look at the plastic glasses. They're usually wrapped in cellophane. However, one has been unwrapped. We can safely assume that it was unwrapped after our victim checked in. Get the C.S.I. people back in here before they leave. Tell them they're going to be packing up some glassware for transport back to the lab. I want prints, DNA, everything. I want a complete analysis." As the officer, left to get the C.S.I. people, Taylor thought to himself, "That guy really is detective material."

Coming Upon Rough Seas

It was a beautiful June morning. There was a slight breeze in the air and the air smelled clean and fresh. In New York City, the air is not always clean and fresh, but today it was. Joseph Duffy, the Assistant Director in Charge of the New York Office, was going to be a little late for work today and he did not care. On his way in, he thought he would stop at the bank. He would make a deposit then walk to the post office. He would pick up some stamps and mail a few personal letters. Then stroll back to his office. It was a beautiful morning. He was going to take a little break from his demanding schedule and take a stroll. He would stroll the long way to his office. Most F.B.I. offices are commanded by a Special Agent in Charge, commonly called the S.A.C., but the New York Office is one of the few managed by an in-house Assistant Director. He would get in about forty minutes late, but he was the A.D.C. No one would note anything official about him being late. It was a perk the boss could give himself. He never flaunted the fact that he was the boss. He never took advantage, but today, he would. Today was a beautiful day for a walk. He parked his staff car in its designated spot, secured it and walked off in a direction that would take him away from the office. It was a nice day and he was taking a morning walk. Period! At 9:15 am, his cell phone rang. He looked at the caller identification screen. It was his secretary calling.

"This better be important," He said as he answered the phone.

His secretary George said, "I think it is sir. A small group of VIP's has stopped in to see you. The director is with them. I've given them some coffee and a plausible excuse, but I think they are becoming impatient."

No one could make the Assistant Director in Charge of the New York Office of the F.B.I. rush to be anywhere he did not personally wish to rush to, but the director waits for no man, not even for Joe Duffy the head of the New York Office.

"Shit! The Director?" Joe asked in disbelief.

"Yes, I told him you called to say you were stuck in traffic and that I expected you in at any moment."

Joe took a deep breath and said, "Ok...good...what's it about?"

George replied, "I don't know, I asked the director, but he said it was on a need to know basis. I guess he figures I don't need to know, because he didn't say anything more than that. ... Where are you?"

"Not far, I'll grab a cab and be there in ten."

When Joseph Duffy got to his office, there was no time to be briefed as to just who was waiting for him. He entered his conference room and found a group of people seated around his conference table. "I'm sorry for the delay gentlemen, but you know how New York traffic can be." Joe knew some of the people there but not all of them. He said, "Ok, for the benefit of those of us who might not know one another let's go around the table and introduce ourselves. I'm Joseph Duffy Assistant Director in Charge of the New York Office and I'm sure you all know Director Madison of the F.B.I. who is seated at my right."

The next gentleman to speak was seated next to Madison. "I'm Deputy Commander Johnson, U.S. Naval Intelligence." Then each, in turn introduced themselves as follows:

John Cobble, Naval Criminal Investigative Services N.C.I.S.

David Tees, National Security Agency

Frank Dwarman, F.B.I. S.A.C. of the New Haven Office

George Franks, Washington Office F.B.I. computer crimes section

Robert Fulfree, Homeland Security

Thomas Trulane, Immigration and Customs Enforcement

George Whentz N.C.I.S. computer analyst.

Finally, the lone female in the room said, "I'm Special Agent Michelle Thompson, New York Office F.B.I."

Director Madison spoke first. "Some of you already know the purpose of this meeting and some of you do not. I've gathered you all here so that we may enlighten each other as to what is going on." He then turned to Joe Duffy and said, "Joe, I hope you don't mind, but I took the liberty of asking your secretary to invite Special Agent Thompson to join us for part of this briefing."

Actually, Joe was quite annoyed that Thompson was in his office. She was a junior member of his staff. She had been invited to this high level meeting in his office and she was not invited by him. She was a rookie. She did not belong at a meeting at this level.

Of course, Joe could not hold it against her for being where he felt she did not belong. When the Director gives one instructions to attend a meeting, one attends, but this was way out of protocol for the Director to have invited her without first advising him, her superior. He was pissed at Madison, but as he thought about it if he had not been late he most likely would have been brought up to speed and he would know exactly why she was there. He knew this was no time to stand on protocol. He replied, "No sir I don't mind. I suppose it was the expedient thing to do. If you have determined that her presence is necessary, it is necessary."

The truth was that Madison knew very well that inviting a low-level agent to a meeting in the boss's office without first having the boss approve was out of protocol, but it was his way of teaching Duffy that one ought not to come in late on a whim.

Madison began the meeting, "A few days ago Agent Thompson opened a case file on one Stanley Adamski, a Polish National, who indicated that he had some information that he thought would be of value to the F.B.I. According to the agent's report at the first interview the complainant refused to offer anything about what he intended to report until he had assurances of protection. Such events often occur. It is a rare occasion when the information is actually that valuable or dangerous to the informant. However, our Mr. Adamski offered proof that he did indeed have something of value to offer. According to Agent Thompson's report, to establish credibility this Mr. Adamski handed over a series of computer disks that he said would serve to validate his claims of having valuable information. The disks were not compatible for use in our computers and Agent Thompson sent them to our computer lab for translation. Am I correct so far?"

Agent Thompson replied, "Yes sir."

"Ok Agent Thompson please take over."

Michelle began, "The disks that he gave me were not compatible with any computers here. I had no way to open the files on them. I had no idea what could be on them and the man who gave them to me was not inclined to tell me. I had no choice but to send them to our lab for deciphering. The complainant told me that if we could not understand the files that I should consult with Navy personnel. I sent the disks to the computer lab with a notation in the comments field to share the analysis with N.C.I.S. if clarification was necessary."

George Franks from the F.B.I. computer lab then interrupted, "I had no trouble opening the files. They were in an old but simple CP/CMS format.

They were a few text files and a series of drawings that, to me, looked like blueprints for a boat. There was also more recently created documents that looked like parts for a ship. To be more specific, it looked like design plans for a boat propeller. I went ahead and called my good friend, George Whentz over at N.C.I.S. I asked him to look at the files. I hoped he could fill me in."

Whentz from the N.C.I.S. computer lab then took over the conversation. "As soon as I saw the documents I immediately suspected that they had something to do with the Sorge investigation."

Kline asked, "The Sorge investigation?"

John Cobble, the lead investigator for N.C.I.S. answered, "We have been conducting an investigation that spans nearly twenty years. It has been a top priority for our agency. The case has been handed down from one generation of investigators to the next, but we have made little progress. Finding Sorge could well lead to us breaking one of the most prolific and long lasting spy and organized crime rings operating anywhere in the free world."

Michelle Thompson interrupted, "Sorge? Are you talking about Richard Sorge? I know that he was once considered to be one of the Soviet's most effective international spies, but he's been dead for years. In fact, I think he died in 1944!"

Duffy looked in her direction with a slight look of surprise in his eyes. First of all he, himself had no idea who Sorge was. He never heard of him nor did he know Sorge was reportedly dead. He was surprised that this new agent would know about the former Soviet spy. He wondered if she was some sort of expert on spies. Does she possess skills that he was unaware of? Moreover, if Sorge was dead what was this investigation about?

Director Madison answered, "Richard Sorge was indeed one of the Soviet's best spies. However, we are not talking about Richard Sorge. We are talking about an individual who fancies himself as the new Sorge. He fancies himself as the new, world's greatest spy. His name is not Sorge that's just a code name he uses. We do not know his real name, but we have code named the investigation as the Sorge Investigation. Let us get back to the disks.

Whentz said, "Okay… When I learned the nature of the files that were on disks, I asked if I could see the actual disks themselves. Franks and I got together and he showed me the disks. Sure enough they were the actual Groton Disks."

Duffy asked, "The Groton Disks?"

Commander Johnson said "I'll explain shortly, but I want to find out from this young lady what she knows about the man who gave her the disks."

Agent Thompson started, "He was apparently a well-educated man in his late fifties, perhaps early sixties." Michelle failed to mention that her initial assessment would not have included the phrase: well educated. "He spoke in broken English and refused to give any personal background information until he had some assurances of protection. He would not say where he was staying or leave a phone number, insisting that he would contact us when he was ready to do so. I could not hold him so I let him go and asked him to contact me in a few days. I went ahead and did some background on him."

Madison asked, "So did that background check produce anything of value? I mean after all you seem to have little to go on."

"Yes, actually, it did... During our conversation, I did get his name, Stanley Adamski. I contacted our western European office and asked if they could sniff around on a name check. It turns out that Adamski is a very popular name, one of the most popular in Poland. However, I did have some info that would narrow our search. I had concluded that he had just arrived in New York only shortly before he came here."

Duffy interrupted, "What made you come to that conclusion?"

Michelle went on, "When he was leaving the building he stopped at security and retrieved a suitcase that he had checked in. It still had airport tags on it. The tags were JFK tags... Anyway, he also said that he was Polish, but he mentioned working in St. Petersburg. He said something about building boats.

Therefore, I conducted a search on Polish nationals who had been recently issued visas in Poland for travel to the United States. I found a visa application filed by one Stanislaus Adamski. This Mr. Adamski listed job title as 'marine engineer' and his place of employment as the Northern Shipyards at

Gdansk in Poland. A little more checking and I found that this Adamski purchased airline tickets for a flight that landed at Kennedy on the very day that my Mr. Adamski came in to see me. I'm quite sure that my Mr. Adamski and Stanislaus are one and the same."

She continued, "From there it got easier and better. I learned that this Mr. Adamski was a well renowned engineer in his day. He had been involved in ship designing for a number of years, but began to come to prominence in the mid 1980's. He was well known, not only for projects in Gdansk, but he also was instrumental in working on designs for Russian naval ships in the eighties. A number of his projects were secret operations. He held a top-secret security clearance from the Soviets for work on their naval vessels.

In the years of The Solidarity Movement, when it started to look like the Soviets were losing their grip in Poland, the Russians moved most of the Soviet ship building operations that were being conducted in Gdansk to St. Petersburg in Russia. At that time, our Mr. Adamski went to Russia to continue a project he had been working on. It was there that he became somewhat an acclaimed ship designer."

Madison asked, "Do you know what the project was?"

"I don't know the details, that is to say I do not know exactly what he was doing, but I understand that he had worked on something called Project 877."

As she said those words, Deputy Commander

Johnson and NSA Agent Tees immediately made eye contact. The looks on their faces sent a message to everyone seated at the table. There was just an eerie silence in the room. Everyone present knew Thompson must have just said something profound, but only a few in the room understood the implications. That eerie silence took over the room. For the next few moments, the people at the table just sat in silence.

A New Member of the Crew

Back in the Bronx, Detective Taylor was doing a by-the-book follow-up in his investigation of the death of an unidentified male found dead in a hotel room. All of the pertinent information related to the death was placed in the appropriate databases for sharing the info with others in law enforcement that might have useful information in the investigation. All the information was uploaded to the FBI's Violent Criminal Apprehension Program database, known as ViCAP. The purpose of the program is to allow the police to share information with other agencies that might be investigation similar crimes. The ViCap database was reserved for the most violent crimes. The database was full of data on serial murder cases. Most were weird sex crimes. Taylor was not sure that his case belonged in the ViCap database but he was adding his info anyway. His victim was naked; there could have been a sex angle. He uploaded a file with all the known facts and circumstances of the death at the hotel. Photos of the victim and a physical description were provided, as was a close-up photo of the tattoo.

There were no similar crimes in the database but one piece of useful information did emerge. The tattoo that Taylor had been describing as a tattoo of a bird was actually a Polish Eagle, a national emblem of Poland. He had already learned from the NYPD lab that the glassware was made in Poland. Taylor was sure his victim would turn out to be Polish.

Given the fact that the hotel clerk said that the victim spoke with an accent Taylor summarized that his victim was most likely a Polish national. Next, he contacted I.C.E. The Immigration and Customs Enforcement is a law enforcement organization. They quickly provided him with a list of all Polish nationals who had entered the country legally in the last 90 days. There was a good chance that his victim had actually been in America for many years but the last 90 days was all that Taylor could handle right now. Taylor restricted himself to those who had indicated that their destination was New York City, but the list was still extensive. He was going to need help on this one.

Taylor went to his captain with a request. Taylor knocked on the captain's door and was invited in.

"Capt.' I have a request," Taylor said.

The captain replied, "Everyone who knocks on my door has a request; what's yours?"

Taylor went on, "I'm working this homicide at the hotel ... and I'm going to need some help. There is a lot of legwork to be done. ... Anyway, I was wondering, ... there is this kid Bradner... he's a uniform assigned to the precinct downstairs, he was one of the first on the scene and he did a pretty good preliminary. I was wondering if we could have him placed on temporary plainclothes assignment to work with me on this."

The captain just smiled. It was hardly the reaction that Taylor expected.

Then the captain spoke, "You know the truth is I like that kid a lot. His work is consistently above average. I knew his father back in the day when I was a detective. His father was in the safe and loft squad in the old days. You know the kid is on the list to go to Suffolk County. The pay is a lot better there. I'd like to see him stay here. His old man still has many friends in the job. If the kid does the right thing he could go places here. He'll never make the money here that he can make in Suffolk, but he can have a very exciting career here. Perhaps a chance to work in plain clothes might……" The captain never finished his sentence. He just began to look off into the distance as if he was remembering his old days in the squad, before he was trapped behind the desk.

"They'll kill me upstairs. We're short on uniformed personnel right now. I'm over my budget on uniformed overtime as it is. Pulling a uniform for another plain-clothes assignment will raise eyebrows. They will kick my ass downtown, but the hell with it! I'll have the kid report to you tomorrow." The captain then waved toward the door. It was a clear signal for Taylor to get out.

As Taylor left the room the captain said, "Hey, get me some good shit out of this soon. Get me something that I can lay out at the next CompStat meeting. While they're kicking my ass for doing this I need to have something in the way of positive results to talk about."

The next morning Tom Bradner reported to Taylor. "So, you had them send me upstairs?"

Bradner asked.

"Yeah," Taylor responded. "I need a little help on this and since you already know a lot about the case I figured …"

Bradner interrupted, "Did my old man have anything to do with this? Do you know him or owe him something? I'm not looking for a Rabbi!"

"No," Taylor replied, "I never met your old man. I asked for you because you did a good prelim. I will say that I most likely got approval for you because the captain knew your old man, but I just asked for you because of your prelim work. I don't think your old man even knows about this."

"Okay," Bradner said, "What do you want me to do?"

Taylor told Bradner why he thought the victim might be a Polish national. He told him to go over the list of recent Polish arrivals. Narrow the list down to those who seemed to be about the same general age. He was to look for anything that might connect the dead person. Foreign nationals are questioned by customs when they arrive. Sometime their responses are noted. Bradner was told to look for persons who indicated that they were going to the Bronx. He was advised to look for anything that might seem unusual. If he got a feeling about any of them, he could work on getting a picture. Perhaps they could identify the victim. Taylor also told Bradner to contact the forensic people and see if there was any evidence gleaned from the glassware.

Tom did the latter first. He contacted the lab

for the forensic results and went directly to Taylor with the news.

"Good news! We got a lead", Bradner said.

"OK, lay it on me", Taylor replied.

Bradner went on, "The lab got prints off the glasses. Both of the tall glasses had our victim's fingerprints on them. Those prints are not in the system. He's never been printed in the past. We got the match from his dead body. Therefore, we still don't know who our victim is, but he handled the glasses. The good news is that there is another set of prints on the glasses, just one other set of prints on the glasses. As I said our victim's prints are on both glasses, but one of the glasses has two sets of prints our victim's and another person. In addition, that other guy has a criminal record. He was arrested in Boston about twenty-five years ago for felony assault! His name is Adam Mickiewicz. At the time of his arrest he listed a Yonkers home address."

Taylor was actually somewhat excited by the finding. First, it proved that the glassware was indeed a valuable piece of evidence. Secondly, the lead came back to a Polish sounding name. Taylor thought his victim might be Polish. Having a person with a Polish sounding name leave prints on the glass tended to support the theory. The Yonkers address was a positive indicator. The murder was quite near the Yonkers border.

However, Bradner had some bad news as well. "The bad part is that this Adam Mickiewicz guy seems to have dropped off the planet after his arrest.

He was charged with two counts of felonious assault in 1984. He made bail and disappeared off everyone's radar. He paid the bail bondsmen's fee with a credit card. We know the card number, but the card was never used again.

The Boston cops traced the billing address on the credit card, but it came back to a post office box at a private mail drop location up in Yonkers. They tried the work address that was associated with the owner of the account; it was another mail drop location, a place in Manhattan. None of the employees at the mail drop locations could provide any info on who might have rented the drop box. The New York driver's license he had when he was arrested expired and DMV does not have archive files for the photos. We have the mug shot picture from Boston, but it's over twenty years old. We have no way of knowing if it's an accurate depiction of what he might look like today."

Taylor asked, "Did he have a social security number?"

Bradner replied, "Yep! ... But again, it's a dead end. The number was never used for anything, but to secure a single bank account and the credit card. Oh, by-the-way only one credit card was ever issued in that name. The bank accounts were abandoned with just a couple dollars in them. The credit card was linked to a checking account with automatic payment of the bill. Each month the minimum payment due was automatically deducted from the checking account and applied to the bill. All the deposits to the account were made in cash. Therefore, there is no record of any alternate address from which the bill might have been being paid.

When the balance in the checking account ran down to zero, there was no further activity in any of the accounts.

The Boston P.D. believed this Adam Mickiewicz was an out of state felon, they asked the F.B.I. to assist in the case. The F.B.I. obtained a fugitive from justice warrant against Mickiewicz. The F.B.I. flagged the accounts and asked the bank to keep the card active as they felt any use of the card might lead to an arrest. So despite the fact that there has been no activity the card number is still flagged. If Mickiewicz ever tries to access any of his accounts, notifications will be sent to the F.B.I., The Massachusetts State Police, and the Boston Police Department, The New York State Police and just about every other person on the planet. The flag never got a hit."

Taylor asked, "Wasn't this Adam Mickiewicz required to put up collateral for the bond?"

Bradner replied, "Yes he was, but the bail was only two thousand dollars that was less than the credit limit on the card so the bondsmen accepted a credit card voucher as collateral. There wasn't a lot of verification on the background of the applicants.

There's more, both the bondsman and the Boston cops tried, at the time, to get background info on the guy. To their surprise, they found that he seemed to come into the world around 1980. That was when he applied for the social security card. Prior to that time, there is nothing on him. No school history, no birth records, he paid no taxes. The only things they could find were a few magazine subscriptions and mail order catalog purchases made with the credit card, all sent to the drop box location in Yonkers. It looks very much like a phony ID from the start. Whoever he, is he is an expert at creating false identity, or he had very professional assistance in creating a false identity. He's an expert covering his tracks. Given the fact that we are dealing with a victim who is a foreign national, my guess is that this is some kind of spy thing. This is a guy who knows how to hide."

Taylor said, "Yes, until now. A person who seems to have come out of nowhere is arrested then disappears for twenty to twenty-five years. Suddenly, his prints appear at a homicide scene, a homicide scene that looks like a professional hit. Someone who drops off the radar for so long must have been out of the country. Perhaps he's been living under an assumed name in a foreign country. Either that or he's some sort of international hit man, a pro. If he's been a pro in the past, he slipped up this time for sure. If he popped up once, he will pop up again unless he gets back out of the country. Put out a B.O.L.O. I know there is not much to put out but put out what we have. Mark it 'Special attention Yonkers Police.' Also, put another flag on the credit card account. Make sure we are on the list of persons to be notified if he turns up somewhere. Put everything we got in the ViCap profile to share with the F.B.I... Update it to say we believe that our victim is a Polish national. Also, advise them that our Adam Mickiewicz is a person of interest. I'm not ready to call him a suspect yet, although he sure looks like our best bet. This was good work Tom, very good work."

Tom said, "There is one more thing. The plastic glass had no fingerprints on it, but there was a set of lip prints. I know we don't keep extensive files on lip prints, but I asked if they could get DNA. The lab tech thought it could be done, but it would take time. I told him it was a very important case. He said he would do what he could."

Taylor got up from his chair and headed for the door. Tom asked, "Where are you headed?"

Taylor smiled and said, "I have to get this info to the captain. He's got CompStat this afternoon."

Project 877

David Tees of the National Security Agency broke the silence in Duffy's office meeting room.

"You asked about the Groton Disks. Let me give you the background. There is a slogan used by our people in the naval submarine service. It's Run Silent - Run Deep. The operative word is silent.

The key to submarine warfare is that the enemy does not know where you are. You run deeply under the waves and strike from a secret position under the water. You cannot see a sub coming. It does not show up on radar. The only way you can effectively hunt for submarines is to listen for them. You use sonar. Sonar is essentially an underwater listening device. Big battleships, destroyers and even other submarines carry all sorts of sonar equipment. They listen underwater. They listen for enemy submarines.

Now, there are basically two types of sonar. There is active sonar and passive sonar.

Any movie about submarines will have a scene in which active sonar is used. The captain who is seeking to destroy a submarine activates his sonar equipment. The equipment makes a pinging sound that is broadcasted underwater. Then everyone watches as the sonar operator listens for the ping to echo back off the hull of the submarine. He hears the ping bounce back through his headset and bingo he knows where the sub is. We watch the movie and see the submarine crew nervously listening as they hear the ping, ping, ping and everyone is in suspense wondering if the sub will be found. Battleships ping the enemy subs, destroyers ping enemy subs and even subs will ping other subs in an effort to find and destroy them. That is how attack submarines attack other submarines. The problem with active sonar is that everyone hears the ping. The crew of the sub hears the ping so they know someone is looking at them. More importantly, when you ping the enemy you give away your own position, because when the enemy hears your ping his onboard sonar will report where the ping is coming from. You can only really use it effectively when you know that the enemy already knows your position and giving away your location is already a moot point. There are other circumstances where active sonar can be effectively used, but I don't want to bore you with the details. We're also developing a new type of active sonar wherein the ping cannot be heard by the enemy."

Commander Johnson interrupted, "Let's not discuss that now. You're going into an area that is a highly guarded top secret."

Dave Tees resumed his briefing, "I'm sorry, you're right. Anyway, that's too complicated to go into now. Besides that's not relative to our current discussion.

A more widely used method is passive sonar. With passive sonar, there is no ping. You just listen.

We use the most sophisticated listening equipment in the world. With that equipment we can listen for the sound of the enemy subs' motor. We listen for the sound of the props churning the water. The hull of every submarine makes its own unique moans and groans as the pressure of the water against the hull changes. We listen for the moans and groans. The crew talking and walking around in the sub can make noise that can be discerned. Therefore, we listen.

We run as quietly as we can and we listen for the other subs. Our subs were the quietest in the world. When the enemy is listening for us, he has one hell of a time finding us; we are so damn quiet. At one point in time, during the cold war, we had a tail on every Russian sub at sea. We followed right behind them underwater. In some cases, we followed them right into their homeports. We went behind them, under them and alongside them. We took underwater photos of them. We recorded their every sound and they never knew we were there. They simply could not hear us. The technology we used to keep our subs silent was all top secret.

Then in the 1980's the Russians began work on Project 877. They developed a new style submarine; The Russians call them the Varshavyanka. It means the Lady from Warsaw. Only because of the name, we have long suspected that the Polish ship designers had a significant role to play in their development. Now we may have more reasons to conclude that this Pole named Stanislaus Adamski may have had a more direct impact on the development of the 877. We call them Kilo Class submarines. There is much to be said about the improvements in the 877 over earlier Russian subs. There were some improvements that we would have expected them to develop, longer range, better weaponry, etc. However there was a new development in the later part of the 1980's. A second generation of 877 started to be built. There were minor changes that had major results. They were quiet! They were quiet, as quiet as our latest subs at the time, perhaps quieter. It seemed like somehow the Russians got a new insight on how to build subs. Of course, we put our people on it right away. We researched the design.

We spy on them; they spy on us. We all know that. We could expect that they would try to copy our designs. Hey, when they come up with something good we copy them. The basic question was this: How did the Russians make the quantum leap to such a silent sub so soon after our latest designs came out? Of course, they could have been expected to make many improvements on their own but we suspected we had a spy who was supplying our designs to the Russians.

We started looking at our design operations in Groton Connecticut. It's where our best stuff was coming from. We did extensive background checks on our staff and found nothing. We put them under surveillance and found nothing. Then we decided to look at our computer security to see if it had been compromised.

Now mind you back then we were not nearly as astute about computer data theft as we are today.

We learned that one of our designers had made back up files of his work. He stored the files on floppies. When we asked to see the backup disks, he proudly opened a file cabinet drawer and showed us a box of floppies. We took them to see if we could determine when they had last been accessed. Guess what?

They were blank! That is right blank! Someone had removed the floppies that had the back-up data and replaced them with blank disks. Since they were only backup copies of work that had already been submitted, no one would be looking at them. They were secured in a file cabinet that was protected by a four-dollar lock! Whoever stole them did not need to be an engineer or design specialist. He only needed access to the room.

From what we could gather from the designer who had made the backups, the disks themselves would not have given away the whole picture, but they contained enough data that a talented nautical engineer would be able to fill in the blanks and design a very sophisticated silencing scheme for any sub."

At that point, George Whentz resumed his part of the briefing. "The disks that Agent Franks had asked me to look at were not copies of the disks taken from the Groton lab. They were the actual disks taken from the lab. We know this because at the time our government was working on ways to improve the storage capabilities of floppy disks. The Navy had a supply of experimental disks. They were better than what was in general use at the time. They were not much better, but they were better. They never went into development because other more effective means for data storage were developed before these disks left the experimental stage. Anyway, because they were part of an experimental development project each and every disk was imbedded with a unique serial number. Through the number, we could trace not only where the disks were sent, but also we could identify the very person to whom they were issued. The disks that were in Mr. Adamski's possession are the very disks that were taken from the lab back in the early 80's. They were not similar disks…not copies of the disks…*the* disks!"

Commander Johnson then spoke up, "The improvements that the Soviets employed made our job a little more difficult. However, we could still find them and they still could not find us as easily. Our listening equipment was so far superior to theirs, but we had to gear- up to cope with their newfound silence. In this game if you can't hear the danger approaching you get killed.

Today we have the most sophisticated listening equipment in the world. We don't just rely upon the sonar onboard our ships. We have an entire array of permanently installed underwater listening devices that are networked together to listen at all times for underwater activity. If the captain of an enemy sub has Rice Krispies for breakfast, we can hear the snap, crackle and pop.

From our work in trailing their subs, we were able to develop a sort of computer-generated voiceprint for every one of their subs. We cataloged the unique sounds produced by each of their subs. You let our boys listen to one of their subs going by and we will tell you the sub's name, ID number, her captain and what type of toilet is on board. We call it the acoustical signature. We have cataloged the acoustical signature of virtually every ship at sea that is owned by any of our enemies. We even catalog the acoustical signature of the ships owned by allies and ourselves. After project 877 it was more difficult to hear the Russian subs. To hear them we had to develop even better listening equipment, but we were still way ahead in that game. As quiet as the 877 subs were they still had noisy props. If they were under power, we could hear those props churning from miles away. Then all of a sudden, they showed up on the scene with no prop noise.

Later we learned that our friends, the Japanese, were selling milling equipment to the Russians; milling equipment that could be used to reproduce the props that we had designed for our subs. We thought we had an international agreement that the milling equipment developed for us by the Japanese would never be sold on the open market, but the Japanese double-crossed us. A very well-known Japanese corporation sold the Russians the tools necessary to make their subs even quieter! We had designed a specialize prop for our subs, the quietest prop in the world. The design was so radical that it could only be built using highly specialized milling equipment. The milling unit, known as a MF-4522, was absolutely necessary to make props to our standards.

Before we knew it, the Russians had our prop. They could have never made the prop without an MF-4522.

Now it's one thing to get the milling equipment, but where did they get the prop design? How did they even know that they would need that Japanese equipment? We knew that they had to have our design or they would never have approached the Japanese in the first place. They knew about our props. They knew they needed the milling equipment to make the props. Ten years of development on our part and the Russians get it overnight. How? We knew that someone was selling us out!"

Duffy interrupted. "Did we ever seek damages against the Japanese company? Did our government ever go after them? Did we arrest anyone? Did the Japanese government cooperate?"

Johnson said, "That's another long story, perhaps a story for another time. If you want the details of the whole story, it was reported in the New York Times, look it up. The more disturbing part for us was the fact that we knew that there had been a leak of our info to them.

At first, we looked at the John Walker crowd. They were the premiere naval info spies of the day. Most of them were already in prison by the time the Groton Disks were stolen and Walker was already cooperating with the authorities by that time. He was telling what he knew in an effort to get a reduced sentence for his son who had been implicated in the scheme. He swore he knew nothing anyone who called himself Sorge." If he knew, he most assuredly would have told us. His son was looking at life in prison. John Walker was already locked up for life, but he was giving up info like mad to spare his son. We told him that if he gave up Sorge his son would benefit. Walker gave up a lot, but he swore he knew nothing of Sorge.

Agent Frank Dwarman spoke next. "We got called into the case in the late 1980's. There was a homicide involving a member of the design team at the Groton shipyards. Again, we still were not using the kind of measures that we should have been using in regarding computer security. A member of the design team was doing work at home and transporting disks from his home to the office on floppies. There was a break-in at his house. The thief broke in at night and stole the home computer that the designer was using along with a large number of floppies. Well, apparently the intruder was interrupted when our team member came home earlier than expected. Our person put up quite a fight. He had two fistfuls of the attacker's hair apparently pulled from the head of the thief. Unfortunately, the attacker had a .380 semi-automatic handgun, we think it was a Walther PPK/S; our person was shot once through the head and was killed instantly. We don't have any way of knowing what fragments of his data might have remained on his hard drive or what might have been on the floppies, but shortly after the theft of the computer, the Soviets began work on project 636.

Don't ask me why a project named 636 came after 877. One would think that their projects would be in sequential number order but they're not. The 636 is the newer design. That's the Russians for you. Anyway, I digress. The 636 is also a kilo class sub. It too had features that were remarkably similar to those in a project that our murdered engineer was working on prior to his death. It is loaded with design features that were exclusively ours. Our designer, who was killed in Connecticut, was working on stuff that later turned up in the 636."

Duffy spoke next, "You said the member of the Groton design team who was killed put up a fight. He had a fist full of hair. Do we still have the hair? There could be DNA."

Dwarman replied, "No actually we never got the hair. The case was initially handled as a local homicide. The local PD in Groton handled the case. The locals notified us after the initial investigation. We were called in only after it was learned that the victim was a federal employee."

Duffy asked, "So we did a coordinated investigation with them?"

"No" said Dwarman, "We could not tell them about the nature of our guy's work; top secret you know. We did our own investigation, separate from the local investigation. At one point in the investigation we found a witness who said that he saw a Groton Police car parked outside the victim's house around the time of the murder. Once the locals learned that we might have suspected one of their own personnel, any chance of cooperation was gone. The local PD got to the evidence first and they kept the physical evidence. I can only assume they kept the hair, but I don't know. DNA evidence was unheard of then. We did not consider the hair to be that important at the time."

George Whentz of N.C.I.S. rejoined the briefing. "In the early 1990's we discovered an alarming spyware program had been loaded on a number of governmental computers. The person or persons responsible had inserted a floppy disk into a number of our desktops that were connected to the Internet. The floppies installed a program that would cause the email function to create a blind copy of the emails produced on the computer. When the user sent an email, a blind copy would be sent to a wide array of federal and local government agencies, hundreds of them. The F.B.I. offices, Postal Services offices, National Guard stations, police stations, fire houses, Social Security Offices and many others. All would receive a copy of the original email. Among the recipients would be someone named Sorge. It was the first time the name Sorge turned up in any of our investigations.

Now when someone got one of the errant emails from the Navy, they would simply assume that they had received the email by mistake. Some of the emails were routine junk mail. However, a few contained data that should never have been sent over a non-secure line. Some secret stuff got out, sent to random recipients. Most of the unauthorized recipients would just throw away the emails as misdirected junk mail.

The beauty of the virus was that our spy could be working at any of those agencies. He could simply look for those emails that listed the recipient Sorge. He could then print them and keep them. He could take them somewhere and sort out those that looked like they contained something of value to our enemies from those that did not. He could then deliver the important ones to his contact. If you looked for a suspect, you would find thousands. The scam was not in operation very long. After a while, numbers of government employees began reporting that they were the unintended recipients of naval emails. We found the bug and killed it, but by then much of the damage had been done."

Agent Dwarman spoke again, "There have been a number of intrusions over the years that have to a greater or lesser degree compromised our national security that seem to have the Sorge signature. It would take all day to explain how we have connected the dots, but we have connected them. From the theft of the Groton Disks to the murders of a number of our personnel, we have connected Sorge to an ongoing criminal enterprise. We have been connecting him to a number of incidents spanning a twenty-year period. There have been at least three murders associated with the theft of government info that have been tied to him. In addition, he has branched out from naval affairs to other matters of national security. He began with very crude smash and grab jobs then went on to somewhat more sophisticated computer schemes and over the years has caused us pain. He's still very crude in his attacks, but more supplicated attacks have also occurred."

Robert Fulfree of Homeland Security spoke next. "Since 9/11 we have been taking a look at all sorts of data that might be helpful to terrorists. Sadly, much of what they need to know is available on the Internet. Still, however, from time to time we find that something we thought was a well-guarded secret seems to get out. Information about our ports, our airlines and our counter-terrorism initiatives gets out and we believe that this Sorge guy somehow gets access to our data and sells it to the highest bidder."

Thomas Trulane from the United States Immigration and Customs Enforcement agency known in law enforcement circles as I.C.E. spoke next, "We do not know if Sorge has ever physically moved contraband in or out of the country, but my office has been involved in this Sorge investigation ever since our agency became part of The Homeland Security Department. We are deeply concerned that anyone who can move information out of the country might also be involved with bringing harmful materials into the country. That is why I have insisted that my office be appraised of every facet of this investigation."

Director Madison began to speak. "At first we believed him to be an agent of the Russians and perhaps he was. Since the break-up of the Soviet

Union, the Russians have downgraded their spy operations. There have been many KGB agents in Soviet bloc nations who were out of a job. However, they still have their contacts, their network. Today many of them freelance. They are in organized crime. The old underground connections that once moved stolen intelligence now move stolen property, stolen gems, and stolen cars. It moves narcotics and occasionally it still moves stolen intel. It is sold, not necessarily to the Soviets, but to the highest bidder. The line between espionage and organized crime has become blurred. Both operations can be profitable and the masters of the spy game have become the masters of crime. It is all interwoven and this Sorge person is in the thick of it. We once believed that our Sorge was in the U.S Navy. Perhaps he was. We do not believe he is currently in the Navy, but he works for the government at some level and he is still doing damage.

More importantly he has a comrade, someone to whom he delivers his information. That someone quite likely has others planted around the country. He may be the controller of sleeper cells. If we can get Sorge, we may get his contact man. We get the contact man and the whole enterprise comes down. When we caught Walker his contact man, Aleksei Tkachenko got away. He made it back to Russia before we could grab him. He was never heard from again. To this day, we do not know if the Soviets gave him a new identity or if they simply killed him themselves to close up loose ends. We just know we never got him. He knew the whole organization and he got away. We got Walker and his cronies, but the main organization remained undercover. There can be no doubt that the Soviets would have replaced Tkachenko, but with who? It is more important to get the contact person. We must find the Sorge contact."

David Tees spoke of NSA next, "There is so much talk these days about our country spying on our own people...that we listen to everyone's phone conversations. Well, that's bullshit. There are billions of phone calls being made every day. We could never listen to everyone's calls. We do have a very sophisticated system for listening to selected overseas phone calls. Every phone call that goes overseas goes through a computer system that links various fiber optic lines to transmit the calls. We at the NSA tap into that system and our computers monitor the calls. We program the computers to listen for key words in conversations between persons talking to other persons in specific countries or areas where we suspect terrorist activity might be afoot. These are multi-million dollar computers with multi-million dollar programs. The computer can decipher codes and can warn us when coded conversations are taking place. For example, after 9-1-1 we learned that certain terror groups were using the term 'light the candle'. Through our computer system we came to find out that 'light the candle' was a code phrase used to initiate the terrorist 9/11 actions."

Robert Fulfree from Homeland Security interrupted, "After 9/11! You people knew something was up before 9/11. You knew that "light the candle" referred to taking terrorist action against the US, and you guys never told anyone that a planned attack was about to occur!"

Tees shot back, "Yeah and the F.B.I. knew that suspicious persons were taking flight lessons that did not include how to land a plane and they did not tell anyone. A US attorney refused to apply for a search warrant that an agent asked for that might have disclosed the plot. Don't lay 9/11 at our door. A lot of agencies dropped the ball!"

Madison jumped in, "Look let's not go down those roads again. By now, everyone knows that the failure to share info contributed to the fact that we did not know what was going to happen on 9/11 until it was too late. The NSA did not tell the F.B.I. what they knew; the CIA did not divulge what they knew, so on and so on. Those days are over. You hear me! Those days are over. The presidential directive mandates that we share info. It is essential to our survival as a nation! We are here to share what we know. That is the new mandate. That's why we are all here. We share what we know with each other. That way nothing falls through the cracks. Now, let's get back to Sorge."

Tees resumed his briefing, "The computer system is self-evolving. We program it to listen for given coded phrases that we know are in use. When it hears a conversation that it earmarks as a suspicious conversation it analyzes it and adds new watchwords to its database. The computer reports any new terms or words that it believes are attached to suspicious conversations. In our monitoring of selected suspicious conversations our computer from time to time picks up the term Sorge. It alerts us that the name is associated with conversations that might be trying to compromise our national security. The term shows up in Middle Eastern conversations and also in a number of dealings with criminal enterprise in the countries that made up the country formally known as Yugoslavia. The F.B.I. refers to persons in these associations as YACS. Am I correct Mr. Duffy?"

Assistant Director in Charge Joe Duffy gave the politically correct answer, "There are persons who have emerged on the scene as part of a known criminal enterprise that can trace their ancestry to Yugoslavia and some to Albania or Croatia and I suppose if you were to try to create an acronym to describe them you might use the term YACS."

Tees resumed, "Okay…When we hear conversations involving the YACS we hear references to Sorge. In conversations involving Sorge, we hear the reference "The Russian." We do not know who 'The Russian' is, but it would seem that there is a team…Sorge and The Russian. There are probably many others at various levels. Perhaps even others in government jobs. It looks to us like "The Russian," whoever he is, is the boss. We know that "the Russian" is likely to be an arms dealer who supplies weapons to a number of terrorist groups.

Find Sorge and perhaps we find The Russian. Find the Russian and the whole enterprise comes down."

Madison spoke next, "Mr. Adamski may have had the Groton Disks, but we do not believe he is actually the spy. His work for the Russians is open and documented. He is not undercover, he is not our spy, he is the recipient of the stolen disks. He is pretty high in the food chain, but not the spy. He is just a person who worked in the communist ship building industry that benefits from having access to U.S. technology. He does not hide his affiliations with the Russians. The master spy is the unknown "Russian." I suspect that 20 years ago the Russian gets the disks from Sorge and delivers them to his Russian handlers. The disks work their way through the system and end up on the desk of a marine engineer by the name of Adamski. Adamski just is a person who does his job and builds ships based on a design he gets from the disks. He's a functionary, not a spy."

Commander Johnson interrupted, "With all due respect I disagree in one aspect. These disks were, at the time, dynamite. The Russian would not have entrusted them to an underling. He would not have sent them through a chain of command. I believe he would have personally delivered them to Adamski. I believe that Adamski is right in the middle of this. For whatever reason he may have, Adamski no longer wants to be associated with the spy ring. My friends, Adamski knows who The Russian is! I'll bet he's ready to tell us. If we know this, you can bet the Russian knows this. We need to find Adamski before The Russian does."

Fulfree spoke next. "I'm concerned. If this Russian is freelancing, if he is selling to the highest bidder, then there may be a more serious and immediate issue. Perhaps our Mr. Adamski is aware of secrets that have been sold to terrorists. Perhaps, he feels the matter is too dangerous for his own well-being. Perhaps, he is here to warn us of an impending attack. If that's the case, you can bet the terrorists will be looking to kill him. I think we will need help. Time is of the essence. I suggest we get the CIA involved. They may have some intel on this so-called Russian. In addition, our Mr. Adamski disappeared somewhere in New York City. The NYPD has a very sophisticated intel unit. I suggest we bring them in ASAP."

Thomas Trulane from the United States Immigration spoke out, "Are you crazy! The CIA? Do you have any idea how reckless those people are? They have no regard for procedures. They will run amuck over everyone here. As for the NYPD…What do they know? This involves top-secret military info. We can't just let it out. I'll bet that they have people in their intel unit that do not have top-secret clearances from us. No way…No way.. We need to keep this among ourselves. There are already too many different agencies at the table. We need to maintain a single, well-focused investigation. If this "Russian" or this Sorge character has something like a dirty bomb, they will be trying to smuggle it into the country. That's why we should be at the lead. I trust our relationship with the F.B.I., but the C.I.A.? NYPD? No way! We need to close ranks on this one. Furthermore, New Haven Office of the F.B.I. has a head start on this I think the lead for this investigation ought to remain there. The New York Office ought to just turn over what they have to New Haven and let New Haven continue to run this operation with us."

Joseph Duffy began to rise in his seat to reply when Madison raised his hand and motioned for Duffy to remain seated and silent.

Madison said, "Calm down. First off, The C.I.A. is out of the question. Trulane is right. They have no regard for procedures. We need proper procedures if we are to get a conviction. When this thing goes to court, I don't want to have to run around trying to clean up evidence that was obtained through C.I.A. tactics. They'll get all our evidence tossed out of court with their tactics. Secondly, we are classifying this as a terrorist investigation. By presidential directive, we in the F.B.I. get first crack at all terror cases and that means no N.Y.P.D., at least not yet."

Fulfree said, "I think I would call this an espionage case. There is no evidence that any of this ever resulted in or is likely to result in an act of terrorism on the homeland. It's a military matter more likely to result in losses in combat. It's a spy case. The CIA and N.Y.P.D. belong on the job."

Madison reiterated, "You can call it what you like. I'm calling it a terrorism case. The F.B.I. will be the lead agency on this and we will handle it ourselves!"

Next, the New Haven office has had this for a long time and there has been little in the way of results. I think a fresh look by the New York Office might be helpful. The New York Office will take charge. We need to find this Adamski person before the Russian or Sorge find him. Let's get on it."

As the personnel began to leave Duffy's office Madison stopped to talk to Duffy. "That Thompson girl actually did a hell of a job. Linking her Adamski person to project 877 is what makes this case. Keep her in the loop. At first I thought that you might have made a mistake by assigning her to the job, but as it turns out she was an ideal selection. I want her to be the lead investigator on this. Make sure she gets whatever assistance she needs. Give her guidance, but let her pick her team. Most of all give her your best people to work with her, but make sure they know she's the lead. Keep me in the loop and keep me appraised on the progress. Keep up the good work."

The last person to leave the conference room was Frank Dwarman the F.B.I. SAC of the New Haven Office. He paused to speak with Duffy. "Joe," he said, "Can I have a moment?" Joe nodded and they walked back in to Duffy's office and closed the door.

Dwarman continued, "I was a little surprised myself that you would assign that Thompson girl to this case. We have an investigation looking for a person who has killed federal employees. I think you know the heat that will generate around this if it actually gets any traction. She's brand new. She can't handle a case this big. I don't care what the director says. She's in over her head."

Joe Duffy responded, "To tell you the truth, I did not actually assign her to *this case.*

When Adamski came in, he was insisting on seeing me. I was told that some raving conspiracy theorist was looking to talk to nobody but the boss. You know the type. They come in all the time.

Thompson was put on it as a simple preliminary matter. I actually wanted her to get rid of him. I thought it would be a simple matter that she could handle herself. She did more with it than I expected. Now, I think I am stuck with her. The director thinks she's on a run. I'll have to let her carry the ball."

Dwarman replied, "She does not have to carry it alone. I have a person on my staff, Alan Chapson. He's been on the Sorge thing on and off for a few years now. He most assuredly knows how the dots are connected. I could make him available to the New York Office. You know, on temporary assignment to you. You could pair him up with this Thompson girl and he could lead her by the nose. You could allow her to believe she's the lead, but my guy could steer her a little. I think the director would be just as happy to see us cooperate. Chapson is an experienced man … lots of time on the job and a lot of background in the Sorge matter."

Duffy did not hesitate for one moment. He

127

just said, "Send him down and I'll hook them up!"

Another Old Salt

Alan Chapson had been with the bureau for over fifteen years. He was an experienced agent with an impressive arrest record. He had a strong desire to move up the ladder in the bureau, but he remained at the entry level as a special agent for all the years he remained in the agency.

The F.B.I. is organized as relatively flat agency. That is to say, there are relatively few supervisory positions given the size of the agency. One can have a very good career, a nice position, lots of excitement and good pay, but moving up the ladder to become a supervising agent or an S.A.C. is very difficult. Chapson wanted to do that. He wanted to be in charge. He often told friends that hooking to some sort of specialty would be the way to move up. Between his regular assignments, he would study cases involving suspected spies. He always wanted those investigations. He told his superiors that he considered the Sorge investigation to be his case. Most of the Sorge related activity seemed to be centered in the Connecticut area. There had been incidents in New York City, Washington D.C. and California, but Chapson strongly insisted that Connecticut was where Sorge started and Connecticut would be where he would be caught. After the break-up of The U.S.S.R. the bureau put the Sorge investigation on a back burner. There were occasions when Sorge activity seemed to go away, but every now and then another piece of secret information would be found in the possession of some foreign agent or YAC and the investigation would heat up again. When that happened Chapson insisted the he get the case. His superiors complied despite the fact that Chapson seemed to be making little progress. His superiors knew that Sorge was an elusive figure, a hit and run man. He was not always active and that made finding him more difficult than an agent who is continually active. There seemed to be no one who knew the intimate details of the numerous Sorge cases better than Chapson and so he seemed right for the job.

Now there had been a break in the case at the New York Office.

Chapson had mixed emotions about being temporarily assigned to the New York office. He wanted to work the lead, but there was an obstacle by the name of Michelle Thompson.

This was his case. He worked it for years. By some random stroke of luck, someone just walked into the New York office and now a new agent was in on his case. She would be the lead investigator. Worse still, she was a woman. He believed the bureau would fawn over her. The bureau needed female heroes. He was sure the bosses would give her more credit than she deserved if the case went well. He would have done all the legwork and she would get the lion's share of the credit. To make it worse he had heard that she was a very attractive woman. If there were any press frenzy, he would be pushed to the rear. Those press people would be making a star of her. He needed to be the star. Fortunately, she was inexperienced. Somehow this was going to be his collar. He'd make sure of that!

It was a few days after the big meeting when Alan arrived at the New York office and met with the Assistant Director, Joseph Duffy. He was waiting in the outer office talking to George, Duffy's secretary.

"You must be Agent Chapson from the New Haven office," George said.

Alan replied, "Yes I am. I'm here to see Mr. Duffy."

George went on, "I'm sure he'll be with you in a few moments. Please take a seat. I guess you're here to work with Agent Thompson on the big case. To tell you the truth I'm glad they sent you down. Michelle is a lovely girl, but this seems like big stuff to me and she's so new. I know Mr. Duffy did not want to assign her to the case, but the Director insisted."

"Director Madison?" Chapson asked.

"Yes, the one and only. It seems that he was impressed by what she had done so far, and he insisted she remain on the case. Mr. Duffy was upset, she is so inexperienced, but what could he do? He was quite relieved when your Mr. Dwarman offered your services."

Chapson needed to analyze what was just said about Thompson. Duffy did not want her on the case, but Madison did. Most assuredly, one does not want to piss off Madison, but Madison is a busy man. He is in Washington. Duffy is in charge here. Chapson would make Duffy his ally. If he was overbearing on Thompson she most assuredly could not complain to Madison. She would have to go through Duffy and Duffy did not want her on the case in the first place. Suddenly, things were looking up for Chapson. He knew he would really be the one in charge. Thompson would be a minor distraction in the case.

Duffy greeted Chapson and took him directly to Thompson's office to introduce them to each other. Michelle was waiting for them. She had been advised that an agent from the Connecticut office would be joining her investigation. She was upset that an agent from another office was getting involved in her case. She knew she would need help on the case. However, she also knew that Duffy had been told to let her be the lead investigator. The helper worked for a different boss who had no such orders. This new guy might be here to take over.

She had just learned that her big case now had a big problem and she needed to advise Duffy and her new partner of the bad news A.S.A.P.

Joe Duffy introduced Chapson to Michelle and Michelle responded, "It's very nice to meet you, but I'm afraid that I must start off by giving you bad news. I have every reason to believe our Mr. Adamski is dead." Duffy and Chapson just listened as Michelle explained, "I just got this off the intel service. It seems that N.Y.P.D is investigating a homicide in the Bronx. They have an unidentified D.O.A. in a hotel. The description fits Mr. Adamski. I've seen the crime scene photos. The victim was

132

shot in the head. There is a lot of facial damage so I can't say for sure that it is Adamski, but the officers on the case note that they believe their victim may be Polish. After reading the transcripts, I agree. In addition, they are looking for a person of interest, a man named Adam Mickiewicz. They are calling him a person of interest, but I'll bet he's their suspect. He has a criminal record for felony assault and he's a fugitive from justice."

Chapson asked, "A fugitive from justice?"

"Yes" Michelle replied, "He's wanted as a bail jumper from the assault charges pending from the 1980's in Boston. There is more. It looks to me like he fits the profile of a professional hit man or foreign agent."

"Why?" Duffy asked.

Michelle continued, "He has no history to speak of. He is someone who has gone to great lengths to cover his tracks. There is nothing on him prior to the early 1980's. No birth records, yet he has a valid social security number. He has no job; he never had a job, as far as I can see. He has a very limited credit history. Only one bank account was ever opened in his name, only one credit card with very limited activity on the card. He had a New York driver's license, with many summonses in a limited period of time.

Then there is the arrest in Boston and then nothing. All of a sudden there is nothing, no accidents, no tickets, no banking activity, no anything. It's as if he dropped off the planet after the arrest. No bank activity, no more traffic tickets, and no death record, nothing for twenty some odd years and then … Bingo! His fingerprints show up at a homicide crime scene. A crime scene that looks like a professional hit carried out against a foreign national who is under investigation by the F.B.I. as a possible spy. It's either a person who's been out of the country or someone with access to a very supplicated means of developing a phony history for himself. You know like a spy, or something." Duffy nodded in agreement.

Michelle continued, "I was just getting ready to call N.Y.P.D. or to go up there to speak with this Detective Taylor. I think we will have to coordinate with them on this."

At once Chapson said "No! Don't do that yet. N.Y.P.D. has no idea what they are looking at yet. There is probably very little they could give us. This case could have implications for national security. Besides just about anything they could tell us seems to be in their intelligence report for ViCap. We need to develop this a little further on our own first."

Duffy said, "I agree. Michelle brainstorm this with Chapson and we will meet in my office later." With that said Duffy left the office and Michelle was left alone with Chapson.

Chapson spoke to Michelle, "It seems you have done a great deal of work on this already. Apparently you impressed Madison."

"So I hear," Michelle said. "The truth is that at first I thought the guy was a kook. Apparently, I inadvertently communicated my impression to Mr. Adamski and he dressed me down, seriously. Then I took him a little more seriously. After he left, I started to think that his information might be related to Russian spy activity. I figured I had better study up on the spy business. Just to be a little better prepared to discuss those kinds of investigations should the need arise. I went through our library on spy cases and learned about the history of Russian spies. Before I knew what was happening, I was called upstairs for a meeting. Much to my surprise, the meeting was about Russian spies. I guess I looked like the expert of the day. I really did not know much about the spy business; it just happens that I was reading up on it just before the meeting. I got the assignment. I thought here is my big chance, but now Adamski is dead, N.Y.P.D. has the body and the crime scene and their suspect is some sort of ghost. He has no background except for the Boston arrest and that arrest case reads like a script from an action movie."

Chapson asked, "What do you mean?"

Michelle replied, "I contacted the Boston P.D. for a copy of their case file. They advised me that the N.Y.P.D. had just done the same thing. They sent them the file yesterday, so N.Y.P.D. already has a one-day head start on us. Anyway, it seems that twenty years ago two young men show up at Fenway Park for a Yankees versus Red Sox game. The young men were wearing Yankee shirts. As you can well imagine, they drew the ire of the crowd. They are cheering the Yankees and jeering The Red Sox. At first there is little more than verbal abuse going back and forth. At some point, the two Yankee fans go to a concession stand for a few beers. While they are on line, a fight breaks out. A half-a-dozen Red Sox fans jump in. However, our two Yankee fans are like a couple of Ninjas. They start kicking ass all over the place as they beat a hasty retreat toward the exits. Several patrons were seriously injured by these two. The cops show up and grab one of them. The other escapes into the crowd and out of the arena never to be seen again. There are several complainants, but only two of them willing and able to identify their assailant. They pick Adam Mickiewicz out of a line-up. They ID him as one of the Yankee fans who had assaulted them in the melee. They both have broken noses so Adam Mickiewicz gets charged with two felonies. He makes bail and is never heard from again. That is until the other day when his fingerprints show up at a crime scene in the Bronx. I'm very sure that the body in that crime scene will turn out to be Adamski. I don't see how we can avoid contacting N.Y.P.D. on this, but we have specific instructions not to."

Chapson said, "Perhaps you are right, but we need not contact N.Y.P.D. right away. Let's go over everything we have on this Mickiewicz fellow. There might be a lead there that we have not yet considered adequately. We'll put our heads together before we do anything rash." Michelle went to get the file. Chapson was pleased. It seemed Thompson was going to follow his lead. He was going to get this Adam Mickiewicz before anyone else even knew where to begin looking. He was sure of it. He could feel it in his bones.

The Sailor and the Girl

Buddy left the pilot boat dock area, closed the gate and went back to his car. What he had to do next would be the most uncomfortable part of this visit home. He had to visit his ex-girlfriend. The only girl he ever loved. Of all the things he missed of his former life, it was Terri Wilkowski that he missed the most. He left her twenty years ago without a word. Not even a simple good-bye. He wondered, what was wrong with him. Had the death of his parents driven him mad or was it his quest for revenge that did that? Now he had to see her. He could not help but wonder what life would have been like if he had stayed around. Would they have gotten married? Would they have children and if they did, what would his kids be like? Would he and Terri have been happy? He knew he'd be happy to have won her love, but would he have developed into a person who she could continue to love or would he have ended up the same bitter man that he was today.

He wondered what the meeting would be like. Would he feel the rush of love's emotions? Would she? Would he be able to control himself or would he break down and tell her that he loved her. He always loved her. He always would love her. Would he tell her that over the last twenty years she was the only woman he ever thought about? Would he control himself? He knew that no matter what he felt he must control his emotions. This was a condolence visit. He was going to pay a visit to the widow of his best friend. He was going to visit Mrs. Ray Cassini. No matter what, he had to respect the memory of Ray. He would say nothing; he would do nothing that would cast any doubt on his respect for Ray's memory. Still, he wondered.

When Buddy and Ray were young men, they were a handsome pair and they knew it. They were well-built muscular athletes. Buddy was considered the toughest person in the neighborhood. He was lean and well skilled in just about every form of martial arts. He was well groomed with a handsome face and a quick wit.

Likewise, Ray was also an athlete. He actually even bore some facial resemblance to Buddy. Many people thought they were brothers. He was a golden gloves boxing champion in his weight class. He was an outstanding baseball and football player. He was fast. The coach of the track team wanted Ray to join the team but Ray was content to stick to three sports: Baseball, Football and Boxing. He was dark and handsome with shiny, black, wavy hair and a beautiful smile. Wherever they went, the young girls would trip over themselves vying for their attention. The boys tried to behave modestly, but they could not help but know that they were a sought after commodity among the young girls.

Ray enjoyed having a cadre of girlfriends. He enjoyed the company of the ladies. He did not go out behind their backs. He openly dated quite a few young ladies insisting that he was not looking for a steady date. The girls he dated knew that this was his style and they accepted it, but each hoped that she would one day become his exclusively.

Quite a few young ladies also pursued Buddy, but he dated only one girl, and that was Terri.

He loved her intensely and he was sure that she loved him, but she refused to accept his ring. She would say that she loved him and occasionally thought she'd like to be his girl exclusively, but she had reservations.

Buddy was a dedicated athlete and scholarly young man. He devoted tremendous amounts of his time to study. When he wasn't at the gym practicing his martial arts, he was at the library studying languages, art and history. He had been number one in his class at school every year since entering the educational system. If he was not working out or studying, he would have his nose buried in some sort of automotive sports magazine or he would be watching car races on TV. He had purchased a car and he was always under the hood trying to make the car faster.

Terri lived in a happy home, but she often felt bad for her mother who seemed, at times to be lonely. Terri's mother often complained that she was a golf widow because Terri's father was a workaholic and when he was not at work, he was playing golf.

Terri was always concerned that if she married Buddy that she would be a widow to any one of Buddy's numerous passions. She thought she might be in love with Buddy, but a girl needs more attention than she believed Buddy would give.

Her other love was Ray. It seemed ironic to her, and to everyone else, that the only other boy she would consider going out with happened to be Buddy's best friend, Ray.

He was good to her. He treated her like gold. He often said he would give up all his other girlfriends if she would agree to date him exclusively. Terri Wilkowski could not believe that. She felt that Ray would always have a wondering eye. Ray just did not seem like the type who would settle down with one woman. If Terri was going to get serious about one man, she had to be sure that she would be his one girl. She had doubts that Ray would remain monogamous. She was torn between the two. Each would be a great catch, but each had undesirable qualities as well. If it was possible for any girl to love two men, Terri was that girl.

Buddy and Ray never fought over Terri. They competed for her affection. Each, in his own way, would try to win her heart. They each knew that one day one of them would have her. In a true spirit of friendship, each was prepared for the other to get the girl. Each knew that one day one of them would be broken hearted, but no matter what they would always remain friends … no matter who got the girl.

Ultimately, Ray got the girl. Buddy had developed a new agenda for his life's plan. The new agenda would require him to travel. He traveled far and wide and for long periods. He knew that in his absence Ray would win Terri's heart. It was the price he knew he would have to pay. He thought he was

141

prepared to pay the price, but he never accurately calculated what the cost of heartbreak would be.

Ray was still his best friend, but Terri Wilkowski was no longer Buddy's girl.

Buddy knew he had to see her. He would see her at the wake of course, but he had to see her alone first. There had been too many years between them. He needed to talk to her. He needed to talk about Ray. He needed to talk about himself. He needed to hear her talking to him, about Ray, about herself and about their past. He needed to do that in privacy. The only way to do that was to visit her at home. It was going to be a few days before the wake would be held. If he went to her home, he was sure he could get a few private moments with her. It would be a painful visit, but it was a visit he needed to make.

He could put it off for a little while. There were a few things he wanted to do first. He wanted to secure a room at the Royal. He would be coming back from Terri Wilkowski's place late at night and he needed to make sure he had a room to stay in tonight. Moreover, the room had to be at the Royal!

He also wanted to visit the Polish Center. He had not been there in years. Besides, he was hungry and he was sure that the Polish Center was still a place where one could get a good meal and a few drinks at a reasonable price. So first he would go to the Polish then to the Royal and then to Terri Wilkowski's house.

Port of Call

Buddy drove to the Polish Center. From the outside, the building looked as it had always looked. It looked like an armory. It was a huge building with spire turrets and huge doors. Only the large sign on the side of the building proclaimed it to be The Polish Center. Two awnings covered the walkways to the two separate entrances used by the public. One led to the banquet room entrance and the other led to the public restaurant/bar. Buddy chose the latter and walked in.

In many ways, the place looked the same. Maple paneling covered the walls. The old oak bar still stood where it always stood. The large mirror across the wall provided a backdrop for the shelving that held a wide array of assorted liquors. In the old days, the barstools consisted of small round, red-plastic upholstered cushions that revolved atop a chrome frame. Now, the stools were black leather upholstered cushions with comfortable high backs that revolved atop a chrome frame … different, yet very much the same. A glass partition separated the bar from the public dining room as it always had, but the dining room had been completely refurbished. New tables, wall accents, lighting and flooring gave the place a very modern and comfortable appearance. The gift shop had been removed to provide more space to the dining area and a new salad bar had been installed. Other than that, the place looked pretty much the same. It felt like home to Buddy and he was glad he came.

Some things were different. After so many years, there were no familiar faces in the room. There were a few old timers at one end of the bar. Buddy did not recognize them. They were quietly talking to each other in Polish as they drank their beers. The people seated in the dining room seemed to be enjoying their meals in quiet comfort, but the faces were different faces. Buddy was sure if some of the old timers were around he might recognize some of them, but it had been a long time.

Buddy walked straight from the front door directly to an open stool at the bar. He could see that there had been a few changes since the last time he was there. What he did not see were the changes that had been made along the wall that had been to his back as he walked through the doorway toward the barstool.

He could see that the bartender was a new face. He was a young man, much younger than Buddy. Buddy took a seat at the bar and asked the bartender if a full meal could be had at the bar. The bartender replied that full meal service was available at the bar and he offered Buddy a menu.

Buddy ordered a typical ethnic meal of stuffed cabbage, kielbasa and pierogies. He ate and washed down the meal with a few beers. As Buddy was finishing the meal, he ordered one more beer then stood to go to the rest room. As he got up from his seat, Buddy turned around to head toward the restroom that was located down a hallway that was

144

behind his chair. As he did so, he faced the wall that had, up until this point, been to his back. For the first time he noticed that the on wall behind him, next to the main entrance door, there had been installed a large trophy case.

The trophy case displayed an assorted array of trophies that had been awarded to members of the athletic club. It also contained a number of photographs of events and of persons that had been significant in the Polish Center's history. There were testimonials from a number of civic associations, proclamations from political leaders and photos of the opening day of the center. There were photos of the past presidents of the center and photos of important events that had been celebrated at the center. In the very center of the display, case was a large photograph of Buddy's parents. They were embracing each other in dance. The photo had apparently been taken in the upstairs ballroom during a party. It was the kind of photo that a roving photographer might take during a dance at a wedding or New Year's Eve party. They had posed during a dance with their heads turned together facing into the camera and they were displaying tremendous smiles. They looked so happy. A small black bunting was draped over the photo's frame and a small brass plaque beneath the photo simply read -

This Display Case Has Been Erected in
Memory of Bob and Anna.

The sight of the photo astounded Buddy. He stopped, dead in his tracks and starred at the photo. He stood there, staring for more than a few moments.

His statuesque stare at the photo caught the attention of the bartender. The bartender came out from behind the bar and approached Buddy. "You look like you know those people," he said. Buddy did not respond.

The bartender went on, "I did not know these people, but everyone here knows the story of them. I understand that they were very nice people. He taught sports programs for the teenagers here. She taught English to people arriving here from Poland. The people here liked them very much. He was a person who learned martial arts in Korea, in classes that were held in the basement of a Korean brewery. One day there was to be some sort of reunion of the students of the brewery school. It was to be a big celebration in Korea. All the original brewery students were going to receive honors. Bob and Anna had their honeymoon in Korea. … A strange place for a honeymoon, no? …But that is what the people who knew them say. .. Anyway, they were returning to Korea for the celebration and to have a second honeymoon. But on the way to Korea their plane crashed and they were killed."

Buddy remained silent for a few moments continuing his gaze at the photo. Then he slowly turned to the bartender and quietly said, "They were not *killed* in a plane *crash*. They were murdered! The Russian Communists murdered them! If you going to tell their story; please tell it correctly. They were not killed in a plane crash; they were murdered by the Russian military."

Buddy went on, "September 1983, they flew on Korean Air flight 007. The flight was to go from Kennedy Airport to Seoul, Korea by way of Alaska. It was an ordinary commercial airliner on an ordinary flight. It was a large commercial plane, a 747. It was carrying two hundred and forty-six civilian passengers and a crew of twenty-three. Sixty-three of the passengers were Americans. There was even one who was an American Congressmen.

They say that as the plane approached Korean airspace the pilot accidentally drifted off course. The plane drifted into Soviet airspace as it hugged the Russian coast for its approach into Korea. It apparently flew in and out of the edge of Soviet airspace several times. According to the Soviets, they warned the pilot that he was violating Soviet airspace and if he failed to leave the area, they would shoot him down. Again, according to the Soviets, the pilot of the civilian aircraft did not respond. So they shot the plane down. Just like that! They shot it down!

A commercial passenger plane, with two hundred and sixty-nine innocent, civilian, men, women and children was shot down! They knew it was a helpless civilian aircraft. It was not a bomber; it was not a fighter or a spy plane. It was a commercial passenger seven-forty-seven! There was no mistake about it. It was a civilian craft that had gone off course and the Russians knew it. It was shot down. It was murder. It was mass murder. There was no war going on. They were not military personnel. They were ordinary folks, women and children. It was mass murder, plain and simple. Those murdering Russian bastards shot it down! The bastards denied shooting it down at first, but when the Americans proved that the Russians shot it down; the Russians then claimed the plane was on an American spy mission. That was bullshit. It was a civilian aircraft with civilian passengers and the Russians knew damn well what it was when they shot it down."

The bartender just stood silent. He had heard rumors that the plane was shot down before, but until that moment, he only half believed that the civilian aircraft had been knowingly and intentionally shot down by the Soviet military. "They knew?" he said.

"They knew." Buddy turned back to the bar where his drink was waiting for him. He drank down the beer in one long gulp. He forgot about the bathroom and began to walk out of the premises. As Buddy reached for the door the bartender asked, "Did anyone ever do anything about it? Did anyone make them pay for their crime?" Buddy pretended that he did not hear the bartender's question. As he walked out, he said under his breath, "I made them pay."

Buddy made his way back to his car and began to drive to the Royal Buena Vista. He drove much slower than he normally drove. He was in deep thought. He was comforted by the fact that the managers of the Polish Center chose to have the small

148

memorial in memory of his parents. He could not get his mind off the day he learned of their deaths. Oddly enough, he had been eating lunch at the Polish Center when news of the incident was announced over the television at the bar.

It was their deaths that caused him to live at the Royal for the short period of his life in the immediate aftermath of their murder. He quite likely could have found some relatives to live with. He most assuredly could have stayed in the home his family owned in Woodlawn. The mortgage was paid up and Buddy would have a substantial sum of money from his parents' estate. However, staying in the house brought him considerable pain. He could have moved in with any one of his family's friends for the short term, but he wanted to be alone to think out his plans. He wanted to go where no one would find him, where no one would think to look for him. He wanted to go somewhere where he could quietly plan his future; a place where he could plan his revenge. Oh yes, he would have his revenge!

He thought back to that evening, twenty years ago when he told his friend Ray of his plans to live at the Royal for a while. It also was at the Polish Center that Buddy met Ray for dinner that evening to tell him of his short-term plans for living at the Royal.

As Ray entered the center, Buddy was already at a table in the public dining area. Ray pulled out a chair and sat to join his friend at the table. "How you doing Buddy?" Ray asked sympathetically.

Buddy replied, "Okay, I guess, for an orphan."

149

Ray just nodded and said, "You'll be Okay you know? You will get over this. You're strong; you have a lot of friends. Life will go on. It happens to people weaker than you and they survive. I know it's hard but you'll get over it. If there is anything I can do just say the word. If you want to stay with my family for a while, I'm sure it would be OK. Whatever you need, you just let me know."

Buddy replied, "Thanks but I've settled on a place to stay. I want to be alone for a while. I'll let you know, but I don't want anyone else to know where I'm staying. OK? Just make sure you don't tell anyone where I'm staying Ok"

Ray nodded and said, "Okay, but where are you staying?"

"I'm staying at the Royal Buena Vista," Buddy replied.

The look on Ray's face told his reaction before the words came from his mouth, "Are you crazy! It's a rehab place! It's full of whores, junkies and ex-cons! You can't live there!"

Buddy responded, "It's not full of whores and junkies. It's full of ex-whores and former junkies. People who are trying to get their lives back together. They're people who mind their own business. That's what I want. I want to get my life on track and I don't want a bunch of nosey neighbors knowing my business. I just want to be alone for a while to sort thing out. It's cheap, it's clean and they don't ask a lot of questions."

Ray interrupted, "Your seventeen! They're

not going to let you stay there alone."

"I've worked that out," Buddy said. "Our 'very special friend' has make the arrangements."

Ray said, "Our, so called 'very special friend', has done a lot of crazy things for us over the years, but this is a little over the edge. It will never work!"

Buddy said, "The people at the Royal have already accepted 'our very special friend'. It's a done deal. Now, I just need you to keep quiet about it."

Ray looked resigned to the fact that Buddy was going to be staying at the Royal. He nodded and said, "Whatever you want Buddy, I'm here for you."

And so it was. Buddy would be staying at the Royal and Ray was the only one who would know. He would never tell anyone.

Today, Buddy was returning to the place that Ray would never tell about. He was again going to stay at the Royal one more time. Again, he was staying there to try to sort out his life. He was again trying to get his life back. This time it was not the death of his parents that played so heavily on his mind. It was the death of Ray Cassini.

As Buddy parked his car in front of the place, thoughts of his past raced through his mind. His memories were as vivid as one could imagine. It was as if the past was occurring right now. Emotionally, Buddy was seventeen again. He was a lost and lonely kid about to walk into a rehab place hoping to get a room where he could sit, alone and sort things out. For the next several minutes, he just sat in his car, parked right outside the Royal Buena Vista Hotel blindly staring off into the distance. It began to rain again. This time it was raining hard. The sound of the raindrops on the roof of the car provided a chaotic yet soothing rhythm in the otherwise silent car. Buddy just sat there, listened to the raindrops and let his mind go blank. Buddy's mind wandered to an old tune from the sixties by Lou Christie, 'Rhythm of the Rain'. Buddy preferred the '80's Dan Fogelberg remake, but the theme was the same. It was a song of love lost. Buddy could not help to think of the people he loved and the love he lost.

The Bunk

After about ten minutes, Buddy refocused. He could see that the rain was not going to stop anytime soon. The rain continued hard, but still Buddy walked slowly from his car into the Royal. He did not care if he got soaked. Perhaps the rain could wash away his depression.

As he entered the lobby, it was as if he had been transported back in time. Everything in the lobby looked exactly the same as it did when Buddy lived there. In the lobby, there was an imposingly large reception desk with an equally large imposing clerk. Just for a moment, Buddy was reminded of the movie The Green Mile. If they ever needed another person to play John Coffee, he was standing behind that desk.

Buddy smiled. He remembered the clerk who worked the desk when he lived there. Buddy knew that the man at the desk was more than a clerk; he was the peacekeeper a bouncer, an enforcer.

Buddy approached and asked if he could have a room and the clerk responded, "I don't think so! You better just be on your way."

Buddy said, "I'm not a troublemaker, a snoop or a snitch. I just want a room for a few nights."

The clerk replied, "This ain't no regular hotel. You don't look like a regular client. You look like some kind of troublemaker; or maybe you're some kind of do-gooder or worse still a cop or a reporter. You ain't no regular client. This is a rehab place.

You need a referral, so be on your way."

Buddy replied in somber tones, "Look I used to be a client here a long time ago. I got myself straight and moved on. Now ... Well let's just say I need a little more rehab time. I need to get away from the world for a while. It's not as if I'm on the lamb or anything. I just need to reflect a little. I don't know if you understand but I'd like to stay here a few nights. I'll pay cash in advance if necessary. I will not be any trouble. Can you understand?"

The clerk said, "No I don't understand. I can't imagine why a straightened out person would want to come here, but it happens. From time to time people come back for short stays. The foundation that runs this place ... they seem to think it's ok. I'll never understand it but they do. They say, sometimes, successful people who are allowed to come back, leave here with a desire to make a donation to the foundation. You know the foundation lives on donations. Anyway, they make provisions for returnees. They leave it up to me. If you meet my requirements, I'll let you stay. Now, I'm not looking for anything for myself. The foundation takes good care of me, but the foundation needs donations. You get my drift?"

Buddy felt ashamed. Of course, the foundation needed donations, and he was now a very wealthy man. He never before even considered giving back to the foundation. He replied, "I get your drift. Yes, I can, and will, do something good for the foundation. Just let me stay a few nights. I will not be any trouble. Believe me I'm no troublemaker."

The clerk said, "OK what's your name."

Buddy replied, "My friends call me Buddy. That's it Buddy."

The clerk did not look amused. He said, "Look pal, this is a legitimate place. You have to sign in with your name, your real name. I have to look you up in the computer to see if you were actually a former resident. If you were, we have your info and your picture in the computer. I look you up. If you're in the computer, you get in. If not, you can get you lost!"

Buddy answered, "But I was here a long time ago. They did not have any computer back then. They gave each resident an ID card and took a picture of all the residents back then, but it was a Polaroid, not a computer picture. Even if you see the picture, it's an old picture. I don't look the same. They did not have a computer system back then. I'm not going to be in your system."

The clerk smiled and replied. "This is the twenty-first century, my friend. Some time back the foundation hired an intern to copy all the old paper files into the computer. If you were ever here, you're in the computer, photo ID card and all. I don't expect the picture to be the same, but it should have some resemblance. So let's have it …. Your name please, your real name.

Buddy nodded and replied, "I understand, ... Mickiewicz, my real name is Adam Mickiewicz."

Logistics

Once the clerk had looked up Buddy's record in the computer, he was satisfied that Buddy was indeed Adam Mickiewicz. Buddy's face had not changed very much, even in the more than twenty years since he had stayed at the Royal and his signature was still the same. The clerk agreed to let Buddy stay. "Good news, the room you stayed in back then is currently vacant. You want your old room?" The clerk asked.

Buddy was delighted. "Absolutely." he said.

Buddy took out a roll of cash from his pocket. The clerk spoke up, "I can't take no cash here. We don't keep any cash on the premises. It invites trouble. I can take a credit card." Buddy looked quite dejected. "I don't have my cards or my checkbook. Just before I came here, I got ripped off. Someone stole my briefcase from my car. Everything was in it. I lost my wallet, my ID, all my credit cards and even my checkbook. I probably could get a postal money order by tomorrow, but I need the room tonight. Look, I'll not only come back with a money order, but I can also make a good donation to the foundation. Besides, I got the cash right here. I'm offering to pay in full, in advance. You're the person who is refusing to take the cash. If I were going to screw you, would I be offering cash up front? Just give me a room key and I'll pay up. I swear."

The clerk said, "OK ... OK I'll probably regret this, but here's the key. If you screw with me, I

156

guarantee I will fuck you up. Understand!"

Buddy said, "I understand. Believe me I can be trusted. I'm no troublemaker. Listen, I have somewhere to go. I'll be back late, any problem?"

The clerk said, "We lock the front door at eleven PM. If you ain't in by then you're out for the night. Got it?"

Buddy just said, "Got it" and he left.

Checking the Log

As Buddy drove off, the clerk spoke aloud to himself as he thought, "Did I do the right thing? Maybe I should have just taken the cash. AAHH it's too late now."

Still uneasy about not getting a credit card from Buddy, the clerk was staring at the computer screen. There, on the computer screen was all of Adam Mickiewicz's vital info from his previous registration. Included in the data that was displayed on the computer screen was the credit card number that Buddy used when he checked in all those years ago. The clerk thought for a moment. Perhaps that old credit card was still good. Just as a back-up precaution the clerk decided to try the account number and ran a credit charge against the number on file. His computer instantly notified him that the account was expired. He thought to himself, I should have known.

What the clerk did not know was that simultaneously, as the credit card company's computer was notifying him that the card was expired, a long list of persons and agencies that had been looking for Adam Mickiewicz were being advised that someone had just tried to use his credit card to check into the Royal Buena Vista Hotel in Yonkers, New York.

Another Shipmate?

Kirill Petrov called the man he called Maestro. "Well my friend, we seem to have a problem. You assured me that Adam Mickiewicz was dead before Adamski checked into the hotel in the Bronx. Yet Mickiewicz's fingerprints were found in the hotel room. Mickiewicz must have met with Adamski at the hotel! You cannot explain this. Now, I have learned that a man named Adam Mickiewicz has just checked into a hotel in Yonkers."

The Maestro responded, "It can't be the same Mickiewicz. It must be an imposter. Perhaps it is some sort of police trick. I'm telling you Mickiewicz was dead before Adamski checked in."

Kirill responded, "Sorge is quite upset. This new Mickiewicz has checked into The Royal Buena Vista Hotel. Sorge has some sort of personal history with that establishment. He is concerned that there may be some sort of police file that connects him to the place and now this Mickiewicz fellow checks into the very hotel where Sorge has had some history. He cannot accept the possibility that it is just a coincidence; in fact neither can I. He is insisting that he be allowed to eliminate this new threat."

Maestro replied, "You know my resources are almost limitless. I'm telling you that I have used all the available resources at my disposal to locate anyone named Adam Mickiewicz in America. There was only one that fits the profile of the man we were looking for. I can tell you, that the one who was eliminated and the one whose fingerprints were found in the hotel are one and the same person. I cannot explain how his fingerprints came to be there, but I assure you that man was dead while Adamski was still in F.B.I. headquarters.

You know that Sorge is a lout. He is brutish and crude. He will fuck us up eventually. You better tell him to leave this alone until I can look at it."

Kirill said, "I'm afraid that he is hell bent on this matter. It seems that he himself may have been implicated in some sort of assault incidents in the area of this Royal Hotel. It was many years ago, but the coincidence of having this Mickiewicz register there is too much for him.

He has already begun his plan to eliminate this new Mickiewicz fellow. Besides it could be that Adamski knew this Mickiewicz who has registered at the Yonkers hotel and not the one who was killed. I don't like loose ends. If we eliminate this one too, it will be safer." With that said Kirill Petrov terminated the conversation.

The Maestro could not help but believe that disaster was on the wing.

Sailing to See the Girl

Buddy drove a short distance from the Royal to the Main Street post office. There, he obtained a number of Postal Money Orders. There were a sufficient number of orders to pay for a few nights' lodging at the Royal and a few more to make a donation to the foundation. Buddy figured he would drop them off with the hotel clerk when he returned to the Royal later that evening. By the time Buddy got back to his car, the rain had stopped and the June sun had come out bright and strong. It was becoming a hot, humid and muggy day. Buddy could have turned on the air-conditioner in his car but he preferred to drive fast with the windows open. The wind rushing through the car at high speed again reminded Buddy of his youth. It reminded him of the days when he could not afford a car with air-conditioning. Although he was no racecar driver, he still liked to drive fast. Buddy took the Saw Mill River Parkway to the Taconic Parkway and then on to Route 9A. He was headed for the little village of Garrison New York. It was where Mrs. Terri Cassini, the former Terri Wilkowski, lived. There was no need to rush to get there. Buddy only drove there fast because that was how he liked to drive, fast with the windows open.

Garrison is a beautiful little village. It lies on the eastern banks of the Hudson River directly across the River from The West Point Military Academy. The views of the river are spectacular from that little village and there are beautifully quaint homes on the eastern shore. Many of the homes are of a late 19th century design. Ironically when the 1969 movie Hello Dolly, starring Barbra Streisand, was filmed, Garrison was chosen as the location to shoot the outdoor scenes that were to depict 19th century Yonkers.

Ray had purchased the home on the Garrison riverfront just before he and Terri married. Although Ray had given up on his dream of becoming a river pilot, he never lost his love for the river. He and Terri had a good life living along the river. Although they had no children, they enjoyed a life full of activities that they did together. They ran the postal drop business that Ray's father had started. They built it into a very large and profitable business with a number of storefronts throughout the metropolitan area. Eventually, a major national chain offered to buy Ray and Terri out. Ray and Terri kept only one store, to keep their hands in the business and received a sum of money for the others that would make them very wealthy for the rest of their lives. They traveled extensively, enjoyed Broadway plays often and lived an idyllic life in their home on the Hudson.

Now Ray was dead and Terri was alone in the world. Buddy wondered how she was holding up. As he approached her home, he slowed his car to a crawl. Evening was beginning to fall and the lights were on in the house. Through the window, Buddy could see Terri sitting in her living room. She just sat on a big couch with her hands folded in her lap, staring off to nowhere.

Buddy parked in the street and slowly approached the front door. He wondered if he should knock, or if he should just get back in his car and leave. He knocked on the door.

A few moments passed and then the door slowly opened. Terri just stood at the door for a moment then sighed, "Oh, Buddy; Buddy it's so good to see you. Please, please come in."

Buddy slowly walked in as he said. "Terri, I don't know what to say. All this time, all that I could think about is that I must come here and talk to you. Now that I'm here, I don't know what to say. I'm so sorry. I wish there was something I could say, something I could do. I wish ..."

Terri interrupted, "I know Buddy, and everyone who talks to me has the same reaction. No one can believe that Ray is gone, but he is gone. I don't know what to say to anyone myself. Please come in, sit, sit down." Buddy wanted so badly to take Terri in his arms and hug her. It would not be a bad thing to do. People hug each other in times of grief. However, Buddy wondered; if he hugged her, could he keep from kissing her. If he kissed her, could he stop kissing her? His respect for Ray was strong. Yet, all he could think about was taking Ray's widow in a loving embrace and whisking her off to be his own. He knew he had to suppress his emotions. He had to be the caring friend who would simply do whatever a good friend could do in her moment of need. "What happened?" Buddy asked.

Terri turned and stared out through another large picture window overlooking the Hudson. "We don't know. It was a minor procedure. Ray was having his gallbladder removed. It was a laparoscopic procedure. In the early days of those things, there were some unnecessary deaths, but today it's a minor thing. One day in the hospital and you're home again. Something went wrong. Ray's doctor insists that everything went fine until Ray went to the recovery room. Ray was sent up to a recovery room while he was still under anesthesia. The plan was to release him once the anesthesia wore off. Ray never woke up. Of course there will be an inquest, but for now who knows? The medical examiner has taken the body. It been several days and I can't even plan a funeral. They say it may be a week or more before the toxicology reports are back." She stopped talking and an uncomfortable silence filled the room for quite a while. Then Terri spoke again, "Please let me get you a drink. Sit here with me a while. Tell me what you've been doing with yourself. Let's talk about the old days, the good times. Enough of this talk of grief. I need a little good conversation. Tell me about yourself ... God! How long has it been?"

Buddy replied, "Too long." Terri handed Buddy a Jack Daniels on the rocks. Buddy sipped the drink and continued, "I guess we, ... Ray and you and I, just drifted apart. As you know after my parents died, I went to live at the Royal Buena Vista for a while. I got a brainstorm while I was there. There's a National Guard unit headquartered in Yonkers, The

164

One Hundred and First Signal Battalion. It's a communications unit for the Army National Guard. They do all the radio, telephone, and computer communications technology stuff for the Army. Anyway, I figured that if I joined the Guard, I'd earn a few bucks and get a few months free room and board while I was in basic training. A communications unit can always use people like me who can speak multiple languages. They not only communicate with Army units they also intercept enemy communications, break codes, that sort of thing. It's all stuff I'd be good at. So I waited 'til my eighteenth birthday and signed up.

After my basic training, I started getting deployed all over the place. Usually, one does not get called for active duty unless the whole unit is called, but an individual member can volunteer to be activated.

We were not at war at the time. Very few Guardsmen were called for active duty back then. I volunteered quite often for individual activations. They always need persons who can interpret foreign languages, so whenever I volunteered I went. I spent a lot more time on active duty than the average person in the Guard did. They sent me all over the world, mostly to the Middle East.

During one of my stateside stays, I took the test for the N.Y.P.D. and I got the job. I worked the patrol unit for a while. They found out about my martial arts background and assigned me to the training unit as an instructor. I did that for a while, but I hated it there. I wanted to be out in the streets. Then I got my sort of "Dream Come True Job." I got into the motorcycle squad. It was a good gig.

The police department will give you time off for National Guard duty during deployments. It was perfect for me. I stayed out in the streets and was free to go to my National Guard duties as needed. I most likely would have stayed with the N.Y.P.D. and made a career of it, but during one of my deployments with the Guard, I met this guy in Taiwan. He was a Chinese-American businessman. I helped him out of a jam. He got jumped by a couple of thugs looking to rob him outside a nightclub in Taiwan. I jumped in and helped him out. Actually, he credited me with saving his life. I don't know if I actually saved his life, but he thought I did.

He was in the import and export business. To show his gratitude he turned me on to an opportunity to invest in his enterprise. I had a lot of cash. You know how it is, no family, no responsibilities and a steady income from both the PD and the Guard. That combined with the proceeds from the sale of my father's business and the house I was pretty well-off. I had amassed a lot of cash. I had no idea where to invest it. It was just sitting in a savings account. I decided to roll the dice. I threw it all in with this Taiwanese businessman. We were importing Taiwanese products for sale in the American market. It proved to be a very lucrative business. I amassed wealth far beyond my wildest expectations.

I stayed with the Guard and made a few more

deployments here and there. I happened to be deployed to the Middle East when my commitment to the guard was up. I did not re-enlist. I just accepted a discharge while overseas and stayed in the Middle East for a while. The thought struck me that I was making so much money with the import stuff that I did not need to do police work anymore. I was in the Middle East, on leave from the department for the deployment and when my National Guard tour ended, I stayed in the Middle East. I just never went back to the N.Y.P.D.

I made a few deals to import stuff from the Middle East for sale here in America similar to the deals I had in Taiwan. I stay in touch with my former business partner. We're still good friends, but I have my own import / export business now. I own warehouses near the seaports in Texas, New Jersey, California and here in New York. I move shipping containers of stuff all over the world. My old partner and I will still do a joint venture every now and then, but mostly I do my own thing now. It requires me to travel all the time. I'm basically a homeless guy. I bounce from hotel to hotel. I have a couple of condominiums here in the states and in foreign countries, but mostly it's the hotel routine. I have no roots to speak of, just a rolling stone.

What about you? What have you been doing?"

Terri explained, "Ray and I have done very well for ourselves. A national chain of mailbox drop stores offered to buy up all of Ray's storefronts for a very handsome price. There was an initial cash payment with royalties spread out over many years. We ended up very well off. The terms of the agreement included a provision that would allow Ray to keep one store. He operates it under their corporate name, but it's his store. You know Ray, he wanted to stay busy and keep his hand in the business a little. We bought this house. Ray insisted that we have a home with a view of the river. It's beautiful, isn't it? Ray could stand here and just stare out this window for hours. He'd be in a trance like state. Just daydreaming, I guess. I often wondered what he was thinking. I asked a few times, but he'd just say, "Oh, nothing." I think he liked daydreaming about the river more than anything else.

We have no children. We tried, but no luck. We gave up on that a few years ago. Now Ray's gone and I have no one. You don't think about it when you're trying to have kids. You just want a kid. However, when you get older you realize that it's the kids that give people comfort in their old age. They keep old widow's company."

As a teardrop began to form in the corner of her eye, Terri said, "I'm sorry, I said no gloomy talk." Terri wiped the tear away and continued to tell Buddy of the years that she and Ray had lived together. Over the next few hours she and Buddy spoke of old times, good times, times the three of them spent together and of the times, they spent apart.

As the evening drew to a close Terri asked, "Have you got a place to stay? You're welcome to stay here."

Buddy had to fight the impulse to stay. More than anything in the world, he wanted to stay but he fought off the urge. "I have a place in Yonkers for the next few days. I'll be staying there." He slipped her a piece of paper with a phone number on it. "It's my cell phone number. If you need anything, please call. I'll stop by again soon. As soon as you know, the funeral arrangements let me know. I'm here for you, you know. Anything you need call."

They walked to the door. Terri said, "You too. I'm here for you too. Even though you have been away, I know Ray was like a brother to you. You must be feeling pain as well. I'm here for you too. Anything you need just call. I'm here for you too."

Buddy was in need. He needed her, but he could never tell her how badly he needed her. He just said, "Thanks."

They walked toward the door together and they said goodnight. As Buddy walked toward his car, he felt ashamed. He was here to honor his dearly departed friend, to give comfort to his widow, yet all he could think about was the fact that the biggest mistake he ever made in his life was letting her get away. He made some big mistakes in his life. They were very big mistakes by anyone's standards, but letting her get away was the biggest. Although he fought the thoughts as hard as he could, occasionally he would get the flash of a terrible thought; in a small corner of his mind he was happy that Ray was gone. Buddy did what he could to suppress such thoughts.

He wanted to think of Ray. He wanted to mourn Ray, but all he could think about was her.

Terri had a habit of closing her door with her back. She did it all the time. She would hold the doorknob turn her back against the door and walk backwards to push a door closed. Closing the door tonight was different. As Buddy walked down her walkway towards his car, Terri placed her right hand on the doorjamb and her left against the door. She leaned her face against the hand on the doorjamb and with her other hand, she slowly closed the door gently until it came to rest gently against her face. She stared intently at Buddy as he entered his car then, she slid her face out of the way, and she gently closed the door. She stood by the door staring at her hands, as they lied pressed together against the door near the seam between the door and the jamb. With her hands still pressed against the door, she thought, "Perhaps it is better that he did not stay the night."

She returned to her seat on the couch. She thought she'd like to listen to a little music. For some reason she felt like listening to Dan Fogelberg, perhaps she'd start with 'Same Old Lang Syne'. She turned on the stereo listened to the music softly and stared out through her window on the Hudson. It was dark now. She looked upon the river lighted by the dim glow of the moon. She could see the lights on a few boats that were traveling slowly along the river and she wondered where they were headed.

As Buddy drove back towards Yonkers, he was angry with himself for deceiving her, for not having told her the truth about himself. Most of what he said was at least, in part true. It was what he did not say about himself that made it deceptive.

Memories of a Long-Ago Cruise

It was about ten at night when Buddy arrived in the Buena Vista Avenue area. The nighttime appearance of the neighborhood streets seemed menacing. He felt that this was no place to leave a brand new Dodge Charger parked on the streets overnight. A brand new car like his would bring unwanted attention from car thieves as it was, but a Hemi Charger would be more than any punk could resist.

Buddy remembered the new parking garage near the corner of Buena Vista and Main Street. He recalled that it had what appeared to be a sophisticated security system. There were cameras everywhere. Buddy decided to park his car there and walk the four or five blocks to the Royal. It was a hot muggy night and Buddy was walking slowly along the sidewalk. The walk invoked another memory of years gone by.

The last time he walked from the area of Main Street to the Royal Buena Vista was more than twenty years ago. It was not a hot muggy night back then. Quite the opposite, it was a freezing cold February night. The temperature hovered around zero and a freezing rain coated everything in sight with ice. Earlier that day Buddy and Ray had planned to go to the Polish Center for dinner. Buddy worked out at the P.A.L. facility. He planned to walk to The Royal to get a few things from his room. Ray was supposed to meet Buddy at the Royal. They planned travel to the

Polish Center together. As Buddy walked from the P.A.L. building to the Royal he was being cautious. Not because the sidewalks were slippery, but because he had been warned to be on the lookout for trouble.

Word had been going around at the Royal that threats had been made against the management of the hotel and its residents. Hate mail was being sent charging that the Royal and its tenants were ruining the neighborhood. In truth, the neighborhood had gone bad long before the Royal began its mission in the area, but the writer of the hate mail did not seem to think so.

The letters spoke of the old days when the neighborhood was good and how the scumbags that were living at the Royal were ruining everything. There were threats to burn the place down and death threats against the residents. Only two days previous, a tenant had been severely beaten by an anonymous stranger with a baseball bat. During the beating, the assailant made it clear that the attack was motivated by hate against the Royal, its mission and its clients. Everyone at the Royal had been warned not to travel alone at night.

It was only six-thirty at night but in the northeast in winter, nightfall comes early. It was dark and Buddy was traveling alone. As he did so, an event occurred that would have a profound consequence for Buddy and for Ray as well.

Neither of them knew it at the time but this day and this night were going to have implications beyond anything they might imagine. On that night, long ago, as Buddy approached the front steps of the Royal, the figure of a large man in a blue coat stepped out of the shadows to confront Buddy.

At once Buddy could see that the man was holding a baseball bat. The man took a classic batter's stance and wound back with the bat over his right shoulder. It wasn't any baseball that the man was looking to hit. His sights were set on Buddy's face. Although his stance and wind-up would lend considerable force to a deadly swing, it exposed the whole left side of his upper body in Buddy's direction. Literally, before the big man knew what hit him, Buddy had placed a roundhouse kick into his would-be assailant's rib cage, just below the left armpit. Buddy knew from the sound of the thud that a few ribs had been broken by the impact of the powerful kick.

The man momentarily froze. Buddy could see the man attempting to inhale, but the stranger had the wind knocked out of him and he could not breathe. The bat slowly fell from his fingers and dropped to the ground. The large man then attempted to come forward with a powerful punch from his right hand, but Buddy quickly blocked the punch. Two quick counterpunches from Buddy landed squarely in the man's face and the assailant crumbled to the sidewalk like a bag of rags. He was out cold.

As Buddy looked at the man lying on the sidewalk, he was shocked to see that under the blue coat, the man was wearing the uniform of the United States Navy. Buddy knew that this was going to be

174

big trouble for him if he hung around.

Even though he was the would-be victim, a police investigation would reveal that he was living at the Royal under false pretenses. He was not really a homeless person. He had used phony credentials to get in. He was underage. The cops did not care for the residents of the Royal as it was; they all had bad reputations or criminal records. His assailant was a member of the armed services. If this unconscious serviceman told the cops that Buddy was the initial aggressor, they would more likely believe the serviceman. They would never believe that the sailor was the bad guy in this. There were cops on the force who knew Buddy from his activities at P.A.L. They might vouch for Buddy's good character, but having any of them learn who he was and where he was staying seemed just as undesirable an outcome. He did not want his cop friends, his father's former friends, to know where he was staying.

Buddy was set to enter the National Guard in just a few days. He believed that if he were implicated in this mess they would not take him. Buddy thought his best course of action would be to leave the area. The man did not know who Buddy was. He only knew that he was a resident of the Royal. It seemed unlikely that he would call the police; after all, he could end up in more trouble the Buddy. If Buddy disappeared this whole thing might blow away. He would go to the Polish Center, meet Ray and figure out his next move.

That night he did meet Ray at the Polish and

after talking to Ray, Buddy decided that he would never go back to the Royal. He was afraid the police would be looking for him there and there was no way he could explain the age thing. Nor could he explain how his "special friend" got the room for him. He did not have many personal items at the Royal. He simply would not go back. He still had the house in Woodlawn. It was on the market, but had not yet sold. He'd stay there for a few days then ship out with the National Guard. He'd be in the wind.

Now it was more than twenty years later and the fight that had taken place on that street was a forgotten event. No one would be looking for Buddy now. Buddy was walking that same path again. He was walking from Main Street to the Royal. He was walking alone at night. He had been "in the wind" for a very long time. It was time he worked his way home. He remembered that night he walked home in the cold. Tonight he was walking home in the heat of a hot humid night. This night would be different. Things would be better. This was a walk to recovery. He was going to find himself. He could feel it.

Ray- A Hero on the River

Ray had spent that same freezing February afternoon of twenty years ago as he had spent so many other days back then. After school, he drove his car to the P.A.L. building and made a brief stop there. Then he drove on to the pilot station. It was a bitter cold afternoon and a light rain began to fall. The wind was beginning to kick up and the river was showing its violent side. Waves were crashing about into higher and higher swells. It was going to be a rough and stormy day on the Hudson. It was going to be stormier than Ray imagined.

Ray knew that the launch captain would enjoy a hot cup of coffee. He picked up a couple of cups of coffee on the way, one for himself and one for the captain of the pilot launch. As soon as he arrived at the dock, he climbed on board the launch and sat with the captain. Drinking the coffee, without spilling it, was difficult as the waves tossed the launch about but they enjoyed their coffee all the same.

When they finished their coffee, the captain said that he needed to fuel up the launch and he was going to take a short ride to the fuel dock about two miles downriver. He did not have to ask Ray if he wished to come along. He knew Ray would be thrilled. The captain fired up the diesel engines and told Ray to throw off the lines. Ray complied and they were off.

They were hardly under way when an emergency call came over the marine radio. A

Yugoslavian freighter was broadcasting a request for immediate medical rescue assistance. They were reporting that a deckhand had fallen from the top of one of the cargo shipping containers stacked on the ship's deck.

Shipping containers are stacked high on the deck of the ship. A fall from the top would be the equivalent of falling from the rooftop of a four-story building. Falling from that height on to the steel deck of a ship would undoubtedly cause very serious injuries. The panicked voice of the ship's radioman made it clear to anyone who might be listening that someone was seriously injured.

At once, there was a clamor of voices on the radio. Seamen everywhere were asking how they might help. They were asking how badly the individual was injured. Most importantly, what was the location of the freighter? The launch captain could hear the Yonkers Police Patrol Boat requesting information on the ship's exact location.

The launch captain knew that the ship was likely still in the area of the Yonkers waterways, as he had just placed the river pilot on board only moments before Ray had arrived at the launch dock. The launch captain began to race toward the freighter as he radioed to the police boat the likely location of the ship. The launch captain knew that all the crewmembers of the Yonkers Police boat were emergency medical technicians, trained in all forms of sea rescue as well as in law enforcement. They were surely up to the task, but he knew they would need help, so he continued his race to the ship.

The police boat was the first to arrive alongside the freighter. It happened to be the closest vessel when the call came in. While the police were trying to figure out how to get aboard the huge vessel, the pilot launch went directly to the area of the ship where the pilot boards the larger boat through the shipside doorway.

The police quickly followed and tied up alongside the pilot launch.

The waters of the Hudson were unusually rough. There were high winds and rough waters. The boats were bouncing violently against one another as the wind and waves trashed them about. The police officers ran across the boats that were tied together as they formed a bridge to the freighter. They entered the larger ship via the pilot entry door in great haste. The pilot launch captain remained at the helm of his launch. It would fall to the pilot launch captain to keep the smaller boats alongside the freighter while the rescue mission was underway aboard the freighter.

A man who spoke impeccable English met the rescue team. "Gentlemen," he said, "I am the ship's security officer. Please follow me." He led to an area of the ship below the main deck. There a seaman lay in a pool of his own blood. The bleeding from the nose mouth and ears gave the dire signs of a fractured skull. The twisted positions of the legs told the story of broken legs and an elbow, bent in a direction that elbows do not ordinarily bend, disclosed additional serious injury. The man was in dire straits, but he was breathing. He was alive! He was barely alive, but he was alive. The man had not only fallen from the height of the stacked containers, he had the unbelievable misfortune of hitting the deck at the edge of an open hatch. He hit the edge of the hatchway at deck level then tumbled through the open hatch to the floor below. He was now below deck.

The rescuers knew that they needed to get the man off the ship and to a hospital fast. Ordinarily, a man so severely injured would be placed in a Stokes basket. It's a sort of steel wire mesh stretcher. A person can be strapped into such a device and be immobilized. Then the basket, with the injured individual strapped in, can be lifted by ship's winches and lowered to another craft or be airlifted by helicopter. However, having the injured man below deck presented a problem. They could strap the man in the basket, but the ceiling above them prevented them from using a winch to raise the basket. The man would have to be lifted horizontally to prevent further injury, but the hatch above them was too narrow to lift the Stokes basket through it horizontally. Instead they would have to hand carry the Stokes basket to the pilot entry door through which they had come. While the rescue crew did some preliminary first aid to ready the patient for removal from the ship, the ship's crew rigged a wood and rope gangway to connect the ship to the launch.

Quickly the improvised gangway was tightly tied between the huge vessel and the smaller launch.

The captain of the launch continued to maneuver his boat close to the larger vessel in the rough waters so as not to rip the rigged gangway apart as the boats bobbed in the rough waters. It was his task to keep the boats close together. He had to maintain some slack in the ropes that formed the gangway tied between his boat and the freighter. A violent wave or an errant turn could push the boats apart, pull on the gangway, and rip the ropes asunder. That would spell disaster.

The rescue crew worked feverishly to ready the patient for transfer to the launch. The whole time they did so the rigged gangway was attached between the larger vessel and the pilot launch. The whole time the freezing rain was falling upon the gangway. As the officers picked up the stricken man in the Stokes basket the security officer spoke up, "If you are going to take a citizen of Yugoslavia off this boat, I must go with you. I am the security officer. I am responsible for the safety and security of this ship and all her crew. I must insist that I come along. The officers felt they did not have time to argue the point, they just said "fine." The security officer led the group back to the doorway. He was the first to go down the gangway to the waiting pilot launch. He arrived safely onboard the launch and waited for the others to arrive.

Ray was anxious to help if he could. He put on a raincoat that was hanging by the cabin door. He stepped out onto the launch deck and stood in the freezing rain next to the security officer, watching the doorway to the great ship. As the wind and rain pelted Ray and the security officer, Ray saw the rescuers approaching the doorway and watched as they stepped out onto the gangway. They were carrying the injured man in a Stokes basket. As they approached the midpoint of the gangway, Ray watched in horror as one of the police officers, the one furthest from the launch, who was carrying one end of the Stokes basket, slipped on the ice covered frozen planks and fell, dropping the basket.

The basket fell to the floor of the gangway and the officer who had fallen was sliding off the improvised gangway. He was on his back and slid head first over the edge. The officer locked his legs on the rope but he was now bent over backwards over the edge of the railing. The basket with the injured seaman, who was still strapped in lay on the deck of the gangway. The officer on the side of the Stokes basket closest to the launch was prevented from lending aid to his fallen comrade. If he released his grip on his end of the Stokes basket to go to help his partner, the injured seaman would surely fall into the river. Even if he could let go of the basket, the basket itself would fall to the deck and block his path to the fallen officer.

Now as he was holding the basket alone, that officer was struggling to hold on. His fingers became enmeshed in the steel webbing of the Stokes basket. The waters were still tossing the smaller boats about the waves and the gangway was being violently tossed about. As the Stokes basket slid around on the deck of the gangway the officer was thrown into

182

excruciating pain as the basket webbing was causing multiple fractures to the cop's fingers with each thrash of the waves. Despite the pain, the officer refused to let go of the basket. Nevertheless, his partner needed help!

Ray ran from the deck of the launch, up the ice-covered gangway and grabbed the side of the basket closest to him, relieving the officer from his need to hold the basket. Now as Ray held his end of the basket up on the gangway it completely blocked any passage. Persons on the gangway were unable to pass to the launch. Quickly, the cop with the broken fingers climbed over the man in the basket to grab his partner by the gun belt. With all his fingers broken, he screamed out in pain, but miraculously held on and pulled his partner back onto the gangway. Now it was more imperative than ever for the pilot boat captain to maintain a proper distance between the boats. If he were to allow the waves to throw his launch up against the larger ship, it would crush the men stranded on the gangway. If it pulled away from the larger ship, the gangway would be ripped in half and all of the remaining men on the gangway would be hurled into the freezing waters.

By now, the security officer had made his way back up the gangway to assist. Another man, who until now had not been involved, suddenly appeared at the gangway and began to assist in the rescue. Together Ray, the security officer and the newest volunteer carried the injured seaman to the launch. The officer with the broken fingers followed carrying his partner.

With the gangway free from personnel, the captain of the launch turned his boat hard toward the starboard and gunned the engines. With the roar of the powerful twin diesel engines, the launch quickly pulled away from the side of the great ship. The flimsy, concocted gangway broke, sending bits of broken rope and splintered boards into the raging waters. Ray quickly threw off the ropes holding the police boat to the pilot launch, sending it adrift. Free from the encumbrance of being tied to other boats the pilot boat captain headed for shore. On board the launch was Ray, one police officer with a badly mangled hand and another officer who complained of severe back pain, the ship's security officer and a man whom nobody seemed to know.

An ambulance and additional police cars were already waiting at the pilot launch dock. The launch captain raced toward the dock to the waiting ambulance. The injured seaman and the officer with the injured back were both placed in the ambulance. The security officer argued that he must accompany the injured seaman in the ambulance. Again, no one believed that they had time to argue the point he was permitted to get in the ambulance. The officer with the broken fingers was placed in a police car for transport to the emergency room of the near-by St. Joseph's Hospital.

By now, a couple of other river pilots had gathered on the pilot dock. Once the injured were on their way to the hospital, a number of pilots climbed on board the pilot launch, and they went out on the Hudson to retrieve the police boat that had been sent adrift.

That left just Ray and the unknown man who had joined the rescue effort alone on the dock. There seemed to be an eerie silence on the dock as the ambulance and police car sirens faded off into the distance. Ray had just been through the most exciting episode of his life. Now he was winding down. He stood in the freezing rain, alone on the now silent dock, alone except for the presence of one man, a man who only moments before was a passenger on a Yugoslavian freighter. He was the man who helped Ray save a life. A man he did not know at all. He was a man with whom he had just shared a most exciting adventure. Ray had no idea how much this chance meeting would mean in his future.

Ray did not know if the man spoke English, but he held out his hand and introduced himself, "Hi, my name is Ray Cassini."

The man replied, "My name Stan Adamski."

Pandemonium

Ray waited with Stanley at the pilot dock for some time. Ray realized that Stan's knowledge of the English language was very limited, but he managed to communicate with him somewhat. Ray was surprised to learn that Stan was not Yugoslavian, but that he was in fact Polish. Ray wondered why a Pole would be on a Yugoslavian ship, but dismissed the thought, as more pressing issues seemed to be at hand.

Ray asked Stanley if he wanted to join his shipmates at the hospital to find out what was happening. Stan indicated that he would like to do so. Ray made his way back to his car, he drove Stan the short distance to the hospital, and they entered through the emergency room door. The scene within was unbelievable. Doctors and nurses were running about the facility in frenzy. When the persons injured in the river incident arrived at the emergency room, it was already crowded with a number of other slip and fall accident victims as the rain covered frozen sidewalks were presenting a dangerous surface on which to walk. The icy roadways were not helping either. A number of motor vehicle accident victims were also being treated when a rush of police officers raced in with their severely injured seaman and two of their own. The officer with the back injury was very seriously injured. The seaman in the Stokes basket was in critical condition.

At once, the new arrivals were given top priority for treatment, as it was clear that they were the most severely injured persons in the crowded emergency room at that moment. The doctors were calling for crash carts ... stat! The speaker systems at the hospital were announcing, "Arrest at Emergency Room! - - Arrest at Emergency Room!"

In hospital jargon, the announcement "Arrest At" does not mean that someone is going to jail. It means that there is a cardiac arrest occurring. Someone is on the verge of dying and all available personnel are to respond as quickly as possible to the area where the arrest is occurring. It means we need help! We need it now! Medical personal from every area of the hospital were running toward the emergency room.

The officer with the broken fingers was in substantial pain; he was told that he would just have to wait. He understood triage and knew that he was not going to be treated for some time. He turned down an offer of pain pills. He was too concerned about his partner at the time to think of his own problems, he wanted to remain alert.

Into this madhouse of activity arrived an array of police supervisors and federal officials. This serious accident, on the waters of the Hudson, required a federal investigation. This was the Cold War era and a person from a communist country was at the center of the action. Foreign nationals had been taken ashore without proper clearance from The U.S. Customs Department. Their personnel had already been on the scene. This could have international ramifications. State Department personnel arrived.

Police brass were concerned about their personnel, but they also had to make sure that the accident investigation was thorough and that all proper authorities were notified.

The ship's security officer hovered over his injured seaman and refused to let him out of his sight. A nurse gently persuaded him to go to a waiting area and take a seat just outside the emergency room door. He only agreed to do so after he was assured that there were no other exits from the ER. No one was going to sneak his charge out a back door. No one was going to defect on his watch.

As Ray and Stan entered the emergency room, they saw the security officer sitting in the waiting room and they joined him there. The security officer reminded Stan that he too was under his command and Stan simply nodded in agreement. Soon thereafter, an official of the U.S. Immigration and Naturalization Department introduced himself to the security officer.

"Hello. I am from the United States Immigration Office. I need to speak with you for a few moments. I have spoken to the police already. They tell me you speak English very well. May I have your name please?"

The security officer replied. "My name is Kirill Petrov. I am the security officer and business agent for the Yugoslavian shipping line."

The immigration officer said, "Well, your English *is* quite good. Your accent seems almost British, but Kirill Petrov? That would be a Russian name, would it not? I thought you were Yugoslavian."

Kirill responded, "My parents were Russian. They moved to Yugoslavia before I was born. My father was with the Russian Diplomatic Corps. They lived in many foreign countries. I was born in Yugoslavia. My father was assigned to Yugoslavia just before I was born. Shortly after I was born, he was transferred to London. I spent my formative years growing up in England. I went to school there. When my father retired, we moved back to Yugoslavia. Since I was born in Yugoslavia, and since I was living in Yugoslavia as an adult, I claimed Yugoslavian citizenship. I am a citizen of Yugoslavia and I travel on a Yugoslavian passport."

The immigration officer responded, "I see. Were you close to the injured seaman? By that I mean were you good friends or just shipmates?"

Kirill responded, "No, I did not know the man other than to say I know he is a member of the crew."

The immigration officer seemed relieved. He said, "Well, I'm sorry to inform you, but you shipmate has passed away. Since you are the ship's agent, I'm assuming that you'll be handling his affairs."

Kirill said, "Yes, I suppose that it is my duty to do so. I can take care of notifications to the family and anyone else who needs to be notified. I can arrange for his remains to be returned to his homeland. Of course I'll have to see the body and confirm for myself that he is indeed deceased."

The immigration officer said, "Of course.

You can go in to see him right now. However, his body will not be released for several days. There will be an inquest by the medical examiner before the body can be released. It seems like a straightforward accident, so under the circumstances I'm sure it will be a quick routine inquest. Even so, I am afraid that might take a few days."

"I can wait a few days," Kirill said.

The immigration officer continued, "You realize that you do not have a visa to be here in this country. As a crewmember, your rights to travel in this country are limited to the ship and its prearranged ports of call. Technically, at the moment, you are an illegal alien in this country. You cannot go wherever you want while you wait. Your travel will be restricted. I can issue a temporary emergency visa. It will permit you to remain here while you are handling your crewmember's affairs. It will also permit you to travel within the country as necessary to deal with the matters at hand on a limited basis. I will need to contact my superiors and advise them as to my recommendations. I am not so sure as to what those recommendations might be just yet. I have to look at the whole situation before I can recommend approval for a temporary limited visa. To get approval for that I will need to know where you will be staying. Do you have any idea where you might be staying?"

"Yes", Kirill replied. "I am familiar with this area. I travel the Hudson often. I know I am not far from the Russian mission residence in Riverdale. My father is well known to them. I have already contacted them and they have agreed to send a car for me. They will let me stay there." The look on the immigration officer's face suggested that Kirill's choice of the Russian residence, as a place to stay would be a troubling issue.

There was an empty office next to the emergency room. The door was open and the lights were on in the room. There were a few desks in the room and a couple of phones. The office was available on a regular basis. It was made available by the hospital to provide space for people to fill out paperwork. Undertakers, ambulance workers, police officers and other visitors who needed to write reports or fill out forms related to hospital business often used it. At the moment, the office was vacant.

Kirill continued to talk, "Look, there is an empty office here why don't we go in here and sit down? We can go over my papers in private. I am sure that once you review my paperwork you will agree that all is in order and that I pose no threat to your national security."

The immigration officer said "Okay." They entered the room and closed the door. About ten minutes later, they emerged and the immigration officer was talking to Kirill as they exited the room.

The immigration officer was saying to Kirill, "It looks good. I'll handle my end of the paperwork and you'll be good to go shortly."

It seemed that in the confusion at the emergency room the immigration officer did not realize that Stanley Adamski, who happened to be seated right next to Kirill, had also gotten off the ship without proper authorization and that he too was there illegally. He paid no attention to him. The immigration officer went back into the emergency room to gather more information from the police about the accident. He emerged from the emergency room and returned to the office that was available for report writing. By now, several police officers had entered the room and they too were seated at desks writing reports. The immigration officer took a seat at a desk next to a Police Officer Leslie Maker, who was writing reports about the accident on the Hudson.

The officer spoke to the immigration officer, "What do you make of that guy? He seems to be very pushy. He says he's the security officer for the ship, but he seemed to hold more authority aboard the ship than the captain did. He was the one making all the decisions as to what should be done."

The immigration officer responded, "I see a lot of that in my business. He's a security officer with a lot of authority. He will never admit it, but I am sure he is with the U.D.B.A. It is the Yugoslavian equivalent of the K.G.B. The communists are paranoid about sending their citizens here. They think they will all defect, or worse that we will get them, turn them into spies, and send them home to do our bidding. All these communist countries put anti-espionage personnel on board their ships. You know 'Big Brother' is always watching.' Our friend Kirill Petrov is U.D.B.A., a communist enforcer, a watchdog."

The cop said, "I should have known. Do I have to notify the C.I.A. or something?"

"No. You see all these federal officials here? No doubt, they have identified themselves to you as members of the National Safety Transportation Board, or the Federal Occupational Safety Administration, or the National Trade Commission, or anyone of a dozen other federal agencies that have a legitimate interest in investigating an accident aboard a foreign trade ship in our waters. Well, take this to the bank; one or more of them are actually C.I.A.... C.I.A agents often identify themselves as being agents of other governmental agencies. They have their professional liars. Just remember 'Big Brother' is always watching. I'll just do my paperwork and you do yours and rest assured that the C.I.A. will do theirs."

Suddenly, it seemed that the police had a new problem on their hands. An unruly person had just arrived at the emergency room and he was demanding to be treated at once. He was trying to intimidate the staff at the hospital to treat him at once, yet he did not seem to be nearly as badly injured as the others who were receiving treatment. He refused to understand that the more seriously injured needed to be treated first. Finally, one of the nurses requested that the police contain the man.

An officer took the man by the arm and escorted him to the waiting room. The man sat down across the aisle from where Ray, Stan and Kirill were seated. He continued to complain loudly about his need for treatment. The very large man in a blue coat complained to the police officer in a very loud voice. "I need to see the doctors right now! My fucking ribs are broken, my face is swollen and I might have a broken nose. I've been beaten up and no one seems to give a shit!"

The cop asked, "Okay, calm down and tell me what happened?"

"I was minding my own business walking down Buena Vista Avenue when I got jumped! There were three of them. I would have kicked all their asses, but one of them had a bat. That punk kid hit me one the left side of my chest with the bat and broke my fucking ribs. I'm telling you it was them scumbags from that fucking Royal Buena Vista. That fucking place ought to be shut down!"

The officer said, "Just sit here for a moment. I'll see if I can get you some help. There are many seriously injured people here. We got a cop with a broken back, another with broken fingers. We got guys frozen half to death and a Yugoslavian sailor who just died in there. Just calm down and they will get to you in due course. Just give me a few minutes and I will take a report on your assault and I'll try to get you some help." With that said, the officer returned to the emergency room.

As the officer left, the man in the blue coat began to complain to anyone who would listen to him. Kirill sat and listened to him as he continued to complain. "You know this fucking country sucks! I go off and join the Navy. I go away and they open a

194

fucking rehab joint in my neighborhood. I got drunks, whores and junkies in the streets to contend with when I come home on leave.

I join the Navy to see the world. They promised me I would be visiting all sorts of exciting, exotic, and romantic places. Where do they send me? ... Fucking Groton Connecticut! I spend the last few years pulling full time guard duty at the shipyards in Groton ... Pretty fucking exciting! Don't you think? Now, I come home on leave and the neighborhood punks beat the shit out of me. I come to the hospital and I'm last on line. For Christ's sake, I'm a fucking U.S. serviceman. Don't I get any extra consideration? NO! The cops are the fucking heroes here. They go first. Okay ... okay ... They go first, the cops go first, but a foreigner ... a fucking foreign sailor gets priority over me! What is this fucking world coming to? A fucking foreign sailor gets preference over a U.S. Navy sailor! What kind of shit is that?"

Kirill began to speak to calm the man down. "You know sir; it seems to me that you are a man who deserves the consideration you seek. After all, you perform vital service to this nation.

Groton? ... Is that not where the United States develops its submarines?"

The man responded, "Yeah."

Kirill continued, "And you are assigned to full time guard duty there?"

"Yeah."

Kirill went on, "It seems to me that you offer your very life in the defense of the American

195

submarine fleet yet you are treated so badly. Tell me;
at what facility do you perform these mundane guard
duties?"

"At the research and development lab," The
big man responded.

Kirill continued, "You know I am a seaman
myself. My friend here is also a seaman and a
shipyard worker. We, who have a common
connection to the sea, ought to take care of each
other, don't you think? Where I come from, we take
very good care of our seamen. When I find myself in
trouble, they help at once. I am presently stranded
here. I have notified my countrymen that I am
stranded here. You know what they are doing for
me? My friends are sending a limousine to pick me
up. They will take me to a very comfortable place to
stay until I can arrange to get home. Where they are
taking me, we have medical services on the premises.
Please allow me to help. I am quite sure I can obtain
excellent medical care for you at once. It would be
superior to any service you might receive here and I
assure you it could be obtained free of charge.
Besides, if you stay here that policeman will, no
doubt, come back and ask many questions to fill out
his report. Once he learns you are a member of the
armed services he will arrange for copies of his
reports to be sent to the military. Next thing you
know the Navy will be asking questions. They never
take your side in these matters, do they? They will
find fault in you, no doubt. You can avoid all that
and get medical help at once. You might ask why I

would do this for you. Well, I too am a seaman. That fellow who is being treated in there is one of my crew and I have just been informed that he has died at the hands of these incompetent emergency room doctors. Please it would be an honor for me to get you some help. You would get better treatment than my shipmate received here."

The man just responded by saying, "Thank you. You know you're right. That cop is just going to cause more trouble for me. Did you say the service would be free? It wouldn't cost me anything?"

Kirill replied, "Absolutely nothing."

Ships in the Night

At the hospital, Kirill went off to another room with the immigration officer to do what he had to do to secure his temporary emergency visa. When he returned to the waiting room, he spoke with Stan for some time in Russian. It was a language that both Stan and Kirill spoke well and, at least for Stan, it was much easier than trying to communicate in English.

Ray saw Kirill hand Stan a roll of money and then Kirill approached Ray. He said to Ray, "Unfortunately, the immigration officer was unaware of the fact that my good friend Stanislaus was also a crew member from the boat. He is somewhat unprepared to issue a second visa. He will, of course, have no choice but to do so. After all Stan is here and it will be much easier to issue a visa and exit papers than to deport him. Besides, under the circumstances, it is the right thing to do. It is simply that the immigration officer must first re-contact his superiors and apprise them of the circumstances before he will issue the documents. I have secured a place for myself to stay and my car has arrived. I must go now. I have given Stan some money and a phone number where I can be contacted in the morning. By then I should have made plans to help Stan return to his homeland, but he will need a place to stay for a few days. If you would be so kind as to stay with Stan until he gets his papers and help him to find lodging? I would be most appreciative." Kirill then handed Ray two hundred dollars. Ray accepted the assignment and Kirill left to go to the waiting car. Ray could see through the glass doors that the man in the blue coat was already outside standing by the limo. He watched as Kirill and the large man entered the car and drove off.

Stan went off to another room and returned shortly thereafter with the necessary papers.

Ray spoke to Stan, "I suppose you're hungry. I'm supposed to meet a friend and go to dinner with him. As luck would have it, he speaks Polish very well. Would you like to get something to eat?" Stan replied in the affirmative.

Ray and Stan drove to the Royal Buena Vista and together they entered the establishment. Ray went to the desk and asked the man at the desk to ring the room of Adam Mickiewicz. Upon hearing the name Stan asked, "Your friend, ... his name is Adam Mickiewicz?"

Ray replied, "Yes."

Stan went on, "But Adam Mickiewicz is famous poet of olden times in Poland."

Ray said, "Errr ... I know. Adam's mother was a Polish college professor and she married an American man named Bob Mickiewicz. She thought it would be good to name their son Adam in honor of the poet. I do not think there is any blood relationship. It is just his name. Besides, he does not use that name often. His friends call him Buddy." Stan nodded to indicate that he understood. By that time, the desk clerk was telling Ray that Adam was not in his room.

Ray thought it odd that Buddy was not in his room. He was sure that he was supposed to pick Buddy up and take him to the Polish Center for dinner. Ray decided that perhaps there was a misunderstanding. Perhaps Ray was supposed to meet Buddy at the Polish Center. He decided to go to the Polish Center.

Sure enough when Ray and Stan arrived at the center Buddy was there waiting for them at the bar. They approached Buddy and Ray said to Stan, "This is my friend Buddy."

Stan extended his hand and said, "I am pleased to meet you Mr. Adam Mickiewicz."

Buddy extended his hand and as he and Stan shook hands, Buddy looked at Ray and said, "You told him my name was Adam Mickiewicz?"

Ray replied, "He was with me at the Royal when I asked for you at the desk. He overheard me asking for Adam Mickiewicz. Apparently, he knows about the poet and fixated on the name. Anyway, I told him to call you Buddy."

After the introductions, the group moved to a table in the dining room. Buddy and Stan spoke extensively in Polish and Buddy related the conversation to Ray. Buddy learned that Stan was a young nautical engineer and computer expert who worked for a large Polish ship building operation. His company built large commercial ships that were in service mostly in communist bloc nations. The ship where the emergency on the Hudson occurred was a brand new ship on its maiden voyage. Stan had been sent along on the voyage as a technical advisor to the crew. His job was to assist the ship's engineer in learning the new onboard operating systems. The ship had many innovations including numerous computer-operated systems. Stan's job was to advise the crew on how to best use the new equipment. He was to report to the company any malfunctions that the crew might bring to his attention so that proper repairs could be made, if necessary. Stan did not know why the crewmember chose to try to climb up on to the top of the containers during an ice storm, but clearly, there were no safety issues for which his company could be held responsible.

They talked for hours. Ray told Buddy about the events of his day and Buddy was deeply interested in the story of his friend's heroic actions. Buddy told Ray about the fight he had earlier that evening and of his determination never to return to the Royal. Ray agreed that Buddy should return to his Woodlawn home until he was ready to ship out with the National Guard. By then Buddy had learned that Stan needed a place to stay for a few days and he offered to allow Stan to live with him until he was ready to return to his homeland. Stan was extremely grateful and accepted the offer. Having a Polish-speaking comrade would be very helpful.

Living together for the next few days Buddy and Stan became quite close. Buddy tried to convince Stan that communism was a bad thing and that Poland ought to be making efforts to break its ties with the U.S.S.R. Buddy made it quite clear that he regarded

201

the Russians as the worst people on earth.

For his part, Stan tried to make Buddy understand that he was not a politically active person but he was careful not to say too much to contradict his host. Stan knew better than Buddy knew that politics is not a good topic for friendly conversation.

Over the next several days, Buddy and Stan traveled together. They went to the Polish Center every day to eat and enjoy a little conversation. Stan made many friends among the Polish immigrants who frequented the center and among a number of American-born people of Polish descent who also went there. He had to endure the numerous suggestions from his new, well-meaning friends that he should remain in America. They told him he could plea for asylum in America. They would tell him how much better life would be for him here. He knew that they meant well, but he just wanted to go home. He would promise to work hard to improve his English and perhaps he would come back to America one day. For now, he just wanted to go back to Poland.

After several days with Buddy, Stan received the call. It was time to go home. Kirill arrived at the Polish Center in a limo, he picked Stan up and together they drove to a dock in New York City where a ship was waiting to take them aboard and bring them home.

A New Crew

On board the ship, on the way home, Kirill had a proposal for Stanley Adamski to consider. He called Stan to his room and offered him a glass full of good American whiskey on the rocks. Then he began a conversation. Speaking in Russian Kirill said, "My friend you and I have shared quite an adventure. I consider you to be a comrade. You are a man to be trusted. I have a proposal for you.

During my brief stay at the hospital, I made a friend. I did him a few favors and supplied him with some much-needed cash. In return, he promised to provide me with something of value. Just before we left the U.S.A. he gave me these." Kirill opened a box and showed Stan its contents. It contained a large number of computer disks. Kirill went on, "My new friend assured me that these would be of substantial value to my people. However, I have a problem. I do not know for sure how much value they have. I was told these disks contain valuable information on American submarine design. I was told that if I were to show these to a nautical engineer that such a person would vouch for their value. You are an engineer and a computer expert.

Now if someone were to tell me that they had value I would be more confident in turning them over to my superiors. I would not want to hand in worthless disks and look like a fool. Beyond that, I have another idea. If these are very, very valuable and if I turn these over to my superiors at the U.D.B.A., I am quite sure that they will deliver them to a higher authority in Moscow and they will give me no credit for having secured them. We in the U.D.B.A. may be in the employ of the sovereign government of Yugoslavia; we all know that Moscow and the K.G.B. call all the shots.

I am considering going over the heads of my superiors and delivering these disks directly to the K.G.B. myself. Now if the disks are very valuable, the K.G.B. will be quite grateful. Given my father's service to the U.S.S.R. and my ability to deliver valuable information about American submarines, I am sure there will be a highly desirable position in the K.G.B. for me. My new friend in America assures me he can, and will, supply more valuable information in the future, there-by assuring my continued value to the K.B.G. I could end up in a very comfortable life. If on the other hand the disks have little value, the K.B.G. will not be grateful at all. In fact, they will be upset that I failed to follow their chain of command. They will report my failure to follow necessary channels to my superiors in the U.D.B.A. and that would have very serious consequences for me.

You can see my dilemma. Now, if I had a partner, a consultant, one who could evaluate what is on the disks, then I would know what route to follow. I might gain much influence in Moscow. I could bring my consultant along. Perhaps I could get him a prestigious assignment at the shipyards in St. Petersburg. I will continue to need his good counseling as more data arrives from my new American friend. It could be very profitable for both my engineer partner and myself. What do you think? Do you know a nautical engineer who knows computer systems and who might be interested in helping a poor Yugoslavian attain greatness in the U.S.S.R.? I think you are a smart man. I think you can realize the value that such a partnership might have."

Stan had been sincere when he pledged to improve his English skills. He was sincere when he said he would like to return to America one day. Nevertheless, that day, on the high seas of international waters, Stan entered into an agreement with Kirill Petrov. In effect, it was an agreement to become a Soviet agent. It was an agreement that would bring him much acclaim in the Russian shipbuilding industry. It would improve his lifestyle for some time. It would improve his life until the day it would end in an untimely death in a Bronx hotel.

Back at Port Royal

Buddy arrived back at the Royal just before eleven. He was not surprised to find the same clerk at the desk. In the old days it seemed that the same clerk was on twenty-four hours a day. Some things never change.

Buddy handed the clerk a stack of money orders as promised. He and the clerk talked for quite a while about the old days at the Royal. They compared notes on who they remembered and how the facility had changed so little in all the bygone years. It was after midnight before Buddy went up to his room.

As Buddy opened the door to his room, light from the hallway streamed into the darkened room. To Buddy's delight, the room looked exactly as it had more than twenty years ago. Buddy entered the room and closed the door behind him without turning on the room lights. The room went dark as the door closed. Some small narrow streams of light from the streetlights below leaked into the room through the opened window past wispy thin curtains. What little light there was sparingly illuminated parts of the room. Emotionally, Buddy was transported twenty years back in time. Twenty years ago he would sit, in the dark, for hours contemplating his world, planning his future, planning revenge for the death of his parents. He did some of his best thinking there. It was what he would do again. He would just sit in the dark. He would just stare out the window, think and plan his future.

Buddy prepared to undress. He walked over to the dresser against the wall near the door. He took off the Hawaiian-style shirt he was wearing and threw it on the nearby bed. He reached around to the small of his back and removed from his waistband his fully loaded Kimber Arms model 1911 .45 caliber automatic pistol. He held the weapon up near his face and admired it for a moment. It was one of the finest weapons of its kind. He felt a personal connection to the weapon. The gun had been a gift, a presentation, from a person who had been an important figure in Buddy's life. It had been manufactured in Yonkers, and it was one of Buddy's most prized possessions. He placed the fully loaded .45 on top of the dresser.

He walked across the room sat on the edge of bed near the window. He stared out the window at the street below as he had done for so many hours in years gone by. A gentle summer breeze rustled the curtains shifting the light and shadows around the room. The breeze felt good against his face, although it did little to cool the room on this hot muggy night. Still, he knew it was more comfortable here than it was in the many of the un-air-conditioned rooms in the city that could not benefit from the cool breezes that came off the Hudson. There was always a little breeze by the river.

Buddy turned on a radio that was on the nightstand next to the bed. He turned the volume down very low and tuned to a station that played oldies. He sat quietly while he listened to the music of his youth. A small round red light on the face of the radio was the only light on in the room. Hours passed. The street below looked as it had years ago. Lined with tenement houses, with old cars parked at the curb and a quite stillness that only these early morning hours would provide, the street looked like a picture of the late 70's poverty that defined this part of town.

As Buddy sat on the edge of the bed, he almost unconsciously, reached down towards his lower left leg. He raised the pant leg and removed the Walther PPK/s.380 caliber pistol from the holster that was Velcro strapped to his ankle. Carrying only one gun was never sufficient for Buddy. Too many people were looking to kill him. Just for a moment Buddy wondered, what kind of man have I become? What kind of man needs to carry at least two guns at all times?

That second gun, the PPK, he placed in the nightstand drawer next to the bed. He closed the drawer and just stared at the street below and let his mind go blank once again.

Buddy's empty mind soon became aware of a presence in the street below. He had spotted a white suburban parked on the east side of the street, across from the Royal Hotel. It was parked near the T-intersection corner just to the south of the Royal. The vehicle was parked quite close to the intersection facing north with the front of the car quite close to the corner. The vehicle moved, ever so slightly, rocking side to side, as if a person was moving about within.

Buddy looked more intently at the suburban. He could just barely see the outline of a person in the car. Buddy had been at the window for more than an hour. The car had been there the whole time. The person within must have been there the whole time as well. Buddy knew it was a surveillance of some sort. The positioning of the vehicle gave the person seated in the driver's seat a clear and unobstructed view of the Royal and all points north of the Royal along the street below.

Buddy pondered for a few moments. It could be a private detective watching for some sort of infidelity on the part of wayward spouse, but people in this neighborhood could not afford a private eye; they attended such matters themselves. It could be a jealous husband waiting for a wondering wife to come home, but Buddy did not think so. He was sure that it was a police surveillance. Most likely, it was a narc looking to spot a drug deal going down. In this neighborhood, a police surveillance of that type would not be an uncommon event. Buddy smiled. He thought it was amusing that while the police were watching some unsuspecting criminal, he was watching the unsuspecting police officer.

Buddy would not have been so amused if he had known that the hotel clerk had run a credit card account number bearing the name Adam Mickiewicz through the system. He would not have been amused if he realized that people from a dozen law enforcement agencies were being advised that a certain Adam Mickiewicz was back on the radar or that Adam Mickiewicz might be staying at the Royal Hotel in Yonkers. He would not have been amused if he knew the man in the surveillance vehicle was not looking for a wayward spouse or an unsuspecting drug dealer. The man in the suburban was looking for him!

As Buddy continued to stare out from his sanctuary, he saw something that he knew was an all too common occurrence. A marked police radio car pulled up behind the suburban. The officer in the marked vehicle activated the red lights on the roof of his patrol car, got out of the car and approached the driver.

Buddy surmised that the detective had failed to notify the local precinct of the surveillance. Now a uniformed cop had spotted the man in the car and deemed it suspicious. He was going to question the person in the suburban. With those overhead red-flashing lights, he was going to draw attention to the white suburban. He was most likely going to blow the surveillance. As Buddy watched, the officer got out of his car and began to approach the suburban. The driver of the suburban exited his vehicle and met the uniformed officer in the street and they began to converse.

Buddy imagined how the conversation might be going. The man from the suburban would be complaining to the uniformed cop that he was blowing the surveillance. The uniformed cop would be complaining that he had not been told of a surveillance in his sector. Eventually, they would chalk it up to experience and resume their normal routine.

As Buddy looked on, he saw the two men shake hands and they began to walk back to their respective vehicles. The uniformed officer got to his vehicle first. He got in, sat down and closed the door behind him. At that point, the man from the suburban stopped at the door of his car. He turned around and returned to the marked police car. As he approached the marked car, he motioned to the officer to open his window. The uniformed officer complied. The uniformed officer remained seated in his car and the driver from the suburban stood alongside the patrol car by the driver's open window. The two men spoke to each other through the open window for a few moments and then without warning ... BLAM! ... BLAM!

Two shots rang out and the uniformed officer slumped over in his car ... He was dead.

All Hands on Deck

"Holy shit!" Buddy yelled out loud. "Holy shit!"

Buddy jumped from his perch on the bed and leapt to the dresser. His first reaction was to grab the .45 and run after the shooter, but he knew the first order of business needed be to get medical help for the officer. Buddy was sure the cop was dead, but if there was to be any hope for his survival he needed an ambulance and he needed one now.

Buddy fumbled in his pocket for his cell phone. He dialed 911. He knew that virtually every 911 call is answered within three rings, but waiting for those rings seemed to take an eternity.

The police dispatcher answered, "911, what's your emergency?"

Buddy knew that most 911 systems display the location from which the 911 call was being made and that it is usually unnecessary to tell the dispatcher where you are calling. He also knew that the system that discloses the location of the call does not always work for cell phones. He knew a 911 call from a cell phone might just as easily connect him to the State Police rather than the Yonkers police. He knew that a controlled voice would be best to describe his situation. Buddy composed himself and said, "This is for the Yonkers Police 10 - 13 .. Shots fired .. Officer down ... 167 Buena Vista Avenue ... officer down! Send a bus! ... The shooter is in a white suburban!"

Buddy knew his call was being recorded and that the dispatcher would have access to instant replay of his message. There was no need to stay on the line. Buddy threw the phone down, grabbed the .45 and ran out toward the street. As he ran past the front desk, he could see the desk clerk was alert and alarmed. Apparently, he had heard the shots. As Buddy ran to the street with his gun in hand, he yelled to the clerk, "A cop's been shot call headquarters!" Buddy knew that a second call from a hard-wired phone would surely go to the local police and that it would provide additional information. It would confirm the location for the 911 system. Buddy continued to run out to the street.

  As Buddy got to the street, he was shocked. The marked radio car was gone! The shooter was gone! The officer was gone! There were no signs of them. He looked up the street and saw that the white suburban was still parked at the curb, but its driver was gone!

  Buddy's mind was astir. Holy shit! ... The shooter took the radio car to make good his escape from the scene. He must have taken the fallen officer's body with him! As Buddy looked toward the north, he saw the faint glimpse of the radio car's taillights turning to the right, going around the next block to the north

  Quickly he thought - the suburban! It's still parked at the curb! Perhaps the shooter left the keys in the car! If he did, Buddy could use it to give chase. Buddy ran as fast as he could toward the suburban, opened the door and jumped in. Alas ... No keys! Shit!

As Buddy sat in the car, he could hear the sounds of dozens sirens coming from every direction. As he looked to the north, he saw what looked like an unmarked police vehicle speeding in his direction. There was a siren blasting from the direction of the approaching vehicle. There were no rooftop lights on the vehicle, but red lights were flashing from within the grill and the headlights were flashing, as were the emergency flashers in the bumper area. It was most definitely an unmarked police car.

"Damn!" .. Buddy thought, "That unmarked car and the marked unit being driven by the fleeing shooter must have passed each other. Shit! Did he not notice that the radio car was going away from the target area?"

As the unmarked radio car got closer, Buddy began to exit from the suburban. As he did so, the driver of the unmarked car locked up the breaks and skidded sideways, sliding to a stop directly across the street from Buddy. In one motion as the car was still skidding to a stop the door opened and a man stepped from the vehicle. The man had a gun in his hand. It was pointed straight at Buddy. As the man jumped from the car, he shouted, "Police! Drop the gun!"

Just for a moment, things seemed to go into slow motion. Buddy looked at the man shouting at him to drop the gun. Reflexively, he looked down at his hand and realized he was holding the .45 out in plain view.

Instinctively, he knew the proper thing to do at that moment would be to drop the gun at once and put his hands over his head. Buddy had been a cop at one time. He knew the rule for armed plain-clothes confrontations. The rule is: If you are not in uniform, yield to the known authority. Drop your weapon and put your hands up. Buddy knew the man yelling to drop the gun was a law enforcement official. His training told him to drop the gun.

Yet, strangely, sometimes under stress, unusual thoughts can enter one's mind. Such strange thoughts can cloud and overshadow good judgment. Oddly, Buddy's first thought was that this gun was his prize possession. It was a presentation piece, awarded to him for outstanding service to his country, his favorite gun. If he was to drop it on the ground, it might get damaged. It was just a fleeting thought. It was a thought that occupied his mind for only a split second. However, in tense situations, even a fleeting, errant, thought can consume valuable time. Fleeting thoughts lead to serious mistakes. Buddy hesitated.

Suddenly, Buddy felt an incredible slamming, crushing pain in his chest. It felt like he had just been hit in the chest by a sledgehammer. He never heard the shot. He just felt the pounding chest pain. Clutching at his chest, he felt his gun slip from his hand and he saw it hit the ground. As his hands made contact with his chest, they were instantly covered in blood, his blood. Buddy tried to hold on to the open door of the suburban to brace himself up, but he felt his knees weaken. Slowly he went to his knees. Then he fell, face first, to the pavement. His eyes remained open, but slowly his world faded to black.

The Scene of the Shipwreck

The scene on Buena Vista Avenue was a sight to behold as Yonkers Police Captain Richard Dent arrived. There seemed to be radio cars everywhere. The streams of red light flashed all over the area as the overhead lights of the numerous emergency vehicles, that choked the street, bathe the entire area in a strange flashing red glow. Captain Dent saw the man lying on the ground with a gaping hole in his chest being feverishly worked on by the paramedic ambulance crew.

Across the street, one of his uniformed officers was standing by an unmarked radio car. He could see skid marks on the ground indicating that the unmarked car at the curb had come to a screeching halt. His officer was questioning a man in a business suit. The man looked like he might be a detective, but the captain knew he was not one of his men.

The captain walked over to his officer and said, "Okay officer, what we have so far?"

"Cap' we received a call - shots fired officer down and responded, apparently, along with every other car in the precinct. The radio transmission stated that the shooter was in a white suburban. We were the first Yonkers unit on the scene. When we arrived on the scene we found this gentleman, already on the scene; he's with the F.B.I. He said he happened to be in the area. He had been monitoring our radio frequency. He had also heard the call and responded. He arrived only moments before us. He says he saw that guy (the officer pointed to the wounded man on the ground) exiting from that white suburban. The radio transmission said the shooter was in a white suburban. He says the guy had a gun in his hand. The agent says he identified himself as a police officer and ordered the guy to drop the gun. The guy did not drop the gun and the agent fired." The captain just nodded.

After a few moments the captain asked, "What about the officer down? Do we have an officer down?"

"No sir. We have no indications of any officer down. However, we have witnesses who state they heard three shots. Our friend from the F.B.I. says he only fired once and as far as we can tell, our friend on the ground over there never fired at all. We have the radio room calling each of our units, one by one, to determine if we have any MIA's but so far all are accounted for."

Captain Dent approached the F.B.I. agent who immediately introduced himself. Holding out his hand he said, "Permit me to introduce myself, I'm Special Agent Allen Chapson."

Angry Seas

Captain Dent was anxious to question Special Agent Chapson, but a sergeant at the scene interrupted him. The sergeant said to the captain, "Sir, we have a traffic unit that is not answering his radio. Communications has been calling car 807 over the radio and they are getting no reply! Both he and his vehicle are MIA!"

The captain ordered all cars, not needed at the scene to begin a search of the area for the missing patrol car. If they could find the car, they might find the officer. Quickly, the captain was amassing as much information as his brain could process. Indeed, it seemed that an officer had been shot and his radio car along with his body had been removed from the scene. The hotel clerk had come forward. He said that he had heard two shots coming from the area of the street. Shortly thereafter, he saw one of the guests at the hotel running from his room, toward the street. It was that guest who had told him to call the police. He identified the man lying in the roadway as the hotel guest. He said the guest was registered as Adam Mickiewicz.

The captain learned that some of his officers had already entered Mickiewicz's room. On the floor, they found a cell phone. It was the phone that had been used to make the first call. They also found another gun in the room, a Walther PPK/s .380. The captain already knew that the clerk's call was the second call made about an officer down. The man lying in the road was in the hotel when the first two shots were heard from the street. Furthermore, neither of his guns had been fired and it appeared that it was he who called in the crime. It seemed unlikely that he was the shooter.

Captain Dent knew the substance of the first call: "10 - 13 .. Shots fired .. Officer down ... 167 Buena Vista Avenue ... officer down! Send a bus! ... Shooter in a white suburban!" ---

The captain knew that it was N.Y.P.D. jargon. 10-13 was the N.Y.P.D. radio call for officer needs assistance, Yonkers cops used a different code, and New York City cops often say "send a bus" when they want an ambulance. Could it be that the man lying shot in the roadway was an N.Y.P.D. cop?

New information came in. The suburban was a stolen car. Yonkers cops traced owner through the license plate, to a doctor from the Riverdale section of Yonkers. They had already contacted the doctor's emergency answering service. They quickly learned that the doctor was on vacation in Mexico. Using the doctor's emergency answering service, they were able to contact him at his hotel. The doctor told them that he left the suburban in his garage at his home when he left for vacation. As far as he knew, it was still there. He said if it was on Buena Vista Avenue and not in his garage, then someone must have stolen it.

Suddenly the captain saw that Chapson seemed to be alarmed about something.

Chapson began to shout, "Hey! What are they doing? They're disturbing the crime scene! They are moving the body!"

All eyes turned to the body of the man lying in the roadway and they saw that the paramedics were placing the body on a stretcher. The captain, Agent Chapson and a few other officers went over to the paramedics. Chapson spoke out, "Don't move that body."

The paramedic replied, "We have to get him to the hospital."

Both Chapson and the captain said, "What!!" Chapson went on, "You don't take a dead person to the hospital. You leave the body in place. You take the living to the hospital and he can't be alive. He's been hit in the dead center of the chest with a .40 caliper S and W round. Look at the position of the wound! It's dead center of his chest. Nobody survives a hit like that."

The paramedics responded, "Well, he is alive. He's got a strong heartbeat and pulse and all things being considered he's got a good BP. If we get him to a hospital, he's likely to survive." The paramedics placed Buddy in the ambulance. Captain Dent told one of his officers at the scene to go with the ambulance and guard the injured man. The cop got in the ambulance with Buddy. The ambulance made its way through the maze of police cars in the roadway and took off for the nearest trauma center.

Shortly thereafter, a Yonkers P.D. detective approached the captain and pulled him aside to brief him on information from the New York State E-justice database. He had run a name check on the name Adam Mickiewicz. The captain learned that Adam Mickiewicz had a criminal record for felony assaults, he was wanted on an outstanding warrant for bail jumping out of Boston and he was a person of interest in a New York City homicide. There was also federal fugitive from justice warrant. There were active BOLO's (Be On Look Out) recently issued against that name and a notation that the suspect might be at the Royal Hotel in Yonkers had been included in the BOLO. He also learned that there was a long list of agencies and persons to be notified in the event that Adam Mickiewicz was located. One of the agencies to be so notified was the F.B.I. and a certain Agent Chapson. The captain went over to the officer who had briefed him on the events when he first arrived at the scene. He asked the officer, "Did that F.B.I. agent tell you he just happened to be in the area?"

The officer replied, "Yes sir. He said he just happened to be in the area."

The captain would have to call the deputy chief at home and apprise him of the situation. He made the call, gave a quick summary to the deputy chief. Next, he wanted to turn his attention to Special Agent Chapson, but first there was a missing officer to be found.

A Vehicle for Land Only

Over the years, Sorge had developed all sorts of plans for stealing police cars. In his business, he always knew that driving a marked police car had many advantages.

A police uniform could be obtained fairly easily. A badge could be gotten. Looking like a cop could get you past checkpoints. It put you above suspicion. Having a police car to go with it was a home run. It meant you would not be stopped for routine traffic stops. The lights and siren were very useful. There was that, ever valuable, police radio where one could listen to what the authorities were doing. Yes, having a police car could be of tremendous value.

Sorge routinely maintained lists of business establishments that had contracts with municipalities for repairing radio cars. There were body shops, transmission shops, front-end alignment stations and even new car dealers on his lists. These locations would often leave the radio cars parked in outdoor, unguarded, parking lots while they were in for service. Sometimes they would be left outdoors overnight. Even better, sometimes they would be left outdoors over the weekend.

Sorge had a key making machine and a book that gave the key codes for every make of automobile based on the ID number that was clearly displayed on vehicle's dashboard. He made keys to steal cars all the time. Sorge could take a police car from a repair shop on a Friday and return it before Monday morning and no one would be the wiser.

He had used police cars before to make getaways. Many years ago, when he shot a researcher in Groton, he used a police car to make his getaway then, but that was different. Then he had a plan. This theft was impromptu. He initially had no plan to take this police car. None of his previous plans included the killing of a cop. This unplanned theft was going very bad.

What Sorge set out to do was simply to kill Adam Mickiewicz. He and his cohorts thought they had already killed Adam Mickiewicz. They were sure that they had killed a man who used the Adam Mickiewicz name. However, they now received a notification that another Adam Mickiewicz had used his credit card to book a hotel room. If there was a person who used the name Adam Mickiewicz, he had to be killed too. They were taking no chances that Adam Mickiewicz, the American friend of Stan Adamski could be left alive.

Sorge had checked out the residents of the Royal earlier in the day. He had spoken to someone in the Royal Hotel staff. He identified himself as a social worker looking to place clients in a rehab. He asked a lot of questions about facilities at the hotel, but mostly he asked about current residents. He learned that the facility catered to inner city young adults of all races and creeds. The clients were all in their twenties. Although there were some older adults who occasionally stayed there, currently there was only one person who was not in his twenties in residence. That one person was older and currently he was only one white male staying at the place. That was Adam Mickiewicz. Sorge would know for sure which resident was Mickiewicz when the residents stepped out in the morning.

Sorge was set up in his suburban waiting for that one and only white male, Adam Mickiewicz to come out. When Mickiewicz came out in the morning Sorge would shoot him from within the suburban. If he did not get a clean shot, he would start the suburban gun the engine and run Mickiewicz down. Simple.

He hoped Mickiewicz would cross the street as he came out, but if he did not, Sorge would drive up on the sidewalk if it were necessary. He was going to kill Mickiewicz. He'd shoot him down or run him down. Maybe he'd do both. In any event, he would make sure he was dead. He was going to kill him.

Sorge had parked close to the corner so no one could park in front of his suburban. He did not want to run the risk that another car could park close to him and hem his vehicle in. Being parked close to the corner ensured him that he could pull right out, fast. All was going well until the cop showed up.

The cop had pulled his radio car in behind Sorge and turned on his overhead lights. Sorge knew that the cop could not have known the car was stolen. The owner was away and would not yet have reported the theft. He was quite comfortable getting out to talk to the officer.

Sorge had fake ID that showed him to be a private detective. He got out, walked to meet the approaching officer. He told the cop he was a private eye doing a matrimonial infidelity case and that he was watching out for a cheating wife. The cop believed him. The cop said the only problem was that his suburban was parked too close to the corner. The officer explained to Sorge that he was on his way to provide a police escort for a large crane that was to be delivered to a construction site near-by. The officer explained that large cranes are moved on the midnight shift when there is little traffic on the streets. His job was to check the planned route to make sure there were no cars parked too close to corners at intersections before doing the escort. Large equipment cannot maneuver their turns through the narrow streets if other vehicles are parked too close to corners. There was a sign 'No Parking Here to Corner - Tow Away Zone'. The suburban's front end was parked in the tow-away zone. The suburban had to be backed up or it would be towed away. Sorge agreed to move the suburban and the cop agreed not to issue a summons if the car was moved back a little.

The cop returned to his car to drive away. As Sorge watched the cop return to his radio car Sorge noticed something that was very disturbing to him. The radio car had a dashboard camera!

Sorge approached the cop seated in his car and said, "Officer, before you go perhaps you could tell me a little something about that dashboard camera. In my business, I often have to take pictures from within my car. I've given some thought to getting a dashboard camera myself. Does that camera take good video at night? Is it on all the time or only if you have to turn it on?"

The cop replied, "It works very well at night. I don't specifically have to turn it on. I can turn it on manually if I want to, but it also comes on automatically when I activate the overhead lights."

Sorge replied, "So our little encounter here has been video recorded?"

The officer said, "Yes it has been." Those were the officer's last words.

Sorge had to get that camera equipment. By tomorrow, Mickiewicz would be dead. The police would focus an investigation in the area. Any surveillance tapes taken in the area would be reviewed. He was on tape. He had been photographed in the area. He had been photographed with the suburban. He felt he had to get that tape and to get the tape he had to take the radio car. To get the car he had to shoot the officer. He shot the officer twice in the head with a two-shot .22-magnum derringer; he had hidden in the palm of his hand. The gun manufactured by High Standard is very small, but the .22 magnum round travels very fast and hits very hard. Unlike the regular .22 caliber round the magnum round makes a lot of noise when it goes off and at close range, it makes a hole like a .38.

Sorge ran around to the passenger side of the car and pulled the stricken officer's body over into the passenger's seat. Then he went back around to the driver's side, got in and drove off. That's when he realized that things were going to go very bad.

There was blood everywhere. It was all over the seats and it was dripping from the headliner. There was blood on the windshield, on the steering wheel and now it was all over Sorge. His clothes were soaked in it. Now Sorge was a prisoner in the car. If he got out on a street corner, he would run the risk of being seen. Even in this bad part of town, a blood-covered man running through the streets would evoke a call to the police. Once in the past he escaped from a crime scene by simply getting on an inner city transit bus. It was his favorite means of escape. The police never look at bus passengers when looking for suspects. A blood-covered man could not just get on a bus without drawing attention.

He could hear over the police radio Yonkers police dispatchers sending all cars to the scene of the shooting. Someone had already called the cops! If those cops driving to the scene saw that his radio car was seen driving away from the scene it would be suspicious. This was perhaps the only radio car on the planet that would be stopped by the police this night. Then there was the problem of the camera. The recording module was securely locked. Apparently, the tape cannot be removed from the recorder without a key. He expected to find the key on the cop's body, but the officer did not have the key on his person. Sorge realized that most likely, only police supervisors would have the keys that would provide access to the tape. Sorge was in a state of panic. He was sweating profusely. Now covered in blood and perspiration, Sorge was losing all rational thinking. All he knew was that he needed tools to break into the recorder. He needed a place to work on the car where he would be out of sight. He needed a place to clean up and he needed a change of clothes.

Sorge suddenly realized where he could get what he needed. The home where he had gotten the suburban was vacant. The homeowner was away. The garage was unlocked. He left it unlocked when he removed the suburban. There was a toolbox in the garage. If he could get back to that garage unseen, he could put the radio car in the garage. As he recalled, the garage had no windows. If he closed the garage door behind him, he'd be out of sight. He could use the tools there to break into the recorder. Once he had the tape, he could break into the house. There he could wash up and steal some fresh clothes. With clean clothes, he could walk away a few blocks and get on a bus and be gone. It would be dangerous to go back there, but desperate times call for desperate measures.

Searching the Seas

Captain Dent began to coordinate the activities of personnel on the scene. First, he grabbed a detective and told him to get a search warrant for the doctor's garage where the suburban had been parked prior to its theft. "Wake up a judge if you have to, but get me a warrant for that garage. While you're at it, get a warrant for the house as well. The lock on the suburban was not compromised. The thief must have had a key. Perhaps, he broke into the house to find a key. Take a crime scene investigation team with you. Check the house for entry. Get anything that looks like it could be evidence from the house as well as from the garage."

Next, he arranged for a grid search of the area for evidence at the scene. He called for a lieutenant to coordinate an area search for the radio car and the missing officer and then he turned his attention to Special Agent Alan Chapson.

The captain asked Chapson, "So as I understand it you just happened to be in the area?"

By this time, Chapson knew that his story that he had just happened to be in the area was not going to fly. He said, "Look, captain I'm not going to bullshit you. I happened to be in the area because I was checking out the hotel. I had received a hit on a BOLO that I put out on an Adam Mickiewicz. He's wanted on a federal fugitive from justice warrant. I was going to do a drive-by to see the place. I planned to come back with a team and take him in the morning. I was scanning your radio frequencies when I heard the shots fired call. The rest is history. When I arrived, Mickiewicz was in the process of stepping out of the suburban. He had a gun. I told him to drop it and he refused. That's basically it."

While the captain was talking to Chapson, another detective approached. He said, " Hey Capt.', we have another agency here. There are a couple of N.Y.P.D. officers here." The captain went with the detective to meet the N.Y.P.D. investigators.

Detective Taylor and Tom Bradner introduced themselves. They advised the captain that they too had a BOLO on Mickiewicz. They explained their perspective on the case.

The captain's interest increased when the N.Y.P.D. officers mentioned that they thought there might be a spy component to the case. He said, "I have an F.B.I. agent here who said he was looking at Adam Mickiewicz on a fugitive warrant."

Taylor smiled, "That's a very old warrant. It was originally issued about twenty years ago. In addition, I put this investigation into the DEX system. You can check. Why didn't I get any hit that the F.B.I. was on him? If there was an F.B.I. DEX on the guy I would have known to coordinate my investigation with them."

Captain Dent was familiar with the DEX. It is a slang term use by cops to describe a national computer database where police officers from multiple jurisdictions can enter the names of persons or locations that they are investigating. It is particularly useful when an agency is conducting undercover operations outside their own jurisdiction. It can help to prevent undercover cops from being improperly identified as criminals by a separate agency investigating the same group of people. It works to prevent cop on cop shootings. If another agency is actively conducting an investigation of the same person or location, the system notifies the agencies to contact each other so the investigations can be coordinated. If this was a bigger investigation, the captain wondered why the F.B.I. hadn't DEX'ed it.

As Taylor was continuing to advise Captain Dent about his findings, the captain became more assured that the F.B.I. agent wasn't telling all he knew. A few more hours passed at the scene.

Once the captain was comfortable that everything that should be done was being done at the scene, he asked all the principal persons to meet at Yonkers Headquarters. When they arrived the building was surrounded by the press. The press corps badgered the cops for information. The captain offered a brief, verbal overview of the incident. During the overview, the press was told that a police officer was missing and was presumed to have been shot. They were also told that a person identified as Adam Mickiewicz had also been shot at the scene, but at the present time he was not considered to be a suspect in the officer's disappearance. The press was advised that Adam Mickiewicz had been taken into custody on an unrelated matter. When the press asked if Mickiewicz was expected to survive, Chapson interrupted and answered, no.

The captain resumed his overview and said, "The man suffered what appears to be a life-threatening wound. However, paramedics at the scene indicated that they believed he will survive." With that said, the captain ended the session and entered the building.

As they entered the captain said to Chapson, "You better hope you're wrong about that guy dying. You better hope he lives. I think we might have a 'cop on cop' shooting here. If we do and he dies you're in some deep shit!"

Chapson responded, "I identified myself and ordered him to drop the gun. He never identified himself as a cop."

The captain said, "I believe you, but the shit is still very deep."

Police officials from just about every agency interested in Adam Mickiewicz showed up.

The meeting at Yonkers headquarters was contentious. The primary focus of the Yonkers officers was the ongoing investigation of their missing and presumed dead officer. N.Y.P.D. was more interested in their homicide case. There was also the shooting of Mickiewicz that had to be investigated to determine if the shooting was justified. The other agencies were only interested in the bail jumping and assault issues.

As soon as N.Y.P.D. higher officials realized the importance of the Yonkers interest in the Adam

Mickiewicz matter, they offered their full cooperation. They suggested that their officers could be assigned to work side by side with Yonkers detectives until the missing officer matter was resolved. They seemed quite willing to forgo questioning Mickiewicz until the Yonkers matter was resolved.

Chapson had, by that time, advised his command of the situation. Joe Duffy had to be roused out of bed, but he showed up at the meeting, as did Frank Dwarman.

Without any of the usual courtesies, Duffy entered the conference room and made an announcement. "Gentlemen, by the authority of Presidential Decision Directives 39 and 62, we are declaring this matter to be a matter involving terrorism against the United States of America. We are assuming command and control of the entire Mickiewicz matter. Henceforth, all actions taken in relation to Adam Mickiewicz shall be subject to the discretion of the F.B.I. I have already directed our security contractor for this region to assume custody of, and to provide security for, Mr. Adam Mickiewicz while he is detained at the hospital. Any Yonkers Police officers or N.Y.P.D. officers that may be securing him at the hospital are to be relieved.

As soon as he is medically fit to be moved, he will be moved to a secure federal detention center. Until such time as we shall see fit, no one is to question, or even speak to Mr. Mickiewicz without first receiving written permission from this agency.

Now, gentlemen I will be taking my agent and we will be leaving here to proceed to our Manhattan Headquarters. If you have any further need for our full cooperation, I can assure that you will receive it. You merely need to contact us there."

Duffy motioned to Chapson to follow him and they walked from the room. As they neared the door the captain yelled, "Mickiewicz is a material witness in a cop shooting!"

Duffy replied, "Mickiewicz is a terrorist!" Then he and Chapson left the building.

The others in the room were shocked and for a few moments, they just sat quietly trying to digest what had just occurred. Then a Yonkers detective entered the room. He approached the captain and said, "I'm afraid I have bad news."

The captain held his breath and nodded. The detective continued. "Our team secured a search warrant for the garage and house as you directed. They went down to Riverdale to execute the warrant, but we were unable to search the garage. It's a large house on a large lot with a detached garage. When they arrived at the house, the garage was on fire. It is a fully involved inferno as we speak. The fire department was already on the scene when our people arrived. They tell us there is a Yonkers Police Radio Car in the burning garage and it looks like there is a body in the car."

An Angry Shipmate

Michelle woke up at her Stuyvesant Town apartment in lower Manhattan. She took her usual morning shower. She stepped out of the shower, wrapped herself in a white terrycloth robe, and wrapped a white terrycloth towel around her long wet hair. She walked to the kitchen and poured herself a cup of coffee. Then she walked to her door. She opened the door and picked up her morning paper, closed the door and walked to her kitchen. She calmly sat at her kitchen table, drinking her morning coffee. She opened the paper and began to sift through the various articles. She came upon an article about a shooting and police officer missing in action in Yonkers. The early edition went to press before the news of the fire and discovery of the officer's body was known. It did not yet have the grim details of the officer's demise. Halfway through the article she exploded.

Aloud she screamed, "Chapson! That son-of-a-bitch! He got a lead on Adam Mickiewicz and went after him without me!"

This was supposed to be her case. Chapson was just to be an assistant. Now he had gotten a lead and followed it to Yonkers. He went there without her and he shot Mickiewicz! She was supposed to find Adam Mickiewicz and question him. The paper quoted Chapson as saying that he did not believe that Adam Mickiewicz would survive. If she could get her hands on Chapson's throat, right now she was sure that *he* would not survive.

She left her hot cup of coffee on the table. She was dressed, out the door and on her way to F.B.I. headquarters before the coffee in her cup was cold.

Arriving at her office she was surprised to find Joe Duffy and Chapson there waiting for her. As she approached, they could see she was furious. Duffy spoke first, "Michelle, I'm glad you came right in. We need to discuss the events of this morning."

Michelle shot back, "We sure do! What the hell is going on here? I thought I was the lead investigator on this! The Lone Ranger over there goes out, without me, and kills my best hope for a crack in the case! I was supposed to find him and question him, remember? We were going to try to get insight into a spy ring, remember? I'm sure I'll have lots of luck questioning a dead guy!"

Duffy replied, "Please calm down. He is not dead and from what I understand it is unlikely that he will die. His wounds are actually superficial."

Again, Michelle shot back, "That's not what Matt Dillon over there told the press. Oh, and by the way, tell me what business did he have talking to the press on my case and why was he up in Yonkers shooting my suspect?"

Chapson looked terrible. He had not gotten any sleep. He had been up all night with the Yonkers detectives and went directly to Federal Plaza when he finished up with them. He was still wearing the same clothes he had on the day before. His tie had been loosened from around his neck and his shirt looked like he had slept in it.

He spoke in contrite tones. "Last evening when we quit for the day, I was headed home. My home is near the New Haven office. I decided to stop in at the New Haven Office to wrap up a few reports on pending matters that I had been working on before I was assigned here. I ended up working late into the night. As I was preparing to go home, for the second time that evening, I decided to take a quick look at my inbox. There was a message. Late last evening our flag on the Mickiewicz credit card produced a hit. I'll bet if you look at your inbox, you'll find that the same message came in to your computer while you were off duty last night. If I had not gone to the New Haven office last night, we both would have found our messages this morning and we would have gone to Yonkers together, I swear.

It was simply a matter of chance that I got my message before you got yours. I could see in the heading that at least a dozen other agencies were also notified about the hit. I was afraid that one of the other agencies would get to him before we did.

It was after midnight. I knew you be away from the office and I did not want to disturb you at home. I decided to take a drive just to take a quick look at the location. While I was there, this call came over the Yonkers frequency that a police officer was shot in front of the very hotel where the credit card hit came from. What was I supposed to do?"

Michelle responded, "I'm not buying any of that crap. How dare you indicate that I should not be disturbed? Am I some kind of delicate child? Do I need my beauty sleep? I'm a F.B.I. agent who has been assigned to what might be the most important spy case since the Rosenberg's and you did not want to disturb me? Fuck you! You were grandstanding! If we were acting like partners you would have call me at home and woken me up! You wanted to grab the collar for yourself, you scumbag!"

Joe Duffy tried to calm Michelle down. Under ordinary circumstances, her use of foul language would not be acceptable in the workplace, especially in front of her superiors. Under other circumstances, she would be getting a stern reprimand, but Duffy knew he was in serious trouble himself. If there was any hope of surviving his next meeting with Director Madison, he needed to calm Michelle down. He needed her on his side.

The director had told him to make Thompson his lead investigator on this. Duffy brought Chapson in without an approval from the director. Now Chapson had screwed things up royally. He would be facing difficult questions.

Why did Duffy bring Chapson in without consulting with the director? Why was Chapson acting like a lead investigator after the director told him to let Michelle run with this ball? How could this happen? This was supposed to be a quiet clandestine investigation. It had been going well. No one knew the Sorge investigation was continuing with a new lead. The Adamski murder had not even made the papers. He was just another nameless person killed in a Bronx hotel. He was just one of New York's millions of unknowns. There was no fanfare about his death. There were no sexy front-page stories. The F.B.I. could quietly investigate.

Now everyone in New York knew about the murder in the Bronx. Now everyone knew the Mickiewicz name. Suddenly, the Bronx Hotel murder was front-page stuff. Now a Yonkers cop was dead. The cop shooting was front-page stuff. Now an F.B.I. agent shot someone at the scene of the police officer disappearance. Now the F.B.I. involvement in the case was front-page stuff. Everybody would know of the F.B.I. interest in the case prior to the shooting of Adam Mickiewicz. Surely, Sorge and everyone else in his circle of spies would know that they were under scrutiny. Now, they would be going deeper underground. There was no way this could proceed as a clandestine investigation. The director was going to be pissed and he was going to be pissed at Duffy. No doubt, there would be another high-level meeting with the director and the others who had been at the previous meeting. No doubt, Michelle would be invited again. There was no way Duffy could keep her out of such a meeting. If Michelle Thompson got her ass in an uproar at the next meeting, Duffy would be finished as the head of the New York Office. If this got any worse, he might be finished as an F.B.I. agent.

Whenever an F.B.I. agent talks about a fellow agent who might be in trouble on the job they like to say, "He's going to get transferred to Butte Montana"; as if to suggest that Butte Montana is the worst possible assignment one could get. Joe did not want to end his career in Butte. Michelle was not going to be reprimanded. Michelle Thompson was going to get whatever she needed, whatever she wanted to make her happy.

Michelle was still seething when she asked, "Did you say he is going to survive?"

Before Duffy could respond, Chapson jumped at the chance to say something that he thought would please Michelle. "At first glance it looked like a fatal shot. He was hit in the dead center of his upper chest. I was sure he was dead at the scene. I did not believe he would survive. Then we got reports back from the crime scene crew that was at the scene of the shooting. We also got a report from the medical crew at the hospital.

It turns out that my round did not hit him directly. When I fired, he was standing in the space between the vehicles doorjamb and the partially open door. My shot apparently hit the steel frame around the driver's side door window. It seems that portion of the doorframe is thick double folded steel. There is the outer steel frame, the steel window track and the inner steel frame. The bullet went through each of those components before it hit him. There was very little kinetic energy left in the round by the time it hit him. The bullet would have already mushroomed out as it exited the frame. A mushroomed bullet with little residual kinetic energy has very little penetration capability. It hit him square in the sternum. That's a heavy bone. The enlarged round blew away a sizable chunk of flesh; lots of bleeding, but it did not penetrate the sternum. Beyond that, there was little internal damage.

It may have caused a slight non-displaced fracture of the sternum, but the bullet was stopped right there. It never entered the chest cavity. No internal organs were hit. He suffered hydrostatic shock from the impact. It may even have stopped his heart for a while, but he is not going to die. We will have an opportunity to question him."

Duffy answered, "Yes it is likely that we will get to question him soon. He is not presently conscious, but he is in our custody in a hospital. The security firm that holds a contract with us for guarding prisoners at public facilities is guarding him. They have strict instructions not to allow anyone to see or question the prisoner until you personally question him. No one gets to him before you and no one gets to him after you speak to him without first having your approval."

Michelle was relieved and to some extent, her ire began to subside, but she was not in any mood to forgive Chapson any time soon.

Who's at the Helm?

Captain Dent was distressed by the heavy-handed tactics of the F.B.I., but not overly distressed by them. He was well schooled in Presidential Decision Directives 39 and 62. Few local police officers were aware of PDDs 39 and 62 until after 9/11. In the wave of anti-terrorism training that followed 9/11, everyone learned that there was a written directive from the Office of the President of the United States that declared that the F.B.I. would automatically become the lead agency in any investigation involving terrorism. Besides, he was more interested in finding the person who was responsible for the death of one of his officers. His focus on that kept him from having time to brood over the F.B.I. superseding him on the Mickiewicz matter.

He was already convinced that Mickiewicz was not responsible for the officer's death. He believed that Mickiewicz truly was trying to help the fallen officer and that he got shot for his efforts. In the back of his mind, he could not shake the idea that Mickiewicz could be an undercover cop. Maybe an N.Y.P.D. undercover, but he knew that N.Y.P.D. detectives get in serious trouble if they fail to DEX their cases. Taylor and Bradner DEX'ed the Royal Hotel, but there were no other DEX filings for the location. Perhaps Mickiewicz was a C.I.A. agent. The captain wondered, "Do C.I.A. agents DEX their cases?" He doubted that they did. Taylor had suggested that the case might involve spies and Duffy had declared it to be a terrorism matter. The C.I.A might well be involved.

The next day Taylor and Tom Bradner brainstormed with the Yonkers Police. They compared notes and shared data regarding their separate, yet linked cases. Taylor and Bradner advised Captain Dent that there was never any N.Y.P.D officer named Adam Mickiewicz. They had entered the name Mickiewicz in every database available to them. If an Adam Mickiewicz were ever on the job, they would have gotten a hit. They did not. Moreover, the fingerprint hit they got from the glass in the room would have made a hit in the police officer registry, a statewide database that contains all the vital information on police officers in New York State. It includes copies of their fingerprints. Adam Mickiewicz's prints were not in the registry. Adam Mickiewicz was not now, nor was he ever, a police officer.

Yet, the .380 found in Adam Mickiewicz's room was last registered, in the police officer registry, as a weapon that had been legally owned by an N.Y.P.D. police officer named Robert Kern.

Oddly enough, Police Officer Robert Kern was also an MIA! It seemed that this Officer Kern had been placed on military leave for duty with the National Guard nearly twenty years ago. At first, he was placed on paid military leave from the department. However, the time allotted for his paid military leave ran out. When his paid leave ran out the department placed him on unpaid leave. Having his personnel files moved to the unpaid leave file cabinet was akin to placing them in a black hole. No one ever checked up on the officers on unpaid leave unless they applied for reinstatement. The N.Y.P.D. had no idea where Police Officer Robert Kern was.

The .45 caliper, automatic pistol found on the ground next to Adam proved to have a most interesting pedigree. Kimber Arms manufactured the weapon. The factory was located in Yonkers and the captain received full cooperation from the management there. The weapon was never registered in the United States. The management at the plant, where the gun was made, told the police that the gun was part of a run of three identical, specially designed, weapons of the highest quality. They were what were called presentation pieces. They were engraved with eagles, American flags and other patriotic symbols and they were inlayed with gold leaf engravings. They were astonishing beautiful guns to look at. The .45 found at the scene was part of a collection of guns that would be awarded to persons as tokens of appreciation for valiant service to The United States of America. The guns were ordered through a congressional appropriation and paid for with a federal government check. This was one of three guns that were specially manufactured, to be presented by Congress to American heroes. Beyond that, the manufacturers could provide no further information.

The captain learned that his detectives had

gone to the hospital to check on the condition of Mickiewicz before the F.B.I. had cut off contact with him. When they were there, Mickiewicz was still unconscious, but they learned that Mickiewicz's condition was not too serious. More importantly, before they left the hospital they fingerprinted the unconscious Mickiewicz. The F.B.I. had not yet done so.

The captain did not yet know much about his investigation yet, but he knew something that the F.B.I. did not yet know. Whoever the man in the hospital might be, one thing was for sure...

The man in the hospital was not Adam Mickiewicz.

The Captain

Captain Dent got copies of the fingerprint cards prepared at the hospital. He could have run the prints through AFIS, the Automated Fingerprint Identification System, and a computerized fingerprint analysis computer. It would have analyzed the prints in moments and the system would have identified, by name, anyone whose prints were among the millions of prints on file. However, the system is run by the feds. Most likely, they would have flagged Mickiewicz's file. If anyone accessed the file, if anyone submitted prints that matched Mickiewicz, The F.B.I. would be notified.

Right now, the captain did not want the F.B.I. to know that he had the fingerprints of the man in the hospital. At least he did not want them to know yet.

The captain had the Boston Police fax him a copy of the Mickiewicz fingerprint card that had been taken on the day of his assault arrest. Then he had one of his fingerprint experts visually compare that card to the fingerprint card prepared at the hospital. The results were conclusive. The captain did not know for sure who the man in the hospital was, but one thing he did know for sure. Whoever the man in the hospital was, he was not Adam Mickiewicz.

At least he was not the Mickiewicz wanted in the fugitive warrant. He was not the Mickiewicz who was arrested for assault all those years ago. He was not the Mickiewicz whose fingerprints were found in the Bronx hotel. He was not the Mickiewicz that

246

Chapson and the F.B.I. thought he was.

The captain made sure that Taylor and Bradner knew of his findings and he invited them back to Yonkers Headquarters to compare notes.

By the time, Bradner and Taylor returned to Yonkers Police Headquarters a number of interesting developments came to light.

The captain was sure he'd get his cop killer. Evidence at the Riverdale crime scene disclosed the killer had entered the house after parking the police car in the garage. Footprints in blood were found leading from the garage to the house. The CSI team found a jimmied window where the intruder had entered the house. Tools matching those in the tool set in the burned out garage had been used to open the window. The bloody footsteps continued inside the house and led to an upstairs bathroom.

Inside the bathroom, the officers found that their suspect had taken a shower. In the shower, they found trace evidence of blood. Later tests would show that the blood was that of the slain officer. In the shower, they found pubic hairs that they believed would yield DNA evidence that might identify the killer. However, it was equally possible that the pubic hairs might have belonged to the homeowner. The CSI officers rightly concluded that the killer must have stolen clean clothing from the home.

However, it was in the burned out garage that they found the most remarkable evidence. Apparently, the murderer first parked the radio car in the garage. Then using the available tools from the garage toolbox, he broke into the video recorder. He removed the tape then using other tools from the garage broke into the house. After showering and getting clean clothes, he returned to the garage with his bloody clothes tied up in the towel that he used to dry himself. He then doused the radio car and the garage with gasoline from a gas can that was kept with the lawnmower that was stored in the garage. He threw the ball of clothing on top of the car. Then he started the fire and fled.

The car and most of the items in the garage were severely damaged by the fire. The wood frame garage collapsed in the fire and it was necessary for the CSI team to rummage through the debris, to look for further evidence. Their diligent searching paid off.

The murderer had placed every piece of evidence that he wanted destroyed in the garage before starting the fire, including his bloody clothes. What the killer failed to realize was that items packed tightly together do not burn so well.

The towel, and some of the clothing wrapped inside the towel, was slightly charred around the edges, but the densely packed clothing that had been wrapped in what was apparently a wet towel, did not burn completely. At the very center of the knotted ball was a pair of men's underpants. A smattering of blood could be seen on the exterior of the underwear. The CSI team rightly concluded that it would prove to be the officer's blood that was on the outside of the underpants. Their years of experience in evidence collection told them that there was a very good chance that the killer's DNA would be found inside. They were right!

Blood on the outside and DNA on the inside irrevocably linked the killer to his victim.

Captain Dent was quite pleased to share that information with Taylor and Bradner. Taylor and Bradner had developed some additional information from their crime scene that they shared with the captain.

They had obtained DNA evidence from the Bronx Hotel crime scene. The N.Y.P.D. lab was able to develop a DNA signature from the lip prints found on the plastic glass. A DNA signature is a series of coded initials that can be derived from a DNA sample. The code can then be loaded into a computer that can analyze the code and match it to other DNA signatures. This DNA sample matched that of a murder suspect in another unsolved case. Taylor had submitted the DNA from the plastic glass to the CODIS system. CODIS is The Combined DNA Index System, a federally operated data bank for DNA signatures. It contains the DNA signature codes of known criminals who are required to provide samples upon conviction. It also contains DNA signatures from unknown persons whose DNA has been found at crime scenes. It includes DNA from active cases and cold cases and links the DNA to case files. The computer system constantly monitors the submissions from all police agencies and notifies the respective departments when matches are found.

While the system is maintained by the F.B.I., the data is available to all law enforcement agencies.

CODIS produced a match to DNA sample found in the lip prints on the plastic glass. Taylor described the nature of the hit to Captain Dent. Taylor said, "We sent a sample of the DNA from our crime scene to CODIS, we got a match to an unknown person who is wanted in connection with an unsolved cold case out of Groton Connecticut. It seems that the Groton PD had an old homicide where a large hair sample was found. They did a cold case follow-up recently and submitted the hair for DNA analysis and their findings were loaded in CODIS. I already spoke to their detectives. The hair sample was recovered from the grip of a victim at the crime scene of a murder that occurred several years ago. They believe the hair was pulled from the attacker's head during a struggle that preceded the shooting of the victim. The victim was a naval engineer, who worked at the submarine base there. He was murdered in his home and his computer was stolen. You get DNA at a murder scene and run it and it comes back to a match at another murder scene that's too much to be a coincidence. I'd say whoever left the DNA was responsible for both murders."

Tom Bradner then offered the following, "I had been assigned to review the paperwork on recent emigrants from Poland, to try to determine the identity of our hotel murder victim. We do not have a positive match, but oddly enough one of our recent arrivals at JFK is a Polish naval engineer who has gone missing. We now have two crime scenes that are linked by DNA evidence and in both cases the victim was a naval engineer. Now that really is too much to be a coincidence. I speculated that my victim in the Bronx is a Polish national named Stanislaus Adamski. I made my suggestion that the victim was Adamski in my official report. We gave out that information to the press a few days ago in the hope that someone would come forward to ID our victim. The press was not interested in the story then, but sooner or later they'll make the connection and Adamski's name will be all over the front pages."

Taylor said, "At the hotel crime scene we have fingerprints that match Adam Mickiewicz and DNA of an unknown person. There is no DNA sample of Adam Mickiewicz on file. We have fingerprints from Adam Mickiewicz, but based on fingerprints we know the man in the hospital is not Mickiewicz. We have nothing that links the DNA to any known person. If the DNA from the hotel is the same as the DNA of the man in the hospital, that would put both him and Adam Mickiewicz at the hotel crime scene. If it's not the same, then we have nothing to link the man in the hospital to the hotel crime scene. Then we need to resume our search for the real Adam Mickiewicz. If we get him we can take a DNA sample from him. If the real Mickiewicz is a match to the DNA at the hotel, then he'd also be a match to the DNA from Groton. We will have solved two murders, the one in Groton and the one in the hotel. If he is not a DNA match then both he and whoever left the DNA would both be suspects."

The Yonkers CSI team had the bloody clothing from the man who had been shot by Chapson. The captain agreed to have it submitted for DNA analysis also. If that was a match to what Taylor had, then the man in the hospital was likely responsible for both murders. Somehow, the captain did not believe that it would not be a match. The captain was sure that the DNA in the underwear found at the fire scene would be the match. He was sure that whoever murdered the two naval engineers had also murdered his officer.

The captain, Taylor, Bradner and a few members of the Yonkers investigation team were headed down to F.B.I. Headquarters for a meeting with the F.B.I. They agreed that they would withhold information until they could hear what the F.B.I. had to tell them. They also agreed that in the interest of solving the case they would ultimately share their information even if the F.B.I. were less forthcoming, but they were going to hear what the F.B.I. had first.

Admiral's Staff Meeting

Another high-level meeting was held at Joe Duffy's office. All the persons who had been at the previous meeting in Joe's office were summoned back for this second meeting on developments in the Adamski investigation. They were meeting at eight AM so that they might be better prepared for the next meeting that would take place at 10:30 a.m. Officers from the N.Y.P.D. and the Yonkers Police would be attending that later meeting and it was necessary that these federal investigators all be on the same page before the local police arrived.

The participants were advised that Adamski had apparently been killed only shortly after leaving F.B.I. headquarters. They were also advised that the N.Y.P.D. had developed a person of interest in the case and that the so-called, person of interest, was Adam Mickiewicz. They told the persons present that Mickiewicz had a dubious background at best. They were filled in on the outstanding charges pending against Mickiewicz. They were further advised that Mickiewicz had been located at a hotel in Yonkers, but before they were able to coordinate a response events unfolded in Yonkers that would lead to Mickiewicz being shot by Chapson.

Duffy was pleased to report that Mickiewicz was in federal custody in a hospital under guard by a private security firm that was under contract to secure federal prisoners until they could be moved to a secure federal facility. Duffy told those present that

Mickiewicz's injuries were not life threatening and he expected him to be moved to a more secure facility soon.

Director Madison took over the meeting. "I must say that we at bureau headquarters are very unhappy with the way this is going. Just a few days ago, we had a clandestine investigation that was not going very well, but we had one thing going for us; the investigation was clandestine. The Adamski murder did not even make the papers. A man gets killed in a Bronx hotel. It's not big news in New York City, but a cop gets killed, an F.B.I. agent shoots someone, that is news. The papers are all over this and everyone is talking to the press. Now much of the case is public record. The newspapers have the following facts: They know that a foreign national, who on the record looks like a homeless man, was murdered in the Bronx. They are sniffing around with the name Adamski. I'm sure that they confirm that a Stan Adamski is missing they will put the name in the papers. They know that someone named Adam Mickiewicz has something to do with that investigation. They know his fingerprints were found at the crime scene in the Bronx. They know the F.B.I. is in the case, which begs the question - Why is the F.B.I. investigating a simple murder in the Bronx? They know that Mickiewicz has been a fugitive from justice, at large for twenty years, and they know an F.B.I. agent shot him. They know that something about this matter is of a high enough profile that someone murdered a police officer over it and they

254

know that the 'someone' who killed the cop' was not Mickiewicz. They also know, notwithstanding the fact that Mickiewicz tried to save the cop, we took him into custody.

Presently, we do not seem to have any federal charges, beyond the fugitive from justice warrant, which dictates that we secure him for the Boston Police. Yet, we are holding him in federal custody on what has been reported to be some sort of terrorist plot. All of that forgoing information has been reported now in the newspapers. The press is demanding to know what sort of terrorist incident we foiled and what city was the target. In fact, we know nothing of any terror plot to speak of yet. That's already bad enough, but it is going to get worse.

The press will dig into Mickiewicz and they will find what we found, which is essentially nothing. They will find that he is a man of mystery. That will only raise the level of interest. The justification for the shooting seems to exonerate Chapson, but the jury is still out on that."

Chapson started to rise to his feet to protest, but Madison waved him off and said, "Calm down I'm sure that in the final analysis you will be exonerated, but for now it's still a hot ticket for the press. They're going to be kicking our asses over the fact that this person, whom we now say is a terrorist, has been allowed to remain at large for twenty years while we sat on a warrant for him. A-N-D ... they still do not yet know, that Adamski came here, to our offices, to report something only hours before he was

255

murdered. When that comes out, and it will come out, they will have a field day."

Duffy tried to respond, "Sir, Agent Chapson only went to Yonkers to verify that Mickiewicz was actually there when the officer shot call came in and ..."

Madison interrupted, "What was Chapson doing on this case? This was the Adamski matter. I told you to let that Thompson girl run this case and she was not there." Madison began to scold Michelle for not accompanying Chapson to Yonkers. Before she could reply Duffy interjected, "Sir, that was my fault Michelle, was not notified that Chapson was going to Yonkers, or that we got a hit on the credit card flag."

Madison asked, "Why not!" and Duffy responded, "It's a long story." Madison said, "I've got time, but you've only got until 10:30. I better know everything I need to know before the locals get here!"

Over the next two hours, Madison and everyone else in the room were briefed and they came to know the full status of the case. At least they knew all that was known to the F.B.I.

At that point, Michelle Thompson spoke up, "Gentlemen, we have continued to run this case as a clandestine operation for too long. While we were sitting on Adamski, the N.Y.P.D. was developing leads. Hell! We did not even know he was dead until N.Y.P.D. put the homicide on the wire. We found out from them that Adam Mickiewicz was a person of interest. Who knows what clse they might know about our case. They may be sitting on an important piece of evidence and not know its relevance or importance. Now Yonkers is knee deep in this. They are looking for someone who killed one of their cops. Don't you think we will be tripping over them everyplace we go on this? Whatever happened in Yonkers involved Adam Mickiewicz. You can bet your career on it. It's just too much of a coincidence that a cop gets shot right outside the hotel where Adam Mickiewicz was staying. This case hardly has any elements anymore that are not in the public record. The papers have most of the story already and will be printing follow-up reports for the next several days. If Sorge and company does not know they're hot, they'd have to be brain dead. I, for one, want an opportunity to work with the locals on this."

Before anyone else at the table could speak, Joe Duffy spoke. "She is right, if nothing else we need to know what the locals are doing in this matter. I say we share what we can and extract as much information as we can from them." Joe sincerely hoped that his support of her suggestion would keep her from blowing up at him.

Thomas Trulane from the United States Immigration disagreed. "I think we need to limit the investigation to those matters of federal interest. Let N.Y.P.D. do their homicide and let Yonkers look for their cop killer. If it turns out that they arrest someone to be of interest to us, we can use federal authority and supersede their jurisdiction." Trulane went on to say, "We are talking about the security of our borders. The Sorge stuff could have implications anywhere around the country. Who knows what might be getting smuggled in? We need to concentrate on ports of entry. Every day I need to concern myself with the thousands of shipping containers that are brought into our ports. We have every reason to believe that Sorge may be importing weapons of mass destruction while exporting American intelligence. N.Y.P.D. and Yonkers PD officers don't have the mobility or resources that we have. We also have the Patriot Act. We can do a lot that they can't do. I say we keep it federal. Do not bring the locals in on the Sorge part of this. Share what we know that might enhance their case against the cop killer but keep the rest confidential."

Robert Fulfree, from Homeland Security chimed in, "I must disagree with Mr. Trulane. I agree with Michelle Thompson. We need the locals and anyone else we can get to help on this. I said so from the onset. I'll tell you something else. The C.I.A. can read the newspapers just like anyone else. You can bet your ass they are all over this. Do you want them working without us? They most likely have some intel on the operation already. They are going to learn the implications of this sooner or later. We have to bring them in. Actually we need to hope that they bring us in."

Madison gave serious consideration to the matter and agreed that the local law enforcement personnel needed to be brought in, but he was still skeptical of C.I.A. involvement. He said, "I'm afraid of their radical approach. Their methods result in evidence getting tossed. They can, quite likely, help us to get Sorge, but their methods might cost us the conviction. We will coordinate with other locals, but I need time to think about the C.I.A." He went on to say, "Agent Thompson, you will be our liaison with N.Y.P.D. and the Yonkers P.D."

The Rest of the Crew

When the local law enforcement people arrived at F.B.I. headquarters, they were escorted to Duffy's office. As they entered the room both the captain and detective Taylor were duly impressed by the ostentatious, well furnished, immaculate meeting room. They were used to much more meager conditions at the local police precinct meeting rooms.

The young Officer Bradner hardly noticed the conditions of the conference room or its furnishings. He was most duly impressed by the very beautiful female F.B.I. agent whose simple presence in the room made it a place where he wanted to be. Ignoring all others in the room, he walked directly to her and introduced himself. The others in the room could not help but smile inwardly. They were young once themselves.

After introductions were taken care of the locals were given a brief overview of the case from the F.B.I. standpoint. Essentially, the F.B.I. admitted that the fugitive from justice warrant was just a convenient subterfuge. They were most interested in the Mickiewicz matter because of the alert put out by Taylor and Bradner indicating that Mickiewicz was a person of interest in the Bronx homicide. They told Taylor that they were sure that the victim in his homicide case was a man known as Stanley Adamski. They did not elaborate much beyond that except to indicate that they believed the Adamski murder had implications affecting national security.

They truthfully told Captain Dent that they had no idea who might have killed the Yonkers police officer or why he was killed. They conceded that they felt that there was some connection between the killer and Mickiewicz. They stated however that their conclusion that Mickiewicz was somehow tied to the death of Adamski was based solely on the fact that N.Y.P.D had found his prints at the crime scene, the fact that Mickiewicz had a mysterious past and the fact that he had a criminal record. They themselves had developed no specific evidence that tied Mickiewicz to Adamski. Whether he was a confederate of Mickiewicz or an enemy of Mickiewicz they did not know, but they were sure there was a connection.

The captain advised those present that the officer's radio car had a dashboard camera. He told them that the murderer had tampered with the recorder and that the suspect removed the tape. It seemed apparent that the officer's camera must have captured something that the murderer did not want photographed.

The captain was about to reveal that he knew that the man in the hospital was not Mickiewicz, but he wondered if the F.B.I. had already known this as well, so he asked Duffy if the bureau had verified Mickiewicz's identity through fingerprints.

Duffy began to respond, "We just sent a team of agents to the hospital to question Mickiewicz. We understand that he has regained consciousness. Our agents will fingerprint him while they are there and we should have his identity verified soon."

The captain was just about to say that he could save the F.B.I. the time and that he knew that the man in the hospital was not Adam Mickiewicz when Joe Duffy's secretary, George, entered the conference room. He said to Duffy, "Sir, I hate to interrupt, but I have an important message from our team at the hospital. They said they will be unable to question Mickiewicz at the hospital. ... Sir, I'm afraid he's gone."

Duffy gasped, "He's dead? ... I thought his wounds were not life threatening?"

George replied, "No, sir, I do not mean he is dead. I mean he's gone ... He has escaped."

Sick Bay

When Buddy awoke in the hospital, he was shocked to find that he was alive. He did not know what it felt like to be dead, but he was sure that he was dying when he hit the ground. As he went to move, he saw that he was handcuffed to the headboard of his bed. At once Buddy's mood changed. He was no longer in a melancholy mood. It was like an electric switch had been tripped in his brain. He shifted to survival mode. The adrenaline was flowing. It was a feeling that he knew well. Buddy did his best work in survival mode. Adrenaline was flowing and his mind quickly rose to a new level of alertness.

The presence of the cuffs told Buddy he was a prisoner. He did not yet know why he was a prisoner, but he knew he was a prisoner nonetheless. Buddy had been a prisoner before. He had escaped before. His previous escape involved killing two people. He was planning to escape again. Hopefully, this time he would not have to kill anyone, but he was determined to escape. He would work on trying to figure out why he was a prisoner later. For now, he needed to plan a peaceful escape.

First thing was to assess his own physical condition. He had some chest pain, but it felt more like an impact pain than a heart attack. He looked up at his IV lines, one was saline and the other was an antibiotic. There was no heart monitor. His chest was bandaged, but beyond that, he did not believe there was serious injury. Okay ...these are not serious measures he thought, I must be in fairly good shape. Next, he accessed the level of security he was under. Looking at the handcuffs, he knew they were not standard issue handcuffs used by street cops. These cuffs had a longer chain than the standard cuffs. They were cuffs specially designed to lock a prisoner to a bed. However, at once he noticed they were not properly attached. One cuff was around his wrist and the other was around the leg section of the headboard just above the bedspring. At first glance, one would think this was a secure way to keep a prisoner attached to his bed, but the bedspring frame was attached to the bed by way of slip joints. If one pulled up sharply up on the frame it would separate from the headboard. Then the cuff could be lowered down the headboard leg to a point below the area where the spring attached to the headboard. Once the cuff was lowered below the spring connection, if one lifted the leg of the headboard off the floor the cuff could then be slipped off the end of the leg and be freed from the bed.

Next, Buddy gave a gentle squeeze to the cuff around the headboard leg and it clicked one notch tighter. It was a sure sign to Buddy that the cuffs were not double locked. He knew that once he got the one cuff off the bedpost, he could easily pick the lock on the other cuff. Every cop is trained to double lock their handcuffs, but so few do it.

Next Buddy needed to figure out where his guard was located. The guard should be in the room or at the door, but it seemed to Buddy that his guard was somewhat lax in his duties. Just how lax was he? Was he relying solely on the cuffs or was he watching from nearby?

Buddy decided to find out. After a few practiced attempts to get out of bed, Buddy quietly arose. He popped the bedspring slip joint and slipped the cuff down and off the bottom of the bedpost. He tiptoed to a position behind the open door to his room and peeked out through the open space between where the hinges attach the door to the frame. The door being open provided a space about two inches wide through which Buddy could see the hallway.

About ten feet to the left of Buddy's room, on the same side of the hall as his room, was the nursing station. Directly across the floor from the station, there was a chair and seated in the chair was a large man in a blue uniform. The man was armed. Buddy did not recognize the uniform, but clearly, this must be his guard. From where the guard was seated, the door to Buddy's room was to the guard's left, but clearly, it was well within the guard's line of sight. If Buddy were going to get away, he'd need a distraction. He needed something that would cause his guard to have his attention called to his right. If he could just make his guard stare to the right for a protracted period of time, Buddy was sure he could slip out of his room scoot across the hall and a few doors down away from the guard. He could slip into a different room and make a get away from there. The guard would be looking for someone to exit from

Buddy's room. It was unlikely that he would pay any attention to someone exiting from a room across the hall and four or five doors down the hall. Escape from his room would be difficult, but leaving from a different room could be a proverbial walk in the park.

As Buddy was considering his options, he spotted a nurse stepping out from behind the nursing station. She began to walk towards his room. Buddy scurried back to his bed and pretended to be asleep.

Through partially opened eyes, he saw the nurse enter his room. The nurse was one of the most stunning women he ever saw in his life. She had a most attractive face, long blond hair and an unbelievable shapely body. She had on a very tight white blouse and the buttons down the front were clearly strained under the pressure of containing her large breasts. As she turned to leave the room, Buddy could see that the view from the rear was quite pleasing to the eye as well. Buddy knew why the guard had positioned himself between his room and the nursing station. He was a man enjoying the view. He was far more interested in talking to and watching the nurse than he was in watching Buddy. Buddy knew that this nurse would be the key to his freedom.

Once the nurse left the room, Buddy repositioned himself behind the door. On the back of the door to his room, there was a map of the floor plan. The map of the floor plan was there to show the room numbers, their location on the floor and their proximity to the fire exits. Buddy determined that the room furthest from his to the left of his was room

6087.

Buddy picked up the phone in his room and dialed the operator. When the operator answered Buddy simply said, "Would you please connect me to room 6087?" The operator complied. When the patient in 6087 answered the phone, Buddy said, "Hello, I'm with the phone company. We are servicing the phones here in the hospital, and there is some sort of trouble on this line. Some of the lines are crossed. Are you Mr. Kramer?"

"No," The man replied. "I'm Mr. Goldstein."

Buddy said, "I see. Apparently your line is crossed with Mr. Kramer's line. People who are trying to call you are being connected to his room by mistake. We can fix that right away. I'll just need for you to leave your phone off the hook for a few moments. Can you do that for me?"

Mr. Goldstein said, "Sure."

Buddy said, "Okay as soon as I have the line fixed I'll send a nurse down to put the phone back on the hook. It will not take long."

Buddy hung up and dialed the operator again. When the operator got on the line, Buddy said. "Would you please connect me to the nursing station on the sixth floor?" Just as Buddy hoped, nurse beautiful answered the phone. Buddy said, "Perhaps you could check on the welfare of the patient in room 6087 for me. I have been trying to get Mr. Goldstein on the phone for some time and I can't get through. When I call the switchboard, they tell me the phone is off the hook. I'm afraid that he may have fallen or something and that he dropped the phone or knocked it over or something. He could be lying on the floor. Could you please check on him for me?"

The nurse said, "Of course, just hold on."

Buddy scurried over behind the door again and watched as the nurse started to walk down the hall. Just as he hoped, the guard could not resist taking in the view. He stared down the hall to his right to watch the nurse as she walked down the long hallway to room 6087. As the guard stared at the nurse, Buddy's doorway was no longer in his line of sight. Buddy was confident that the guard's eyes would remain fixed to his right for the nurse's entire trip to the room. He was equally confident that the guard's eyes would remain fixed to the right for return trip as well. He was right. While the guard's eyes were fixed in the wrong direction Buddy hurried on tiptoes. He went seven or eight doors up the hallway and across the hall when he spotted an empty room. He slipped into the room and again got in a position behind the door where he could watch the guard and he could watch for the nurses return trip. He needed to make one more call. As the nurse got close to the desk, Buddy called the nursing station again so that the phone would be ringing as she got back. Again, she answered the phone. As she did so Buddy said, "I'm sorry to have to call back, but I guess I got cut off. Is Mr. Goldstein okay?"

The nurse said, "He's fine. The phone company was fixing his phone and he had to leave it off the hook for a while, but it's back in operation now."

Buddy said, "Oh, thank you so much. I was worried for nothing." Buddy knew that if there wasn't a worried person on the line when the nurse got back to the station it might arouse suspicion. That last call would buy a little more time, but Buddy could not know how much time he bought.

Now Buddy needed street clothing to make good his escape. Buddy went to the phone again and called the operator. When the operator answered, he said, "Hello, I'm with the phone company. I'm supposed to install a new phone in the housekeeping department for their men's locker room. I'm presently working on 6 West. Could you tell me how I get to the men's locker room from here?" Buddy knew that hospitals provide uniforms to the hospital housekeeping staff. The hospital laundry cleans the uniforms for their workers and keeps a sizable supply of spare uniforms of all sizes on hand for the housekeeping staff. If a maid's or a porter's uniform gets soiled with contaminated fluids while cleaning up the hospital, they need to have a change of clothing. Hospital uniform shirts and pants of all sizes are usually available in the locker rooms.

Buddy was sure he could simply walk out of his new room without drawing any attention to himself, as long as he kept his face out of the view of his guard. He was right. Buddy just walked out of the room, turned to his left and walked away with his back to the guard. The guard never suspected that the person walking out of the room so far down the hall

269

was his prisoner. Buddy made his way to the locker room and managed to slip in unseen. Just as he hoped, Buddy found a uniform that fit him. Knowing that hospital workers often change shoes between work shoes and street shoes, Buddy looked for a pair that would fit him. The porters often do not put the shoes in the locker, but instead they will place them on top of the locker. He rummaged around the room until he found a pair that would fit him.

Knowing that the porters are a trusting lot, he tried each of the locker doors until he found one that was unlocked and had some money in it. He took the money from the locker and wearing a porter's hospital uniform; he strolled out of the hospital.

As he walked along the street he could not help to think, "Perhaps I should get a job with the phone company; it can open a lot of doors."

Buddy spotted a subway station just a block from the hospital. He walked to the station and he descended into the New York City underground, the IRT subway system.

Buddy needed a sanctuary. He needed help. The pain in his chest was becoming unbearable and he could feel his bandages oozing blood. In the adrenaline-filled action of the escape, Buddy felt invincible. Now that the crisis period had passed, he once again became aware of his pain and he felt exhausted.

He had only a few dollars. He saw a subway station and knew where he had to go. He bought a metro card and got on a southbound subway headed for Grand Central Station.

Grand Central Station is one of the most magnificent railway stations in the world. Its grand rotunda area has been used for the backdrop in many classic movies. Scenes from Alfred Hitchcock's North by Northwest, Robert DeNiro's Midnight Run and Robin Williams' Fisher King were filmed there, but Buddy was not going there to film a movie. Buddy needed to get out of the city. He needed a train that would take him beyond the limits of New York City. The IRT is a fabulous transportation system, but its tracks do not go beyond the city limits.

At Grand Central, one can change trains, from a New York City Subway Train to a commuter line and that was exactly what Buddy intended to do. Buddy could think of only one place where he could find sanctuary. He was going to see the one person he could trust to help him. He was getting off the IRT subway line and getting on a Metro-North commuter train.

When he arrived at Grand Central Station, he purchased a few newspapers. If he wanted to know what was going on in his life, if he wanted to know why he was a prisoner, he was sure the newspapers would tell him.

Next, he went to the ticket booth in the grand rotunda of the magnificent station. He told the ticket agent there that he needed a one-way ticket for the northbound Metro-North Hudson Line. The ticket agent said. "Very good sir. What station will you be going to?" Buddy replied, "Garrison."

Sailing Back to Garrison

The commuter train ride along the banks of the Hudson River through suburban New York State is very different from a ride on the New York City Subway. The train cars are much larger and the tracks have turns that are more gentile. Rather than the jolting bumps and grinds of the subway, the commuter trains have a sort of soothing gentle rocking motion. The trains are not crowded masses of human flesh pressed into uncomfortable cars. The Metro-North trains have large comfortable seats and large windows that permit one to observe the countryside vistas as one travels, above ground, in the relative comfort of the large commuter cars.

Buddy sat in a comfortable seat and read his newspapers as he rode. He was alarmed to learn that an agent of the F.B.I. who was looking for a notorious criminal named Adam Mickiewicz had shot him. Buddy most assuredly knew that Adam Mickiewicz was a fugitive from justice, but he never considered him to be a dangerous felon. He hardly believed that anyone would think him to be a terrorist. The statement attributed to the agent also shocked him that Adam Mickiewicz was not expected to survive. As Buddy rode along, he stared out at the beautiful Hudson River Valley and wondered how he could get so enmeshed in more international matters while he was simply seeking some peace and solitude. Still, Buddy knew that the course of his life was such that these events did not seem as improbable for him as they might be for anyone else. Buddy was concerned about every aspect about his current predicament. He was saddened to learn that the police officer was dead. Right from the start, he believed that the officer was instantly killed with the first shot, but still he held out hope that he might have survived. Buddy wondered what might have provoked the attack, but he was sure that the officer had unwittingly witnessed something that the shooter did not want known. Once Buddy finished learning all he could he put down the papers and watched the scenery go by.

Soon the train rolled gently to a stop at Garrison station and Buddy got off the train. It was only a short walk through the quaint tiny village to the home of Terri Cassini.

Although it was only a short walk Buddy was exhausted by the time, he arrived at Terri's house. His injuries were not life threatening, but they did take a toll on his stamina. He needed some T.L.C.

Once again, Buddy glanced into the picture window of the Cassini home. Once again, he saw Terri seated on her couch. She was dressed in a black pants suit with a black vest and white blouse that had a large, black, ornamental, feminine bowtie. The slender cut of the garments, although reserved, showed off the curves of her body in a most enticing manner. Terri looked good in black. To Buddy, Terri looked beautiful regardless of what she was wearing. She was seated on her couch crying. Buddy knew the shock of his arrival, in his present condition, might be more than she could stand, but he was already past the point of no return. Buddy knocked on the door.

After a few moments, the door opened. Buddy could tell that Terri was shocked to see him. As Terri looked at Buddy she burst into tears. Throwing her arms around his neck, she cried out, "You're alive! Oh, thank God in heaven, you're alive. My God, what would I have done? First Ray dies, then you? I could not bear it if you were gone too! Oh my God. Thank God in Heaven!"

As she embraced him, the tears were flowing from her eyes. She began to kiss him passionately on the lips, only occasionally breaking off to utter the words "Buddy, Buddy" and then she would resume her embrace and passionate kissed.

Buddy embraced her as well and returned her kisses with a passion like he had never felt before in his life. There were no thoughts of Ray now. All Buddy could think was that he was glad to be alive. He knew that he had wasted so much of his life in loneliness. Life was not meant to be wasted in loneliness. The woman that he loved was in his arms. Was she kissing him out of her love for him, or was it just the emotional outburst of a woman who thought a long lost friend was dead? Buddy did not care. At that moment, he did not care about anything, but holding the woman he loved; a woman he had loved in silence for years. He would savor these moments as long as he could. He was determined not to let her go. He hugged her, kissed her and loved her like never before.

Buddy began to feel weak again. He felt as if

he were about to pass out. The damage to Buddy's body was not deadly, but it was serious. He needed to lie down.

Without another word, Terri helped Buddy to her bedroom and put him to bed. She removed his shirt and gasped at the sight of the blood soaked bandages.

Buddy looked down at himself and said, "I don't think it's as bad as it looks."

Terri said, "Please tell me you're not dying Buddy. I'll take care of you; you'll be okay." Buddy felt himself slipping into unconsciousness. He wasn't sure that he was not dying. If he was dying, there was something he had to say before life slipped away. As he slipped from consciousness, he said, "Terri, I love you; God forgive me, but I've always loved you."

The Nature of the Seaman

Over the next few days the principals of the various law enforcement agencies continued to meet. The captain provided the F.B.I. with the fingerprint cards that his men had secured at the hospital. This time the cards were submitted to AFIS, the Automated Fingerprint Identification System. AFIS confirmed that the prints were indeed not those of Adam Mickiewicz, the man wanted for assault and bail jumping. Rather they were those of Robert Kern, a police officer, who seemed to be on an extended leave of absence from the N.Y.P.D. As the captain suggested, the fingerprints had indeed been flagged, but they had not been flagged by the F.B.I. They had been flagged by the C.I.A. The C.I.A. was, therefore, automatically informed that the F.BI. had run the prints of Robert Kern, a man whose fingerprints were flagged. Whether they liked it or not, by running the fingerprints through AFIS, the F.B.I. had unintentionally invited the C.I.A. to the table.

At the next meeting in F.B.I. Headquarters, C.I.A. agent Peter Cage took a seat at the table. He had a lot of information to offer regarding the now notorious Mr. Kern. He addressed the group, "We now all know that man who registered at the Royal Buena Vista as Adam Mickiewicz is, in fact, Robert Kern. What you may not know is that Mr. Kern might well be one of the most dangerous persons on this planet. He is a survivalist and a killing machine. I cannot tell you if he killed Stanley Adamski, but it is not out of the realm of possibility. If as you say, Mr. Adamski worked for the Russian military, then he would be at risk of being killed by Mr. Kern, but it seems unlikely. As far as we know, Mr. Kern has never committed any crime on American soil. I cannot tell you why he would have registered as Adam Mickiewicz. As far as we know, he has never used that name as a cover. We do know that his friends and acquaintances call him Buddy, but we have no record of him ever being referred to as Adam Mickiewicz. He is a master of deception and if he chose to use that name, you can be sure it is for some strategic reason. I can't tell you whether he might have been up to something legal or something nefarious. I can tell you that we try our best to keep tabs on him, but occasionally he eludes us and when that happens shit can hit the fan. I can tell you that he believes himself to be an extraordinary patriot and champion of American democracy. Some people, at our higher levels of government, would agree, but many would not. He has on many levels set back American efforts at diplomacy and for that he is not held in high regard. But as far as America is concerned, he has not ever been a criminal. Here is some background.

Mr. Kern is a highly educated man. He is a very successful American businessman, a martial arts expert, a linguist and a man bent on revenge.

His parents were killed when a Russian military fighter shot down a commercial airliner flying over secure Russian military airspace. You may recall it was in all the papers, Korean Air flight 007.

As a result, he hates the Russian military. At the height of the Cold War, he joined the National Guard and became a code breaker and translator. He also served as a martial arts training officer and a general topics trainer for the U.S. military. For a short time he served as a New York City police officer. He joined the military for one reason, to kill Russians. At first he was satisfied knowing that his code breaking and language skills were having a negative impact against Russian military efforts. However, over time, he began to feel that he needed a more 'hands on' activity to satisfy his need for revenge against Russians. As luck would have it, a group of insurgents, calling themselves the Mujahideen were fighting against the pro-Soviet government in Afghanistan. The Russians sent troops in support of the pro-Soviet government. Of course the U.S. sent financial aid to the insurgents. We supplied some low-tech weapons and a limited amount of training. We had just come off the Vietnam War and the U.S. was not inclined to get heavily involved in Afghanistan. Our support was very limited, very low key. We tried to be as inconspicuous as possible about our aide. We actually thought we could support them without the Russians or the American people finding out.

Surprisingly the Mujahideen did quite well against the Russians. The Mujahideen ground troops were holding off Russian ground troops and were at the verge of toppling the pro-Soviet government. The only thing holding them back was the Russian air supremacy. The Russians were using attack helicopters against Mujahideen ground troops and the Mujahideen had no weapons that could take out a helicopter.

A certain Texas congressman was pushing for the United States to take a more active role in the support of the Mujahideen in their war with Russia. He pressured his fellow congressmen and the C.I.A. to supply the Mujahideen with latest anti-aircraft weapons, Stinger missiles. The Stinger missile was the perfect weapon for the Mujahideen. It is simple to use. A foot soldier can carry a launching device on his shoulder. The shoulder-held device fires a heat-seeking missile that can hit a target flying at 11,000 feet. The Russians had nothing like a Stinger and no defense against it.

Most of the U.S. administration officials were against it. The pentagon feared that the Soviets might capture a working model of a Stinger and they could reverse engineer it. Then they could develop a Stinger type weapon of their own.

The State Department feared that the use of the Stinger would be proof positive that the U.S. was supplying weapons to the Mujahideen. That was something we were denying all along. Congress was concerned that the obvious use of Stingers might bring us into direct war with Russia. Nevertheless, the Texas congressman succeeded in getting Stingers for the Mujahideen.

When Robert Kern learned of this, he contacted the congressman and convinced him he was the best-suited man to teach the Mujahideen how to use the weapon. He spoke the language, understood training techniques, had been trained in electronics and was already a member of the National Guard who was willing, indeed, anxious to go. The congressman pulled some strings and Mr. Kern became the only member of the National Guard assigned to active duty in Afghanistan at that time.

Now, here is the official story of how the Mujahideen shot down their first Russian helicopter. Reportedly, the leader of the Mujahideen took the first shot at a Russian helicopter, but his missile was a dud and it did not launch properly. His second in command then took a shot and made the kill.

Our people in the field tell a different story. They say that when the Mujahideen leader took the shot he fell on his ass, dropping the launch device. The missile traveled about 300 yards, hit the ground and exploded, giving away their position. Mr. Kern, who was on the scene as a translator, to give technical advice only, picked up the launcher, reloaded and fired the second missile, blowing the Russian helicopter to kingdom come. After that incident, he began to travel with Mujahideen foot soldiers shooting down Russian choppers left and right.

When word of his exploits got back to Washington, they went ballistic, no pun intended. This was supposed to be an operation by the Mujahideen. Our official position was that America

280

was not involved. Now we had a member of the American military, actually in the field, killing Russians! Every member of the administration who was briefed had the exact same reaction. They would say, 'The guy is starting WW III.' They wanted to court martial him, put him in prison, kill him if necessary, but stop him at all costs. When saner heads prevailed, they agreed that a court martial would only bring public scrutiny to the whole matter. The State Department reached out to the Russians and learned that they were tired of the Afghan debacle and they were planning to withdraw anyway. However, they wanted the ass of Robert Kern. Finally, the American military simply issued a general discharge to Mr. Kern. They actually discharged him 'in country'. They did not even give him a plane ride home. They left him in Afghanistan! He was out of their hair. With Mr. Kern out of our military the Russians had a green light to kill him if they could find him.

For his part Mr. Kern stayed with the Mujahideen as a freedom fighter without any American sanction. However, because the Afghans still had Stingers, Mr. Kern continued to shoot down the Russian aircraft. It was still a mess, but fortunately the Russians pulled out soon after. The Kern incident did not become the major international issue that everyone feared it would.

However, at the end of the war, we were unable to account for all of the Stinger equipment that had been sent to the Mujahideen. There are those in our government who suggest that Kern stole the Stinger equipment to sell on the black market. However, it never turned up. Some say he managed to keep some of the Stinger equipment and that he has it stashed away for future use. Anyway, you know how it is in war. Equipment gets used up, it gets destroyed in the field, and it gets lost. We were never able to prove that Kern ever appropriated any of the Stinger missiles for himself, but you never know. We try to keep tabs on him. If any evidence that he has the Stingers ever turns up, we'll have to arrest him, but so far there hasn't been any hint that he ever tried to sell anything like Stingers or the launching equipment needed to use them.

Many people in our government considered him to be a renegade, but some considered him a hero. The Texas congressman managed to have him and two other Afghan fighters awarded congressional tokens of appreciation. He and two unnamed C.I.A. agents were awarded the Kimber Arms .45 firearm by congressional decree.

After the Afghan War with the Russians, the Mujahideen experienced internal strife. Ultimately, they split into separate groups. Some in the group wanted to set up a democratic state in Afghanistan. Others, who called themselves the Taliban, wanted to set up a theocracy, a Muslim State. Infighting among Mujahideen fighters broke out. For a while Mr. Kern fought alongside those members of the Mujahideen supporting democracy. He killed a number of Taliban fighters. For that, the clerics issued a Fatwa against him, directing Muslims to kill him on sight as a religious dictum. Yet he survives

Once the Russian forces moved out of the region the American government lost interest in Afghanistan. Without additional American support those supporting democracy lost control and the Taliban established their Muslim state. We all know how that turned out. Despite Robert Kern best efforts, Afghanistan ended up as a terrorist state. However, he managed to get away alive.

Somewhere along the line, after the Afghan War, he traveled to Taiwan. There he hooked up with a very successful Taiwanese businessman who also lost loved ones on flight 007. He too had been running a campaign against Russians. It was only natural that Kern and he would eventually become business partners. That led to business connections that made Mr. Kern a very rich man. He gained control of a large shipping company that moves shipping containers all over the world. He has warehouses in Texas, New York and California and a few overseas as well.

The Taiwanese businessman also uses his resources to seek revenge against Russians, but I digress. That's a story for another day.

Mr. Kern' next encounter with the Russians took place in the Russian breakaway, Republic of Georgia. As the Soviet Union was collapsing, the Soviet Republic of Georgia broke away and became an independent state. There was infighting in areas of South Ossetia and Abkhazia. Russian loyalists staged a rebellion to maintain Russian sovereignty over that area of Georgia.

Of course the Russians backed the rebels of Abkhazia and South Ossetia. They supported them with intelligence, money and troops. So this small country of Georgia found itself fighting against one of the most powerful armies in the world. However, the Georgians had Mr. Kern on their side. Using the cover of his import and export company, he shipped large container ships of weapons to Turkey. He then arranged for them to be delivered from Turkey to Georgian forces in need. It is alleged that he personally went into Georgia and fought side-by-side with Georgian forces, killing many Russians in the process. In the final analysis, Georgia was forced to cede some of its territory in South Ossetia and Abkhazia to the Russians, but the Russians lost a lot of military personnel in the process. The Russian intelligence community had to know of Kern's activity, but they never succeeded in killing him.

A few years later there was a dispute between the Russians and Chechnya. The Russians sent in troops. Robert Kern went to fight for the Chechens. He supplied weapons and offered to fight in the field. Our Mr. Kern was captured by the Russian military in Chechnya. He was accused of assisting the Chechen rebels by supplying money and weapons. He was also accused of being an American spy and he was charged with killing Russian military personnel. The Russians finally had their man. They directed the 'new KGB' to take custody of Mr. Kern and deliver him to Moscow. They wanted a public trial where they could accuse the U.S. of supporting the insurgents. It would have been a major political victory for the Russians, but for one thing. This so called 'New KGB' does not have half the savvy or ruthlessness that the old KGB had. The Russians had sent just two KBG agents and a car to deliver Mr. Kern to Moscow. Mr. Kern escaped.

Their agents were found dead on the side of the road. Apparently, they were beaten to death in hand-to-hand encounter with Kern. From what we summarized, the KGB agents were over confident and failed to accurately access the threat that transporting Kern presented. We learned that Kern was placed, handcuffed, in the back seat and the KGB agents chose to sit in the front. They apparently relied on handcuffs holding Mr. Kern hands behind his back and the locked rear door as the only means of securing him. It looked like Kern had slipped his handcuffs from behind his back to in front of himself. With his hands still chained together he reached over the front seat throwing his arms over the head of the driver. Then he used the handcuff chain to strangle the driver from behind while kicking the passenger in the head. Mr. Kern killed his captors and escaped.

Reportedly he returned to the field and resumed his activities with the rebels.

At first it was a simple matter of people opposing Russian dominance, but it proved to be a very disturbing dilemma for Kern.

The Chechen war involved Muslims fighting

against Russians. These Muslims created a Mujahideen of their own. The conflict drew the attention of Muslim extremists. Before too long al-Qaeda was supporting the Chechen rebels. A splinter group formed within the Chechen movement. They resorted to terrorism in their battle with the Russians. They were targeting civilians. Many of the rebel leaders were opposed to using terror tactics against the civilian population, but the leader of the splinter group, Shamil Basayev, also had a lot of support for the use of terror tactics. They placed bombs in public shopping malls killing many Russian civilians. In 2002 they took over Moscow's Dubrovka Theater and held the entire seven hundred audience members as hostages. Many civilians were killed when Russian authorities tried to free the hostages. In September 2004 Basayev ordered an attack on a school in Beslan, a town in North Ossetia, Russia. More than three hundred people died in the siege, most of them children.

Our intelligence tells us that Kern was outraged. He complained to the rebel leadership that his weapons were for use against Russian military only. He warned them that if they did not eliminate the Muslim extremists from within the movement he would turn his resources against them. The terrorist rebel leader, Shamil Basayev, insisted that Russian civilians were legitimate targets. He refused to back off. Basayev ordered his people to kill Kern. Then, remarkably, Shamil Basayev had a so-called 'accident'. A truck he was driving exploded. He and a number of his followers were killed. There is a lot of secrecy about the incident. No one really knows how he came to be killed. One would assume that Russian intelligence killed him, but that's not clear. The Russians delighted in the kill, but they never took full credit for it, nor did they ever explain how they might have killed him. There are those in the Russian government and many in Muslim extremists groups who believe Kern carried out the execution. As far as the Russians were concerned, anyone who would kill Basayev is a hero. It seems that after Basayev's death the Russians forgave Kern's past transgressions against Russian interests. They never sought to regain custody of Kern after that. There are those within al-Qaeda who insist it was Kern who killed him and they have marked Kern for death. Yet he survives.

Mind you, none of this activity was ever sanctioned by the U.S. He was never an agent of ours. Kern is just a man who fights everything Russian. Sometimes there is a good outcome for American interests so we might have turned a blind eye to his affairs. However, not all of the outcomes have been ideal. The Taliban ended up in control of Afghanistan, something Kern did not anticipate. Georgia lost territory to the Russians despite his efforts to prevent that, the Chechen rebels killed innocent civilians. Now, we have seen many of the former members of the Afghan Mujahideen turning up among al-Qaeda and we have good reason to believe that Chechen Muslim extremists are also plotting against America. Terror tactics developed in

Afghanistan have been deployed against America. Most experts in American foreign affairs doubt that our assistance to the Afghan Mujahideen or our subsequent the withdrawal of that assistance resulted in the attacks of 911, but many believe that if the communists were still running that part of the middle east our troubles would be significantly diminished. The actions against Russian civilians and the events of 911 weigh heavily on Kern's mind. He feels somewhat responsible.

Kern has doubts about himself and his own involvement in world affairs. The events at the school in Beslan were extremely disturbing to him. Some say he went into clinical depression after the children were killed, but he never lost his zeal for harming Russian military personnel. Kern is a troubled man. He dropped out of the international war effort to kill Russians after the attacks on innocent Russian civilians. He is said to be very remorseful over the deaths of innocent Russian civilians, yet he believes their complacency empowered an evil empire to bring pain on the world. He is in a state of personal inner conflict. He may even be mentally ill at this point. He is a patriot, no doubt, but he is also a loose cannon and a very troubled man.

We are looking for a man who has been marked for death by al-Qaeda, the Russians, Muslim fanatics and who knows who else. He has managed to survive. In the act of surviving, he has killed many people. The U.S. government does not consider him to be a terrorist, but I cannot say the same for governments of other nations. All of this stems from his hatred of the Russian military. Might he have killed a Pole who worked as Russian naval engineer? It seems to be the kind of thing he would do, except for the fact that Mr. Adamski was killed on American soil, just as he was apparently about to reveal something important to Americans. Kern has steadfastly avoided committing crimes on American soil and if Adamski were here to offer information that would be harmful to Russia, Kern would not want to silence him.

There is no evidence to place Kern at the crime scene. It's not his DNA on the plastic glass; it's not his fingerprints on the glass. I doubt he'd kill Adamski. There can be no doubt that he is somehow connected to the Adamski thing, but I doubt he'd kill anyone in America. I think, as far as your investigation goes, there is no need to bring him in right now. If I were you, I'd refocus my attention elsewhere."

At that point Agent Thomas Trulane of the United States Immigration and Customs Enforcement spoke, "Mr. Peter Cage, is that what you said your name was?"…Peter Cage? I have heard that a certain Mr. Peter Cage is the C.I.A.'s chief minister of misinformation. You're their most professional liar. Are you not? When the public needs to be lied to you are the one called upon!"

Cage responded, "I perform many duties in the interest of national security. Today, I am here to provide our best accurate information to this task force. You be the judge."

Trulane went on, "You guys at the C.I.A are hot shit. You have this guy Kern running around the world performing all sorts of tasks that we at home would consider to be acts of terrorism if they were committed against us. However, because his acts affect people hostile to us, you think it's okay. You say our government does not sanction his actions, that he is a renegade.

I'll bet you and your agency do whatever can be done to cover his tracks and leave him free to do what our leaders would like to do, but can't because of legal or diplomatic restrictions. You let him roam free; perhaps while he still possesses Stinger missiles and silently hope he does more damage to our enemies. You don't want him brought in because a trial would expose how deeply your agency is involved in maintaining him and the world unrest he creates."

At that Cage responded, "That's just typical anti-American bullshit! You just want to believe our leadership is inherently evil. The real evil lies in those who would let our enemies kill our people just so they can say they followed all proper procedures. You say you stand on principle. I say you hide behind the dogma of proper procedures to cover your own ass while the American people pay the price with their lives. That being said, I'll tell you this, we don't cover for *anyone* engaged in unlawful actions. Period! I'm just telling you the guy has not violated any laws in America as far as we know. If you think it is better

290

to waste time and valuable resources trying to bring in one of the most elusive men in the country, who is unlikely to have committed any crime here, knock yourself out."

Joe Duffy spoke next, "He's been wanted on a federal fugitive from justice warrant and now he is wanted for escape from custody. He pulled a gun on a federal agent and refused to drop it when ordered to do so. We're bringing him in and that's that."

Crew Building

The members of the different law enforcement agencies working the various components of the related cases decided to form separate task forces to investigate the many aspects of the case. All at the table volunteered to work those aspects of the case that were of primary interest to themselves.

The New Haven SAC, Frank Dwarman, his agent Alan Chapson, Thomas Trulane from the United States Immigration and the members of N.C.I.S. would continue their main focus on the investigation to identify Sorge.

Taylor would remain primarily focused on the Adamski murder, but would closely work with the Yonkers captain on the police officer shooting, since they were sure that the two murders were related.

Police Officer Tom Bradner quickly rose to suggest that he should work closely with Michelle Thompson to review the records of all that was known about the cases to establish flow charts that would indicate how the various persons in the related cases might have come to know one another and to see if anything had been overlooked. Michelle quickly agreed. Most at the meeting believed her quick acceptance of Tom Bradner's suggestion was more hormonal than professional, but no one objected.

Duffy suspected that Michelle's quick acceptance of Bradner's suggestion was merely an attempt to break free from Chapson, but he was not going to interfere.

Taylor believed that Bradner's suggestion was merely an effort to get closer to the very beautiful Ms. Thompson. Bradner's interest in Michelle was evident from the moment he entered the room. Taylor also believed Thompson might be attracted to the young and handsome Tom Bradner. Perhaps she was a little better in concealing her interest in Bradner, but Taylor could see through it. Taylor's instincts were honed by many years as an N.Y.P.D. detective. He could read people. He surely was right in his assessment of the Bradner-Thompson mutual attraction, but he did not think a little pursuit in the interests of love, in their off hours, would have a negative impact on their investigation. Whatever the reason, Bradner and Thompson would now be working exclusively as a team.

Cage from the C.I.A. and David Tees from the National Security Agency seemed like a natural fit to brainstorm international events to determine if there was a link between what had already occurred and world events.

Other sub-groups were formulated and all agreed to regularly scheduled mass meetings where ideas could be shared.

Back at the Garrison Sanctuary

When Buddy awoke he found himself naked and he realized he had been sleeping in Terri's bed. She was lying in the bed next to him, still asleep, still fully clothed in her black pants suit. She had her arm across him in a loving embrace. As he stirred in the bed she woke up. She looked up at him and said, "Oh Buddy, thank God you're okay. I don't know what I'd do if you had died. I know Ray is not yet in his grave, but I wept more for you than I did for him. I could not go on if you died too.

It would have been you, you know. Had you stayed it would have been you that I would have chosen. All these years I knew I loved you, but you were gone and Ray was still here. Ray always knew he was my second choice. It bothered him, but he accepted it. He loved me enough to want me even though he knew. He loved you too, you know. You were his best friend. I think that sometimes he felt guilty for having won my hand. Yet, God forgive me, we both knew he won by default. We made the best of it. There were many loving moments between us, but somehow your presence was always there, in our minds, haunting us. Now ... now Ray is gone and you are here. I'm so confused.

The papers said that the F.B.I. Agent Chapson doubted you would live and ..."

Buddy interrupted her. He put his index finger first to his lips then to hers. He gently whispered, "Shhhhh. I know ... I know. I have done so many things that I regret, but I regret leaving you behind more than anything else. I do love you and I want to take you right now, but Ray is still on my mind. Perhaps we can get past this. Perhaps we will come to believe that it was our destiny to be together, just you and me, but for now Ray is still between us. Perhaps we will come to know that even Ray would understand, but for now, even I don't understand. How can I lie here in Ray's bed holding his wife, wanting her? I think you know that. Right now we're both confused, we're in pain, and we're troubled, on so many levels. You're so vulnerable right now.

As for me, my life has been a bit of a train wreck lately. I've done so many horrible things in the name of honor and duty. But it was all by my own standards of honor and duty. I'm not so sure the world or God would agree that the things I've done are so honorable. I've come home to honor Ray's memory, to attend his funeral and all I can think about is taking Ray's wife. God forgive me. What kind of man am I?

In part, I have come home to seek redemption and until I can redeem myself in my own eyes I can never be the person I was when I left home all those years ago. Right now I'm no good for you. If I am to be redeemed, I must begin to do honorable things; truly honorable things. Right now I have to do the most honorable thing I've ever done in my life. I want to take you in my arms and make love to you. I want to satisfy a yearning that has burned in me for years, but I must constrain myself, we must constrain

295

ourselves, until the time is right. I must constrain myself until we both know for sure the time is right. I love you. I'll always love you, but we must wait. We need to think this out."

Terri nodded in agreement and slowly rose from the bed. As she did so, Buddy held her arm for a moment and said, "I must ask a question. When I first came to your door, you said you thought I was dying. This morning you said you read in the papers that the F.B.I. agent said I was dying. I've read all the papers none of the stories mentioned me by name at all. The newspapers identified the victim of the shooting as being Adam Mickiewicz.

I can understand how the authorities and the newspapers might have thought, at the time, that I was Adam Mickiewicz, but whatever made you realize that I was Adam Mickiewicz?"

Terri looked confused, but she answered, "Well, first of all, there was the mailbox."

Buddy replied, "The mailbox?"

Terri went on, "Yes, the mailbox. When you first left, I went to work for Ray's father at the mailbox store as a part-time bookkeeper. One day I noticed that there was a mailbox for a person named Adam Mickiewicz. I noticed that the rent for the box had not been paid in years. I told Ray and he got upset. He made me promise not to tell his dad about the delinquent account. He told me that the box belonged to his 'very special friend'. He said he had arranged for this 'very special friend' to get a free mailbox. It was a little secret that he kept from his dad. I thought nothing of it. Ray's dad was turning the business over to Ray anyway so, if Ray wanted someone to have a free box, who would care? I let it go.

Then about ten years later, an F.B.I. agent came to the store. He said that he was working old cases in connection with a cold case task force in Massachusetts. He said he was looking for a person named Adam Mickiewicz who had listed the address of the mailbox store as his home address.

Ray told the agent he never heard of anyone named Adam Mickiewicz. Well, I knew Ray was lying. We no longer had the Adam Mickiewicz mailbox, but Ray had once told me that Adam Mickiewicz was his 'very special friend." Now Ray was telling the F.B.I. he never knew the guy.

In the conversation that followed Ray learned that the case against this 'Adam Mickiewicz' was about ten years old. That meant that it occurred right around the time you left town. Ray asked the agent, "Hasn't the statute of limitations run out on that?" The agent said, "No! If they could prove that Adam Mickiewicz had continuously lived outside the state of Massachusetts, during the time gone by, he can still be arrested." He said the clock for the statute of limitations does not run while the suspect is out of state and that they had reason to believe he was out of state the whole time. I could see that Ray was very upset when he heard that, but he stuck with the story that he had no knowledge of who Adam Mickiewicz was or where he might be.

I was careful not to contradict Ray in front of the agent, but when the agent left, I asked Ray about it. I pressed Ray to tell me about Adam Mickiewicz. Ray said that he had taken a blood oath with his best friend never to reveal anything about Adam Mickiewicz. He said that it could be a very dangerous matter and it needed to be kept secret. He asked me never to speak of Adam Mickiewicz again. He was so upset that I decided that I'd drop the subject.

However, what struck me most about what Ray said was the fact that he said he took a blood oath with his best friend. Buddy, you were the only person that he ever referred to as his best friend. I figured it had to be something secret between you and him. He said it was something very dangerous. I knew you were involved in dangerous things with the military, so I just assumed it was a name you used.

Then there was the fact that this 'Adam Mickiewicz person' was shot at the Royal Hotel. I knew you had been staying there as a kid. I could not figure out why you would ever go back there, but it reaffirmed my suspicions that you and Adam Mickiewicz were one and the same. I assumed that it must have had something to do with some sort of dangerous undercover military assignment or something. I know your real name is Robert Kern, but tell me Buddy, are you also Adam Mickiewicz?"

Buddy took a deep breath and sat up on the edge of the bed and said, "There is no Adam Mickiewicz. There never was any Adam Mickiewicz, at least not the Adam Mickiewicz who is in the middle of this mess. He was just a guy created out of the minds of two young kids looking to dupe their parents. That's all. No big conspiracy, no military action or C.I.A. cover name. It was nothing like that at all. He is just someone in the imagination of two mischievous kids.

One day when Ray and I were about fourteen or fifteen years old we walking along the Hudson riverfront. We came upon another boy who was shooting at soda cans with a BB gun. I asked the kid if I could take a shot and he said, 'Get your own BB gun'.

Well, of course we wanted to get our own BB guns. We had after school jobs. We had money. We could buy BB guns, but our parents were too strict. You needed parental consent to buy a BB gun and we were not going to get parental consent. There would be no BB guns for us.

Then Ray told me about an idea that had been brewing in his mind for some time. There were things we wanted that our parents would never let us have: BB guns, slingshots, Ray wanted Playboy magazines and I wanted car magazines, you know, Car and Driver or Hot Rod magazine etc. but my mother would not let me read that stuff. She said it detracted from more important studies. There were all sorts of things that we wanted, but were not allowed to have. Ray was working part time for his dad at the mailbox store and I had an after school job. We both had money. What we did not have was parental permission. Ray suggested that he could dummy up a mailbox account at his dad's Yonkers store. Then we could mail order whatever we wanted. Hell, Sears sold anything a boy could want through their mail order catalogs at the time. You could buy a bow and arrow set, BB guns, hell, you could buy real guns from the catalog. All the stuff that young boys want, but parents often forbid. Magazine subscriptions were cheaper than newsstand prices and you did not have to worry that the clerk might refuse to sell Playboy to a kid, or worse tell your parents that you tried to buy one. You could even mail order wine and beer if you wanted it. Ray could easily set up the box himself, but he needed an accomplice, someone to retrieve the stuff that came in. He could not do it. The other workers would see him removing stuff from the store. They might tell his dad. He needed an accomplice, someone who was unknown to the workers at the shop who could be the pick-up man. I thought it was a great idea; Ray would secure the mailbox and I'd be the pick-up man.

Next we needed a name for the mailbox account. We did not want to use something like Smith or Jones. In our adolescent minds, we were afraid our stuff might get sent to the wrong Mr. Jones. We needed a unique name. I reached into my book bag and pulled out a book that my mother had given me to read on the life of a well-known Polish poet, Adam Mickiewicz. Bingo! That would be the name on the mailbox.

And so it came to pass that Adam Mickiewicz got a mailbox. Then Adam Mickiewicz used money orders to buy all sorts of stuff. We used him to order magazine subscriptions to all sorts of adult magazines and automotive magazines. He bought us beer and wine...and yes he bought us BB guns. Whatever we wanted, Adam Mickiewicz would buy it. We started to refer to him as our 'very special friend'. At first it was harmless kid stuff, but it got complicated.

We did not know it at the time, but having Adam Mickiewicz order magazine subscriptions got his name put on mailing lists for junk mail. I just threw most of the junk mail away, but one day Adam Mickiewicz got a letter from the magazine sweepstakes. It said '**Adam Mickiewicz; You May Have Already Won a Million Dollars!'**

We were ecstatic! We thought for sure Adam Mickiewicz won a million bucks! We did not know that millions of such notices went out regularly. We thought only the finalists would get such letters. We thought we'd be rich! Every day I'd go to the box and look for the million-dollar check. However, we began to wonder, how would we cash the check? Adam needed a bank account. That's when things really got cooking.

We went to a bank to open an account for Adam Mickiewicz. We were told he needed a social security number. At the time there was a government program where young people were being given part time jobs at government facilities. Ray knew a girl who was working at the city clerk's office. He used his father's photocopy equipment to dummy up a birth certificate. It took a lot of cut and paste work, but we changed successive photocopies of Ray's birth certificate to make a birth certificate for Adam Mickiewicz. When he was done, it looked pretty good.

Of course the winner had to be twenty-one years old to claim the prize so we made Adam Mickiewicz twenty-one years old. Then Ray had his girlfriend at the city clerk's office take the dummy birth certificate to work with her. When no one was looking, she put the city seal on it.

We took the dummy document to the social security office where another of Ray's girlfriends was working.. Bingo! Adam Mickiewicz had a social security number.

Next, Adam Mickiewicz got a checking account. It was all so foolish. We were kids we didn't know we were being foolish. We were going to win a million dollars!

Then it got even better. One day, sometime after we opened the checking account, Adam Mickiewicz received an unsolicited, pre-approved credit card application in the mail. It actually said 'because of your good credit history you qualify for a credit card!' What credit history? Adam had no history. Yet all Adam had to do was sign the application and return it. Sure enough the application was approved! There would be no further need for us to buy postal money orders. Adam Mickiewicz had credit.

We use the card to buy all sorts of stuff. We always paid the bill; we would not want Adam

Mickiewicz to have bad credit.

When I turned sixteen, I got my driver's license. Then I got a brainstorm. A sixteen-year-old cannot drive at night in New York, but Adam Mickiewicz was twenty-one. I took all the tests over again, this time as Adam Mickiewicz. Now Adam had a license and I could drive at night. When Ray got his license, I reported the Adam Mickiewicz license as being lost. The D.M.V. promptly issued a duplicate. Then each of us had two driver's licenses, our own and one in the name of Adam Mickiewicz. Back then there was no computer cross reference that would invalidate the original and there was no photo on the licenses. Similar things occurred on a fairly regular basis. By the time we were eighteen years old, Adam Mickiewicz had every conceivable form of ID. He even registered for the draft. We used his ID whenever it seemed covenant to do so.

One day Ray and I went to a Yankees versus Red Sox baseball game that was to be played in Boston at Fenway Park. We bought the tickets with the Mickiewicz credit card. We were wearing Yankee shirts. Of course we drew the ire of the crowd, but we thought it was fun. We were on line to buy beer and someone, a Red Sox fan, threw a beer on Ray."

Terri interrupted, "I'm guessing that was a big mistake. Ray would have flattened the guy."

Buddy resumed, "Yeah, and I flattened another guy who tried to jump in on Ray. A major fight broke out. Hell, we were in the middle of a riot.

303

The next thing you know it seemed like we were fighting everyone in the place. In the confusion, Ray and I got separated. Somehow I got away, but Ray got arrested.

At the time, Ray had pockets full of Adam Mickiewicz ID. Ray never told them he was Adam. The Boston cops just found the ID on him and took him to be Adam Mickiewicz and booked him under that name. Ray did not protest. If the cops thought his name was Adam Mickiewicz, he was not going to correct them. Ray expected Adam to be charged with disorderly conduct. He figured he would pay a fine and be let go. No one had to be any the wiser, but two seriously injured Boston fans identified Ray as the assailant. He was charged with two counts of felony assault. He jumped bail and never went back. I tried to convince him that he should turn himself in, but only a week before a Yankee fan was sentenced to three years in prison for an assault at Fenway. And that guy did not give the cops a false ID. How could that be explained? Ray wasn't going back.

We agreed it would be best for us to kill and bury Adam Mickiewicz forever. We would never use the Adam Mickiewicz name or credit card again.

Terri, when the F.B.I. came to the store, they were looking for Adam Mickiewicz, they were actually looking for Ray. They thought the man arrested in Fenway was named Adam Mickiewicz, but the man they wanted, the man arrested for the fight was Ray. He's the one whose fingerprints are on file as Adam Mickiewicz. That's why he was upset when he found out that the statute of limitations clock does not run when you are out of state. He was afraid he would be arrested if anyone found out he was Adam Mickiewicz. He could not tell you. That would make you open to a charge of aiding and abetting, or obstructing justice, if the authorities ever found out you knew. Mind you I was Adam Mickiewicz also.

I never intended to use the name again, but recently when I wanted to stay at the Royal they would not rent to me, or at least they would not rent to Robert Kern. I learned that they would rent to any person who had been a previous tenant; it's sort of an alumni thing. When I lived at the Royal, I was a juvenile. They would not have let me live there, so at the time; I registered as Adam Mickiewicz and used the Adam Mickiewicz credit card to pay the rent.

Nowadays Robert Kern cannot rent at the Royal, but the former tenant, Adam Mickiewicz could. I lied to the clerk. I told him I was Adam Mickiewicz. I told him my wallet was stolen, so I would not have to use a credit card or show ID. He looked up a picture they had on file for Adam Mickiewicz, but of course it was a picture of me! He let me register as Adam Mickiewicz without any further ID.

I only told the clerk. I cannot figure out how the F.B.I. came there looking for Adam Mickiewicz at the Royal, but according to the newspapers that's why they came. However, they could not have been looking for me; I'm not the Adam Mickiewicz whose fingerprints were found at the Bronx Hotel. I'm not the one named in the warrant. They were looking for Ray, he's the one wanted in the warrant.

My fingerprints are not in any file associated with the Adam Mickiewicz name. Ray's fingerprints are on file as Adam Mickiewicz as a result of the Boston arrest."

Terri spoke out, "But Ray could have nothing to do with this. He never even knew this Adamski guy. Besides, Ray died on the very morning of the day that Adamski was killed."

Buddy shouted, "Adamski! Not Stanislaus Adamski! What does he have to do with this?"

Terri replied, "Yes Stanislaus Adamski. While you were asleep, I went out and got some late additions of the newspapers. The latest editions say that Adam Mickiewicz's fingerprints were found in the hotel room of a man named Stanislaus Adamski who was murdered in the Bronx hotel. That can't be correct, not if Ray is Adam Mickiewicz. Ray died in the morning on the very day that Adamski was murdered. He was never at that Bronx hotel and he most certainly did not kill anyone. I don't believe he ever knew anyone named Stanislaus Adamski."

Buddy continued to speak in excited tones as he said, "Ray did know him! So did I!" He asked, "Did Ray ever tell you about his role in the Yugoslavian shipping accident?"

Terri replied, "Of course, he did."

Buddy went on, "Stanislaus Adamski was a crew member of that ship. Adamski was temporarily stranded in the U.S. and he spoke little English. He was a Polish national. Ray brought him to the Polish Center to get him some help. I met them at the center. Ray introduced us to one another. However, he first tried to find me at the Royal. Stan heard Ray ask for Adam Mickiewicz at the desk and so Adamski believed that to be my name. Of course neither Ray nor I ever wanted anyone who knew us to refer to either of us as Adam Mickiewicz. We just told him to call me Buddy and let it go at that. I let him stay in my house. We lived together for a while and ...

Holy shit! ... It just dawned on me; I never told him my real name! I just told him to call me Buddy! I never felt it necessary to tell him my real name. Buddy just came naturally and we let it go at that! It never dawned on me that he would have gone back to Poland still believing my name was Adam Mickiewicz. I had told him that he should defect to the United States. I tried very hard to convince him to do so. I told him that if he ever wanted to defect that he should contact me, I would help him. However, I never told him my real name! If he were going to defect, he would be trying to contact Adam Mickiewicz. I just assumed he'd contact me through the Polish Center and he'd ask for Buddy. At the time I did not know the events in my life would take me away from Yonkers.

Terri, I don't know how to tell you this, but we have to consider this - - For Ray to have died on the same day as Adamski -- for Adam Mickiewicz's fingerprints to be at the scene -- it is just too much to be a coincidence. We have to consider the possibility that Ray was murdered!"

Terri said, "That's absurd."

"No it is not! Suppose Adamski knew something important, something secret. Suppose he was trying to find Adam Mickiewicz to get assistance in defecting. Suppose communist agents knew he was trying to contact an American named Adam Mickiewicz. They would surely kill Stan Adamski. They would try to find and kill Adam Mickiewicz as well.

Suppose they were trying to find the Adam Mickiewicz whom they knew had once promised to help Adamski defect. In other words they were trying to find me. Suppose, by mistake, they found the Adam Mickiewicz who was wanted by the Boston Police, Ray. If they realized they killed the wrong Adam Mickiewicz they might come looking for me. I can't figure out how Ray's fingerprints got in the room, but I know for sure that the fingerprints they found must be Ray's.

Now I'm sure that the guy in the suburban was there to kill me and somehow the cop got in the way. The cops are looking at this all wrong! I've got to contact them. If we are going to get justice for Ray, we need to have his death investigated as a murder. I have to contact the cops."

A Tighter Crew

Tom Bradner was not the type of guy who could be easily dissuaded from performing his duties. He was a young cop who saw his job as an endless adventure. He was driven to make the most of it. He was the type of cop who would go on vacation and spend the whole time off wishing he was back at work, fearful that he would be missing some of the excitement. He had been assigned to busy precincts. He saw a lot of things that few people ever see up close and personal and he knew there was a lot more to see, to learn. He lived in the city and made almost as many off duty quality arrests as some cops make while working. He was always on, always working, always a cop. However this assignment had a major distraction attached to it. Michelle Thompson was stunning. She was smart and beautiful. Bradner was going to be a professional cop all the way, but even a professional cop can be distracted. Michelle was going to be an asset in this investigation, but she was going to be a distraction as well. For Tom this case was going to be one of the more pleasurable adventures even if he could not keep his mind on his work.

Michelle Thompson was an eager F.B.I. agent. She was eager to get her first taste of something real. Until now she had been relegated to the mundane follow up duties that are given to rookies, cleaning up the loose ends of someone else's adventure. Now she would get her bite at the apple. She could taste it.

This was a real case. Murder, espionage, a cop killing, a mystery man and the case was hers to make or break. She was not going to phone it in. This was a rush, her first.

Yet, when that young N.Y.P.D. cop Tom Bradner entered the conference room, there was a different sort of rush. She had to compose herself for a moment before she could present herself as the professional F.B.I. agent she knew herself to be.

She was in favor of having the F.B.I. working with N.Y.P.D. cops from the early stages of the case. She told herself that the fact that she was assigned to work with Bradner was just a natural by-product of a professional investigation. It was inevitable that if an N.Y.P.D. officer came into the case that she should be assigned to work with that officer, whoever he happened to be. There was nothing else to it. He was handsome. There could be no denying that. If they made something out of working together that would please her, but first things first. There were dangerous people who had to be taken off the streets.

Over the next few days, they worked tirelessly reviewing reports from every agency that ever had any involvement in any part of the Sorge investigation. Neither of them was going to let anything interfere with their pursuit of this most dangerous person. However, on as the late afternoon of their third day together approached, Tom finally felt it was time for him to begin a pursuit of a different sort.

Tom spoke, "Michelle, we've been working

hard on this. My brain is going into overload mode. If we don't relax and let off a little steam, we'll crash and burn. I think we need to take a few hours to relax. Perhaps we can go out for dinner or something. I mean go for a real dinner. Go to a real restaurant, not a fast food joint. Not studying over take-out burgers and pizza, a real dinner, just you and me. Wadda ya say? We can still discuss the case, but we need to unwind. Wadda ya say?"

Michelle just smiled a little and said, "You're right. We need to get away from this for a while, but I have a better idea. In addition to being a world-class investigator I am also somewhat of an outstanding chef. Why don't you go home and freshen up a bit and I'll do the same. Here is my address. You show up around seven with a bottle of a fine red wine and I'll do the rest." With that said she closed the file that she was looking at and began toward the door to leave the office. For a moment Tom was a bit frozen in his tracks. There was certain warmth in the tone of her voice during the invitation to dinner. Tom knew that Michelle was somewhat pleased that he had asked to dine with her. He could not help but believe that there was something more than an invitation to a good meal.

She stopped at the office door, opened it and said, "You know you have to be escorted out of the building. You're not allowed to roam the halls here by yourself. I'm opening a door for you. If you don't come along now, you'll have to get someone else to escort you. You coming?"

With that said, Tom followed her lead.

Tom arrived at Michelle's apartment right on time and he brought a bottle of fine wine, as he had been instructed to do. They dined on an excellent dinner then retired to the living room to relax a little, sip a little more wine and discuss their case.

Michelle began the conversation by saying something that caught Tom's attention.

"There is something that is bothering me about my review of the files," She said.

Tom inquired, "What's that?"

"Well, during our original briefing at F.B.I. headquarters, before you guys came into the case, Frank Dwarman, the SAC of the New Haven office said that he did not know if the hair samples recovered at the Gorton murder scene were preserved by the local police, but according to the Groton P.D. reports they notified the lab that processed the hair sample that it was a joint investigation with the F.B.I. I can't believe that the lab would not have sent a copy of their findings to the Connecticut F.B.I. office. Another thing, he also said that the Groton P.D. broke off cooperation when the bureau told them that they suspected that a person operating a Groton P.D. patrol car was parked at the victim's home at the time of the murder. The implication being that a Groton cop could be a suspect."

Tom replied, "So?"

"Well according to the Groton P.D. reports, filed at the time, they did consider that a possibility," Michelle said. "The reports indicate that at the suggestion of one of their detectives they checked the vehicle mileage logs for all of their cars to see if there were any indications of unauthorized use. In doing so, they found that one of their vehicles had been sent to a body shop for repair. The officer who delivered the car to the shop noted the mileage. When they went back to the shop to pick up the car, there was an additional forty miles on the odometer. Initially, they accused the shop owner of using the car to run errands. The shop owner insisted that the original officer must have made a mistake noting the mileage when he brought the car in. He insisted that no one on his staff used the car. At first Groton was just going to write it off as some sort of bookkeeping error, but when this car at the scene of the crime thing surfaced, they re-opened the investigation. The shop owner admitted that he had left the car outdoors overnight where it could have been stolen and returned without anyone knowing it was gone."

Tom said, "So."

Michelle went on, "It's all in the record. The record complied by the Groton cops at the time of the Groton murder. The Groton cops were not uncooperative. Their findings were all forwarded to the F.B.I. If the Groton cops were prepared to acknowledge that their car could have been stolen and used in the crime, why would they break off cooperation with the bureau? They had a plausible explanation as to how one of their cars might have been there without necessarily implicating one of their own. It looks to me like they were cooperating all the way. Furthermore, when they sent the hair in for DNA testing they indicated that the F.B.I. was a cooperating agency. Would they do that if they were being uncooperative? I think Dwarman is lying."

Tom thought for a moment and said, "The original case was a long time ago. Perhaps he forgot the details."

Michelle shot back, "My boss at the New York office took some time off on the morning of the meeting so he was not briefed in advance. He did not know the director was coming in for that meeting, nor did he know why. However, Frank Dwarman did know why he was there. He had to be notified in advance in order to know enough to report to the New York office to be there for the meeting. He knew there was a meeting to be held, he knew why and he knew he would be meeting with the director. He had plenty of time to prepared himself. He knew he was meeting with the director. You can bet your ass he'd make sure he would know what was in the file. There is some reason why he is not telling all he knows. I think he's withholding info so his man, Chapson, can make the collar. So his office can get the credit."

Tom looked at her and said, "You know there is another, more troubling possibility." Michelle knew there was, but she was refusing to allow herself to believe the thoughts racing around her head.

On the Radar

The captain believed that the efforts to bring in Robert Kern, a.k.a ., Adam Mickiewicz, were a waste of resources. By this time the results of the DNA analysis of the bloody clothing taken from Kern on the night of his shooting had come back. Kern was not a match to the cop killer! He was not the owner of the hair found in Groton. He was not the person who used the cup at the Bronx Hotel. From the DNA samples taken from the clothing at the garage fire, the captain knew that whoever left the clothing at the fire scene was the same person who left DNA at the Groton murder scene, he was the same person who left DNA at the Bronx hotel, and he was the same person who murdered his police officer.

While Captain Dent sat at his desk contemplating his next steps, a detective burst into his office unannounced and excitedly said, "Sir there is a man on the phone who says he is Adam Mickiewicz. He's asking to speak to you!"

The captain said, "Start a trace!" Then he picked up the phone and said, "Hello Mr. Kern. It's nice to hear from you."

Buddy began to speak, "Captain, I know that by now you would have figured out that I am not Adam Mickiewicz and I assumed you'd know my true identity. I can see from your comments in the newspapers that you know I am innocent. I am very reluctant to tell you this, but I must do so if I am to get justice for my friend who was murdered."

The captain replied, "Your friend who was murdered? What friend would that be?"

Buddy replied, "Ray Cassini."

Inquisitively, the captain said, "Ray Cassini? Who the hell is Ray Cassini?"

"Ray Cassini was my best friend. He died on the same day that Stan Adamski was murdered. He was killed because someone thought that he was Adam Mickiewicz. I'm quite sure that the man who killed your cop on Buena Vista Avenue was there to kill me. He wanted to kill me because he believed that *I* was Adam Mickiewicz. They need to kill Adam Mickiewicz and they will kill anyone who even looks like Adam Mickiewicz.

This is speculation, but I believe Stan Adamski would have been trying to contact Adam Mickiewicz from the time he arrived in America and very dangerous people, Russians, did not want that to happen."

The captain asked, "Who the hell is this Adam Mickiewicz, why would Adamski want to contact him and why does everyone want to kill him?"

"All I can tell you now is that Ray was an acquaintance of Adamski and I believe Ray's death is connected to the attempts on the life of Adam Mickiewicz and the murder of Stan Adamski. It is quite likely that his death is tied to the murder of your police officer as well. Ray's body is currently in the possession of the medical examiner. His remains are being held pending the outcome of a medical examiner's inquest into the cause of death. Currently, most people involved in the inquest believe that the cause of death is some sort of medical malpractice, but I'm telling you he was murdered!"

The captain replied, "The medical examiner's office is very thorough. I'm sure if there is any evidence of foul play they'll find it."

Buddy said, "Not if they are not looking for evidence of foul play. I'm sure that whoever killed Ray would have had the expertise to make it look like malpractice. Without an air of suspicion of murder, the medical examiner's office might not look in the right areas. They move at a much slower pace in malpractice cases than they do in criminal cases. Criminal cases get top priority.

Ray was positively identified through his hospital admission records and by his family. There would be no pressing demand to confirm his identity. They might not have even fingerprinted him yet. If they did take his fingerprints, they would not have been submitted as part of a criminal case. It can take months to get a fingerprint report back on fingerprint submissions that are not tied to criminal cases. Fingerprint submissions in criminal cases can come back in one day."

The captain said, "Let me ask two questions. First of all, why should I believe you that this Cassini fellow has any connection to Adamski or my murdered cop? Secondly, how would a rapid return of Cassini's fingerprints have any impact on the case?"

Buddy replied, "I can answer both questions. First, Ray Cassini met Adamski in Yonkers back in the early 80's at the scene of a shipping accident involving a Yugoslavian freighter on the Hudson in Yonkers. A number of Yonkers Police officers were injured in the rescue efforts. At least one was seriously injured. He most likely went off the job disabled. I'm sure that if you search your own records from that era you'll find volumes of reports linking them. Both Adamski and Cassini will be in those reports. Perhaps others, who might be potential suspects in the Adamski case, or in your murdered cop case, will also turn up in those reports. Secondly, an analysis of Cassini's fingerprints would disclose that Ray Cassini and the man, known to law enforcement, as Adam Mickiewicz is one and the same person. The medical examiner will likely determine that Cassini, a.k.a. Adam Mickiewicz, died before Adamski did. That would eliminate him as a suspect in the Adamski killing!" Right now I do not know who killed Adamski, but it was not Cassini or anyone called Adam Mickiewicz!"

The captain said, "If this Cassini fellow, who is also known as Adam Mickiewicz, did not have anything to do with the Adamski" murder, why were his fingerprints in the hotel room?"

Buddy asked where the prints were found and the captain explained in detail where the glasses were found, what they looked like and how the fingerprints of Stanley Adamski and one Adam Mickiewicz were found on the glasses.

Buddy said, "Those glasses were part of a bar set that was kept in a leather case. Did you find the leather case from which the glasses were taken?"

The captain said, "No."

"Those glasses were part of a gift set that Cassini gave to Stanley more than twenty years ago. The three of us shared a drink together from that set just before Stan Adamski went back to Poland. Stan said he was going to close up the glasses in their leather case and never use them again until he returned to America. Sealed in a leather case the fingerprints could still be on the glasses from that long ago. There have been cases of fingerprints being recovered from similar conditions that were known to have been placed more than thirty years before they were recovered. Stan and Ray drank their drinks over the rocks and used the tall glasses. I drink my whiskey straight up. I joined the toast, but drank my drink from the shot glass that was in the set. If you had recovered the case and the rest of the set you might very well have found my prints on the shot glass."

Buddy went on, "Stanley Adamski had reason to believe that Adam Mickiewicz was a man who would help him to defect to the United States. That is why I believe he would be trying to contact him. There are people who could not let that happen. They misidentified Cassini as Adam Mickiewicz, because he used that name at one time. Because of that he was killed.

For much the same reason those same people want to kill me. Somehow your cop got in the middle of that. I'll do whatever I have to do to help you get

319

Cassini's killer and when you get Cassini's killer you'll get your cop killer. Check it out and I'll be in touch."

As those words were said, the phone went dead.

Captain Dent knew he had a new lead and perhaps he had a new ally in his quest for his cop killer.

A detective entered the captain's office. "Sir," he said, "The trace shows that the call was from a disposable cell phone. We triangulated the call. The call was made from the area of the Bear Mountain Bridge."

The captain said, "So we can assume that the phone is now in the Hudson River and our Mr. Kern is in the wind. Get the medical examiner on the phone."

The Report

The medical examiner acted on the captain's phone call information. He soon established a number of facts that seemed to redirect his whole investigation.

Fingerprint results established that Ray Cassini was indeed the same man who was known to law enforcement as Adam Mickiewicz. Ray Cassini's DNA did not match any of the DNA found at the crime scenes. The DNA found at the crime scenes; the garage fire, the Groton murder scene and the Bronx hotel all matched each other, but they did not match Cassini's DNA. More importantly, because Ray's death occurred in a hospital, the exact time of death was known. Ray Cassini was pronounced dead at the hospital at eleven AM. Records at F.B.I. headquarters clearly established that Stan Adamski was in headquarters at that time. Moreover, the receipt found at the hotel room established that Stan had checked into the hotel at one thirty on the afternoon of Cassini's death. It seemed clear that someone other than Cassini, a.k.a. Adam Mickiewicz, was the killer.

The medical examiner found that Cassini had died as a result of a massive overdose of Propofol, by way of what is called a Propofol push. It was the same drug cited in the death of Michael Jackson.

It is a very safe anesthetic used in surgical procedures like laparoscopic surgery. However, it is designed to be given by way of an intravenous drip, one small drip at a time. It puts the patient into a very deep sleep. There are rare occasions, during surgery, when the patient may show signs of waking up during a surgical procedure. On those rare occasions, the doctor might direct that a hypodermic needle be used to inject an extra amount of Propofol directly into the I.V. shunt. That is called a Propofol push.

Someone gave Ray a Propofol push. Whoever did, pushed a lot of Propofol, enough to kill a man twice Ray's size.

However, there was nothing in the medical charts to indicate that a Propofol push was given during the surgery. The doctor swore he never authorized a Propofol push and none of the nurses in the operating room remembered seeing it being done. The hospital pharmacy had a record of Propofol I.V. bags being supplied for the surgery, but it had no record of any of the small bottles of Propofol, that are used for a Propofol push, being used that day. Of course it would be difficult to track down all Propofol bottles without a complete inventory of all the hospitals drugs, but the medical records of the Cassini procedures were otherwise well documented. It seemed unlikely that an authorized push would not have been documented.

Ordinarily, evidence of a death by an overdose of Propofol given by way of a push would be a good indication of malpractice, but given the information from the captain combined with the other anomalies in the record, the medical examiner ruled Ray's death to be a homicide.

The medical examiner's findings firmly established for the captain that Robert Kern was a creditable and reliable source of information. The captain directed that his officers conduct a search of the department's archived records in search of a report of Yugoslavian freighter accident on the Hudson. He learned that his department had volumes of reports in the case of the Yugoslavian freighter accident all those years ago. The captain was sure that those reports would contain a valuable link to his cop killer.

Taylor and the Captain

Captain Dent called Detective Taylor and asked him to come to his office. There, he told Taylor the substance of the Kern phone call and of his most recent findings regarding the accident on the Hudson. He had reviewed the records as suggested by Kern and found the reports that disclosed the link between Adamski and Cassini. Everything in the reports was as Kern said they would be.

Taylor said, "Do you realize the implications? If Cassini is misidentified as Adam Mickiewicz in the national fingerprint files and those fingerprints are the only things that would identify Cassini as Adam Mickiewicz, then we have someone in law enforcement that is aiding and abetting our killer. Only law enforcement personnel have access to those fingerprint files. Only a law enforcement officer could have made that kind of mistake. Man, we are playing with fire here. A regular Joe Cop would have to log on to the system and identify himself to access the file. He'd know he'd be caught unless he had someone else's password. Someone higher up in the chain could more easily access the system and cover his tracks. If this is an espionage matter, we could be dealing with a very highly placed mole.

I have an idea. We need to set up a meeting with all the principles in this case. We need to have it at your headquarters, not F.B.I headquarters. You and I need to keep a few things to ourselves. Also, from now on, we only discuss what we know face to face and in private locations. If I am right about this, these people would not be above taping your phones or mine for that matter. They could even bug our offices. I would not trust my home phone, my cell phone or even the phones at headquarters.

Get a hold of Joe Duffy. Tell him we need to meet with all the principle investigators at your offices. If he balks at coming up here, just tell him you have new evidence to disclose and if they don't show up, they'll miss out on your latest findings. They'll come.

I trust Duffy. He is new to this investigation. If someone in law enforcement were involved it would be someone who has a long-term involvement in the case and that is not Joe Duffy. Nevertheless, we need to be careful around him. He will share what he learns with his investigators. He will report to his superiors what he knows and that could cause a problem. Now let's go for a walk outside and discuss what we must do."

Getting on Board

The principle investigators all crowded into a small interrogation room at Yonkers Headquarters. All the participants who had been at the last briefing were present. It was the type of room normally used to question suspects where video recording of their interviews can be made through a one-way mirror. It was a small room equipped with a small conference table, a one-way observation mirror and one telephone. The walls were stark and the furnishing simple at best, but the room was just about big enough to hold the meeting.

As the captain's aide passed out coffee to each of the participants, the captain began, "First of all I'd like to apologize for the cramped quarters, but we do not have the elaborate conference rooms that you are used to at F.B.I. Headquarters. We make do. Nevertheless, I thought it best that we meet here as we will be discussing reports that are on file here and we may need access to related reports that are also in our files. They are old paper records, quite fragile after all these years. They're too bulky to be transporting around."

To the surprise of all present, the captain announced, "Robert Kern has contacted me by phone. He is not turning himself in, but he offered information that I believe will prove to be enlightening. He has suggested where I might find a connection between Detective Taylor's victim, Stanley Adamski, and the person known to law enforcement as Adam Mickiewicz.

As you know, initially, we all thought that the man shot in front of the Buena Vista Hotel was Adam Mickiewicz, but we subsequently learned that he was in fact Robert Kern, an international assassin, businessman and an intrepid arms dealer of dubious distinction.

Kern has told me that Adam Mickiewicz is an alias that was used by a man whose real name is Raymond Cassini."

The captain informed those present of the substance of his conversation with Kern and his suggestion that they review the decades old Hudson River accident. Then the captain went on to say, "Now we have discovered that Adamski and Cassini were both present at the scene of the shipping accident on the Hudson River and that as a result of working together in an attempt to rescue someone, they became acquainted.

Kern suggested that this Mr. Cassini had also been murdered. Raymond Cassini died on the same day as Stanley Adamski. His death was classified as medical malpractice. At the suggestion of Mr. Kern the Medical Examiner took a fresh look at the case. Now the medical examiner has ruled Mr. Cassini's death to have been a homicide.

In looking at the reports of the Cassini and Adamski connection we uncovered another person of interest, a Yugoslavian national named Kirill Petrov. It seems that he too was present at the accident scene and that he conversed with both Cassini and Adamski at the hospital where the accident victims were taken after the accident. A number of the officers indicated in their reports that they were suspicious of Petrov's actions at the scene of the accident and at the hospital. One officer noted that Petrov indicated that he would be staying at the Russian diplomatic mission residence in Riverdale. Given the status of U.S. Russian relations at the time, the officer considered that to be suspicious. Lastly, our review of the records disclosed that both Adamski and Kirill Petrov both returned to Yugoslavia aboard the same vessel."

At that point Peter Cage of the C.I.A. sat up in his seat and said, "Kirill Petrov is known to us. We do not consider him to be a Yugoslavian. He is a Russian."

The captain was only little surprised that the C.I.A. Agent, Peter Cage would know something about Kirill Petrov, but he was more surprised that Cage would be so forthright about it.

The captain said, "Please enlighten us if you can."

Cage resumed, "Kirill Petrov is a man who occasionally pops up on our radar. He was born in Yugoslavia to Russian parents. As a young man, he was a low level operative in the Yugoslavian intelligence service. At one time, he served as a security officer aboard a number of Yugoslavian vessels sailing into American waters. His main job was to prevent defection by the ship's crewmembers. At the time he was suspected of doing some low level smuggling, bringing small quantities of Turkish drugs into America and returning with American products that could be sold on the black market in communist countries. It was simple stuff like blue jeans and American cigarettes. It was all small potatoes. We became aware of his activities sometime after he had left the Yugoslavian service and joined the Russian K.G.B. We had reason to believe he was a Soviet spy dealing in stolen American military secrets, but his trips to America were so infrequent that we never got a handle on exactly what he was up to here in America. His Russian handlers preferred to use him in England. He was raised in England and spoke the language perfectly, British accent and all. He became England's problem.

After the breakup of the Soviet Union, a lot of K.G.B. agents were put out of work. Kirill Petrov was one of them. At first he defected to Great Britain where he offered to inform them about Russian intelligence operations in that country. He was offered British citizenship and asylum in exchange for intelligence information.

The Brit's are our allies, but they don't tell us everything they know, so we can't say for sure what he told them, or did for them. However, we did learn from them that his main activity for the Russians was procuring military secrets. Information he gave to the Brits eventually led to the arrest of Herman Simm. He was a spy working for the Soviets, a man they called the Spaniard. He was supplying info to the Russians on British military operations. The truth is that the Spaniard had outlived his usefulness to the Russians.

He was living beyond his apparent means and was at risk of being caught anyway due to his lavish lifestyle. The Russians were getting ready to cut him loose. The Britt's could not trust that Petrov wasn't just giving them a convenient scapegoat with Russian approval. They broke off relations with Petrov, but not before issuing him a legitimate British passport.

He then used that British passport to come to New York where he opened an import and export business. He apparently has accumulated considerable wealth. We suspected that he was brokering arms deals overseas, but he abruptly stopped after 9/11. The U.S. heightened security measures after 9/11 made brokering such deals from within the U.S. a very dangerous business. We suspected that he would travel abroad to conduct his business. As far as we could tell, he was not doing any business that posed a direct threat to the United States. We let him travel unimpeded hoping his movements would lead us to learn about more serious threats to America. We occasionally keep tabs on him but we haven't seen anything yet that would warrant arresting him."

David Tees, of The National Security Agency spoke next, "At our first briefing at F.B.I. headquarters in New York regarding the discovery of the Groton Disks I informed everyone here that we've had a person known to us only as 'The Russian'. We got tons of phone conversations involving him. This Petrov guy seems like he could be 'The Russian.' If he is, he's been doing business in the Balkans for some time. We have suspected that he may be the controller of Sorge and he may be at the head of a spy ring that has been stealing American military secrets for some time. Based on what has been said here, I am sure that Petrov is Sorge's contact."

Cage returned to his briefing, "We suspect that he may be a sympathizer with a yet to be named paramilitary group that is developing in Russia, so we maintain an interest in his activities."

The captain asked, "What about this paramilitary group?" Cage replied, "There are people within the Russian military who long for the old days. They believe they can reconstitute the old U.S.S.R. You know, reestablish their potential for world dominance. They believe that their governmental leaders are too soft and are selling them down the river. They want bold action. They want to go back to places like Georgia and bomb the shit out of them. They want to regain power in the Balkans. They believe it is time for a military coup in Russia. They believe the Russian military can take over the Kremlin. With each new embarrassment for the incumbent regime, they rev up their rhetoric.

The current suggestion that American nuclear missiles might be installed in Poland is making them crazy. They recall how America reacted to missiles in Cuba. They expected their government to block the American missile installation in Poland by a show of force, the same way the Americans did when they forced the removal of Russian missiles from Cuba.

Some Russian naval personnel implied they

would go rogue and blast American ships out of the water, with or without government approval, if the Americans ever attempted to deliver the nuclear missiles to Poland.

Of course the government leaders in Russia are doing what they can to contain them, but even Russian leaders fear that military personnel could mutiny and start World War Three, or at the very least cause a civil war in Russia.

The Russian leadership is on a tightrope. They know that the best future for them is to maintain peace. They have bought themselves some time as a result of winning some diplomatic battles. Right now the U.S. has backed off from its plans to put the missiles in Poland, but you never know.

As long as the Russian economy remains in shambles, the paramilitary people have a popular appeal. If the economy in Russia recovers the paramilitary groups will lose steam, but right now they do pose a threat. Fortunately, there is only a very small group within the military and a small group of former military personnel who actually believe they can pull off a coup. For the most part, supporters are just a bunch of boastful fools. Still they cannot be ignored and we suspect that they may have sympathizers in high places in the military command staff.

Now a guy like Petrov could profit a great deal from the efforts to reestablish a communist state. He has the connections to supply weapons to the insurgents and at the present time they are acquiring weapons. Right now, they pose no threat to the free world. If they pose a threat to anyone, it is the current leadership of Russia. Still we need to watch him.

Our intelligence tells us there are highly placed persons in the Russian military that are stockpiling weapons stolen from military bases in Russia and throughout the world. They are getting ready. The official position of the Russian military is that these insurgents are enemies of the state, but a lot of Russian military personnel can sympathize with the sentiment. Little is being done to prevent the thefts and less is being done to capture the thieves. There are at most a few hundred of them, maybe a thousand. The likelihood that they could stage a successful coup is slim. It would be like the Freemen or the Ku Klux Clan taking on the entire American military force. They might have a few sympathizers within the military ranks, but even if they had a general or two on their side the likelihood of success against the entire federal machine is unimaginable. Nevertheless, they could cause quite a stir.

Right now the Russian government tolerates their presence. They do so partially because they privately agree with their sentiments, but mostly because there are more than a few sympathizers within the Kremlin who cover for them and cooperate in their operations.

Right now the Russians are in a financial down turn much worse than anything we've seen here. There is much discontent in the streets and dissidents of all types are popular.   If the incumbent government can turn things around economically the dissidents will lose favor. If the incumbents go after the dissidents right now they could make heroes of them.

Russia has agreed to disarm much of its nuclear arsenal in order to win trade agreements with the west. As the Russian military is in chaos the whole world is watching the Russian nuclear arsenal for fear that nuclear weapons might fall into the hands of radicals, but little is being done to account for conventional weapons. Many of them are being stolen both by the Russian mafia, foreigners and by disgruntled Russian military personnel.

Recently pirates in Somalia seized a Ukrainian ship that was transporting thirty-three Russian tanks, anti-aircraft missiles and massive amounts of RPG's. Some contend that the ship's crew may have been complacent in the ship's capture. It has become so bad that the Russian Army is also arming itself with stolen property. In another incident, members of the Russian mafia broke into a container being used to transport American military equipment and stole four American military Humvees that were in reroute to Georgia as part of a humanitarian relief program. They then sold them to the Russian military. The Russian military is using them right now in the field. The United States has demanded the return of our stolen property. Russia acknowledges the fact that the Humvees were stolen from us, but they refuse to return them. Try to imagine this, the Russian military is actually buying stolen equipment from the mob and deploying that equipment in the field! Dealing in stolen military property has become a way of doing business and the Russian mob is in the thick of it.

Petrov was brokering deals in the Balkans to get weapons to paramilitary groups there and for the Russian mob here. He most assuredly has the connections all over Russia and the Balkans to broker arms deals. However, as I've said we have not seen any activity since 9/11. We believe he has gone into retirement. He's just trying to live out his years in quiet solitude. If someone like Adamski had information regarding Petrov's earlier criminal activities that would surely dampen his plans. He would have a strong incentive to silence people who might know of his past indiscretions. He has a motive for murder.

He stands to profit from chaos if it should occur. Right now that is not likely, but because of his connections we watch him. Not heavy scrutiny, but we watch.

I must confess that when we learned that a Polish national connected to the Russian military was killed in New York, we looked at Petrov. He was under surveillance at the time of the Adamski killing. I can tell you he did not do it."

Taylor jumped in and asked, "Can you tell us that he did not order the killing?"

Cage replied, "No I cannot."

Duffy was furious. "You knew this and you did not tell us?"

Cage replied, "You did not ask. Remember?

You did not bring us in even when you suspected terrorism. I was not invited to the first meeting regarding the recovery of Groton Disks. If I were, I might have been able to identify Petrov as 'The Russian' on day one. As it is the NSA should have supplied their information on 'The Russian' to us in the first place. They did not. We only got in on this because the captain over there ran fingerprints that came back to Kern, a person who was of interest to us."

David Tees of the National Security Agency jumped in to defend his agencies failure to notify the C.I.A. about 'The Russian', "We have taped conversations of persons referring to the name 'The Russian', but those conversations initiate from within the United States to persons overseas. You at the C.I.A. are not permitted to use the conversations of persons from within the United States to investigate American citizens. We send you all relevant portions of the half of the conversations spoken by the foreign nationals from within the foreign nation, but not the words spoken by the people in America."

Cage glanced around the room to see if any of the other attendees were astounded by what Tees had just said. In effect the C.I.A. is given half of the recorded conversations. The words spoken into the phone overseas are given to them, but the words spoken, in the same conversation, into the phone on the American side of the call are not. Cage knew this was NSA policy. He just wondered if anyone else in the room knew. The looks on the faces of the participants indicated that they did not.

Cage shook his head, made a parenthetical statement under his breath, "We wonder why terrorists get away with murder." Then he continued his earlier discussion. "If we did not have Kern's fingerprints flagged we would still be out in the cold on this!" Cage then turned to the captain and said, "Captain you are to be commended. You linked these three people in a way that we would never have suspected. I must confess we never knew that Adamski had ever been an associate of Petrov or that either of them ever knew this Cassini fellow who called himself Adam Mickiewicz. That name was never known to us as either Kern or as Cassini. We simply never heard of the name and I cannot tell you why either Kern or Cassini would have used that name. Now that we know, that they did, I can only assume that it was some sort of cover name for some sort of nefarious plot. However, I still can't tell you what it all means."

Rookie F.B.I. Agent Michelle Thompson listened intently and began to formulate a theory of the crime in her mind. She was a little reluctant to speak at this time. Like Taylor and the captain, she and Tom Bradner had also concluded that someone in law enforcement, who was close to the case, was a mole. Unlike Taylor and the captain they had a suspect. Neither she nor Tom could reconcile why Frank Dwarman, the F.B.I. SAC of the New Haven Office would withhold information that was vital to the investigation. Yet clearly he had. Worse still he had indicated that the Groton police were not cooperative in the initial investigation, but the records at Groton and the delivery of the hair to a crime lab indicated otherwise.

A rookie agent cannot simply march into work and accuse an S.A.C. of espionage without proof. Tom and Michelle agreed that they would discuss their concerns with Taylor and map out a strategy to confront their suspicions. Michelle wished they had done so before this meeting. She was not sure what to do, but a meeting of all the principles did not seem like the type of meeting that would occur often enough and Michelle thought she ought to get her idea out on the table for discussion.

Michelle Thompson began to speak, "I have a thought on the matter. It's just a crazy theory, but here goes. Suppose this Petrov guy somehow gained influence over an American traitor back when he was still a low level smuggler, and he got possession of the Groton Disks. Now, we've known from the beginning that the disks would be of no value to anyone who could not interpret them or utilize them. The thief would need a computer expert and a nautical engineer. Petrov needed a ship's engineer or a computer expert to make use of the disks. Adamski was both a nautical engineer and a computer expert. By sheer coincidence, one day they end up on the same ship. Petrov shows the disks to Adamski and asks him to interpret them. They team up and take their findings to Russia. Petrov becomes the spy who can steal American and British naval secrets and

Adamski is the guy who can make use of those stolen secrets to design better submarines for the Russians.

In time they go their separate ways. Petrov becomes a spy, thief, weapons broker and who knows what else.

Adamski becomes a famous submarine designer, using stolen American ingenuity to make a name for himself.

Eventually the U.S.S.R. disbands and both Petrov and Adamski lose their jobs in Russia. Adamski goes back to Poland and to designing commercial ships. Petrov goes who knows where and becomes an arms dealer.

As an arms dealer, Petrov begins to supply arms to communist resurgents in Russia. These communist resurgents are amassing weapons. If pirates in Somalia could acquire thirty-three Russian tanks stolen from the Russians, imagine how many tanks members of the Russian military could steal and squirrel away within Russia, especially if people in the command staff are co-conspirators planning a coup. Imagine the stash of weapons they could have.

You say that there are not a significant number of people in the group, but even so, there could be a few hundred, perhaps a thousand. No?

What I am about to say may seem absurd, but a few days ago if someone told me that our government suspected that a guy like Kern, a rogue former member of the National Guard, had a cache of stolen Stinger missiles and that we were not turning over every stone on the planet to prove or disprove the accusation, I would have said that is absurd. Yet we all sit in this room and accept that as a possibility. We accept it and do nothing about it as if it was some kind of semi-benign misdemeanor. Something we've hardly investigated. Why? Because we believe that if Kern does have them, he'd only use them against our enemies and in a little corner of our minds we think - Bravo!

You've already said that these resurgent, communist, nuts have some allies in high places in the Russian military. You have also said that some have threatened to carry out attacks against American shipping into Poland even if they do not get governmental leadership approval.

What if the zealots have a stolen submarine? What if they have stolen a kilo class submarine like the ones that Stanislaus Adamski designed? What if after stealing the submarine, they encounter some sort of engineering problem that renders the sub useless to them. I don't know; perhaps there is a broken part or computer malfunction or a password that needs to be hacked through or some such thing. They'd put the word out they need a 'naval computer engineer kind of guy.'

Petrov, in his dealings with these Russian communist zealots, learns they have a submarine, but for some reason they can't use it. They need an engineer who is familiar with their stolen sub in order to utilize it. Petrov offers to get them one for some sizable sum of money. They agree to pay. He in turn goes to his old pal Stan. I mean, why not? Adamski was trusted in the past. They were partners in crime before. So he tells Adamski about his situation. Perhaps he offers a large sum of money for his assistance.

However, there is something Petrov did not count on. Stan is a Pole and Poland is now an American ally. When Poland and Russia were hand-in-hand, it would have been no crime in Poland to assist the Russians so Adamski goes along. Now, to do the same, he would be a traitor. Moreover, when Mr. Adamski spoke to me, it seemed to me that he did not like Russians. He said something to the effect of his Russian bosses looking down on Poles. He was angry about that.

Let's say Stan wants to do his part for the Polish homeland and he wants to stick his finger in the Russian's eye. He can't know who to trust in Poland. Surely they too must have at least some communist zealots there. Instead he comes to America and goes right to F.B.I. headquarters and Petrov finds out about it. It doesn't take a genius to figure out what Stan is going to tell. Petrov knows Stan has got to be silenced."

Deputy Commander Johnson of U.S. Naval Command then leaned forward in his seat and looked in the direction of C.I.A. agent Cage and took over the discussion.

He said "Hey! Cage, what did you say about the missing Stingers? 'You know how it is in war. Equipment gets used up, it gets destroyed in the field, and it gets lost.' Can't the same be said of a submarine?

You mentioned the idea that the zealots in the Russian Navy would destroy an American ship even without governmental leadership approval. I can tell you that a handful of zealots would have serious difficulty pulling that off. If they simply happened to be aboard a battleship or a destroyer, they could not do it. First, their ship would have to just happen to be in the same area of the sea where the American ship was. Next, they would have to have the compliance of the whole crew to get the ship into position to attack the American ship. Finally, they would have to have the cooperation of the gun crew to take the shot. Then they would need the cooperation of the command staff to get away while fighting off the American escort battle group that would accompany such a shipment. They'd need a small flotilla of ships, with multiple crews, working as a battle group, all agreeing to commit treason.

They would have to employ so many people in their conspiracy that the authorities would surely learn of the plot. Further, unless you could employ several ships in a coordinated attack your chances of success are zero.

With a submarine it's a whole different story. A kilo class sub is a lone wolf. It attacks alone. It can carry more than 100 Torpedoes. It can carry 8 guided missiles, 24 mines, and best of all, it can travel underwater! It is a formidable weapon and it can be operated stealthily with as few as 40 crewmembers, if necessary even fewer crewmembers.... A sub can operate with a small crew. A smaller contingent of mutineers could take the boat. If they have a confederate in a high level of the command staff he could ensure that no effort is made to find the sub when it goes missing. *AND* yes, they'd need someone with ship's engineering background to make use of the sub.

The entire weapons and navigation systems are computer-controlled. Every submarine carries a chief engineer on board. If the chief was not part of the mutiny an assistant engineer might be able to perform the duties, but he'd likely need access to the ship's manuals and he'd need to break password protocols. Even if the ship's engineer were part of the plot there would be a problem. Each time a kilo class submarine in the Russian fleet goes on a mission a series of mission specific passwords are set into the onboard computers at the home port by personnel at central command. Different members of the crew are entrusted with different portions of the passwords; usually it's the captain, first mate and another high member of the boat's crew. Each must input his own specific password to engage the weapons system. If any one of them were not part of the plot, the mutineers would not have all of the password components needed to engage the system.

Also the passwords will expire. If the mission is expected to last thirty days, the passwords might be valid for something like thirty-two days. After which they expire and the weapons systems cannot be engaged. If for some valid reason, the mission has to be extended, they must surface and communicate with a Russian satellite to download an updated extension of the valid time period for the passwords or obtain new ones. They'd need someone at the satellite control center to update the passwords. If they do not have a trusted confederate there, their sub becomes somewhat useless. They'd need to get the design engineer to by-pass the password protocols.

If the zealots have just one person in a high command position back at Russian Central Military Headquarters, they could easily arrange for forty or fifty like-minded people to be assigned to the same submarine. Even if they could not gather forty or fifty, they could assign enough likeminded persons to a single sub to stage a successful mutiny and theft of the boat. If the command headquarters believes the sub is on a secret mission underwater and does not return to port, most likely the command staff will assume the boat sank. The last thing they would think of is that it had been stolen.

If our zealot is in a command position he can make sure that no one looks for the stolen sub when it goes missing. Someone who can report it destroyed at sea, or some such thing. Could they hide their stolen sub until they are ready to use it? You bet your ass they can, especially if no one is looking for it."

A submarine would be the best way to take out ships delivering nuclear missile equipment to Poland. You'd only need to take out the cargo vessels then run like hell. You would not even have to engage the escort group. Even if the escort group reacted to the attack after the fact you'd have a good chance at getting away and maybe you could even take out some of that escort group as a bonus.

Think about this. If an Iranian or a North Korean submarine came within firing range of an American battle group, our sonar would identify it as such, we'd consider it hostile action and we would blow them out of the water without hesitation. They know it. They do not screw with us at sea.

However, we are not so cavalier when it comes to subs that we identify as being Russian. We taunt each other with close encounters and such activity all the time. You know what we do when a Russian sub comes within range? We send a harshly worded letter to the Kremlin and complain. A submarine whose acoustical signature that is listed in our catalogs as being Russian could get very close and an attack would be a genuine surprise. They'd have a good chance of pulling it off and they know it. If we were already engaged in a major conflict with Russia right now, it would be a different story, but we would be most certainly caught by surprise if a Russian sub took a shot at us today.

Furthermore, if they were successful in their attack and they were subsequently sunk by our responding escort group, we would blame the incumbent government officials. These communist zealots would benefit from having the present day Russian leaders in a war with us. I think we should listen to this young lady."

Michelle resumed her talk, "If we look at the

facts that are known to us, we can see that Adamski had in his possession, the Groton Disks. We now know that the Groton Disks disappeared right around the time of this Hudson River accident when Petrov was in America engaged in some sort of small potatoes smuggling scheme. We also know that both Adamski and Petrov went home to the motherland aboard the same vessel. Finally, we know that both Petrov and Adamski shortly thereafter went off to Russia and both enjoyed the benefits of being held in high regard in the U.S.S.R. I'm telling you Petrov and Adamski were partners in a scheme to steal American naval secrets and they had a falling out. That is why Adamski came back to America, to tell us that Russian communist zealots have a submarine and that they intend to use it against us. That is why he was killed."

Thomas Trulane from the United States Immigration spoke next, "That's a very interesting theory, but it tells nothing about the case at hand except for a possible motive that this Petrov guy might have. Cage has already told us that Petrov is not the killer and your theory can't tell us who the killer might be. I think we need to focus on Kern. We know he is a killer. He has killed people all over the world. He had two guns with him in the hotel. Why all the fire power if he wasn't there to kill somebody? Why does a rich man like Kern stay in a fleabag hotel?

He pulled a gun on Agent Chapson. If the agent did not react quickly, it is likely that he too would be dead right now. Kern has killed people all over the world who have been allies of the Russians. Petrov is a Russian. Adamski worked for the Russian. Kern hates Russians. What better way to have some revenge against Russians than to kill one of their top naval engineers and place the suspicion on a KGB agent?

As for this Cassini guy, he has a criminal record for assault and he has been a fugitive from justice. He was apparently so adept at his little criminal enterprise that he managed to fool the Boston police into booking him under the name Adam Mickiewicz. The guy gets locked up and he has ready-made phony ID with him? What's that about? Then for twenty years he disappears off the planet until Kern identifies him for us. How convenient.

Our borders are at risk from intrusion by radicals who could sneak a nuclear device into any one of our ports at any time. Our biggest fear is that one of the thousands of shipping containers that are moved on to our shores un-inspected might hold a thermonuclear device that could wipe out a city. What does Kern do for a living? Oh yeah! He moves shipping containers in and out of ports all over the world.

The man is a menace. He poses a threat to world security no less than the Russian radicals do. He's an unlawful weapons dealer. So is Petrov. They could be in business together. This Adamski guy was also connected to the shipping business. Perhaps he was going to tell us about weapons of mass destruction that were loaded onto a ship bound for our shores. Weapons dealers have no patriotism. They sell to the highest bidder. We are all fooling ourselves if we allow ourselves to believe Kern is a friend to America and an enemy to our adversaries. Who knows what weaponry they may have already smuggled into this country. I'm telling you. If we get Kern, we'll get Petrov and all their cronies. We need to bring him in!"

Joe Duffy spoke next, "I must say that I believe the most disturbing possibility seems to me to be that Ms. Thompson could be correct. Deputy Commander Johnson is one of this nation's foremost authorities on world navies. He seems to think it is at least within the realm of possibility and that scares me. What do we do about that threat?"

Cage answered, "Actually that may not be that difficult a problem. What I find ironic is that the last time there was a similar incident, that is, one involving the placement of nuclear missiles in Cuba, most of the issues were resolved here in Yonkers. Few people know this, but when the Cuban missile crisis was a hot item, the two nations, Russia and America, both wanted a diplomatic resolution to the matter. However, none of the high level State Department personnel in either Russia or the U.S. wanted any face to face negotiations to take place unless they knew in advance what the other party would say at such a meeting. Behind the scenes they agreed that a low level C.I.A. agent and a low level

K.G.B. agent would each act as messenger boys and meet so that one could tell what their respective State Department people might agree to. That way if there was no meeting of the minds, there could be no suggestion that a policy maker backed out of some sort of agreement. They could simply say that the low level agents were not authorized to speak on behalf of the principals. Those low level agents held their clandestine meeting at Graystone Station here in Yonkers.

If we go through diplomatic channels and tell the Russians about our theory, they will act accordingly. They certainly know if a submarine has recently gone missing. They just may not know why. If they are smart, they will start looking for it right away. We have to tell them that in the interim any close encounters by one of their sub will be regarded as an immediate threat and we will attack any subs that come within firing range of any of our vessels. They know that we can identify their individual subs by their acoustical signature. If they are smart, their legitimate subs will steer clear of us until they can assure us the rogue sub is no longer a threat. If they are even smarter they will leak to us the identity of the errant sub and let us help find it. I think we need not be over concerned about that. I'm sure our state department can handle it, and if they cannot Deputy Commander Johnson's people can." Johnson just smiled and nodded.

A lively discussion followed, but little more was resolved. At the end of the day all the participants agreed that the meeting was useful and the attendees left the interrogation room. Only Taylor and Captain Dent remained.

After all of the other attendees had left the building Taylor said to the captain, "That went rather well."

The captain replied, "Yes it did. It did indeed. I must say you had a great idea, suggesting that we hold this meeting here. We learned a great deal about this Petrov guy, we may have set in motion a plan to rid the seas of a rogue Russian submarine and best of all they all drank the coffee."

Thomas Trulane - The ICE Man
United States Immigration and Customs
Enforcement

Thomas Trulane was determined to refocus the investigation on the search for Robert Kern who, like Ray Cassini, was also known as Adam Mickiewicz. At the previous meeting with the other law enforcement agencies, he tried to convey his sense of urgency at securing the nation's borders. He told them, "I could not care less if some stupid group of communists are looking to take back Russia with one submarine. I'm sure our State Department and the Kremlin will neutralize that threat. If not, our Navy will. Leave the military affairs to the military.

We represent law enforcement. We are responsible for the protection of the American people here at home. We need to focus on the threat to the homeland. The greatest single threat to our homeland is the constant flow of shipping containers that come into our ports by the thousands every day. We do not have adequate staff to examine them. We are stopping ships on the high seas to intercept containers before they get to our ports, but we actually examine less than five percent of those containers.

Everyone is on some wild goose chase, but Kern holds the key. Even if he did not kill Adamski himself, he's deeply involved in this thing. He is diverting attention from himself and causing us to focus on the Cassini murder. For all we know, Kern could have killed Cassini. Also I am shocked to find that none of you seem to be the least bit disturbed by the suggestion that Kern could have stolen Stinger missile equipment in his possession.

Using his shipping facilities, he could easily have smuggled these weapons of mass destruction into this country. He could sell the stuff to Al-Qaeda. We are trying to stop our enemies from bringing weapons into our country at the borders. The weapons they need may already be within our borders, sitting in one of the Kern warehouses, hidden in a shipping container, just waiting for a buyer. An arms dealer has no loyalties to any one nation. A man who will deal with terrorists attacking our enemies will deal with terrorists attacking us."

Trulane would search for Kern, if he had to do it all by himself.

Kern may have been an elusive person in that, outside the C.I.A., few had any idea that he was an international arms dealer and soldier of fortune. However, in the shipping industry, he was a well-known entrepreneur, import and export businessman and owner of numerous waterfront warehouses. He could usually be found directing the movement of a multitude of his numerous shipping containers through the nation's many ports of entry. His presence in and around the nation's docks was well established. He was someone who would be known to customs agents. He would be given free access to the ports and would be very comfortable in that environment. Trulane was sure that Kern would be hiding in plain sight somewhere in the area of New

York harbor.

Trulane saw to it that customs officers were advised that Kern was believed to be in possession of weapons of mass destruction. They were advised to consider Kern to be armed and dangerous. Thomas Trulane, from the United States Immigration and Customs, put out the word to his men that he wanted Kern located. In no time, he was advised that Kern had been seen at one of New York's Hudson River pier warehouse.

The information that Trulane had received about Kern being at one of his warehouses was correct. Buddy had spent a few days at Terri's home, but her constant presence at his side presented temptations that Buddy knew he could not resist for long. As soon as he felt strong enough, he left her home promising to return once he could reconcile Ray's untimely death. More than any other promise that he had ever made in his life, this was the promise he wanted to keep. He wanted to enjoy a simple life. He wanted redemption. A simple life with the woman he loved was all Buddy wanted now. But first he had to deal with the fact that he was a wanted man. He was sure that the federal authorities would have a warrant charging him with escape. They also likely were drafting charges related to his encounter with Agent Chapson. Kern knew that the encounter required him to drop his weapon. He held no animosity toward Chapson for having shot him. The man did what he was trained to do. Still he hoped that Chapson would come to realize that Kern never posed any real threat to the agent. He was merely trying to respond to the aid of the police officer that was shot. He hoped that if he could help the authorities, the escape charge and any charges related to failing to drop his gun when ordered to do so would be dropped. He did not know that Agent Trulane, and perhaps others, considered him to be a potential terrorist.

One of Buddy's New York riverfront warehouses had a small office set up as living quarters. That is where Buddy would stay. From there he would do as much research as possible to see who might be linked to the case. Whenever he could, he'd slip out of his den at the docks, go to the New York Public Library and pour through archived newspapers to look at any stories that might give some additional insight into the Hudson River accident and its aftermath. At night he'd return to his little room in the warehouse. Little did he know that he had been seen; that he was in extreme danger.

Trulane was on his way to capture or kill Robert Kern.

Best of All They All Drank the Coffee

The captain picked up the phone and placed a call to the director of his forensic lab. The director, who was waiting for the call, answered.

The captain simply said, "They all drank the coffee. Send the evidence collection team up to retrieve the cups."

As per Taylor's plan, each participant at the meeting was handed a cup of coffee as he or she entered the room before they sat down. Each, therefore, had to take the cup in his or her hand as they went to their seats. This meant that each would leave fingerprints on the cups. Then as each drank the coffee, they would be placing DNA samples from their saliva upon the cups. The cups would then serve as a link between that person's fingerprints and his or her DNA. The cups had been especially selected by the lab personnel so as to be of a material that was well suited for the collection process. They were subjected to Laser Light analysis before they were place in the room to ensure that no fingerprints or DNA material was on them before they were introduced to the room. A brand new, clean garbage can was placed near the door so that it would provide a non-contaminated receptacle for the collection of the cups. The aide to the captain, who had passed out the coffee at the start of the meeting, was positioned by the door. At the end of the meeting, as the participants left the room, they found that a garbage can was conveniently placed at the door to receive their used cups. If any participant in the meeting attempted to leave with his or her cup, the aide would simply say, "Please let me take that for you," and he would toss the empty cup into the can.

Now DNA tests would take place. If any of the cups held DNA that matched the DNA from the Groton murder hair samples, the hotel glass and the underwear found at the garage fire, that cup would be examined for fingerprints. Only two sets of prints would be on each cup, the prints of the aide, who handed out the cups and the person who drank the coffee.

Once the aide's prints were eliminated the remaining fingerprints could be used to identify the person who drank the coffee from a particular cup. Any DNA on that cup would belong to the person whose prints were on it. The videotape equipment that was standard equipment in any interrogation room was on to record the action of the participants in the meeting. The tape could be used to show that no one switched cups or drank from any other person's cup. There were elaborate back-up plans for anyone who decided not to have coffee, but none of that was necessary. Everyone had taken a cup in his or her hand as it was handed to him or her. Everyone drank the coffee and everyone's cup was deposited in the clean garbage can. If the killer was one of the law enforcement officers at that meeting, the DNA on the cup would match the crime scene DNA and the fingerprints would tell Taylor and the captain who put that DNA on the cup.

At the Sick Bay

Agent Michelle Thompson decided to follow up on the Cassini murder angle. Cassini's death was not classified as a federal offenSe, but if his death had any connection to the Adamski case, she was determined to find out what it was. Michelle told Assistant Director Joe Duffy she intended to go to the hospital where Cassini died to review the medical records. Although he doubted she would find anything significant, he allowed her to follow her instincts. However, he gave her specific instructions to call and advise him, at once, if she found anything of value to the investigation.

Upon arrival at the hospital, Michelle spoke to the recovery room head nurse, Jill Sampson.

"I keep my own copies of medical records on procedures that have come through my recovery room that go awry," Nurse Simpson said, "After that young man died, I made sure I'd have accurate copies of the medical records. You never know when you might be called to testify in a malpractice case. If those incompetent bastards downstairs lose a file, you could be up shit's creek. I would not put it above the administration to lose an important file then try to put the blame on some nurse, if you know what I mean. That's never going to happen to me. No sir. I keep my own copies and I review them thoroughly."

Nurse Simpson assured Michelle that her records would be very thorough. Then she said, "I can let you read my copies. I pride myself on maintaining most accurate records. Everything that happens here is recorded."

Michelle thanked the nurse and accepted her copies of the medical records. As Michelle scanned through the files, she would occasionally ask the nurse to explain notations that had been penned in the margins alongside the text of the reports. The head nurse explained that she annotated the reports with comments in the margins; her own form of shorthand to note items that might not appear in the standard reporting format. It was a little habit that helped her remember details of events that took place in the recovery room during her watch.

At one point there was a notation indicating that Mr. Cassini's intravenous shunt had been flushed with saline. There was an added note penned in the margin – IV flush- Dr. IA/js.

The agent asked to what did this note refer.

Jill smiled and replied, "I told you I keep impeccable notes." She went on to explain, "When a patient is receiving an IV, fluid is introduced through a shunt placed in a vein. Occasionally, the shunt becomes blocked by a small amount of coagulated blood and the IV fluid stops dripping. When that happens the IV must be flushed and restarted. The shunt is left in the vein, the IV line is removed from the shunt and a syringe is attached in its place. A small amount of water is forced through the shunt using the hypodermic and the blockage is washed away. Then the IV line can be reconnected to the shunt and it will flow again. It is a simple procedure.

358

It's done all the time. It is something that should be duly noted in the record, often it is not. However, like I say, I keep impeccable records."

Michelle said, "Yes I understand that, but what does the note in the margin mean?" Jill responded, "Well, you know how doctors can be. Sometimes when they perform a simple procedure they don't think it necessary to make a record of every little thing they do. A little thing like an IV flush, ... Well sometimes they don't note those things. So I just wrote it in for him."

The agent asked, "The doctor did the IV flush? Isn't that something that is usually left to the nurses?"

Jill replied, "Well, yes, but I guess the doctor was standing near-by, observed the IV not running properly and just decided it would be easier to just flush it himself rather than wait to get a nurse. Anyway, I saw Dr. Anissina flushing the IV with saline and I saw that he failed to record it. So, I recorded it for him after he left."

Michelle reiterated the nurse's statement, "You saw him inject the saline into the shunt in Mr. Cassini's hand?"

"Yes."

Michelle asked, "Are you sure it was saline in the hypodermic?"

Jill shrugged her shoulders and said, "What else would it be? Dr. Anissina would not have been administrating any drugs. Mr. Cassini was not his patient. He just saw the IV was blocked and decided to help out."

"This Dr. Anissina was not supposed to be attending Mr. Cassini?"

Nurse Simpson replied, "No, he was not the doctor of record. We were very busy and he was just helping out."

"Isn't it a little unusual for a doctor to render aid to someone who is not his patient?"

Nurse Simpson replied, "Well, I suppose so, but it happens."

Michelle said, "I need to speak to this Dr. Anissina. Where can I find him?"

"I don't know where you could contact him now. He is not on staff here. He has privileges here, but he is not on staff. He travels a great deal. I don't know where you could find him now."

By now Michelle was getting frustrated and in a huff she asked, "Well, where are his offices!"

Jill smirked and said, "He does not have regular offices that are open to the public. He is the on-staff physician to the Russian Diplomatic Corps. He only treats embassy staff and visiting VIP from Russia. He travels all over the continent. His territory covers all of North America. He is also a licensed pilot. He flies himself to wherever he is called. He could be anywhere in North America where the Russians have an embassy or an official residence. I believe he said something about going on assignment to Mexico."

Michelle was dumbfounded. She simply stared at Jill and tried to digest the implications.

After a few moments, she called Tom Bradner's cell phone. "Tom, you not going to believe this. Ray Cassini was killed by a doctor employed by the Russian government!" She went on to tell Tom what she learned from her review of the records and her discussion with the nurse."

Tom asked, "What is this doctor's name?"

Michelle answered, "Doctor Ivan Anissina."

Tom shot back, "Doctor Ivan Anissina! Michelle, he is the doctor whose garage was burned down with the police car in it! He is the owner of the stolen white suburban! Son of a bitch! The doctor gave the cop killer a car to use. The killer would feel safe using the suburban knowing that it would not be reported stolen until after it was used in the crime. The doctor could go off to Mexico and establish an alibi. He could come home long after the culprit had escaped and report the vehicle stolen after it was too late for the cops to find the car the with thief in it. What they did not count on was the fact that the killer would be videotaped by the police dashboard camera. When the killer needed tools and a place to stash the police car, the doctor's house was the perfect spot. The doctor was still in Mexico. His alibi was still good. Who would think he was a participant. If Kern never got in the middle of this no one would have tied Cassini's death and the cop's death. It was perfect until Kern got in the mix."

Michelle asked, "What should I do?"

Tom replied, "Grab the records and get out of there!"

She said, "But I don't have a court order to seize the records."

Tom shouted. "Screw the court order. If you leave there without those records, we run the risk that someone will learn about them and they'll get destroyed. We can call it exigent circumstances if we must. Just take them, by force if necessary, but take them. Don't even tell anyone what you're going to do. Just grab them and go. Tell that nurse not to tell anyone about her notes. If she does her life will be in danger. Don't let anyone stop you. Most of all do not tell anyone else about this yet!"

"Okay, but Joe Duffy said I should tell him as soon as I know something, but I'm afraid to do that. I trust Duffy, but he will tell Dwarman. Tommy, I can't get my arms around it, but there is something in Dwarman's lack of candor, the fact that he is leaving out essential facts at the briefings. Tommy, I don't trust him, but I don't think I can tell Duffy that an S.A.C. is not trustworthy. I'm just a rookie and I'd be accusing a senior staff member without any evidence. We all are starting to look for a law enforcement mole in this thing and Dwarman is my favorite candidate. If I make this F.B.I. general info, they'll all get it."

Tom counseled Michelle, "Okay, Taylor says we can trust Duffy. I think we can too, but grab the records first. When you get outside hit him from your cell phone. Tell him you have something about the Cassini killing you can't discuss on the phone. Remind him that we have all acknowledged there is a law enforcement mole. Tell him you need to meet face to face with him. Delay the meeting as much as possible. Then go straight home. I'll try to get Taylor and we'll all go to Duffy's office together."

About an hour later, Michelle called Tom back. "I'm home now. Duffy agreed that it was best not to discuss any aspect of the case over the phone. He never even asked for any the details. He agreed it would be best to meet face to face and avoid any phone talk about the case. I told him I'd like to meet privately with just him, you, Taylor and myself. I also told him Captain Dent should be invited. Much to my surprise, Duffy said that the captain had just contacted him and they had arranged to meet in Yonkers tomorrow morning. Duffy said he'd call the captain back and let him know we'd all be coming to the morning meeting, just the five of us."

Tom said, "Great, I'll call Taylor. I think we should get together tonight. You, Taylor and I can make sure we have all our ducks in a row."

Michelle said, "Okay. Duffy suggested that we meet at my apartment in the morning and that we can all go to Yonkers together. That way I can fill him in before we meet with Captain Dent. Right now he does not have a clue as to what I've discovered."

"Okay, Taylor and I will come over to your place this evening about eight."

Michelle said "See you then," and hung up the phone.

Michelle sat down on her couch and breathe a sigh of relief. She thought to herself, tomorrow we will see if we have enough to arrest the doctor. This is shaping up. Giving a car to someone who would use it to commit a felony is, at the very least the crime of Criminal Facilitation. In this case, perhaps even Conspiracy to Commit Murder. A murdered cop ... Michelle felt her career was on a roll. There would be no more mundane follow up assignments for her. This case was going to get her noticed.

As she sat alone in her apartment, she got up off her couch, she looked into a mirror that hung on her living room wall and spoke out loud to herself. "Michelle you're looking good. Why don't you whip yourself up a little something to eat, shower and get dressed? Dress nicely Michelle. This may be a business meeting, but a girl's got to look good for company, especially if the company is going to include Tom Bradner."

Petrov Charts a Course

Kirill Petrov and the man who called himself the Maestro planned to meet face to face. They each took special precautions to make sure that they were not being followed and met, as they often did on Wednesday afternoons, at The Bronx Zoo. Wednesday is free day at the zoo. No admission charge. The zoo will gladly accept a donation of any amount on Wednesdays for admission, but essentially it's a free day.

The zoo is always crowded on Wednesdays. Schools, day camps and social organizations all take advantage of the free admission. Petrov enjoyed the anonymity that Wednesday's crowds provided. Petrov and The Maestro strolled together along the winding, narrow asphalt walkways. They would stop occasionally to admire some of nature's most beautiful and interesting creatures and they would talk. The Maestro filled Krill in on all that had transpired at the law enforcement meetings.

The Maestro spoke first, "I'm afraid that the young lady has figured out much of our plan. She offered a superlative hypothesis regarding the possibility that there has been the theft of a submarine. The people at the meeting seemed to embrace the idea and unfortunately it will lead to an investigation along those lines. Our state department people have suggested that they will inform the Kremlin. However, while they may be establishing a motive for the untimely death of Mr. Adamski, at the present time they do not have a suspect, although I must say your name has surfaced."

Kirill replied, "Yes, that is most unfortunate. I think that I am well enough insulated. They will never find the kind of evidence that would be required by the American system to arrest me. However, I too have bad news of a different sort. From my tap on Agent Thompson's cell phone, I have learned that she is now aware of Doctor Anissina's role in our little enterprise. I am confident that she has not yet reported her findings to her superiors, but I suspect she will do so in the morning.

It seems a certain nurse Simpson made a notation in her medical record that she observed the good doctor giving our Mr. Cassini an injection through his IV. It could be a problem for him."

The Maestro replied, "I'm sorry I chose him for that assignment but ..."

Kirill Petrov interrupted. "No, no do not blame yourself. He was the right man for the job. Our target was in the hospital and the doctor had access. It seemed like a logical choice at the time. He has been so helpful in the past. He is very capable. You picked a capable man for the job. You know, he attended to both Alexander Litvinenko and Viktor Yushchenko for us. He took care of many other less notable patients as well. He's a very capable man indeed. At the time using him seemed like the right thing to do.

I have no fear that the American authorities will ever get him. Even if they can establish his guilt, as a member of the diplomatic staff, he enjoys full diplomatic immunity. He cannot be arrested by American authorities or by the authorities of any other nation with whom Russia has diplomatic relations. I still have enough influence at home to insure that his immunity will not be withdrawn and I can have him transferred to a comfortable post elsewhere. He will be safe from arrest. Still I would much prefer to keep his name out of this. If he is identified, that could lead to other revelations and danger lurks in such revelations.

I do not want to lose him. If I can dispose of that medical record and those who know of its contents, he would be better. We all would be safer. I may be able to keep him here where he can continue to work for me. He is a very valuable asset. He can render medical aid to our friends who get injured on assignment and he can assist with the removal of problems.

I have spoken to the doctor. He assures me that none of the remaining official medical records still on file at the hospital make any reference to his presence at Mr. Cassini's side. There is only a note in the margin of one copy of those records that indicates he gave the injection. That is in the copy of the notes that nurse Simpson maintained and that Agent Thompson now has in her possession. I gather from her phone conversation that only the nurse, Thompson, and her lover, Officer Thomas Bradner, are aware of the notation."

The Maestro asked, "Her lover?"

"Yes the listening device I placed in her bedroom strongly suggests that Officer Bradner and Agent Thompson have enjoyed each other's company in matters that extend beyond the scope of their employment.

Anyway, by now I assume that Bradner would have confided in Taylor. From what I gather they have agreed not to disclose what they have learned until a meeting that will take place in the morning. At the present time only Thompson, Bradner, Taylor and Nurse Simpson herself know of the contents of her notes. Thompson has secured the medical record at her home and she admonished Simpson to tell no one. We have an opportunity to eliminate this small complication.

Thompson has invited Taylor and Bradner to come to her home at eight this evening. Do you think you could get into her home and eliminate her by, let us say, six-thirty, find the file, then set a trap to get Taylor and Bradner when they arrive at eight?"

The Maestro said, "I most assuredly could, but that still leaves Simpson. She could still tell someone."

Kirill continued, "Yes, but I can attend to her. I can make it look like an accident.

We need to time this properly. If we eliminate Simpson first and are unsuccessful in eliminating the others, we make our situation worse. They would know for sure that she was murdered and they would know why. Additionally, they would still have her records.

If we kill Thompson, Bradner and Taylor first and get the records, we can kill Simpson and no one will know why Nurse Simpson died or what she knew. Doctor Anissina will be Okay.

Make an excuse. Get in to see Thompson and do what you must. Kill her and get the file.

When Bradner and Taylor arrive they will not know they are walking into an ambush. The element of surprise will be your ally."

The Maestro said, "Piece of cake."

Kirill continued, "I'll be stationed near Nurse Simpson's home. Call my cell phone as soon as you have completed your task. Then I shall attend to the good nurse. If I do not hear from you by eight forty-five, I will assume you were unable to complete your assignment. I will vacate the area and arrange to put Dr. Anissina beyond the reach of the American authorities.

I suppose I should get word to the submarine crew. They should abandon the boat where it can be quickly found. We would not want a protracted search. The authorities might find other items in our possession if they continue to search our shores. I have spoken to the admiral and we have arranged a new strategy. It seems that our so-called leaders in Russia have invited the Polish president and members of his cabinet to fly to Russia for a ceremony. They do this while Poland conspires with America against Russian interests. Those fools! They have no pride. At the ceremony the Russia will apologize for having killed some Polish officers who were held captive in the Kaytn Forrest in 1940. Our leaders want to admit it was a war crime to win favor from the west! Again Russia will be on its knees begging forgiveness. I can assure you there will be no such ceremony. The admiral and I have arranged for there to be an accident. Those Polish airplanes are so old and our Russian air-traffic controllers are sometimes incompetent. I'm afraid the Polish President and his cabinet will not survive the trip. We have our people in position in Poland to take their place. Our people in the Russian military will investigate the crash and there will be a finding of pilot error. The new Polish cabinet will agree to the findings. There will be a new regime in Poland. This may be better than our original plan. After all if the diplomatic efforts prevent the installation of the American weapons on Polish soil there would be no catalyst to bring about our attack at this time. An attack can wait. With the removal of the current president and his cabinet a quiet political revolution is better. A new policy will emerge; Poland will soon be an ally of Russia again."

Kirill thought he was done, but he asked. "Now tell me. Are there any other loose ends?"

The Maestro said, "I'm afraid there is. Now that the Cassini matter has become a murder investigation I am concerned about his wife. She saw me. She knows I had contact with her husband only shortly before his demise."

Kirill asked, "How so?"

The Maestro went on, "When you asked me to

locate Adam Mickiewicz the first thing I did was look in the F.B.I. record to see if there was an Adam Mickiewicz in the files. I found a file on him that contained his fingerprint cards.

It seems that about ten years ago an agent working on a cold case warrant squad went to Cassini's mailbox store in search of the Adam Mickiewicz who was wanted in the Boston assault case. That agent later filed a report indicating that he felt the storeowner, Ray Cassini, bore a strong resemblance to the mug shot of Adam Mickiewicz. He requested that The U.S. Attorney get a court order calling for Mr. Cassini to submit to a fingerprint examination. The U.S. Attorney contacted the Boston District Attorney and learned that the officers who had arrested Adam Mickiewicz had retired and moved to Florida. Of the two victims, one had died in an automobile accident and the other was himself serving time for an unrelated felony assault.

The case against Cassini was dead. They'd never get a conviction and the Boston DA was not going to go through the time and expense of an extradition hearing on a twenty year old case with no witnesses and no victims who could testify. Because Boston was no longer interested in the case the U.S. Attorney suspended action on the federal case and she never filed for the court order. The agent who had requested the order just went on to other cases.

Following up on the suggestion that Cassini might be Adam Mickiewicz I went to the store. I acted as if I was a clumsy customer who wanted to mail a parcel. I asked Cassini to help me tape up the box. I handed him a roll of wide clear plastic packaging tape and asked him to help me wrap the package. I kept fumbling the box so Cassini would have to handle the tape a lot. You can't handle that stuff without leaving a hard copy of your fingerprints imbedded in the sticky side of the tape. Even after you stick it to the package the fingerprint impressions can be seen through the dry side with the naked eye. Further, the impressions cannot be rubbed out no matter what you do. I simply mailed the package with his fingerprints imbedded in the tape to my home. I did not have to sign on to the computer to do a search. I simply did an old fashion direct side-by-side eye examination comparison to the prints in the file. That's the way we used to do it in the old days. The prints were a positive match to the prints of Adam Mickiewicz from the Boston assault case and the Adamski murder crime scene. That is how I knew for sure that Cassini and Adam Mickiewicz was one and the same person. That is why I was sure that Cassini and Adamski were connected. I could not have known that Kern also used the same pseudonym at one time. The problem is Cassini's wife was at the store when I collected Cassini's prints. She saw me.

They already suspect that someone with access to the fingerprint files identified Cassini as the Adam Mickiewicz. If they question her about his murder, they will expect me to be present. If she recognizes me, I'm done!

I did a run down on her. There is more

disturbing news in her recent credit card activity. On the day after Kern escaped from the hospital, she used her credit card to buy a large supply of gauze and sterile bandages. She purchased high quality antiseptics. She renewed an old prescription she had for painkillers and she purchased three throwaway cell phones. I think she was sheltering Kern at her home and attending his wounds in the days after his escape. I did a surveillance of her home and I do not think he is still there. He is likely to meet with the widow Cassini again. If she tells the tape and package story to Kern, he will figure it out."

Petrov said, "This is disturbing, but I'll tell Sorge to handle her. She does not know him. He can get close. If Kern is not there it will be an easy assignment.

Now, I must ask you, have you seen the wonderful exhibit they have here with Siberian tigers? It is quite something, you know. We have some time to kill, let's go you can see it. You will be impressed."

Tom and Taylor in Tom's Quarters

Tom Bradner called Taylor from his Second Avenue apartment and asked him to come right over. Taylor went over and Tom greeted him at the door. Taylor said, "What's up, you sounded excited."

Tom said, "I am. Michelle called me and told me that she has a line on a serious development into the investigation of the Cassini murder. It looks very much like the Cassini murder and the Adamski murder are connected. Michelle believes a Russian doctor killed Cassini. I told her you and I would come over at eight and discuss a strategy."

Taylor looked a bit puzzled and asked what evidence she had. Tom told Taylor the substance of the phone call from Michelle.

Taylor's eyes widened and he exclaimed, "She told you all that over the phone?"

Tom indicated that she had and said, "We agreed to have no further discussions over the phone. From here on all discussions must be face to face."

Taylor shouted, "It's too late! You've already said too much over the phone! We are dealing with very dangerous and very powerful people. They understand police methods. They have access to police information files and police equipment. If they have a tap on her phone, and I strongly suspect they do, they know too much already. If she is holding records at her home, she is in serious danger. We can't wait until eight o'clock. We need to get in touch with her right now. Call her don't say anything about the case. Just tell her that she is in danger. She should arm herself and be on alert. She lives only a few blocks from here. We have to get over there at once."

Tom dialed Michelle's cell phone and got voice mail. He dialed her home and got the same result. Michelle was in the shower and did not hear the phones ringing. As Tom and Taylor ran from his apartment to Taylor's police car, which was parked right outside Tom's apartment, he used his cell phone to call her over and over. No matter how many times he rang the phone, no one answered. Tom was in a state of panic as he and Taylor raced toward Michelle's home.

As the men were racing to her home, Michelle was enjoying a warm and relaxing shower. As she drenched herself in the soothing waters, she continued to rehash her case in her mind. She was, of course, trying to remain focused on the case, but she could not help but fantasize about her future with the bureau. Suddenly, she was an important player.

Tomorrow morning she would be briefing Duffy about her findings. Most assuredly, her discovery would be conveyed to Director Madison in Washington. He'd acknowledge her as being a top-notch investigator. Duffy was the boss. He'd maintain a general overview of many cases, but she was the lead. She had the details. The solution of the case was in the details. She needed to remember every aspect of the case. She had to be sure that Duffy would know everything he needed to know to properly advise Madison. After all he'd know nothing about this case if it were not for her comprehensive reporting. Tomorrow she would brief Duffy in the car as they went to some sort of important meeting in Yonkers. He would know everything she discovered because she would give a comprehensive briefing. Duffy would have to appreciate that. Surely he'd reward her with new important cases. The boss would look like a fool if the lead investigator did not properly brief him.

As those thoughts went through her head suddenly, Michelle had a shocking revelation. She shouted to herself out loud, "It's Chapson! It's not Dwarman. It's Chapson! I've been thinking it's Frank Dwarman, but it's Chapson!
Dwarman would not have specifics on the case. He is the boss. He only has a general overview of cases. When he needs to know specifics, he'd ask to be briefed by the lead investigator. He only knows the details that Chapson gives in his reports.

Dwarman just regurgitates the facts as Chapson told them to him. Chapson has briefed me. Why didn't he tell me about the hair or the Groton police car? Dwarman believes that the Groton police were not cooperating because Chapson told him so. Dwarman never spoke to Groton cops himself. No wonder the F.B.I. could not find Sorge. The lead investigator has been in on the crimes from the start."

She had to tell Tom. Now she strongly believed that it must be Chapson and not Dwarman who could not be trusted.

While Michelle was in the shower thinking those thoughts, the Maestro came to her apartment door. He knocked, but received no reply. Slowly and quietly he tried the doorknob. It turned effortlessly and the door opened. Michelle had left the door unlocked. As the Maestro entered, he heard the shower water running. His first thought was: This is going to be easier than I thought.

It was a straight walk from the front door down a long corridor that allowed access to rooms on either side. The bathroom door was straight ahead, at the far end of the hallway. The Maestro tiptoed across the parquet oak floor of the apartment as he slowly reached to his waistband to retrieve his gun from its holster. He inched toward the bathroom. The silencer was already attached to his weapon. All he needed to do was to shoot through the shower curtain.

Even a well-trained F.B.I. agent does not take a gun or bulletproof vest into the shower.

As he was nearing the bathroom door, he slowly reached toward the doorknob. Suddenly, the front door burst open! Tom Bradner came crashing through the front door into the apartment.

The Maestro spun around and fired two quick shots in his direction. Tom went right down! He was hit with the first round. As he fell to the floor, The Maestro saw Taylor who was coming in right behind Tom. The Maestro fired twice more at Taylor, but missed. Taylor was already retrieving his weapon and ducking behind the wall adjacent to the doorway as he rapidly pulled his gun and returned fire.

Taylor also missed his mark. His bullets flew past The Maestro, straight down the hallway, right through the bathroom door, through the shower curtain, narrowly missing Michelle. The bullets struck the ceramic tile wall of the shower. The tiles exploded into fragments that pelted the wet and naked body of Michelle. Taylor had no idea that as his rounds were missing The Maestro, they were continuing to travel down the hallway penetrating the door of the occupied bathroom, threatening the life of the very person he and Tom had come to rescue.

Because of the silencer, Michelle had not heard the four shots fired by The Maestro, but even over the noise of the shower she clearly heard Taylor's return fire. The shattering tiles on her shower wall left no doubt as to what was going on right outside her bathroom door.

She jumped from the shower and burst into the corridor that led to her front door. She instantly took in all that was happening. Her eyes first fell upon the hulk of a man with his back to her, standing over the limp, bleeding body of Tom Bradner.

She could see the gun with its silencer in his hand as he had resumed firing at Taylor. She could see Taylor, from a position of cover behind the doorjamb, attempting to return fire.

Now Taylor could see that Michelle was directly in his line of fire. He had no choice, but to cease firing.

Michelle realized at once that her presence in the hallway was preventing Taylor from firing.

The Maestro was still standing and facing the front door as he lowered his weapon to fire another round into the limp body of Tom Bradner, who laid at his feet,

At once, Michelle jumped and thrust her wet and naked body into the air. She landed squarely on The Maestro's back. She grabbed on and held tightly with her legs wrapped around his waist and her right arm around his throat. With her left hand, she ripped at his eyes. His eyelids began to weep blood at once.

The Maestro flared around trying to extricate himself from her clutches to no avail. The pain in his eyes was excruciating and he was having difficulty breathing due to the presence of her arm around his throat. She bit as hard as she could on her attacker's left ear. He let out a scream as she bit off half of his ear and spit its pieces out on the floor. She removed her fingers from The Maestro's eyes, only briefly, to pound a clenched fist against the seriously wounded ear. With each strike The Maestro screamed in pain. Then she would resume gouging the eyes. However, Taylor was still unable to fire. Any shot was as likely to kill Michelle as it was to kill the intruder.

The Maestro was in considerable pain and could not reach his gun to a position around his back where he could shoot Michelle without endangering himself. Missing her he could put a round in his own back and there was still Taylor to deal with. In the commotion, The Maestro could not see where Taylor was. Indeed he could not see at all with Michelle's long fingernails jammed in his bloody eyes. The Maestro wondered if he would be forever blinded. All he knew was he had to get out of there.

He fired shots wildly as he spun around like a bronking bull attempting to unload a rodeo rider. One of his wild shots found their mark. Taylor was hit in the right arm. The wound caused him to drop his firearm.

At one point The Maestro found himself positioned so that his back was to the door. Wildly, uncontrollably, he began stumbling backwards with Michelle still perched upon his back. In doing so The Maestro tripped over Tom's body. Now he was half running backwards and half falling, stumbling. In moments his huge frame tumbled out through the open apartment door into the common hallway. He came crashing down on his back with Michelle beneath him, smashing her naked body against the hard terrazzo floor.

The impact knocked the wind out of Michelle. She was instantly dazed. She involuntarily released her captive.

The Maestro rolled and jumped to his feet. All he could think of was that he had to get out of there. Through his blood-covered eyes, he could see the light of the elevator shining through a small square window in the elevator door. The elevator was stopped on Michelle's floor. The Maestro mustered all his strength and ran toward the light of the waiting elevator. Occasionally, he would turn, look back and fire a shot at Taylor, who was now up and in pursuit. His shots just went wild. As Taylor stepped over the naked body of Michelle lying on the hallway floor, he could see that she was recovering and beginning to get to her feet. Taylor yelled, "Check on Tom! Call 911! Get us some help!"

Taylor was returning fire, but the gunshot wound to his right arm forced him to shoot left handed. He wished he had paid more attention the N.Y.P.D. firearms instructors who insisted that all officers practice shooting with the weak hand, but Taylor was never any good at it and he hated doing things he was not good at. His shots were going wild.

The Maestro reached for the old style elevator door that had to be opened by hand. He pulled it open, jumped into the elevator and pushed a button on the elevator keypad. As the door was closing, Taylor let off another shot. At once he saw an exploding burst of blood blow out from Maestro's hip area and he saw the big man crumple to the elevator floor. The door closed and the elevator began to descend.

Taylor ran to the staircase adjacent to the elevator and ran down the stairs. He had no way of knowing which button The Maestro had pushed. Experience taught him not to assume that a fleeing felon would choose the ground floor. At each Taylor exited the stairway and watched to see if the elevator stopped. When it did not, he would resume the race. Floor after floor Taylor would arrive just in time to see the light of the elevator shine through the small window of the elevator door as it continuing its decent. Finally, he arrived at the lobby level just as the elevator arrived. Taylor pulled the door open.

The veteran police officer, who had seen many gory accidents and crime scenes in his career, wretched at the sight within the elevator. Taylor's bullet had struck The Maestro's thighbone just below the hip joint socket. The round shattered the bone at its uppermost joint to create a razor sharp jagged edge of thighbone that looked more like a crude javelin than any body part. As the weight of the large man came down upon this internal spear within his own leg, the sharpened point of bone tore through the man's inner thigh, severing the femoral artery and piercing the man's scrotum, then ripping upwards through his pants. The man lay upon the floor impaled upon his own leg bone. He laid like a pile of rags on the floor and the exposed bone stood straight and tall pointing directly at the elevator ceiling. The man's hands were wrapped around the standing bone as if he were trying to lift himself up off the bony post. The man's eyes were open and he stared up at a ball of flesh that was once a part of himself, that now sat atop the end of the jagged bone like a piece of beef on the end of a barbecue spit. The femoral artery, which was completely severed, was pumping out blood at an incredible pace. The blood had actually puddled up into a pool that covered the entire elevator floor. The pool ran over the edge of the elevator floor like water in an overflowing bathtub, dripping into the elevator pit below. By the size of the wound in the upper leg, Taylor knew that there would be no way to stop the bleeding. It was probably too late anyway. A severed femoral artery can make a man bleed to death in a few minutes.

Taylor knew at once that the man was dead. If he was not dead yet he would surely bleed to death before any help could arrive.

Taylor stared at the man's face. It was a face that he knew. Taylor stared at his face and he stared into the blank, dead eyes of Alan Chapson staring back at him. Taylor did not know that Petrov referred to Chapson as The Maestro. He called him by that name because it was Chapson who orchestrated Petrov's work in America. Chapson would no longer be conducting business for Kirill Petrov.

Taylor could hear the wailing sounds of responding police cars and ambulances. Michelle had made her call. Taylor, exhausted from his run down the stairs and bleeding from his own wounds, sat on the hallway floor using his legs to prop open the elevator door. He placed his gun where it would be out of sight of the responding officers. He knew how to avoid death by friendly fire. He took the badge that was suspended by a chain around his neck and held it up by his face and awaited the arrival of help.

Michelle was in her apartment tending to Tom's injuries and praying that Taylor was Okay. When the cops and the paramedics arrived at her apartment, they found her dressed in a robe kneeling on the floor next to Tom. They told her that Taylor was okay and that he was on the way to a hospital for treatment of his gunshot wound. They assessed

Tom's injuries. They told her his injuries were serious, but they did not think them to be life threatening. Finally, they told her the man in the elevator was dead.

The paramedic said, "We'll be taking your friend here to the hospital. Do you want to come along?"

Tom managed to choke out the words, "You don't have to come along. I'll be Okay. You know what you have to do here."

Michelle turned to the paramedics and cops and said, "I'd love to go to the hospital with him, but I have work to do here. I'm an F.B.I. agent. The dead man in the elevator was an F.B.I. agent too, a bad apple, but an agent. I'll have to call the bureau."

Jill's Fate Cast Upon the Waves

Kirill Petrov sat in the dark inside his car outside the home of Nurse Jill Simpson. He sat quietly waiting for the call from Alan Chapson, The Maestro. If he received the call telling him that Taylor, Bradner & Thompson were dead and the medical file was recovered, he would proceed with his part of the plan. He would kill Jill Simpson. As he sat in his car, Kirill listened to the car radio. It was tuned to an all-news radio station. He listened as the regular broadcast was interrupted for breaking news. The radio reporter had few details, but some facts were known. There had been a shootout in the Stuyvesant Town section of Manhattan. The reporter said that three men had been shot, one fatally. The news report then gave sketchy details about a man, believed to be an F.B.I. agent, who was killed in a confrontation with a female agent and two New York City Police officers. The reporter promised more details would follow, but Kirill needed no further details. He knew that Chapson was dead and Petrov's plans died with Chapson.

Killing Jill Simpson would be of no value in Kirill's plan now. The other persons who knew of Doctor Ivan Anissina's "treatment" of Ray Cassini were still alive. They still had the nurse's medical records. Tonight, Jill would go to sleep, she would awaken in the morning like every other morning. She would go to work, live another day and never know how close she came to dying in her sleep.

Kirill Petrov picked up his phone and called Doctor Anissina. When the doctor answered, Kirill said, "My friend I am afraid that we will not be able to spare you the embarrassment of being named as a suspect in the death of Mr. Raymond Cassini. I am sorry. I tried. I sent The Maestro to take care of this and now I have learned that he is dead. I fear that your inclusion in the medical records will now be part of the investigation. However, fear not, your diplomatic immunity will remain intact. I have seen to that. The authorities here cannot touch you. Nevertheless, I think it would be best for you to remain at our embassy in Mexico City for now. One of our colleagues will arrange to have you temporarily transferred from the North American Bureau to the South American Bureau. He will have you assigned to the consulate in Venezuela. You will be safer there. That will be the safest thing to do. I shall join you there. I have many friends in Venezuela. In the recent past I have been very helpful to the government leadership there. They believe in our ideas of how communism ought to be. I trust you have your personal aircraft available."

The doctor replied, "Yes, it is being serviced at this time, but it will be available to me in a few days."

Kirill answered, "Good, it may take a few days to arrange your transfer anyway and there are a few matters that I must address to ensure my own departure. There is a bar in Chicago I must visit to meet another associate. There are other projects to set in motion before I can leave. A few days delay will serve both of us well. There is no urgent need to go right now. Your immunity protects you. To be safe, do not leave the compound until your transfer is approved and your plane is ready to go. There is no sense in taking unnecessary chances in the public streets of Mexico. Once you receive your transfer orders go at once. Have a member of the consulate staff drive you to the airport in a consulate vehicle. If you must refuel your plane, do so in Cuba. I know we will miss the amenities of America. However, I can assure you, we will live a very good lifestyle in Venezuela. Americans have short memories. In time we can come back. Be safe my friend. I shall see you in Caracas."

Buddy Checks in With the Captain

By the time Buddy saw the newscast regarding the events at Michelle's apartment, there were more details being made public. Alan Chapson was identified as rogue F.B.I. agent who was apparently collaborating with a Russian spy ring. Agent Michelle Thompson, Detective Taylor and Police Officer Bradner were identified as the team that uncovered Chapson's unlawful activity. They were being praised for their intelligent police work and brave actions in bringing down this dangerous criminal. The newscaster made a brief mention of Chapson's involvement in the shooting incident at the Royal Buena Vista Hotel in Yonkers, which according to the newscaster, was still under investigation.

When Buddy got the news, he called Captain Dent at once. When the captain got on the line, Buddy said, "Well my friend I see that it was apparently no accident that Agent Chapson shot me. All this time I actually believed he came to the scene to assist your officer. I actually felt bad for him knowing that he was undergoing an internal investigation as a result of my failure to drop my gun in a timely manner. I was blaming myself.

Now I know it was just another attempt by the Russians to kill me. They have tried many times before when I was in Asia. I always thought I'd be safe on American soil. I guess in my business you just never know.

If Chapson was in cahoots with the Russians, it is most likely that Chapson was acting as a back-up to the man in the white suburban who was sent to kill me and who ended up killing your officer. I have to believe that the killing of Adamski was in some way connected to the Russians knowing that I had once offered to help Adamski defect to the west.

Tell me something. Do you think Chapson killed Adamski and Ray?"

"No Mr. Kern, I'm afraid not. He was on duty in is his F.B.I. assignments in Connecticut during the time periods when Adamski and your friend Cassini were killed. His presence in Connecticut is well documented. However, we do believe he was involved in the plot that ultimately resulted in their deaths. You're right that the Russians have something to do with that as well. I probably should not tell you this, but just before the attack on Michelle Thompson's home, she uncovered evidence suggesting that a Russian doctor killed your pal Ray, a man on the Russian embassy staff, a Doctor Ivan Anissina. Michelle uncovered evidence of an unauthorized visit and an unauthorized treatment given to Cassini by Dr. Anissina. We believe Chapson was trying to destroy that evidence and kill Thompson to prevent her from disclosing what she had learned. We already called in Mr. Cassini's widow to see if she knew of any connection between Chapson and her late husband. She positively identified Chapson as a man who had been to their store recently. Chapson had been at the store, but did

389

not identify himself as an agent. The way she describes Chapson's conduct at the store, we believe his visit to the store was a ruse to obtain a fingerprint sample from Cassini. Chapson had possession of a file that contained Adam Mickiewicz's fingerprint card. So we are quite sure that it was Chapson who identified Cassini and Adam Mickiewicz as being one and the same person. That identification is what led to Cassini's death. However, all the evidence suggests that the actual killing of Ray, by way of a fatal injection, was done by Doctor Ivan Anissina."

The captain told Buddy all the details of the case, how they came together and Buddy agreed that it was most likely the doctor who killed Cassini. Buddy asked if they were getting a warrant for the doctor.

The captain replied, "Well, Mr. Kern, there are a couple of complications."

"Complications? What complications?"

The captain answered, "To start with the doctor is in Mexico at the present time."

Buddy interrupted, "So get an extradition warrant. Get the Mexican authorities to hold him 'til you get the warrant. Better still, it is an espionage case. Have the C.I.A. grab him in Mexico and hold him for you."

Captain Dent took a long breath and in somber tones said, "Mr. Kern, I'm sorry to tell you this, but the doctor is on the embassy staff, he has diplomatic immunity."

Buddy screamed, "What! Call the Russians;

get his immunity revoked! This is murder we're talking about. Just go get the bastard."

Captain Dent replied, "We are doing all we can. We want to get the son-of-a-bitch too. We believe he supplied the car to the man who killed our officer. We want him as badly as you do. If he can be gotten, we'll get him."

Buddy said, "If you don't get him, I will!"

Dent replied, "Don't do anything foolish. Give us a chance to get him."

Buddy said, "I'll give you your chance, but if you don't get him I'll kill the son of a bitch myself. I swear to God I'll kill the bastard myself!"

Captain Dent went on, "You should turn yourself in. I'm sure that once the facts surrounding you being shot and the subsequent escape from custody are made known any charges against you will be dropped."

Buddy replied, "I'll come forward after the charges are dropped. You should be able to get that done for me. A rogue F.B.I. agent shot me and they think they are going to put me in jail? Those charges should be dropped at once."

The captain said, "I'll talk to Duffy. I'll see what I can do. I'm on your side in this. Without the information you supplied we'd be nowhere in this case. I'll see what I can do, Mr. Kern."

Buddy replied, "Thanks, by the way my friends call me Buddy."

The captain just said, "Okay Buddy."

Then the phone went dead.

Captain Dent sat staring at his phone and thinking he'd like to meet Kern face to face one day.

Suddenly, the door to his office burst open. His chief investigator in the police officer homicide was standing in the doorway. "Captain! We got a DNA hit off one of the coffee cups. I know who the cop killer is. I've already touched base with the F.B.I. They have an enormous background file on our suspect. You're not going to believe all the evidence supporting our conclusion. We have identified the person who killed our officer! We have identified Sorge!"

Down at the Docks

Several hours had passed since his latest phone call to Captain Dent. Buddy was stewing at the thought that the so-called doctor might escape justice because of diplomatic immunity. Buddy had come home for redemption, but those old feelings of wanting revenge were consuming his every thought. Once again a person who meant very much to Buddy had been murdered. Once again it was a Russian who was responsible. Buddy thought he'd go mad. He knew that seeking revenge and seeking redemption were mutually exclusive.

He sat quietly alone for a few moments trying to compose himself. His thoughts wandered to Terri. She must feel so lonely at this point. By now she knew that a clumsy customer who fumbled with a package at her store was at least partly responsible for Ray's death. At least that man was dead. Buddy wondered if she was yearning for revenge or was she sufficiently at peace in knowing that his killer was now known to law enforcement. Did she know that the suspect in Ray's murder had diplomatic immunity? Did she understand the implications? If she did, she must be tormented. Her husband was dead. She was alone. Did she overcome her passion for Buddy while he was away from her? Did she come to believe that it would be wrong to be in love with him while still grieving for Ray? Buddy prayed that she did not. He needed to see her. He decided to go to her.

As he was preparing to slip out of his hideaway, Buddy looked out from his dockside warehouse window. He could see the grand ships moving into the harbor and others setting out to sea. He opened the window to draw in the fresh ocean air that was blowing in from the east. He gave thought to how in ancient times the great ships had to rely upon the winds to blow them about. A life at sea depended upon the winds.

As he looked around these docks that served as his home, it occurred to Buddy that most of his adult life he sailed the seas and worked the docks. He had longed to be a racecar driver or a policeman. Dangerous occupations that could get you killed. Ray wanted to live the tranquil life of a riverboat pilot, a seaman. The winds of fate had blown both Ray and Buddy away from their dreams. Those winds blew him to be closer to the sea than Ray would ever be. Though Buddy faced many dangers, the winds of fate had blown him away to safety. The winds of fate had simply blown Ray away. The winds of fate had given Terri to Ray and now the winds of fate could very well blow her into Buddy's own arms.

As Buddy tried to lose himself in the mysteries of fate, he was suddenly struck by a disturbing reality. There were things that Buddy had come to have an instinct about. Events that Buddy knew well were unfolding on the docks below. From the second floor window of his little hideaway, Buddy could see below the well-choreographed movements of men moving around the dock area. They were the

394

unmistakable movements of an assault team. Customs agents were surrounding and closing in on Buddy's warehouse.

Buddy was enraged. He grabbed his cell phone and hit redial.

Captain Dent answered and Buddy flew right into a rage, "You son of a bitch! You liar! You want me to believe you're on my side that you're trying to help me! You traced my cell phone and gave my location to the Feds!"

The captain shot back, "What are you talking about?"

Buddy said, "Federal agents are surrounding my place!"

The captain asked, "Where are you?"

Buddy replied, "I'm at my warehouse."

Then with some urgency in his voice the captain asked, "What agency?"

Buddy said, "ICE."

In near panic tones the captain replied, "You're in terrible danger! It's Trulane! Buddy he's going to kill you! We've just discovered that he's part of the spy ring! I was just informed that his DNA matches the DNA from the Groton murder site, it matches the DNA at the Adamski crime scene and it matches the DNA from my police officer homicide. He's a murdering spy! He put out a BOLO on you. He's informed ICE that you have weapons of mass destruction, that you're a terrorist! He has told his men that they are to surround your warehouse and keep you contained until he arrives. He just left his office and he is most likely in route to your location. He does not yet know that we are on to him. He thinks if he kills you there will be no way to connect him and Petrov. He tried to kill you on Buena Vista because you know who he is."

Buddy exclaimed, "I know him?"

The captain replied, "I think you do. Around twenty years ago we had received reports that a number of residents of the Royal Hotel had been assaulted. Some of the victims described their attacker as being a man in a Navy uniform. Trulane lived in the neighborhood and he was serving in the Navy at the time. The assaults seemed to occur at times when Trulane was home on leave. His name surfaced as a suspect, but none of the victims could positively identify him and he was never arrested.

It was rumored that one of those residents kicked his ass and sent him to the hospital. After that the attacks stopped. We searched the hospital records at the time, but there was no record of him being treated there. There were no witnesses or victims who were willing to cooperate with the police at the time, so the investigation was dropped. However, according to his naval records, he reported for duty around that time with broken ribs and other injuries that he attributed to being assaulted by a street gang.

When we first interviewed Ray's wife, we asked her to tell us anything she might have known about the night of the Hudson River accident. As an aside, she mentioned that Ray told her you kicked a sailor's ass that night and sent him to the hospital.

Ray told her that he was at the hospital with Adamski when the injured sailor came in for treatment. The hospital emergency room was busy and the sailor was not getting treated. Ray told his wife that sailor left with some Russian guy to see a private doctor. According to our reports Petrov was at the hospital that night and when he left he went to the Russian Diplomatic Residence in Riverdale. Guess who was the doctor at the Russian residence in Riverdale at the time! Doctor Ivan Anissina! We believe Anissina treated Trulane that night.

Guess where Trulane was assigned when he was in the Navy? He was on permanent guard duty at the submarine research center in Groton. It seems evident that Trulane stole the Groton Disks. I'm sitting here with F.B.I. agents brainstorming. We were just getting ready to bring him in. Stay where you are and take cover. We have men on the way!"

Buddy said, "I'll stay put as long as I can. They're not moving in just yet. I guess they are waiting for Trulane to get here, but talk to me. Tell me what you know."

"We have established a link between Petrov, Trulane and Chapson. According to Chapson's F.B.I. personnel file, Chapson was an Immigration agent before he joined the F.B.I. When Petrov went to the hospital on the night of the accident, he needed to get a customs and immigration temporary emergency visa to stay in the country to attend to the dead sailor's needs. Guess who signed his temporary visa? It was Chapson!

Whenever a police officer is required to notify another agency to join an investigation, an agency notification list is maintained. It tells us who notified what agency and when they were notified. We checked all the notification records to see who notified immigration to respond to the hospital that night. No one did! Chapson came on his own and told the officers at the scene that they need not notify anyone else because he was already on the scene. He'd take care of everything. We speculate that when Petrov was still a small time smuggler he must have had an accomplice in immigration and customs. He needed someone who would look the other way when necessary. Chapson, the customs agent, was most likely on Petrov's payroll back then. When Petrov was stuck in Yonkers, he did not want to be questioned by just any immigration agent. Petrov must have called Chapson himself to make sure that no other agent from customs would come. Petrov, Trulane and Chapson all left the hospital together.

At some point Chapson made a career change. He left immigration and customs to join the F.B.I. It was all the better for Petrov. With a contact in the F.B.I. he could advance his own position in the KGB.

If Petrov still needed a contact in customs, he most likely would have encouraged Trulane to join customs when his Navy hitch was up. Customs was giving preference in hiring to persons with military backgrounds. Trulane applied for a job at customs. Chapson was already an F.B.I. agent by that time. Trulane gave Chapson's name as a reference on his

398

application. A reference from an F.B.I. agent and his naval experience virtually assured that Trulane would be hired. It was a perfect set-up. Trulane would commit the Sorge crimes and Chapson would make sure that he was assigned to investigate those crimes. Petrov could come and go through American ports at will as long as he made sure that Trulane was on duty. It was perfect, until Adamski showed up in America trying to locate Adam Mickiewicz. Adamski probably knew the whole set-up.

More importantly, we believe that Adamski was aware of Petrov's connection to a Russian secret insurrection group that was planning to attack an American ship at sea. If Petrov's connection to that group were made known, he'd be a dead man.

We also discovered that Stanley Adamski was subjected to a special search of his suitcase when he arrived at Kennedy Airport. The TSA record shows that Trulane personally did that search. Why would a high-ranking boss at customs be doing baggage searches himself at the airport? We suspect he placed a tracking device in Adamski's suitcase during the inspection so he could track him down and kill him. Remember, we found DNA at the Adamski crime scene and we know for sure that Trulane left the DNA.

When Adam Mickiewicz registered at the Royal Hotel, it was too much for Trulane. He knew there would be a record showing that he was a suspect in the assaults there. He also knew that the name Adam Mickiewicz was somehow connected to

399

Adamski. When you registered at the Royal under that name, he must have figured that someone was trying to connect the Adamski murder and the Royal Hotel assaults from years ago. If that connection were made, Trulane's name would resurface! The videotape from the officer's dashboard camera locked Trulane at the scene at the Royal Hotel. He was the one person who could not be seen anywhere near the Royal. He panicked and killed the cop to destroy the tape.

Once he realized you were the guy who had kicked his ass, he had to be afraid that you and he would meet in this investigation. You could establish that he was in the hospital at the same time as Petrov. If that came out we'd be pulling all his records from that time and find the Petrov connection.

Buddy, he's told his agents you're a terrorist and that you have Stinger missiles."

Buddy exclaimed, "That old clap trap shit again! That's a rumor started by the Taliban to discredit me! They are the ones who made off with the Stingers that were issued to the Mujahideen after they split off from the Mujahideen proponents of democracy. You of all people should know that if there were any real evidence that I took the surplus Stingers after the Afghan war, the Feds would have locked me up years ago. I've been in plain sight this whole time."

The captain said, "We can discuss all that later. Right now you're in danger. As far as those ICE agents know you're a terrorist! A terrorist with

Stinger missiles! Trulane does not know we are on to him. He thinks if he kills you he will be free. I've sent help. They should be there soon."

Buddy simply said, "Don't worry about me." With that said, he hung up.

Buddy slowly slipped into a position where he could observe the movements of the ICE team below without being seen himself.

Clearly, the agents surrounding his warehouse were being extremely cautious and keeping at a safe distance. They had his warehouse surrounded, but held their position for nearly an hour. Buddy was wondering why they were waiting. Then he saw another car arrive. A single agent occupied the car. As that agent exited from his vehicle, Buddy could see the other agents readying themselves. The agents surrounding his warehouse were not waiting for Buddy to come out. They were waiting for this agent to arrive. This must be the boss. This must be Trulane. Then Buddy saw the new arrival leave his car and go to where the group was positioned. He spoke to the agents on the scene. Then this same single agent slipped away from the pack and approached the door of the warehouse. He was coming in alone. It was Trulane.

Buddy was assessing his situation. He could see that Trulane was armed with a shotgun. He was likely carrying a sidearm as well, but it was the shotgun that was Buddy's main focus.

Buddy figured that Trulane had ordered his men to maintain a perimeter. Then he would enter the warehouse alone. That way there would be no witnesses as to what occurred inside the building. Trulane could shoot Buddy, kill him and claim that Buddy attacked him first with a weapon that Trulane would plant on the body.

Buddy's plan was to allow Trulane to come inside and start a search. If Trulane followed through as Buddy expected him to do and came in alone Buddy would know for sure that Tulane's plan was to kill him and have no witnesses. A professional search is conducted by a team.

Buddy would be hiding behind an interior door. As Trulane searched, he would eventually come through that door. The barrel of the shotgun would precede him. Buddy would grab the shotgun by the barrel, twist and pull it from his attacker's grip. Then he'd bust his face with a powerful smash from the shotgun's shoulder stock. It was a movement that he had used in the battlefields. The movement would be followed by a smashing chop to the throat that would crush the larynx and cause suffocation. Many an enemy combatant, who faced Buddy in combat, had died a horrible death struggling to draw breath through a crushed windpipe that would not permit the passage of air. Buddy watched too many who had the same reaction to the crushing blow that awaited Trulane. Looking skyward, they would stretch out their arms as if they could somehow grasp the air in their arms. With their mouths wide open, their chests would heave repeatedly, struggling to catch some small quantity of precious oxygen. The expression on their faces would be the expression of a man screaming for help, but not a sound would be emitted. A man with no air can't scream for help. The man dies slowly and silently. He cannot even cry out in his anguish. The first time Buddy used the maneuver he found it difficult to watch a man suffocate and die slowly before his eyes, but in time he got used to it.

Buddy was many years older and more experienced than he was when he first kicked Trulane's ass, but the years had only made him tougher. In his days as a tough kid in competition, he sometimes worried that he might seriously hurt an opponent. That empathy restrained his prowess. Buddy was not that person anymore. Killing Trulane would be a routine matter. It would be easy.

As Trulane approached the front door Buddy watched with bated breath through a crack between the door jamb and the concrete wall of warehouse. He waited for the right moment to pounce. Step by cautious step Trulane came closer and closer to his rendezvous with the man who would break him in half. Buddy was confident in the first part of his plan. He knew he could take out Trulane. Buddy's mind raced toward what his next move should be. What would he do once he took Trulane out? Customs agents surrounded him. They were agents, good men and women who had every reason to believe Buddy was a terrorist. They were honest, professional officers who would do whatever it took to bring down a terrorist. They were positioned on all sides of his building, waiting, poised to do what their years of training and professionalism had taught them to do. He had escaped from more contentious circumstances before, but in doing so he had to kill people. He did not want to harm innocent agents who were acting on false information supplied to them by their superior. How could he escape without harming anyone beyond Tulane? A new plan sprang into Buddy's mind.

Quickly, he turned and ran silently toward the back door of his warehouse. He threw open the back door and with his hands over his head he walked out and shouted, "I surrender! I'm unarmed, I will not resist! I surrender! I surrender!" He then dropped to his knees and still holding his hands over his head again shouted, "Don't shoot I surrender!"

At once two agents scrambled from behind their cover. They ran up to Buddy, threw him to the ground, twisted his arms around his back and handcuffed him. They dragged him to a waiting agency vehicle and threw him into the back seat.

It was a sudden realization that came to Buddy. Surrendering was something he had never done before. However today he would surrender. He knew he could rely upon the agents' professionalism. He knew that among honest agents, a surrendering man would be taken alive. There was nothing Trulane could do to him now. For the first time in his life surrendering means he wins! At that moment Buddy was safer than he had been in many years.

The Fleet Arrives

As Trulane exited from the warehouse, he was still holding his shotgun. He walked slowly toward the car where Buddy was seated. He was contemplating his next step. He gave some consideration to having Robert Kern transferred to his car for the execution. He could say that Kern tried to escape, but how would he explain why the man who had surrendered tried to escape.

Suddenly, a parade of police vehicles came screaming into the parking lot at the dock. Trulane and his agents stood there somewhat puzzled by the arrival of the N.Y.P.D. It was not unheard of for local police to come running in after a federal raid. Usually, the local precinct is notified that a federal raid is taking place to avoid having the locals crash in on the party, but occasionally there is a mix-up and they do not get the word. Sometimes local residents see the Feds with guns drawn and they call the locals thinking some sort of gang war is under way. However, N.Y.P.D. was notified that this raid would occur. It was put in the DEX system. The locals would know that this was a federal raid. Why would they be rushing in?

Uniformed officers and agents in three-piece suits were exiting from the cars as if it was some sort of new raid. What the ICE agents found most shocking was that the locals were drawing down on Trulane. They were calling him by name and shouting, "Trulane! Drop the gun, drop the gun!"

As Trulane looked at the guns that were pointed at him, he focused on individuals in the group. It seemed surreal. There were people in the group he recognized. There was Joe Duffy. He was wearing an F.B.I. raid jacket over his suit and he was pointing his gun right at Trulane.

John Cobble, Trulane's old friend from N.C.I.S. was yelling, "Drop the gun!" Trulane looked to his men and he saw his own boss Robert Fulfree, from Homeland Security, telling his men to back off. They looked confused, but they were backing off.

At first Trulane could not grasp what was happening. Everything seemed to go into slow motion. Then Trulane saw Captain Dent from Yonkers coming toward him shouting. "Drop the gun!" At the captain's side were several of the captain's men. Trulane could see the anger in their faces and he knew. He knew that they knew. They knew that he had killed one of their own. Trulane realized that good and honest officers had discovered his treachery.

Trulane racked the shotgun making it ready to fire. He pointed the gun at the group that was approaching. Duffy shouted, "Don't be stupid!" and as those words were said, all present heard the unmistakable sound of a twelve-gauge shotgun blast. Everyone heard the blast, everyone except perhaps Trulane. They say you do not hear the sound of the bullet that kills you. If that is true Trulane did not hear the blast. Trulane had placed the barrel of the twelve-gage under his own chin and blew himself away. Sorge was dead.

The men and women present were shocked by the events, but shocking events are the norm for law enforcement personnel. They soon settled in and did what their training had taught them to do. They secured the perimeter, called for the crime scene unit and went about their business.

Buddy was released from custody. As the cuffs were being removed, he was introduced to the people who had been working the investigation. He shook hands with each and gave a hug to the captain.

As they stood there the captain motioned in the direction of Trulane's lifeless body. He said, "The son of a bitch denied us the opportunity to put him through an excruciating trial that would expose him as the scumbag that he was. He denied us the opportunity to fry his ass. I would have liked to see him twist in the wind for a while."

Buddy said, "Yes, but at least we know he can't do any more harm; now what about Petrov and the doctor?"

The captain looked remorseful and said, "I'm sorry Buddy, but we don't know where Petrov is. We're searching high and low for him, but we haven't got a clue. Even if we find him his known accomplices are dead. We can't question them. We may not be able to make a case against him. As for the doctor, the Russians are standing by him. They will not revoke his diplomatic immunity. Our State Department will not push the matter any further. In fact their position is that we have insufficient evidence to even publicly accuse him. They believe any pressure from them to go after Anissina might jeopardize some very delicate negotiations with the Russians that could affect national security. We are under a federal mandate not to mention the doctor's name. We cannot mention any connection between the case and the Russian delegation in any press release. No one will ever know the truth about what happened here. I'm afraid he'll go free."

Buddy pursed his lips, nodded and said, "I understand." Then he asked, "Can I go now? There is someone I need to see."

The captain said, "The U.S. Attorney has dropped all charges against you. If you want to go I can't stop you."

Buddy just kept nodding and went on, "When I checked into the Royal, I left my car at that fancy parking garage at Buena Vista and Hudson, a block from the Royal. Is my car still there, or did you find it and impound it?"

The captain said, "We found it, but we did not impound it. It is still there." Buddy smiled slightly, "You had it under surveillance? I figured you would do that in case I was dumb enough to come back for it. Can you give me a ride? I'd like to get my car."

Buddy and the captain rode back to Yonkers. They did not speak much. Buddy got his car and headed out. He drove fast. He drove faster than was reasonable for public roads. Perhaps he was driving so fast because that was how he let off steam. Perhaps he was driving fast because he so desperately needed to get to Garrison as quickly as possible. In his mind, either reason seemed sufficient to justify the speed.

A New Cruise

As Buddy pulled up in front of Terri's house, she opened the door, stood in the doorway and held out her arms. Buddy rushed to be at her side and they embraced. They kissed passionately and held each other like they would never let go. In time they stopped their embrace only to embrace and kiss again. Eventually, they made their way inside and settled into conversation. Terri knew much about the day's events. The captain had filled her in and the T.V. news had extensive coverage of the shooting at the warehouse. Buddy filled in other details.

They ate dinner and sat on the sofa for a few drinks. As evening approached, Terri looked lovingly at Buddy and said, "We can be at ease now. You're not being pursued. We can be together. Buddy I love you, sleep with me tonight."

As she looked at Buddy, she expected to see a soft loving look upon his face, but the countenance she saw was not what she expected. She could see that Buddy was tormented. He was angry and it showed. Then he said, "Terri, they are not going to get Doctor Ivan Anissina. They are not even going to make any further attempt to get him. He has diplomatic immunity. Terri they are going to let him go. The man who killed Ray is going free."

Terri responded, "Buddy I know, I know. Captain Dent explained it to me some time ago, but what can we do? Bringing him in will not bring Ray back. It disturbs me greatly that he'll get away, but

I've come to terms with it. Buddy I have you now. We have each other. It's what we always wanted. I never wanted Ray to die, but he is dead and there is nothing we can do about it. Let's make what we can of the rest of our lives. We can be happy. At long last we can be together and we can be happy. Please let it go."

Buddy hung his head and said, "I can't. I can't let it go. That Russian bastard killed Ray and he is getting away with it. I can't let it go. I have to get him. I'm going to get him. I have to kill the son-of-a-bitch. Terri, I swear I'll come back for you. I'll love you forever, but I can't let this go. I have to go and get him. I have to avenge Ray's death or I'll never be able to live with myself."

Terri said, "Buddy you can't live with yourself now. You came home for redemption, to put that life of vengeance behind you. You can't get redemption if you are seeking revenge. Redemption begins when you can forgive those who trespass against you."

Buddy replied, "I can forgive those who have trespassed against me. I can't forgive those Russian bastards who have trespassed against my loved ones. I can't let that go!"

Terri pleaded, "Revenge against Russians is what drove you away from me in the first place. We can have each other now. You have me now. We can be happy. Are you going to leave me again to seek revenge again? You could end up dead. Let it go. I need you more than you need revenge. I need redemption too. I've lived a lie. I stayed married to Ray while loving you. Now he is dead. Don't you think I feel guilt, but we can put it behind us? We can be in love and seek redemption together. We can live out our years in peace. Please Buddy, please let it go."

Buddy replied, "I can't let it go. Those Russian bastards killed my parents and now another Russian bastard killed my best friend. How can I let it go? I am going to leave, but only for a short time. When this thing is done, I'll be back for you, I swear. When I come back we can seek redemption together."

She looked mournfully at him and said, "When this thing is done, there will be another thing."

Buddy begged, "Don't give up on us. I swear this will be the end. I'll just take care of this one thing and I'll be back"

Terri said, "Just go. You and I will never know peace, will we? If you're going to go, go now."

Buddy hung his head and walked toward the door. He hesitated for a moment, turned to look at Terri, then turned again and walked out the door.

A tear flowed down Terri's cheek as she closed the door behind Buddy. She reached up to the knob that locked the door and just held it for a moment. She looked at her hand on the knob, but she just turned and walked away, without locking the door. She walked over to her window overlooking the Hudson River. She saw ships on the water. They were heading out toward the sea. She wondered which, if any of them, would come back to these shores.

The Cruise to Venezuela

Doctor Ivan Anissina's small private jet was waiting for him at The General Servando Canales International Airport. It was fueled up and ready to go. The doctor walked out on the tarmac and did his preflight safety check of the plane. He was quite particular about performing all the preflight safety requirements. He had been a pilot for many years, but still checked out his plane with all the enthusiasm and detail of a brand new pilot. He filed his flight plan to fly from Mexico to Cuba. There he would layover for a while, top off the fuel tanks and file a plan for the second part of his journey.

The doctor entered the plane and strapped himself into his seat. He made all the necessary check-ins with the flight tower and received clearance for takeoff. A light rain was falling, but there was nothing in the forecast that would suggest that the flight should be delayed because of the weather conditions. His takeoff was smooth and uneventful. Soon he would be over the Gulf of Mexico.

As his small plane began to climb, he was unaware that another man was onboard his small craft. That man had been quietly hiding in the restroom at the rear of the plane. He emerged from his place of hiding. Slowly, he made his way toward the front and sat in a seat directly behind the pilot. Gently he whispered, "Nice take off doctor; very smooth."

The doctor, somewhat shocked, turned and

looked over his shoulder at the man seated behind him and he let out a deep breath and said, "I am a very good pilot Mr. Petrov; but you already know that. This is a wonderful plane, is it not? I am afraid there are no beautiful stewardesses to hand out peanuts, but there is a bottle of fine Russian wine from the Rostov Region, Semigor Winery, under my seat. I shall be quite pleased to share it with you."

As they drank their wine, Doctor Anissina said. "I was quite surprised to find that you chose to join me on this flight. I suppose it was wise for you to hide in the plane. These days it is so difficult to go through customs."

Kirill Petrov replied, "Yes. I dare not fly nor allow myself to be recorded crossing a U.S. border without the aid of our old friend Mr. Trulane. It is so difficult to travel by aircraft any more. So many searches and security measures for air travel. Yet, there is no inspection of luggage or persons boarding a bus. I was able to take a Greyhound to Brownsville, Texas without much ado. From there it was easy for me to get me across the border. Then it was just a short trip to Matamoros, Mexico. I had to sneak into the airport last night, but that was not too difficult and getting into your plane was easy. So much attention is given to commercial airliners and so little to private planes. Anyway, this seemed like the best way for me to get to Venezuela. Unlike you I do not enjoy the benefits of diplomatic immunity. I think I will hide myself when we land in Cuba as well. You never know who might be watching your activities there.

Those pesky C.I.A. people are everywhere. I understand they have picked up a few of our low level operatives in Yonkers. Once we are in Venezuela I will feel safer. I have a wonderful plan for our comfort there. We shall live a very good life my friend. But let me tell you more about the progress of our operations. The plane carrying the Polish president and his cabinet members took off for Russia this morning it will not land safely. Our people in the ministry of public information are prepared for the sorrowful press release. We are quite sure we can replace many of the cabinet members with people sympathetic to our cause. The next phase will shock the world. Soon they will ignore us no more. There is good and bad in that. Our work is progressing. However if anyone learns the truth of the crash, or the scope of our influence we will need to go deeper under cover. Our mission becomes more difficult as victory approaches, but in the end we shall prevail."

Epilogue

This morning Michelle Thompson awoke in her apartment in Stuyvesant Town. She was sleeping in the nude, but under the covers her bed was warm and comfortable. She longed to stay in bed and snuggle up with Tom who was lying, naked by her side. They were so much in love. They experienced more in their short time together, than most couples share in a lifetime. They saved each other's lives. Tom's injuries were not as serious as first thought. He was held in the hospital only two days and he was sent "home" to recuperate. Now his home would be by her side.

Things were going to be good for them. Tom was advised that he would be promoted to detective for his efforts in the Adamski case. He was going to be detailed to the Joint Terrorist Task Force, commonly referred to as the JTTF. That meant he would be working regularly with the F.B.I. Michelle was being moved from general assignment to Counter Espionage. That meant she would have constant contact with the JTTF. She would again be working with Tom. They had already talked about marriage. There was still a lot of planning to do, but they already agreed that Taylor would be the best man.

Michelle rolled over and gave Tom a strong hug, kissed him and pulled herself out of the bed. She walked into the bathroom and stepped into the tub. She glanced, only for a moment at the shattered tiles on the shower wall; tiles broken by gunfire that could have ended her life. She gently ran her fingers over the tiles that had not yet been repaired. She quietly uttered a small prayer. She made a short thankful prayer to God that her life and the lives of her comrades in arms had been spared. She turned on the water and showered.

It was her usual morning routine. She took her usual morning shower. She stepped out of the shower, wrapped herself in a white terrycloth robe, and wrapped a white terrycloth towel around her long wet hair. She walked to the kitchen and poured herself a cup of coffee. Then she walked to her door. She opened the door and picked up her morning paper, closed the door and walked to her kitchen. She calmly sat at her kitchen table, drinking her morning coffee. The headlines announced a startling story. It was the story of an unfortunate plan crash that took the life of the President of Poland and several members of his staff. The story went on to describe how the accident occurred, the terrible loss to the Polish people and the preliminary crash investigation that concluded that the crash was due to bad weather and pilot error. She wondered if there could be more to the story than meets the eye. She wondered if it might be worthwhile to ask her superiors if she could look into the case. After all there could be a terrorism or espionage angle to it. Then she chided herself and spoke to herself aloud "Come on Michelle, not every bad event is part of some grand conspiracy, accidents do happen." It seemed that the Polish government officials were satisfied that it was an accident. Why should she think otherwise? As she pondered she thumbed through the remaining pages of the paper until another headline caught her eye. She read with renewed interest.

U.S. COAST GUARD RECOVERS WRECKAGE OF PRIVATE JET

South Padre Island, Texas- U.S. Coast Guard officials confirmed that they have recovered most of the wreckage of a small private jet that was hit by lightning and exploded shortly after takeoff from General Servando Canales International Airport, in Matamoros, Mexico on the U.S. / Mexican border.

According to American authorities, the plane was in route to Cuba when it was struck by lightning and exploded in midair, just as it cleared the Mexican coastline. Most of the wreckage fell into American waters. It is believed that the pilot, a Doctor Ivan Anissina was the sole occupant of the plane at the time of the crash.

Near-by local residents and the weather services confirm that there was rain fall around the time of the crash, but there were no reports of lightening on record for the day; which has caused some to question the government's conclusion that lightening caused the crash

"There is no evidence of any other cause for the explosion found in the rubble of the plane. Based on an in-depth laboratory examination of the debris already recovered we have firmly established that the incident was the result of a lightning strike," said the U.S. government spokesperson, Mr. Peter Cage.

American authorities are discounting a report from an American fisherman who said he witnessed the explosion. Mr. John Jacobs said, "I served in the military. I know what I'm talking about. I was out in the Gulf fishing. I heard the plane flying overhead and happened to look up when I saw a flash of light go across the sky. It hit the plane just as the plane exploded; to me it looked like a Stinger missile strike and I witnessed many of them when I was serving with the military in Operation Desert Storm. There is no question in my mind it was hit by a Stinger!"